Vis and Ramin

VIS AND RAMIN

Translated from the Persian of FAKHR UD-DĪN GURGĀNĪ by GEORGE MORRISON

COLUMBIA UNIVERSITY PRESS 1972 NEW YORK AND LONDON

UNESCO COLLECTION OF REPRESENTATIVE WORKS

This volume has been accepted in the Translation Series of Persian works jointly sponsored by the Royal Institute of Translation of Teheran and the United Nations Educational, Scientific and Cultural Organization (UNESCO)

The illustration on the title page is reproduced from MS Ouseley Add. 24, folio 106r, through the kind permission of the Curators of the Bodleian Library.

FOREWORD

One of the chief distinctions of Persian literature, compared with other literatures produced in the Middle East, is its rich store of epics and romances.

Lyric stories begin to blossom almost with the beginning of the Islamic literature of Persia in the early tenth century. In fact, a tradition of lover's tales, sung by minstrels and bards, had long existed in pre-Islamic Persia. Once the consternation and confusion caused by the rapid Islamic conquest in the seventh century subsided and the normal pursuit of the arts was resumed, the old romances, which had for centuries entertained kings and nobles and had relieved the tedium in the lives of the common folk, began to reappear.

Firdausi (10th–11th cent.) immortalized many such stories, notably those of Zal and Rudabeh, and Manizheh and Bizhan, in his monumental epic, the *Shāhnāmeh*, while Nizami (12th cent.), a master of lyric romances, composed lasting poems in which he gave new expression to the tales of other famous lovers.

An early writer, whose poetic gifts have assured the survival and popularity of an ancient romance to this day, was Fakhr ud-Dīn Gurgānī (11th cent.). His *Vīs o Rāmīn*, an exquisite example of Persian narrative poetry, tells the story of two lovers, Vīs and Rāmīn, whose passionate love for each other breaks the bonds of loyalty they both owe to King Moubad, Rāmīn's elder brother and Vīs's husband. The tale, which may have in fact some historical background in the events associated with a branch of the Parthian dynasty (247 B.C.–A.D. 224), abounds in conflicts, intrigues, adventures, romantic scenes, and poetic contemplations. These are all rendered with great sensitivity and skill in Gurgānī's versified version.

The romance is also of interest to the student of comparative literature, for in it he can see many unmistakable affinities with the Celtic tale of Tristan and Isolde. That pair may in fact have been modeled on Vīs and Rāmīn, following the diffusion in Europe of the traditions of Persian minstrels during the Crusades or earlier. Mr.

George Morrison, who has rendered Gurgānī's poem into English prose with admirable ease and fluency, examines the question in more detail in his informative introduction.

Structurally, *Vīs o Rāmīn* does not follow the norms of the modern Western novel, but in its lineal and meandering course provides the reader with frequent opportunities to explore various aspects of love and the intricacies of human passion. In contrast to classical and Western literary construction, individual events are treated as avenues to be examined in their own right, rather than as indispensable parts of a structured whole. Each episode is enlivened by poetic sentiment and embellished by aesthetic devices. As such *Vīs o Rāmīn* is an excellent example of the Persian conception of a love story.

E. YAR-SHATER

Columbia University

ACKNOWLEDGMENTS

I must first acknowledge the generous help I received from Professor Mujtabā Mīnovī during two visits which I made to Tehran for the purpose of consulting him. Professor Mīnovī gave me unstintingly of his time and placed at my disposal his copy of the Istanbul MS Beyazit 5411 when I had not yet obtained my own copy. His suggestions have proved impossible to acknowledge individually because of their number. I consider it a great privilege to have been able to work with this distinguished scholar and am most grateful for his help. I wish to thank Oxford University for kindly helping toward traveling expenses. Professor Vladimir Minorsky, in what was, sadly, to be our last conversation, gave me much helpful advice. I must thank Professor E. Yar-Shater for his attentive assistance. Mr. A. A. Ḥaidarī was kind enough to act as reader of the translation and I am extremely grateful for his many helpful observations and suggestions, which again I am unable severally to acknowledge. I must also thank my pupil Miss Parīrokh Mosteshār for patient work on the preparation of the text for translation. The French translation by H. Massé (Paris, 1959) has been valuable, as have been the learned notes by M. Maḥjūb to his edition of the Persian text. I have to thank Mr. N. C. Sainsbury, Keeper of Oriental Books and MSS in the Bodleian Library, Oxford, and his staff for their help, and my wife for reading proofs. Columbia University Press has dealt expertly with a complicated MS.

It only remains to say that any imperfections which remain in the translation are attributable solely to myself.

Oriental Institute GEORGE MORRISON
Oxford University
October, 1970

SOURCES

For the present translation the editions of Mujtabā Mīnovī (Tehran, 1935) (abbreviated *Mi*) and M. Maḥjūb (Tehran, 1959) (abbreviated *Mb*) have been used together with the Istanbul MS Beyazit 5411 (abbreviated *I*), for a microfilm of which I am much indebted to Umumî Kütübhanesi. The use of readings of *I* has been indicated in certain cases only. *B* refers to Bodleian MS Elliot 273. *NL* refers to the edition of Nassau Lees in Bibliotheca Indica(1864-65). *T* refers to the edition of A. Devonaqulov (Dushanbeh, Tadzhikistan, 1966). The edition of the text by Todua, Gwakharia, and Aini (Academy of Sciences of the USSR, Georgian SSR and Tadzhik SSR, and Cultural Foundation of Iran, Tehran, 1970) has also been used. I owe my copy to the kindness of Mr. M. Ashtiany. Use has also been made of the Georgian translation of *Vīs o Rāmīn* in the English version by Sir Oliver Wardrop (Oriental Translation Fund, reprint 1966) (abbreviated *G*). Minorsky, *Iranica*, refers to *Iranica*, twenty articles by Professor V. Minorsky, University of Tehran Publications, Vol. 775 (1964).

Tristan refers to Gottfried von Strassburg, *Tristan*, translated by A. T. Hatto (Penguin Classics L98, 1960); *Tristan (B)* refers to Benoul, *The Romance of Tristan*, translated by A. S. Fedrick (Penguin Classics, 1970).

ABBREVIATIONS:

B	Bodleian MS Elliot 273
G	Georgian translation
I	Istanbul MS Beyazit 5411
Mb	edition of Maḥjūb
Mi	edition of Mīnovī
NL	edition of Nassau Lees
T	Tadzhikistan edition of Devonaqulov

INTRODUCTION

The poem *Vīs o Rāmīn* was composed by the Persian poet Fakhr ud-Dīn Gurgānī between A.D. 1040 and 1054. This was the time when Persia was being conquered by the Seljuqs, who after taking possession of Khurāsān in the east spread their conquests farther west. The Seljuq Sultan Ṭughril, after taking Isfahan, appointed as its governor 'Amīd Abū'l-Fatḥ Muẓaffar. This ruler suggested the composition of the poem to Gurgānī, as the poet records in his exordium, and it is to Abū'l-Fatḥ Muẓaffar that the poem is dedicated.

Information about the poet himself is unfortunately negligible. He tells us that when the Sultan left Isfahan he himself, having some business in the city, remained behind and was persuaded by the governor to stay until Nourūz, the Persian New Year, which falls in March. A month after this meeting the governor asks Gurgānī, "What do you say about the tale of Vīs and Rāmīn? They say it is a thing of rare excellence; in this country all are devoted to it." He replies, "It is a very beautiful story. . . . I have never seen a better; it resembles nothing so much as a blossoming garden. However, its language is Pahlavī,[1] and by no means everyone who reads it is aware of its purport. . . . At that time poetry was not an art. . . . When a work has meter and rhyme it is better than when it is arranged haphazardly. . . . However dainty and sweet a tale may be, it becomes refurbished by meter and rhyme. . . . If a scholar were to apply himself to it, it would become as pretty as a treasure full of gems."

His patron directs him, "Beautify this story as April the garden." "I shall tell it as best I can," Gurgānī goes on, "and purge it of meaningless expressions. . . . I have girt my loins for the charge he laid on me."

Thus is narrated at firsthand the genesis of one of the earliest Persian romantic epics which we possess. The poem opens according to convention with an exordium beginning literally at the beginning

1. Or Middle Persian, the language of Iran before the Arab Conquest in the seventh century A.D.

with a section in praise of God, in the course of which the creation of the Universe is described. In this section Gurgānī follows closely the Arabic *khuṭbah* of Avicenna. The creation of man follows, then the sending of the prophet Muhammad. The paramount Sultan, Tughril, next receives his meed of praise; his vizier is then eulogized, and finally Abū'l-Fatḥ Muẓaffar is made the subject of an encomium.

As might be expected, this section of the work is very much a child of its time; the reader moves here amid the conventional atmosphere of the eulogistic poetry of the period. With the start of the story proper, however, we find ourselves in a different milieu. The atmosphere of Zoroastrian Iran is vividly rendered, and as the romance develops the poet, faithful to his undertaking at the beginning of the work, brings into play the full gamut of the devices of Persian poetry to embellish the romance.

Gurgānī makes it clear that he is in fact producing a *rifacimento* of an earlier work and reveals an acquaintance with the Pahlavī language. Indeed the romance appears to have existed earlier in ballad form;[2] Rāmīn, its hero, is an accomplished minstrel, a talent which he shares with Tristan, hero of the legend of Tristan and Isolde, to which the Persian story bears a resemblance. Songs of Rāmīn are interspersed in the work, some of which are easily distinguishable in the Persian text since they display a tendency to rhyme at the end of the line of two half-verses, whereas the form of the poem demands only that the half-verses themselves rhyme.

When King Moubad calls on Rāmīn to sing at his banquet, he sings in veiled allusion to his love for Vīs, the queen:

I saw a garden where spring flowers fell in cascades,
Perfect for love's blossoming:
Tall cypress swayed into sight,
Heavenly moon rose and spoke silver words to the night.

Sweet April rose shyly opened its petals and smiled,
Perfumed in far paradise,
In days of joy a delight,
In nights of weeping a balm for a lover's sad eyes.

2. See V. Minorsky, *Iranica*, University of Tehran Publications, Vol. 775 (1964), p. 196; Mujtabā Mīnovī, *Majalleye Adabiyyāt* (Tehran), I, No. 3 (1954), 62–77.

I lost my heart to the garden: now early and late
Through tulips wander my feet,
Slave of the garden of love,
I feast my eyes on the flowers,
Enemies outside the wall like the ring on the gate.

Why should the envious glare at me as they pass by?
God gives each what he deserves:
Heaven was deserving, and so
God gave the moon to it to be the Queen of the Sky.

Lying at the side of Vīs he dreads the break of day and sings of the
night:

Night, you that steal my heart away,
You are to me the day:
Daybreak brings darkness to my eyes,
Sunset my sunrise.

Now once again morning is near:
My sleeping heart, beware!
Swift comes the arrow that you fear
Splitting the dawn air.

However sweet love's rose we find,
Thorns lurk behind!

The poet has devoted especial care to the Ten Letters sent by Vīs
to Rāmīn, in which rich use is made of lyric figures. Passages of
rare beauty occur in them; here as elsewhere Gurgānī's work has
had a marked influence on later Persian poetry.

The long dispute of the lovers clearly engages the sympathies of
the poet and he relentlessly causes them to discuss the successive
stages of infatuation, loyalty, faithlessness, regret, and longing
through which their long-suffering hearts pass. Gurgānī rounds not
infrequently on Fate with great dramatic effect to reproach her for
her harsh treatment of the lovers and of humankind in general. An
Old Iranian motif is recalled when there are references to the souls
of the lovers finding each other in the next life; when they die their
souls are said to be united in Paradise as bride and groom. This

echoes the beautiful passage in the Hādokht Nask of the Avesta
where the soul of the devout Zoroastrian is met in Paradise by a
beautiful maiden whose approach is heralded by a sweet-smelling
breeze; she greets the soul of the dead man and tells him that
whenever he has carried out a good action on earth—or abstained
from an evil one—her station in Paradise has been advanced.

Gurgānī finds occasion, too, to display a shrewd gift for parody
when he lampoons the stock repertoire of love poetry. There is also
an attractive vividness about his appeal to the reader before he
passes from the end of the romance to valedictory eulogies of his
patron: "When you read this poem, man of letters, crave forgiveness
of God Almighty for my sins! Say, 'O Lord, have mercy on the
youth who composed this beautiful tale; it is you who accept excuse
from your servants: forbear to visit his words on his soul!' "

The Persian legend was fortunate indeed in finding such a poet
to give it immortal form; Gurgānī not only displays a cultivated
sympathy with the Iran of ancient times but brings to his presenta-
tion of what is for him the main drama, the vicissitudes of the hearts
of the lovers, a masterly talent for the manipulation of the rich
armory of Persian lyric poetry.

There may be a historical background to the romance of *Vīs o
Rāmīn*. Professor Vladimir Minorsky[3] believes the story reflects the
history of a branch of the Parthian ruling house. The Parthians
ruled in Iran from the third century B.C. to the beginning of the
third century A.D., and the branch in question was founded by a
ruler called Godarz in the first half of the first century A.D.

The story tells of the vicissitudes of the lovers Vīs and Rāmīn.
Shahrū, Queen of Māh, rejects the suit of King Moubad of Marv
and swears that should she bear a daughter she will give her to him
as a bride. She gives birth to a daughter, Vīs, who is sent to Khūzān
to be cared for by a nurse who also brings up Rāmīn, younger
brother of King Moubad. When Vīs grows up Shahrū marries her
to her son Vīrū, brother of Vīs. Zard, half-brother of Moubad and
his vizier, arrives at the banquet with a message from Moubad
recalling the old oath. War breaks out and Moubad's army is

3. Minorsky, *Iranica*, p. 178.

defeated, but an invader from the north threatens Vīrū. Moubad, profiting by this turn of events, makes his way to the castle where Shahrū and Vīs are being kept and suborns Shahrū with gifts; she surrenders Vīs to him. On the way to Marv Rāmīn sees Vīs and falls in love with her. Vīs persuades the Nurse, who is a sorceress, to make a talisman which renders Moubad impotent. The talisman is lost in a flood and Moubad remains impotent for life. Rāmīn seduces the Nurse and prevails upon her to arrange an assignation with Vīs. Moubad discovers their intrigue and makes Vīrū place Vīs in custody; she is banished to Māh, her homeland. Rāmīn leaves Marv on the pretext of a hunting expedition and breaks his promise to Moubad not to associate with Vīs; the lovers spend seven months together. Moubad learns of it and sets off with an army but is placated by Vīrū. He orders Vīs to swear before the sacred fire that she is innocent of connection with Rāmīn. Vīs and Rāmīn elope and Moubad sets off to wander the world in search of Vīs. Rāmīn's mother elicits a pledge from her elder son, Moubad, that he will not harm Rāmīn; the lovers return to Marv where Moubad overhears them whispering fondly at his banquet. Rāmīn wanders on the palace roof and sends a message to Vīs by the hand of the Nurse. Vīs tells the Nurse to lie in her place in the King's bed. The King discovers the trick but is consoled by Vīs. News reaches Moubad that the Emperor of Rome is approaching with an army. Moubad orders Zard to imprison Vīs in a redoubtable fortress. Rāmīn sets off with Moubad's army but falls sick with misery. He is left behind and makes his way to the fortress. He shoots an arrow into the castle as a signal, scales the wall, and the lovers are reunited. Vīs pledges her love for Rāmīn with the wine cup and they remain together for nine months. Their secret is divulged to Moubad, who comes to the castle; the Nurse lets Rāmīn down the wall. Moubad beats Vīs and the Nurse, returns to Marv, and summons Vīs to join him. Rāmīn makes his way into the palace garden, where Vīs comes upon him asleep. Moubad arrives and Rāmīn escapes by scaling the wall. There is later a brawl at Moubad's banquet when a minstrel sings a song with a pointed reference to the situation. Rāmīn parries Moubad's dagger blow and throws him to the floor. A sage counsels Rāmīn to leave Marv and console himself with another sweetheart.

Professor Vladimir Minorsky[5] concludes that the relationship between the two stories is tenuous and quotes von Stackelberg to the effect that both may go back to a common Indian source. R. Zenker[6] suggests a closer relationship and speculates as to whether bards or itinerant monks might have carried the Oriental romance to Ireland. Professor Mujtabā Mīnovī[7] believes that the Persian romance may have been transmitted to the West through minstrels who had free access to both Crusader and Saracen camps in the Holy Land. The poem was translated into Georgian possibly early in the thirteenth century.[8]

Parallels between the two romances may be noted from the point in the Tristan story where King Mark sends for Isolde as his bride and Tristan and Isolde meet. Vīs and Rāmīn in the Persian story have already lived together as children in the care of the same Nurse, the counterpart of Brangane. The triangle Mark-Isolde-Tristan corresponds to Moubad-Vīs-Rāmīn.

Rāmīn, as we have seen, is, like Tristan, a minstrel. Joseph Bédier, in the course of a discussion of certain traits in the character of Tristan unlikely to have been of French origin, writes: "Tristan possède, comme Sigfrid, le don d'imiter à s'y méprendre le chant de tous les oiseaux. Quel poète de France l'eût imaginé d'un chevalier?"[9] No Persian poet, on the other hand, would have dreamt of disqualifying a knight on such grounds, much though Vīrū in the Persian poem may lampoon Rāmīn disparagingly for being given to the minstrel's calling.

Tristan and Rāmīn also share the gift of being skilled archers. There is a marked use of hunting metaphors in the passages referring to Rāmīn's romantic exploits which recalls similar passages in the Tristan story and the hunting prowess of Tristan.[10]

King Mark is depicted as less melodramatically evil than his counterpart King Moubad but both are the slaves of nagging

5. Minorsky, *Iranica*, p. 194.
6. "Die Tristansage und das persische Epos von Wîs und Râmîn," *Romanische Forschungen*, Bd. 29, Heft 2 (Erlangen, 1911).
7. This view was communicated to me orally.
8. Minorsky, *Iranica*, p. 151.
9. Joseph Bédier, *Le Roman de Tristan par Thomas* (Paris, 1902), II, 155.
10. See, for example, p. 225.

jealousy. On the other hand, Vīs, though deceitful to her husband and a victim to feelings of revenge, does not sink to the level of Isolde. In both stories the heroines are more faithful than their sweethearts; Rāmīn even has the epithet "cunning." The episode of Tristan's infidelity with Isolde of the White Hands is closely paralleled by that of Rāmīn with Gul, whose appealing forwardness very much recalls the demeanor of her counterpart. Rāmīn sadly recalls the keepsake of Vīs, as does Tristan the ring of Isolde. The idyllic sojourn of Tristan and Isolde in the Cave of Lovers has a parallel in *Vīs o Rāmīn*. Both Tristan and Rāmīn plead illness to excuse themselves from a hunting expedition. The Nurse in *Vīs o Rāmīn* is persuaded to deputize for Vīs in Moubad's bed exactly as befalls Brangane in *Tristan*. Her counsel to Vīs resembles a corresponding passage in *Tristan* where Brangane similarly admonishes Isolde.

The absence of the motif of the love-potion is noticeable in *Vīs o Rāmīn*. Here, however, the Nurse herself is the baneful influence binding the lovers together and keeping them on their fatal course. A. T. Hatto writes: "The Brangane episode is an integral part of the events which arise from the drinking of the potion, showing as it does how swiftly love can drive Isolde to the depths. In the Brangane episode the malign aspects of love as it was released by the philtre are shown to the full in action."[11]

In the Persian romance the Nurse is a sorceress and uses a talisman to render King Moubad impotent. The tie of a common nurse links Vīs and Rāmīn and the three-cornered relationship is further cemented by Rāmīn's seduction of the Nurse in the garden.

Both Vīs and Isolde are commanded to suffer the Ordeal, though Vīs escapes during the proceedings. The killing of Moubad by a boar recalls the dream of Marjodoc in *Tristan*[12] where a boar rushes into the royal palace, makes its way into Mark's chamber, and soils the royal linen with its foam. Both romances contain the adventures of the lovers under the suspicious eye of the King, including the unexpected arrival of the King on the scene.

11. *Tristan*, p. 23. Cf. p. 97.
12. *Tristan*, p. 219. In *Tristan* (B), p. 63, Tristan, after being wounded by a large boar, leaps on to the king's bed; his wound opens and soils the sheets.

Other parallels are pointed out in the notes to the translation; similarities may also be noticed in the passages which philosophize on the subject of love.

It is notable, incidentally, that the figure of Zard, brother and vizier of King Moubad in *Vīs o Rāmīn*, seems to have appealed particularly to Gurgānī; his characterization is an attractive one and throughout the romance he maintains a chivalrous demeanor, even, for instance, parrying an abusive attack by his monarch with unruffled courtesy; at the end he dies a hero's death.

Vis and Ramin

I.

PRAISE TO GOD.[1]   To the King who brought into being the world
and ourselves, thanks and blessings! Sovereignty and kingship are
meet for him, for he is never separated from sovereignty; God pure,
without peer or companion, far alike from thought and sight. The
eye cannot see him nor the thought contrive to reach him. He does
not suffer detriment like substance, nor does his state alter thereby.
Nor in him is accident associated with substance, for substance must
of necessity have existed after him. It is impossible to describe him by
saying "How" he is, for he is outside comparison and description.
Neither is it proper to say "How many" by way of describing him,
for the conception "How many" implies degree and components. It
is also improper to say "Where," for it would then be neccessary to
postulate something around him. It is also improper to say "When"
he has been, for no period has measured his existence; and if the
conception "When existing" were to enter into a description of him,
he would then have to have a beginning and an end. He is not
conjoined to any other thing, for then they would be equals in
existence. He has no position, boundary, or measure, for then limits
would be evident in him. Neither is his essence associated with place,
nor is the knowledge of that essence hidden. He was in the beginning
the innovator of Time; he needed no colleague in that innovation.
Time came into existence by his order, near the highest substance of
the universe, at the place where motion came into being, and from
that motion time emerged. Limits, too, came into being for place,
many bodies between the two. Will you not, pray, tell me who
might design an edifice in this wise other than an all-wise King who,
without partner, brought force into being and through existence
made it powerful over nonexistence, a Lord whose command ever
thus has currency in his sovereignty?

First he created the substance of the spiritual beings, fashioning it
neither from place nor time; he denuded their form of matter, guides
to felicity all; he clothed them in his own light and created through
them all he willed. His first creation was the angels, then he created
a substance which was the Heaven; from them came those bright

1. This passage follows closely the Arabic *khuṭbah* of Avicenna; cf. *Mb*, p. 12,
and Ahmedmian Akhtar, *Islamic Culture*, IX (Hyderabad, 1935), 218.

bodies, like roses in a verdant garden; they boast the best of shapes, the round; and the best of colors, radiant; there is no form like theirs, for they know no dread or calamity; they are not all alike in degree, aspect, action, or motion. If the wheeling sphere had been without stars, the epochs of the world would not have become different; there would not have been these temporal causations from which the equilibrium of life arises. Had there not been this cause of growing organisms, there would not have been creatures on the earth. Had the stars been without the sky, the world would have been constantly full of light; the radiance of light would have erased darkness; then this coming into being and decaying of ours would not have been. Had he not made the heaven inclined, with such a slight equalizing inclination, there would not have been the seasons of the revolving year, neither summer nor winter would have come round.

Mighty, puissant Creator, who has shown to us his power so vast! Just as his might and power are boundless, even so are his bounty, largesse, and liberality. He is in no wise troubled, however much he exerts his power; his treasure is not thinned a whit, however much he distributes bounty. As he was no less than eternal in displaying power, his generosity and power were boundless.

By his power he created something capable of taking on dimension, susceptible of the power of the creator of the world; the scholar terms it *hyle*; it is susceptible of energy. Boundless as are the creations of God, its susceptibility is no less. It receives from the Creator the imprint of creations as the *dīnār* the imprint of the stamp. It resembles gold, from which the goldsmith fashions every kind of form.

When God willed the creation of this world from which arises the being and decaying of everything, he knew that this would come to pass when its elements were below the moon.[2] One of them should by nature sever connection, another should make connection opposite the first;[3] form should be malleable in crookedness before a third, a fourth should be the guardian of form in straightness. He fashioned for the world from *hyle* four elements each possessing one of these four properties. Of these, Heat proved the severer of connection;[4] next, Cold whereby connection was established; Moisture made bodies

2. *I.* 3. *I.*

4. Reading *paivandbur* (cf. *B*, folio 3).

such that they were malleable at the time of taking shape; Dryness similarly held them down by its property of fixing and rectifying.

When these four elements were created, warmth rose upwards; had the cold risen upwards, it would have become warm by the movements of the sphere; so the two warm elements prevailed; cold, moisture, and softness retreated; air and fire turned out to be the refined ones, thus they raised their heads upwards; he caused them to turn like a revolving wheel; all light passes through them, so that the light of the sun and other bodies may penetrate thence to colors and bodies; the earth is innocent of refinement, so as to be able to retain light; had it not been thus by nature the light would not have remained trained on it.

When these four Mothers, air, pure earth, water, and fire, came into existence, multifarious kinds of progeny were born to them from substances and fruitful seeds; a thousand kinds of every species of creature, all constantly altering their condition; but the world of being and passing away received a different order from God, for in the upper world of beginning the better emerged by disposition; the order in this world was not so; for the jewel was first produced from the mine; things were so disposed that what was better remained till later; nature exercised foresight in equilibrium, as with the material from which man arose. Our God first pruned it, then created bodies of its superfluities, each one of a different species and name; their aspects are plain in the mine, but hidden from men's eyes. First, the species of mineral arose from the mine, below it the categories of varicolored minerals; next, the species of vegetables came into the world; third, the species of animals of a thousand types.

When God refined the ore of man, by the proportionateness that he possessed, he created man from substance and made him chief of creatures of the same clay. The end purpose of all was man, for he had human virtues. The vegetables, animals, and minerals of the world all came under man's sway; once his position was above theirs, a different world came into being in perfection; God gave him a pure substance not of wind or water or fire; some call it holy spirit, some articulate soul. He does not know the limits of universal science, but evolves invention out of invention; since he seeks knowledge and likes it, he learns, then puts his knowledge to use. He is cleansed of the

3

When a people of such deeds and words, their tongue a shower of pearls and their sword bloodstained, heard the Furqān from the Prophet and saw him in the battles of Badr and Khaibar they knew that these two were Godhead, and that acceptance thereof was light for the soul. Leaders submitted themselves willy-nilly and loosed the strap of the fastening of the girdle.[3] They escaped from the claws of the demon of evil nature and smashed the idols of Mecca. Darkness was erased by the light of religion, mercy rained from the cloud of truth. Idol worship departed, the religion of God came in, the sword of faith took the land of heathendom.

How, other than by devoting our souls to thanking God, are we to render gratitude and thanks to him for the felicitous religion he gave us, the prophet he sent for our sakes? The Prophet came, conveyed his messages, and rescued an entire world from his wrath. What a forgiving, clement God! How excellent in action and merciful! to have mercy on our helplessness, give us a prophet, and show us the right way! We accept him as God, his prophet as guide in sincerity; we do not associate any other with him nor accept anything other than his word; we look to him in this world and the world hereafter, none but he holds us dear. Even if swords rained on our heads, none but this religion would be proper for us. We hold to the faith while we have spirit and entrust spirit and faith together to God. O God, we have done what behooved us, entrusted body and soul to your command; we have accepted your religion from the Prophet and multiplied gratitude and blessing upon you. But it was you who molded this body of ours; you who wrote your Destiny upon us; should it so happen that from time to time offense or sin should emanate from our frame, do not visit our deed on our heads, do not mete out to us retribution according to our due! We are the helpless servants of you, our Lord, and are of the communities of Muṣṭafā;[4] though we be marred by infinite sins, we yet hope for your grace and mercy. We call on you, and rightly so, for we know no road but that to your audience hall. The generous do not drive away the weak, especially when they call abjectly upon them. You are generous: summon us to your audience hall when we call on you. We are weak;

3. *I.* The sacred thread worn by Zoroastrians.
4. "The Chosen" (epithet of the Prophet).

it is meet that you should summon us; we are sinful; it is meet that you should not drive us away. Grace and patience are as little surprising in you as in us cruelty and evildoing. Your goodness and mercy are infinite, our interceder kindly disposed. When Muḥammad intercedes for your mercy, how shall our hope in your grace be dashed?

3.

OF THE PRAISE OF SULTAN ABŪ ṬĀLIB ṬUGHRILBEG.[1] Three kinds of obedience are obligatory to the reasonable man, and those three are connected; they spell for the heart enjoyment of desire, and for the soul, good name; honorable life in this world, eternal paradise in the next. Do not turn your head away from the command of these three, if you would gain both worlds! One is the command of the Judge of the world, which liberates the soul forever. Second, the command of the Prophet Muḥammad, which is rejected by a faithless unbeliever. Third, the command of the Sultan that rules the world, splendor of the religion of God in the realm, Abū Ṭālib, mighty king, lord of the lords of the world, King Ṭughrilbeg, that sun of nobility; grandeur and wealth have reached all from him; victory is his guide and generosity his treasurer, constancy his chamberlain, reason his minister.

As he is of the same name as Muḥammad, he has become like him victorious and divinely aided. He appeared from the east like the sun and by his fortune became King of Kings like Jamshīd. He took India and the East with his Indian sword, captured Rome and Barbary with his Turkish warriors. He has girded his loins for conquest of empire, and conquers the world merely to give it away as largesse. Why do you read the story of the Sassanians[2] and the chronicle of the Samanids?[3] Read but once the history of the Sultan and all that will become as nothing in your eyes.

You shall find therein all in the way of prodigies of victory and kingship that you desire; unique turns and changes of fortune, wonders and miracles of God. Read his history so that you may know

1. The Seljuq Sultan, d. A.D. 1063.
2. Rulers of Iran from the third to the seventh century A.D.
3. Tenth century A.D.

6

that no one attains empire without lifting a finger! The territory of Transoxiana and Khurāsān has constituted a battlefield for the King from end to end; he has fought an engagement on every inch of it, defeated thereon a general and a king. When he moved from Tūrān to Iran, crossed the Oxus like Kaikhusrou,[4] his mount was a ship, Fortune his pilot, God his support, and Heaven his aid. See how pure was the certainty of his heart, to cross such a river fearlessly! Since his heart did not quail at the Oxus, why should it do so at any other circumstance? It does not shrink from heat or cold, sand, salt desert, mountain, or sea. The deserts of Khvārazm and Khurāsān are in his eyes like a garden; the folds of the Qārin[5] mountains like a rose plot; he is not a seeker of wine bowls, like other kings, for he is a seeker of fame through endurance of tribulations. No sooner had he left the Oxus River behind than he made two hundred Oxus rivers of enemies' blood flow! A storm rose from his sword which spelled the end of all kings! In the other world the soul of King Mas'ūd was ashamed before the soul of King Maḥmūd,[6] for he rebuked him sorely for giving up Khurāsān foolishly; now because of the multitude of kings who have become co-mates of the fleet wind, all wounded by the Sultan's sword, all giving up kingship and kingdom to him, his soul has been delivered from its shame, for there are many wretched as he: he is excused in his father's eyes, for he has seen many a better king than himself brought low.

What king in the East could enter the lists with the King of Khvārazm at the time of battle? Everyone who has lived in our time knows how Shāh Malik's[7] star rode high in the heavens: he had hundreds of thousands of Turkish cavalry; one cavalryman from their midst was sufficient to take on an entire army. His raids and night attacks were so numerous that he was more formidable than Rustam.[8] The Lord of the World, the Great King, by his unerring

4. Of the legendary Kayānī dynasty. See *Shāhnāmeh*, paperback ed. (Tehran, 1345 H.S.), II, 242.
5. In Tabaristān. See V. Minorsky, *Ḥudūd ul-'Ālam* (London, 1937), pp. 39, 135; Guy Le Strange, *The Lands of the Eastern Caliphate* (Cambridge, 1905), p. 372.
6. Of Ghazna, eleventh century A.D. Mas'ūd was the son of Maḥmūd. W. Barthold, *Turkestan down to the Mongol Invasion* (London, 1928), p. 303.
7. *Ibid.*, p. 304.
8. See *Qābūsnāmeh*, ed. Reuben Levy (London, 1951), p. 82.

strategy and firm counsel rends armies on the day of battle as a heavy anvil glass! The Sultan's adversary not only fled disgracefully from before him but was miserably killed on the march. No matter who it was of the Sultan's enemies, he tasted the same fortune and fate. Any lesser being who tries conclusions with a greater will so fall that he shall never rise again! His body shall become a byword for disgrace, his soul a target for the arrow of destruction.

But had he had no enemy, against whom could he have displayed this prowess? Had darkness not spread its shadow, the radiant sun would not have gained its worth.[9] Even so did the King of the World display his lofty worth to men through his enemies.

Once he had cleared Khvārazm and Khurāsān, he came to Tabaristān and Gurgān. There is no land in the wide world so withered and weird. Three kinds of places are formidable and inaccessible; one, the sea, the others, forest and mountain. Its mountains are like an endless succession of castles,[10] the sea like a moat at their feet. No man however shrewd can describe it, no demon find his way therein. In it dwell warriors, Gīls and Dailamīs;[11] the bravest and most valorous in the world; their profession is plunder and their calling war, learned in that sea and forest; once they saw the standards of the Sultan they fled like demons from the name of God. The Sultan caused blood to flow more copious than the sea of that region. Now they find on the trees there the brains of hapless victims instead of fruit!

When that province was cleared by the King, he advanced his standards thence to Reyy; he sent generals to every part, as I shall mention to you in brief: one general went to Makrān and Gurgān, one to Mosul and Khūzān,[12] one to Kirmān and Shīrāz, one to Shushtar[13] and Ahvāz; one to Arrān and Armenia, to cast the lands of Rome into lamentation. His generals were victorious, his enemies struck by ill fortune.

An ambassador came to him from Arslān Khān[14] and by letter craved of him alliance and treaty. The Khān sent him great quantities of money as a gift and promised him the revenue of the Tartar

9. Lacuna in *I* here.   10. Reading *qal'eh* as in *Mi*.   11. Cf. § 99, p. 340,
12. See n. 5, p. 26.   13. In Khūzistān.   and *ibid*, n. 2.
14. Barthold, *Turkestan*, p. 300. *Mb*, notes, p. 444.

kingdom; the general of the world made a treaty with the Khān, for he saw him very sagacious in kingship. Then came knights and money from Caesar, such as come from a junior to a senior. He sent ten years' revenue of Rome and freed his prisoners from their bonds. Opposite the fortress of 'Ammūriyyeh[15] the Sultan built minaret, mosque, and minbar. The name of the Sultan was written on the minaret, the faith of Islam proclaimed by it. A messenger also came from the king of Syria, nobly accepting a treaty; he had sent great wealth as a gift, among it a royal ruby: a gorgeous red ruby, large and round and rough as a mountain; in radiance it was like the sun in the heavens, the tribute of Syria for a whole year its price; besides its beauty, fineness, and color its weight was thirty-six *misqāls*;[16] in its train came a rescript and a robe of honor, the insignia of sovereignty from the Caliph.[17] The Sultan assumed these insignia in Isfahān; kings congratulated him on them. The kings of the age all the way from China to Barbary became his servants. The powerful became his slaves and disabused their hearts of trickery and stratagem.

Between Tigris and Oxus is a whole world; but to the King it is like a mere garden. He moves at his ease in this royal garden with the servitors of his court. A thousand suns in his Chinese temple, a thousand dragons within his castle walls. Sometimes he dwells in Khurāsān, sometimes in Isfahān, sometimes in Gurgān. They constantly bring him news of some victory from the regions of his realm; I did not sleep in Isfahān for seven months from the noise of drum and horn of messengers claiming reward for good news! There is no period in the month when a present is not brought from some clime. The world is his; he rules it happily and gives largesse generously to small and great alike. He has no objective in this world but chivalry; he fears God and not men. In all parts of the world famous kings crave position and fame from him. Those of them who are singled out by him for special favor rejoice the more at their fortune. Those who are junior to him at his court are senior to Khāns and more than

15. In Asia Minor. Le Strange, *Lands of the Eastern Caliphate*, p. 134. *Mb*, notes, p. 445.

16. *G*, p. 2: "twenty-six drachmas."   17. *I* resumes here.

Caesars; for from year to year different kinds of wealth continually come in from Khāns and Caesars.

Which of the kings of the land have you ever seen with this fame, position, and glory? What king has ever possessed such empire, comprising Egypt, Syria, Mosul, even so far as the wall of China? What king has had the valor to shrink neither from tribulation nor from death? It would be meet for his soul to survive so long as to outlive eternity; may a thousand blessings be upon his soul, the orbit of the sphere be according to his command! The stars be the guides of his desire, Destiny well disposed to his fame! May his sovereignty and fame be eternal, his body at ease, and his soul joyful! Wherever he fights may he be victorious, wherever he banquets may he be attended by pomp and glory! May joy attend his every step, may God aid his every enterprise!

4.

OF THE PRAISE OF KHVĀJEH ABŪ NAṢR IBN MANṢŪR IBN MUḤAMMAD.[1] When God befriends one of his servants, the eyes of his fortune are awake. In triumph he secures his every desire, in fair fortune he secures all fame. Be there a possession fair and royal, be there knighthood apt for warfare, God vouchsafes them wholly to that servant, for he is ever worthy of them.

Try to choose out from all you know in the world the quality of what he has now vouchsafed to the Sultan! All the men of his court are such that other men are but women beside them: but amongst them is one renowned, brave, competent, and sagacious; wise, clever, a good judge of men, generous, good-natured, of excellent counsel; eloquent, a connoisseur of style, blessed with wit, talented, avid in perfecting his accomplishments, refined; for he is the Support of the Sultan's court, laudable in every enterprise and event, divinely aided by victory and good fortune, Abū Naṣr,[2] Manṣūr,[3] Muḥammad;[4] a lord who is a world of excellence, in which his high will is the sky.

Of all things in this world he cleaves to learning and multiplies his pleasure by attaining it. He ever seeks a good name and fulfills

1. Vizier of Ṭughrilbeg.   2. Lit. "father of victory."   3. "Victorious."
4. "Praised."

10

obligation even where none exists. He is gentle and modest before men and (as could be expected) has no enemy. How should one whose soul ever has mercy on his suppliants have an enemy? He has Reason as minister by his side and keeps his heart far from all that is distasteful. He knows all tongues like Solomon; he has thousands of demons in his thrall; in beneficence he is greater than Ḥātim,[5] in knightliness the superior of Rustam son of Zāl. He speaks the tongues of the seven climes so fluently that you would swear his origins had been from the land concerned! The man of Ṭarāz[6] thinks he is a Ṭarāzī; the man of Ḥejāz says he is from Ḥejāz. He not only composes prose felicitously in every tongue but performs miracles in each language too; he speaks Darī,[7] Arabic, and Turkish with a diction that scours corrosion from the heart! He has two swords: one of diamond, one of eloquence; one in his hand, and one in his mouth; the one penetrates adamantine rock at the time of prowess, the other beautifies learning at the time of speech; many the hero who has writhed at the one, many the sage soul that has expired through the other! Great and small in the army of the Sultan of the world swear firm oaths by his soul. He behaves like a father when he is with a junior, like a son when with a senior. With his peers he is like a brother. Can there be nobility greater than this?

A bevy of sages from all disciplines surrounds him, orators, secretaries, scholars; they have flocked round him from every city and have sunk in the sea of his beneficence. Were he not a ready customer for our wares, the poet's craft would lack distinction; though a poet be not learned, he still makes it his business to exclaim profusely "Bravo!"[8] and "Excellent!"; partly to cheer him, and partly to ensure that the reward may be the greater. The Sultan has placed the affairs of the world, from east to west, under his command; this charge causes him less trouble than a single cup of wine does a winedrinker. How great is the beneficence of the world-surveying Creator to vouchsafe such bounty upon men! May this generous, goodnatured man live long! May his state and fortune ever prosper!

5. Ḥātim Ṭā'ī, legendary in the East for generosity.
6. In Transoxiana. Minorsky, *Ḥudūd ul-'Ālam*, p. 119.
7. Lit. "court language," Persian here.
8. *Aḥsant:* the exclamation is still used in Iran to applaud poetry.

May his destiny ever be triumphant, famed for victory and weal!
May the empire of the world attend him, the glory of God favor him!

5.

OF THE TAKING OF ISFAHĀN BY THE SULTAN. When the mighty
Sultan, King of Kings, entered Isfahān with propitious omens he
beheld a city in joy like spring; a wall round the city like a mountain.
The King's opponent had ruined the city, for his opponent is like a
storm. Had the King not been truly just, of generous heart at the
time of love and mercy, he would not have left one brick on another
in Isfahān, and no one would have cultivated it for a hundred years;
but he followed a chivalrous course and pardoned city and army.
He crushed their sin under foot, so that not one single person com-
plained of his wrath. He did not follow out an old feud like other
kings but ennobled the enemy in his eyes; according as God recorded
in the Qur'ān[1] when telling the story of Bilqīs[2] and Solomon: "When
kings enter a new city they wreak destruction and ill, and hand over
a number of those in positions of distinction and state to humiliation
and suffering." The Lord of the World, valorous king, introduced a
better custom than this; he conferred upon every class of men that
there was in the city, one and all, something of his bounty; he conferred on the army territory and rule, and neither treated them ill
nor visited them with destruction.

At that time no one suffered loss at his hand, but enjoyed profit
and happiness. When he had disposed the matter of the troops thus,
no one having so much as a hair of his head harmed by him, he
treated the people even more generously, and gave the whole city
relief from ill-wishers. A group who had oppressed the people and
arraigned the subjects in the Dīvān[3] had their tongues cut off by his
order and their eyes transfixed by red-hot needles. Then he relieved
the city of his visitation and departed leaving it free of disturbance,
in order that no person should suffer affliction at his hand, for people
might not be able to cope therewith.

When he departed he gave Isfahān to the one worthy of being
accorded a hundred worlds, Abū'l-Fatḥ, sun of the illustrious,
Muẓaffar by name, crown of the successful. A complete world in

1. xxvii, 33. 2. The Queen of Sheba. 3. Department, e.g., of taxation, etc.

12

bounty, like a precious son to the King; the King conferred steward-ship on him and also laid the mantle of royal fortune upon him He had won his approval in every task, his heart had never been hurt by him. He had found him competent in every enterprise and experi-enced from him loyalty and reliability.

He summoned him to his presence at the time of his departure and showered gems upon him from the treasure of affection. He said to him, "Though you are sagacious, loyal, and affectionate from the very heart, I yet have no option but to say that I lay a charge on you: I have chosen you as better than all others, for I have seen you worthy in your enterprises. Listen to all I say with the ear of your heart, for it is your glory that I seek in these words. My first compact with you is this: that you fear him who is Judge of the world; fear him and hope in him; implore his help in every enterprise. Do not withdraw your head from his command; perform every task in accordance with his behest. Next, the people in the world, all, like me, his servants; adjudge with equity in their cause, always help the Right. A tyrant is God's enemy, for he is indifferent to his decree. Prune his enemy with the dagger, but bestow kindness upon his friends. As you do not countenance oppression from a tyrant, neither do you yourself indulge in tyranny; for we are indifferent to men's property, holding our heads high in justice and the faith. Make Isfahān prosperous by justice, rejoice everyone by goodness. So maintain the city inside and out that it may be secure from intriguer and traitor. It should be possible for a woman to put gold on her head and walk round the walls day and night and no one dare to eye the gold on pain of losing his head for the offense. I have tested you much heretofore and have been satisfied with your every enter-prise; let met be satisfied with you in this task, too; let not what I seek to increase decrease! Let me sum up my discourse in one point: you well know what my aim is: you well know that we approve what is good and do not fix our hearts on the things of this world; on this side we seek fame from this high state, on the other side a good end for ourselves. Make our name glorious by good works; for goodness makes a man fortunate. As I fear God in this sovereignty, so shall I demand of you all that is demanded of me. Should you discharge my affairs according to my desire you shall have of me any hope you may cherish. We shall not leave your hope and pains to waste, but shall promote you to increase hereafter. As soon as you prove worthy you shall be suitable for higher things; keep hope of good fortune strong in your heart, for my glory shall ally itself to your fortune; it will resolve many a problem, all your desires of me shall be realized. I have told you my desire; I go, and entrust you to God."

Then they drew up rescripts accordingly and made over to him all income and expenditure. The King conferred on him an honorific present than which no one has ever conferred a better. A famous speedy Arab horse, with a golden bridle and royal saddle on it; a Byzantine robe and a gold-woven turban and much else in the way of ceremonial gifts; drums and flags in proper style, such as befit an illustrious personage. Fine as the institution of the robe of honor may be, it still falls short of the degree of his high nobility; how should a heart which is more exalted than a whole world rejoice in a mere Isfahān?

6.

PRAISE OF 'AMĪD ABŪ'L-FATḤ MUẒAFFAR.[1] What more can you wish for, Isfahān, than to have become the capital of the King of Kings? Baghdad envies you, for it has not what God gave you—a king such as the distinguished Sultan, King of Kings of the world in victoriousness, a lord like Abū'l-Fatḥ Muẓaffar, who has been vouch-safed position and glory by the Sultan; great in lineage and fortune, lofty in status and nobility; distinguished in breeding and in his star, laudable in outward aspect as well as in intrinsic worth; his stock was ever like the east, moon and stars continually rising from it. Now there has risen up from it a minister like the sun; the world has placed its hopes of glory in the glory of his radiance. His first name comes from victory, his second from triumph[2]—this is why he has had his fill of both.

When you examine the world, it is a young old man. The famous 'Amīd is like the world: young in years, fortune, and peace, but like an old man in counsel, intelligence, and knowledge. If intelligence

1. Governor of Isfahān (see p. 12). Minorsky, *Iranica*, p. 198.
2. Abū'l-Fatḥ: "Father of Victory." Muẓaffar: "Victorious."

took visible shape it would show itself plainly in that fortunate countenance. His hand with the cup of wine is a stem of joy: but this stem of joy a whole garden of bounty.[3] You would say, from the excellence that his rescript and decree possess, that he was inspired by God. Awe and justice should be thus, so that the very name of tyranny and injustice may vanish away. If he is looked at with the eye of intelligence, you would think he was pure soul; if he is heard with the ear of justice, you would swear he was pure spirit. In the opinion of the learned, past judgments have, by the side of his decree, been mere injustices; their character like a mirage, which is not water and yet resembles it. When his order issues from the court of redress, Providence emerges from the heavens side by side with his decree. Hope says, "My guide has come!" Doom says, "My dagger is here!" Were he to give the order, it would become the law that the mean and cowardly should not be born into the world. When I utter praise of him or pray for his fortune, good luck itself suggests the praise, Gabriel says Amen to the prayer. Though made of clay like ourselves, he is in aspect and action an angel.

Although Isfahān is the pride of Iran, it is below the station of this pride of the world.[4] Nīshāpūr cries in distress of heart because this renowned figure has gone far from her. Isfahān laughs with delight, for she has become full of bounty because of his justice. Isfahān was like a broken limb; what was broken has now become mended by his glory. It is hardly surprising that this year the very trees bear praise of the minister as fruit, or that from the security of his justice the winter wind scatters not a single petal from the garden.

The Sultan who controls the world knew into whose hand to entrust this task; if he has made Isfahān ailing, he has yet given her an expert physician.[5] Assuredly when he sees his work he will choose him out from all others, entrust him with all his domains, for he has no other subordinate like him.[6] Everyone saw the villages of Isfahān, which were each and every one like the desert and the ruined place;[7]

---

3. *I.*
4. *I. Mb:* "the station of that pride of the world is more than its station."
5. See Nāṣir-i Khusrou, *Safarnāmeh*, ed. Dabīrsiāqī (Tehran, 1335 H.S.), p. 123. Minorsky, *Iranica*, p. 198.
6. *I* has an interpolation here.
7. *I. Mb:* "each and every one wasted rivers."

the people wandering out from the villages, all the time without provision and destitute; but when they heard his name they came back from Kūhistān and Khūzistan and Shīrāz. He called them one by one to the Dīvān and treated them kindly, gave them cattle and seed, and saw to their troubles. In the space of two months he has brought the province to a pitch no one would have credited. Those same villages one would have said were like deserts are now in point of prosperity the equal of Kandahār. Truly, had a whole lifetime passed, it could not have so been done by another.

In all these verses wherein I have praised him, God be my witness that I have not exaggerated my description of him. I have written no verse other than in description of what he is, I have merely said what I have seen of his actions. I see that I have omitted one blessing from my expression of thanks to him, namely, my privilege in praising him. By becoming so fortunate as to eulogize him, I have won my dearest wish. You have heard the saying about friendship: "Friendship is brightness." Since this Lord has been my friend, my heart has become brighter than the bright sky itself. Since the hunting lion has been my friend my *kebāb* has been the leg of the wild ass of the plain. As long as moon and sun are in the firmament, so long as fear and hope exist in the world, may that Lord remain in glory, may his body be wedded to health, may the world be his slave, fortune his guide, fate his servant, the Just God his aid. May his soul ever rejoice in prosperity, his ambition in chivalry be realized.

7.

THE SULTAN LEAVES ISFAHĀN; ACCOUNT OF THE AUTHOR. When the drum beat from the Sultan's gate you would have said mountain and rock had split asunder; the shining sun hid its face in the east, the heart of Venus was disturbed in the sky. An army went out from Isfahān, one hundredth of which has not been seen by any king. The Lord of the World, the Great King, left Isfahān happy and joyful; his stirrup possessed the magnificence of eternity, as his pavilion heavenly glory. The Sultan's camp was on the plain, like a mountain range, so many tents and pavilions were there, the warriors its leopards and lions, the dainty beauties its wild ass, deer,

16

and gazelle. The King stopped in Kūhistān, which became as glorious as a garden thereby. Next day he left Kūhistān and went straight to the hills of Hamedān.

I had some business in Isfahān, in the performance of which some time was to pass; I therefore remained in Isfahān and did not follow at the stirrup of the King of Kings. I went to the Crown of the Regime, Khvājeh Abū'l-Fath (may he ever enjoy victory in his campaigns!); in his majestic manner he inquired after the health of his slave; I descried glory in the inquiry. He then said to me, "This winter, stay here and do not go to Kūhistān. When the world is renewed by *Nourūz*[1] the weather will turn pleasanter; then go, I shall provide you with what provender you require; in this regard you shall suffer no loss." I replied, "My lord, you have always acted thus and proceeded in this manner, you entertain guests, treat servants well, crush enemies to the delight of friends. You free your slaves from the trap of pain, draw them up from the Fish,[2] and set them over the moon. Who am I to decline to be your guest, nay, your chamberlain? When dust from this portal settles on me fortune will surround me like a halo round the moon. You have many subordinates better than I, I no superior, however, like you. If you show this affection for the Pleiades, they will approach for you to tread them underfoot!

"When I place my foot on the dust of your archway my place shall be in the Seventh Heaven. My Nourūz will consist in seeing you, my pleasant weather in the pleasure of talking with you. May I not be blest with good fortune if I fail to see the world when I look on your face. In devotion I am even as I have appeared to you; if I have anything other than this in my heart I am a Jew!"

I uttered blessings for some time; a month then elapsed after the occasion of these words. That central point of the Faith said to me one day, "What do you say about the tale of Vīs and Rāmīn? They say it is a thing of rare excellence;[3] in this country all are devoted to it." I replied, "It is a very beautiful story, collected by six scholars.[4] I have never seen a better; it resembles nothing so much as a

1. The Persian New Year, March 21.
2. I.e., the creature supposed to support the earth.
3. See Minorsky, *Iranica*, p. 154.   4. See *ibid.*, p. 153, on this passage.

17

blossoming garden. However, its language is Pahlavī,[5] and by no means everyone who reads it is aware of its purport; not everyone reads that language well, or even if he reads it, knows its meaning. It contains numerous descriptions of all manner of things, but when you read it over it has no great meaning. For at that time poetry was not an art; there was no scholar of quick wit; if only those scholars could see how diction is produced nowadays, meanings unraveled, meter and rhyme superimposed! The volume is read in this region in order to learn Pahlavī from it, as the people of this clime are ever avid for that sweet speech. When a work has meter and rhyme it is better than when it is arranged haphazardly,[6] particularly when one may find therein sentiments which, when one reads them, will one day stand one in good stead. However dainty and sweet a tale may be, it becomes refurbished by meter and rhyme.

"There should be numerous sentiments and expressions scattered here and there in the story, like a royal pearl set in gold, shining out from its midst like stars. Then the nobles and intelligentsia may read it to learn many sentiments from it, whilst the populace and ordinary folk merely read it for the sake of the story. A discourse should be such that when it issues from the poet's mouth it should travel the wide world, not merely stay at home, declaimed by none but its author!

"Now those authorities of the past composed the tale of Vīs and Rāmīn; they used all their art to compose in Persian, for they were masters of Persian.

"Thus they composed a story with strange expressions in it from every language.[7] They took no pains over sentiments and proverbs, nor embellished it with these two. If a scholar were to apply himself to it, it would become as pretty as a treasure full of gems; for this is a famous story, whose incidents contain numberless marvels."

When the Lord heard my words, he placed a crown of pride upon my head. He thus requested me, "Beautify this story as April the garden." I shall tell it as best I can, and purge it of those meaningless expressions; for those expressions have become obsolete; through the

5. Boyce, "The Parthian gōsān and Iranian Minstrel Tradition," *JRAS* (April, 1957), p. 38.
6. *Ibid.* Mīnovī's adoption of the reading of *I* yields the meaning "haphazardly."
7. Minorsky, *Iranica*: "? style."

revolution of time their day is past and gone. I have girt my loins for the charge he laid on me, for his charge scoured the corrosion from my fortune. However much I range I shall not attain fortune better than that of seeking his satisfaction. Perhaps by forbearing to turn my heart from his command I shall attain to ascension in the heaven of his regard. I have never seen an elixir like his satisfaction nor a furious dragon like his anger. So far as I can I shall seek his elixir and shrink from his fatal dragon! Perhaps like his underlings I shall become a noble, or like his servitors, renowned; once my name is conjoined with theirs my ambition, like theirs, will be realized. "Though the grass grows in the garden, they nevertheless water it in the shadow of the rose plot." May this Lord, ruler of the world, live long, ever enjoying the world in good fame; may he survive forever in enjoyment of his desire, the nobles like the stars, he like the sun, purity and joy co-mates of his soul, benevolence and generosity courtiers of his nature. May he have thousands of slaves like me to tell his fame, to seek the award of his pleasure by their cogitations. Now I must begin a tale which the perceptive will term no less than sage advice.

8.

THE STORY OF VĪS AND RĀMĪN BEGINS. I found written among the tales, one of the lays of minstrels about traditions,[1] that once upon a time there lived a king, who in his sovereign rule performed his will and enjoyed good fortune. All kings were his slaves; it was for his sake that they lived on earth. All rulers stood ready to serve him, wishing him well with all their hearts. The sovereigns of the earth were obedient to him; his writ ran parallel with God's.[2]

What a splendid banquet there was in springtime![3] All who were there were nobles; from every city a general and a king, from every march a girl with the face of a fairy, a maid like the moon. The pick of the nobles of Iran—from Āzerbaijān, Reyy, Gurgān, Khurāsān, Kūhistān, Shīrāz, Isfahān, Dehistān;[4] such as Bahrām, Ruhhām

1. Minorsky, *BSOAS*, XXV (1962), 280, n. 2; Minorsky, *Iranica*, p. 154, n. 1.
2. *I* has an interpolation here.
3. See C. M. Bowra, *Heroic Poetry* (London, 1952), p. 280, on the feast as an opening gambit; cf. also Mark's festival, *Tristan*, p. 48.
4. See n. 2, p. 40.

of Ardebīl, Gushasp of Dailam, Shāpūr of Gīlān, Kishmēr[5] the hero, famous Āzīn, Vīrū the brave, heroic Rāmīn; such as Zard, that confidant of the king of the land, at once his brother and vizier; the king seated in the midst of the nobles like the moon among the stars, chief of kings of the earth, Shāh Moubad;[6] the kings like so many stars, Moubad the moon, on his head the crown of conquerors of the world, on his person the regalia of princely lords; from his face splendor shone and the royal glory flashed forth like the sun; warriors sitting before him, maids like moons standing behind him. The nobles like hunting lions, the beauties like gazelles of the plain; gazelle did not shrink from seeing lion, nor fierce lion tire of seeing gazelle. The cup full of wine passed amongst them, like the shining moon among its mansions. Blossoms showered from the trees like a rain of coins upon the fortunate; the smoke of burning musk hung like a cloud, in color and scent like the curling locks of heart-bewitching beauties. On one side minstrels singing to the wine; on the other, nightingales singing to the rose. Wine had made the sweet-lipped beauties even fairer than before, just as the nightingale enhanced the minstrels.[7] There were two kinds of tulips in the face of the lover, from beauty and from the cup.

Though the King's banquet was splendid, others were no less so; for on garden, slope, and riverside constant rain fell from the wine cup; everyone had gone out from his house to the country, taking with him the paraphernalia of entertainment; from every garden, field, and river a different variety of music charmed the ear. The ground was so full of flowers and grass that you would have sworn it was the star-studded sky. Everyone had a crown of tulips on his head; all had glowing embers of wine in their hands. Some enjoyed horse racing, some listened to music and danced; some drank wine in a garden, some picked roses in a rose plot; some sat on the banks of a

5. Minorsky, *Iranica*, p. 171; Minorsky, *BSOAS*, XXV (1962), 285.
6. Minorsky, *Iranica*, p. 184. The name, as suggested by Professor H. W. Bailey (*ibid.*), may mean "ruler of Marv." The city of Shīrāz used to contain a castle known as "Shāh Moubad's fortress" (Minorsky, *Ḥudūd ul-'Ālam*, p. 126). In the *Shāhnāmeh* Jamshīd describes himself as both *Shahriyār* (monarch) and *Moubad* [paperback ed., Tehran, 1345 H.S.], I, 25, 1. 6; *Shāhnāma*, selections translated by R. Levy, p. 9). *Moubad* usually denotes a type of Zoroastrian priest.
7. Cf. *Tristan*, p. 49.

stream, others in the midst of tulips; everyone had gone there for enjoyment, and had made the surface of the earth like brocade.

The King, too, had gone out for the occasion, with kingly ornaments and regalia, riding an elephant mighty as a mountain, but a mountain encircled with gold and decorations; around him were renowned mighty elephants, tried in battle and bravery; so abundant were the silver and gold that the effect was like some sea—if a sea could flow across the plain! In front of him galloped horses fleet as the wind, their hooves of steel fit to try even steel itself; behind came many litters, carrying secluded moonlike beauties; his beasts of burden had become distressed under their loads, so weighty were his jewels. His possessions were heavier than any mountain, his fortune[8] lighter than any straw. He made his court glorious with those riches and beauties; not a jot remained when he rose to depart; he had given all away, scattered all abroad, and done his will with such abundance of wealth.

This is how you should enjoy the world—thus bestow largesse and live! Since neither mean nor generous survive, better to be generous and gay! The King remained thus for a week, celebrating with his nobles early and late.

9.

THE BEAUTIES OF MOONLIKE FACE LOOK ON AT KING MOUBAD'S BANQUET. The beauties of fairylike face of the wide world graced his banquet; like Shahrū, princess of Media, from Māhābād;[1] Sarv e Āzād from Āzerbaijān;[2] from Gurgān, Ābnūsh with form as fair as the moon; charming Nāz from Dehistān; from Reyy, Dīnārgīs and Zarrīngīs; Shīrīn and Parī Vīs from the Land of the Mountains; from Isfahān two beauties like moon and sun, fortunate Ābnār and Ābnāhīd, both by descent daughters of scribes; Gulāb and Yāsman,[3] daughters of viziers; Zarastūn, the famous daughter of the Kanārang,[4] from whom spring itself would steal attractiveness and color;

8. *I. Mb:* "his throne."

---

1. Media (also referred to as Māh).
2. *T:* "like a tall cypress of Āzerbaijān."
3. *T.* takes these words as "rose-water and jasmine."
4. Minorsky, *Iranica*, pp. 165, 169, 191.

Nūsh of the sweet lips from the land of Humāvān,[5] like the jasmine in color, scent, and body; Nāz, Āzargūn, and Gulgūn,[6] with cheeks like snow with blood spattered on it; Sahī[7] by name and "straight" of stature, the wife of the King, with body of silver, lip pure nectar, and face as fair as the moon.

Each of these moonlike beauties had a thousand fair attendants round her, idols of China, Turkestān, Byzantium, and Barbary with curls like violets, cheeks like roses, and jasmine-scented breasts. In stature each was like a tall cypress, her curling locks like myrtle and boxtree; each one with belt on waist and crown on head, the one of purest gold, the other of gems.

Of all these winning and bewitching beauties, with coloring and complexion like peacock and hawk, eyes like the deer of the riverbed, to whose eyes even hunting lions were easy prey, fairest and sweetest was the Royal Princess, in eye and lip at once pain and cure for the soul; like a cypress in stature, but the fruit of the cypress, the sun; ruby-red of lip, but with Venus glinting from the ruby; cheek of brocade and garment of brocade—two brocades matching, as beautiful as could be, lips of sugar, teeth gems, her speech like gems mixed with sugar; her ambergris-scented locks so twined and curling that they were linked together like a chain or like mail; two narcissus eyes full of such fell enchantment and color that you would have sworn here was some magician busy at spellbinding; fifty tresses of her musky hair fell from the crown of her head to her waist, in brightness and color like oozing vitriol; hung from silver, they were spread on ivory. Wherever she sat she was the Moon of Princesses, wherever she walked she was like a swaying boxtree. The earth had become brocade from the very color of her face; the air had become musky from the scent of her hair. Roses fell scattered on the earth from the mere color of her face, the breeze was suffused with ambergris from the perfume of her locks. The spring breeze was ashamed before her face, aloes of Khmer[8] were bashful before her locks; though like a jewel, pure, faultless, and fit for a crown, she still

5. *NL, I*: hāvar. Minorsky, *Iranica*, pp. 166, 171.
6. *T* takes these words as "Charm, fire-hued, rose-hued."
7. Sahī: "straight."
8. Cambodia. Minorsky, *Ḥudūd ul-'Ālam*, p. 241.

decked herself in ornaments; gold and brocade were the more beautiful on one who needed neither.

10.

MOUBAD ASKS SHAHRŪ'S HAND IN MARRIAGE AND SHE MAKES A COMPACT WITH HIM. It came about that one day the King, whom they called Moubad Manīkān,[1] saw that swaying cypress of silvery figure, smiling idol, moon among ladies; he called her before him in private and sat her upon a throne like the new moon. He put in her hand a bouquet of choice red roses, matching the color of the face of that Hūrī of fairy lineage; tenderly, smilingly, gaily, and pleasantly he said to her, "You who are all beauty and grace, how fine to carry out my will in the world along with you! You should be by me, either as wife or lover, for I hold you equal to my very soul; I shall place all sovereignty in your hands; I shall ever stand before you ready to carry out your orders, just as the world waits on my command. I shall prefer you to everything I have, shall see none but you with the eye of affection; to my heart's desire I shall live year in, year out at your side; I shall give you silver, gold, and riches; I shall lay body and soul at your feet; I shall do whatever you may say. Should I have your face with me night and day, my night will be day, my day Nourūz."

SHAHRŪ REPLIES TO KING MOUBAD. When Shahrū heard these words from the King, she charmingly gave him a pretty answer; she said, "World of success, why do you persist in taunting me? I am not the one to seek a lover and husband, for I am unworthy of either. You do not tell me how I am to enter into a marriage bond with a husband after having given birth to several children, all heroes, generals, and kings, gifted, attractive, like the moon in splendor, the best of them noble Vīrū, endowed with more formidable might than an elephant. You did not see me in my young days, all charm and willfulness and gaiety, grown as straight as the lofty cypress; the breeze wafted scent from my twin forelocks, I was in the springtime of my life, like the willow bough by the stream. In broad daylight the sun lost its way at the sight of me, the moon missed its way by

1. Minorsky, *Iranica*, p. 185.

night. Many a face lost its radiance because of me, many an eye became sleepless! If one day I so much as passed along a lane, it would smell of jasmine for a whole year! My beauty made slaves of kings, my scent brought the dead back to life. But now my life has reached its autumn days, the spring of beauty has deserted me. Time has scattered yellow flowers on my cheeks and mixed my musk with camphor; abstracted the glow of beauty from my face, bent the crystal cypress of my figure. The world piles shame and humiliation upon every old person who plays at being young! Should you see me do an improper act, I shall become low in your eyes through disgrace."

SHĀH MOUBAD REPLIES TO SHAHRŪ. When Moubad Manīkān heard these words he said to her, "Eloquent, shining Moon! May whatever mother gave birth to an enchantress like you be ever blest in her desires and happy! May your mother's mouth be full of nectar for having given birth to this lofty cypress figure of yours! Blest be the land that fostered you! May men for ever be joyful and happy in it! You are as captivating as this in your old age—what can you have been like in the days of your youth? Your beauty's flower is like this, when half-faded, meriting a thousand compliments—how fell in charm must it have been when newly budded! How it must have stolen the hearts of the nobles! Now if you will not be my mate and lover, and fill my days with joy, give me a daughter born of you; better for the pine to have its heart's desire and be with the jasmine! Since the fruit will surely be like the seed, your daughter will be jasmine-bosomed like you. My weal and joy shall grow apace when the sun is in my seraglio. When I gain the sun of love I shall not desire the heavenly sun."

SHAHRŪ REPLIES TO SHĀH MOUBAD. Shahrū answered, "Majesty, what better for me than you as a son-in-law? If I had a daughter behind the veil my fortune would now be brilliant thanks to a lucky star. I swear to you that I have no daughter; if I had, why do I not bring her forward? I have not till now given birth to a daughter—and if I give birth to one hereafter, you and you alone shall be my son-in-law."

When Shahrū swore her oath before the King, his heart was glad because of the pledge. They spoke much of the covenant and joined their hands in token of the bond.[2] They mixed rose water and musk and with it wrote the treaty on silk: "If Shahrū gives birth to a girl she shall rightfully belong to none in the world but the King."

See into what tribulation they fell from giving away an unborn child as a bride!

11.

VĪS IS BORN TO HER MOTHER. The world has infinite colors and shapes: reason is in conflict with Creation. Fate knows well how to tie knots that reason cannot undo; see how it set this fabulous snare so that such a monarch fell into it! It set a desire in his heart[1] whereby he sought the hand of an unborn bride; reason failed to unravel for him the secret that his doom was being delivered of its mother. When the two renowned ones made their compact and together took the oath according to Righteousness,[2] although it was astonishing that they should conclude a contract about a thing not yet in existence, Fate played its trump card and added wonder to wonder.

Many years passed after the contract, the memory of these events faded from men's hearts. The dried tree became once more full of sap and bore fruit—in the shape of a gorgeous red rose. The queen bore issue in her old age;[3] you would have said that a pearl lighted on the oyster shell, a pearl from which, after nine months had passed, came forth a shining moon.

You would have said she was no mother, but rather the Orient, for a shining sun showed its face from her, a daughter who, when she was born of her mother, rubbed out dark night like the sun. Great and small alike said the same: "Dear God, can there be a vision such as this?" All gazed spellbound at her face and called her fortunate Vīs by name.

2. *G*, p. 7, adds: "Shahro's husband was Qaran. But Shahro was of nobler birth than Qaran; she was the offspring of King Djimshed [Jamshīd], who was the fifth king after Adam." Reference is made to the killing of Qārin by Moubad in §24. On Qārin see Minorsky, *Iranica*, pp. 176, 186 ff.

1. The Spanish *Don Tristan de Leonís* similarly talks of "variable fortune, which never rests, but always effects changes in human hearts."
2. Cf. the Avestan formula *ašāt hača*, "according to truth."
3. *G:* "the thirty-year-old Shahro."

25

As soon as she was born her mother gave her to a nurse[4] who took her to Khūzān,[5] her own abode and home. She made all her finery of brocade and jewels and nursed that coveted one with a hundred tender cares. She cosseted her with tenderness and with all her heart could desire; musk, ambergris, camphor, spikenard, perfume of willow, myrtle, narcissus, and rose, fur of beaver, marten, ermine, and squirrel, fine ornaments and radiant pearls; on couches of brocade and down she cosseted her with tenderness to her heart's desire; her food as pure, nourishing to the soul, and sweet as were her garments dainty, fine, and fair of hue.

When that royal cypress whose body was of silver, but whose heart was of steel, grew tall in stature, reason was left dumbfounded at her face and did not know what to call that idol. Now it would say: "This is a spring garden where bright tulips grow, its violets her curls, its narcissus her eyes, while its roses and tulips are her profile and cheeks." Now it would say: "This is an autumn garden with the fruit of Mihragān[6] in it; her black curls are ripe grapes, her chin an apple, and her breasts twin pomegranates." Now it would say: "This is a royal treasure, containing the heart's desire of all the world, her cheeks brocade, her limbs silk, her two locks perfume, her tresses ambergris; her body silver, her lips pure ruby, those teeth of hers lustrous pearls." Now it would say: "This is the Garden of Paradise, which God fashioned out of his own light; her body is water, her cheeks milk and wine, whilst those lips of hers are honey."

Well might reason be dazzled by her, for the very eye of heaven became dark before her. Her two cheeks were the springtime of charm, her two eyes the ruination of patience. In face she was the sun of the fair; in glances, past mistress of sorceresses. That pretty face of hers was like the Emperor of Rome, her two locks before him like two black-robed chamberlains; her curling tresses were like the Emperor of Ethiopia, her two cheeks before him like two blazing candles; her twisted curls like a dark cloud, her earring like Venus peeping through the cloud; her ten fingers like ten ivory pipes, each one crowned with a hazelnut; her necklace with pearls set in gold,

4. The counterpart of Brangane in *Tristan*.
5. Minorsky, *Iranica*, p. 169.
6. The autumnal festival, hence "Autumn."

like water frozen upon fire, resembled the Pleiades strewn on a new moon, or a band clasped around a silver cypress. She had the beauty of a Hūrī, the nature of a sorceress, the thighs of a wild ass, the eye of a doe. Two kinds of rain fell from her lips and locks, one raining sugar, the other musk. You would have said fell charm had been personified in order to steal people's hearts, or that the sphere of heaven had displayed in that figure and face all the beauty it possessed.

12.

VĪS AND RĀMĪN ARE BROUGHT UP IN KHŪZĀN AT THE NURSE'S SIDE. The Nurse cared for her so tenderly as to devote her life to the task. Rāmīn, too, was with the Nurse in Khūzān—for his life likewise the Nurse trembled; Vīs and Rāmīn were there together, like anemone and eglantine in a single garden. The two darlings grew up together there, played together day and night; when they had graced that spot for ten years, Rāmīn was taken away to Khurāsān. Who knew, who could suppose, what the heaven-ordained fate of both was? what Destiny purposed for them, what pretexts it would put forward for its work? When they had not even yet been born of their mother, the seed of both not yet fallen on the ground, Providence had settled their plans, their roles were written down to the last detail. Heaven's decree could not have gone otherwise or have been diverted from them by deceit or stratagem. When anyone reads this story he will know the faults of this world; not for us to criticize them—one cannot block the path of God's decree.[1]

13.

THE NURSE WRITES A LETTER TO SHAHRŪ WHO SENDS AN ENVOY TO FETCH VĪS. When Vīs, fair of face as an idol, had so grown in stature that she was as tall as the cypress of the garden, her crystal-like arms filled out, her locks became like a looping lasso; the end of her tress threw a shadow on the rose, cherished sweetheart with tender heart; her name spread abroad in the city, a letter went from the Nurse to her mother. She blamed her copiously in the

1. *G* has here a section (pp. 9–10) describing Rāmīn's beauty and attainments and how Moubad, on hearing of them, sends nobles to bring him to Marv.

letter: "There is no one in the world of such bad faith as you—your soul is not kind either to your child or to her nurse; you neither display fondness for your darling child nor rejoice in the sight of her for so much as a day. When you gave birth to her you gave her to me, but you gave nothing worthy of your daughter. Now she has grown up at my side with a thousand charms—the hawk's chick has begun to spread its wings; I am in terror lest, if it fly, it too will become a hawk and take a mate. I have brought her up as was proper; with every color and scent that was fitting; with brocade and royal ornaments from the roll and tray of every draper and druggist; now she does not fancy our stock, although it is silk and brocade of every kind.

"When she sees gorgeous garments she points out faults in every one: 'This is yellow, fit only for those of ill repute;[1] this is blue, for those in mourning; this is white, which suits crones; this is two-colored, for scribes.' When she rises from sleep in the morning she demands of me Astarābād[2] silk; when the day is at the forenoon she craves of me silk plain and colored; at night she demands double-faced brocade and pretty fair-faced girls to attend her; there must be no less than eighty women by her, for were there less than this it would not be proper in the way of retinue; every time she eats with them she demands gold bowls and plates—be it day or night, early or late, she insists on fifty girls to tend her; with girdles fastened and tiaras put on, standing before her to do her every whim.

"When you read this letter, decide as soon as may be about your daughter, the beauty of any town—I can no more be doing with her —I cannot procure each and every thing she desires; who am I to look after a princess as I or her well-wishers would desire? The work of one head is not to be done by a hundred fingers, nor does the light of one sun come from three hundred stars."

When the Nurse's letter reached Shahrū, she saw fair words in it; she took the news of her daughter to be a good omen, her name auspicious and her star likewise. As a present for good news she gave her messenger a golden crown, and much gold and jewelry besides. She so enriched him with coins and jewels that generations of his

1. *G:* "red . . . for harlots."
2. On the southeast shore of the Caspian Sea.

descendants were rich. Then, as is the custom of royalty, she sent her daughter many golden litters, servants before each litter, each one in stature a graceful cypress; they went happily on their way to Vīs and brought her from Khūzān to Hamedān.

When her mother saw her daughter's face, her straight stature, and her gorgeous form, she scattered much gold and many jewels, and called on the fortunate name of God. When she set her on a throne before her, she could not tell her face from the gleaming moon; she tended the roses of her cheeks, arranged the violets of her locks; she scented her hair with ambergris and musk, and put jeweled bracelets on her arms. She made her blaze with brocade of gold, and burnt fumes of aloes and musk under her breast; she adorned that winning beauty as the spring breeze decks the garden. She adorned that earthly moon as Mānī the design of the *Arzhang* of China;[3] she painted that beautiful idol as Chinese painters the garden of Iram;[4] she made that blessed one as perfect as Rizvān[5] the Hūrīs in Paradise. Although a face be without blemish, passing fair to the eye of all who see it, when it is gorgeously adorned with gold and jewels and colored brocade, it will surely become still fairer with adornment, as gold becomes redder with tincture.

14.

SHAHRŪ GIVES VĪS IN MARRIAGE TO VĪRŪ BUT BOTH FAIL TO GAIN THEIR DESIRE. When her mother saw charming Vīs, laying the garden low with her cheeks, she said to her, "You who are all excellence and glory! Earth and heaven alike are decorated by you; your father was a Khusrou,[1] your mother a queen; I do not know of a husband in the land worthy of you. Since I do not know of a husband for you in the wide world, how can I give you to someone less than a husband? There is no mate in all Iran worthy to be your

3. Name of a masterpiece containing pictures, painted by Mānī (Manes), variously described as a picture-gallery and as a book. See Geo Widengren, *Mani and Manichaeism* (New York, 1965), p. 109.
4. Believed to have been designed in imitation of Paradise by Shaddād ibn ʿĀd (Qurʿān, lxxxix, 7). See *Encyclopaedia of Islam, s.v.* Iram.
5. The guardian angel of Paradise in Muslim belief.

1. Name of kings of the Sassanian dynasty; cf. also the name *Kaikhusrou* of one of the rulers of the legendary Kayānī dynasty; as a title it resembles "Caesar."

spouse except Vīrū, who is your own brother. Be his mate and make your family glorious, and make my days happy by this union. Vīrū's worthy sister shall be his wife, our bride shall be our fair daughter. Vīrū is like the sun in excellence, Vīs like Venus in beauty; there can be no greater good fortune for me than to give a prize to a prize." When Vīs heard these words from her mother her face became like saffron from very shyness, passion welled up in her heart, her silence signified consent. Not a word either way did she say to her mother; for love of her brother was in her heart. Love gladdened her heart, she became as radiant as the moon in the sky. Her cheeks changed color every moment; her twisting lock fell across them; her mother knew there and then that she had chosen the way of silence; being an experienced older woman, having witnessed much of the world's good and evil—she had had the same experience in her youth, and had kept silence in just the same way!

When she saw her daughter suitably minded for love, she summoned the astrologers from every region. She asked them about the heavenly reckoning, what good and what gain and loss should come;[2] when should that chosen day be according to the stars; the evil of Mars and Saturn be countered by it; for her daughter to see a husband, her son a wife; he better than any husband, she than any wife.[3]

All the astrologers brought tables of the stars and reckoned the stars one by one; when they had examined their revolutions, they chose the day of Dei[4] in the month of Āzar,[5] for at that time by the revolution of time it was spring in the month of Āzar; when the day

2. Jivanji Modi, *The Religious Ceremonies and Customs of the Parsees* (Bombay, 1922), p. 19.

3. On the marriage of brother and sister, see Jacques Duchesne-Guillemin, *La Religion de l'Iran Ancien* (Paris, 1962), p. 127 (where Arthur Christensen, *L'Iran sous les Sassanides* [Paris, 1936], p. 323, is quoted). A recent Parsi discussion of the subject is *Marriage in Ancient Iran*, by Jamshid Cawasji Khatrak (Bombay, 1965), which was kindly brought to my notice by Moubad Rustam Shāhzādī of Tehran.

4. The eighth, fifteenth, and twenty-third days of the month are named in part *Dei* in the Zoroastrian calendar. Modi, *Religious Ceremonies and Customs of the Parsees*, p. 434; R. C. Zaehner, *Zurvan: A Zoroastrian Dilemma* (Oxford, 1955), p. 196.

5. Minorsky, *Iranica*, p. 192. Now the ninth month of the Persian year, November-December.

of Dei in the month of Āzar came round and the sixth hour of the day arrived, Shahrū went to the Kayanian palace,[6] took the hand of Vīs and the hand of Vīrū, uttered many blessings on the pure Creator, then many curses upon the demons,[7] praised the angels with propitious titles, offered up countless prayers,[8] and then said to the honored couple, "May you have delight and enjoyment of your desires. A brother and a sister united need no ornaments or captivating finery; there is not even any need for a moubad's[9] seal on the deed. It is also proper that there should be no witness; the just Creator is enough as your witness—the angels, moon and sun, heaven and stars." Then she joined their hands[10] and uttered many blessings on both: "May your months and years be attended by happiness, your works ever marked by chivalry. Be true lovers one to another and enjoy this union; be eternally steadfast in it, shining together like moon and sun."[11]

15.

ZARD COMES TO SHAHRŪ AS MESSENGER. When an affair is to have a bad end, it is clear right from its very start; when it is to be a day of snow and rain, signs of it appear from early morning; when there is to be a bad year in the world, its drought appears in the winter. A tree which is not to be straight of stature shows its crooked-ness when it is a sapling; when there is to be but little fruit on the branch it can be told by blossom at Nourūz; when the arrow is to swerve from the bowstring it is clear from the archer's drawing of the bow.

Just so did the fortunes of the heart-illumining Moon evince a bad complexion that very day; for when Shahrū called down blessings and set her hand in that of Vīrū, they celebrated a reception in the hall and royal palace. A smoke-colored cloud came up from the sea; suddenly night descended on pure day. You would have said it was

6. *Kayānī*, lit. "of the Kayānī dynasty"; one of the legendary dynasties of Iran.
7. Cf. Avesta, Yasna XII.
8. Persian *niyāyish*: prayers to the sun, Mithra, the moon, the waters, fire.
9. Zoroastrian priest.
10. Modi, *Religious Ceremonies and Customs of the Parsees*, p. 31.
11. *Ibid.*, p. 38.

no cloud but rather that a rough wind had fallen on a mountain of ashes.

A rider appeared on the road, like a swift mountain with a fleet steed under it. The horse was black and its trappings and saddle blue; the rider, too, in like attire; robe and boots and leggings and turban all colored the same, like a collyrium needle; saddlecloth, caparison, and sedan of the litter in hue like marsh violets; thus horse and accoutrements and garb of the knight like a blue water-lily and his name Zard,[1] envoy, minister, and brother to the King; both he and his horse as vast as mountains; his eye bloodshot with the trials of his journey, his brow furrowed by great anger; like a lion hunting the wild ass in the desert, or like a wolf leaping upon its prey; with the King's letter in his hand; all his route smelling of ambergris from its scent; for the letter was an inscribed silken parchment, dipped in musk, ambergris, and wine; sweet words were in the letter, a gold seal stamped upon its superscription.

When Zard came to the audience hall of Vīrū, he rode up to Shahrū without dismounting, made reverence to her, and offered many an apology "that I should have approached you on horseback; for thus is the order of the King—and his command is to me even as my religion—thus the monarch has ordered me: 'Rest not by day or by night but ride on; your haste on the road must be such that no wind in the world may catch your dust; your hasty speed must be such that you sleep on your horse's back till you return to Marv from this journey; do not rest from riding, early or late; do not sleep or sit on the way; descry Shahrū from the saddle; deliver the letter, and when you have received a reply, turn your horse's head toward Marv'." Then he said to the Sun of the Hūrīs, "Greetings to you from your relatives-in-law: greetings to you, Shahrū, from the King, your son-in-law of auspicious fortune and good purpose; greetings to you with many respects to your royalty, nobility, and puissance!" He recited all the King's respects, then handed her the monarch's letter.

When Shahrū opened the letter and read it she was laid low like a donkey with its foot stuck in the mud, for there were many words in the letter: the old compact was renewed.

The opening of the letter was in the name of "God the Creator,

1. "Yellow."

꒰ 32

God who ever ordered justice; he founded the two worlds, made them in accordance with righteousness and did not introduce crookedness into them even so much as by a single hair: and just as he made the world glorious in accordance with righteousness he also required justice and righteousness of men. The person who seeks elevation from righteousness will be guided by victory. There is no alchemy in the world other than righteousness, for the grandeur of righteousness does not diminish. I ask you to seek righteousness, ever to act and speak rightly.[2] You know (who better?) what we said to one another; how we took each other's hand in contract. We made a bond in amity and friendship; then both took oath. Do not now forget the oath and treaty; fulfill the demands of good faith and strive in righteousness!

"You gave me your daughter when you bore her after much time; since I was a fitting son-in-law for you, it was through my fortune that God granted you this daughter. By my fortune you gave birth in old age, as a cypress whose fruit might be pomegranate and mallow flower. I am greatly delighted by the daughter to whom you have given birth, I have given abundant goods to the poor. As God has fulfilled my hope, realized my desire in this union, now that God has given me this moon, I am not willing for her to be in Māhābād, for there young and old alike are pleasure-loving, all devoting themselves heart and soul to womanizing; the young are more apt at wenching, full of wiles in their amorous ploys. They ever practice seduction of women, and are minded thus from wantonness; let no woman see their ways, catch their disgraceful character!

"Women are softhearted and weak-headed and will fall into any character which you induce in them. Women take men's words as gospel, surrender their body to them at the first sweet word. However acute and clever a woman be, she is as clay in the hands of a sweet-tongued man. The ruination of woman is assured if you so much as say, 'Thou art as bright as the moon, as fair as the sun. I am restless and wretched because of love for thee, day and night I cry in my misery, I scour the desert like a madman. If thou be not merciful I shall die; I shall lay my hand on the hem of thy garment in the next world; do not cruelly rob me of my life, for I am human like thee,

2. The Zoroastrian triad is "good thought, good word, good deed."

33

young like thee!' Even if a woman be a queen or empress, holy or chaste, she will toe the line at these sweet words, little realizing that she will become ill-famed thereby!

"Notwithstanding that Vīseh[3] is flawless and pure, my heart is full of anxiety on this account. Do not keep her in the land of Māhābād—send her to Marv with happy heart; do not concern yourself about gold and jewels—it is her that I require, not baubles! I have plenty of ornaments and jewels—who is more worthy than she for my treasury? I shall keep her in luxury day and night, give up to her the keys of my treasury; I shall devote my heart to love of that idol-faced beauty, be pleased with whatever is her pleasure. I shall send you so much gold and jewelry that, if you will, you may fill a whole city with gold. I shall make you as happy as my own soul, keep the land of Māh without fear and prosperous. Vīrū, too, I shall hold as my own son; make a marriage for him in my own family; I shall make that family so renowned that its name will be eternally remembered."

When she read the letter and heard these words, Shahrū writhed inwardly, as twisted, on account of this, as the scroll itself; she felt constant shame for her action, her hard heart grew soft from the shame; her brain grew dizzy and her vision dark; from shame she was left dizzy and could do nothing. When Shahrū was struck dumb by the King's letter, so much so that her heart was scarcely aware of the outside world, from shame before the King she became wounded by her own hand, her heart grew helpless because of her own action; her head hung low like those in shame, she writhed inwardly like those who break a covenant; fearful alike of the King and of the Creator, having broken all that oath and covenant; even so is breach of faith—now it brings fear, now shame.

When Shahrū became thus heartbroken, lip closed to speech, breath stopped, Vīs of the face fair as the moon saw her become like saffron from shame and fear. She said to her, "Mother, what has happened that sense and color have drained from your body? You lapsed far from the norm of reason to go and give in marriage an unborn girl! When could reason ever approve such an act? It is proper for everyone to laugh at you."

3. Another form of the name Vīs. Minorsky, *Iranica*, p. 166.

16.

VĪS QUESTIONS ZARD AND HEARS HIS ANSWER. Then she said to the messenger, "What is your name and from whom is your descent and origin?"[1] He replied, "I am one of the King's minions, at his court I am one of the commanders of his army; when the renowned King sallies forth with his host, I precede him on every road; every task which is illustrious the King lays upon me. When he has a secret he tells it to me; he asks me for counsel and seeks the way from me. I am his confidant in every affair, I share every secret with him. I am ever of ruddy face and carry out my own desire; I have a black horse in this fashion and my name is Zard."

When the beauty heard the words of Zard she replied to him softly and laughingly, "Yellow and yellow[2] again be he who sent you, thus wise and learned and just! Have you this custom in Marv that *two* people take a wife with dowry? Who would seek as a wife one who already has a husband when husband and wife are without blemish in purity? Do you not see all this commotion, all these guests, the din of the musicians echoing up to Saturn? the palace decorated like early spring, with the idol-faced beauties of the city and the renowned, with ornaments and royal jewels, gorgeous draperies and gold-worked brocades? famous princes from every city and land, warlike champions from every march and line? idols with faces like the moon from every seraglio, roses with musky tresses from every rose garden? At the color of the faces and the cups of the inflamers of hearts, the scent of musk and aloes of those who burn in helpless love, the heart in every breast has begun to cry in despair, the brain in every head has fallen into distress; everyone is enjoying the company of a neighbor, a blessing is on the tongues of all: 'May this palace be ever splendid, full of joy and charm and riches! May it have happy brides and relatives-in-law, young maidens as brides, youths as bridegrooms.'

"Now that you have seen this bridegroom's feast, heard the song and blessings each and every one, turn the reins of your steed black

1. Cf. the Avestan formula in the Gāthās (Yasna XLIII, 7): "Who are you, of whom are you?" An identical form of address survives in Pashto.
2. Zard: "yellow."

as night, haste on the road like a whizzing arrow. Do not again traverse this road in this hope, for the hand of your hope will fall short! Do not scare us any more with letters, for I hold this message but as the empty wind. Do not tarry here. Take the road, for Vīrū will even now return from the hunt; he will become sore at heart on my account and wrathful toward you. Go, so that there may not be revenge and pain, but say to Moubad by way of a message from me: 'No person of sense is like you! It is a long time, many days have passed since your unwisdom has become clear to me! Your mind has become addled from old age, your time in the world has passed; had any wisdom been your guide, your tongue would not have spoken these words. You would not have chosen a young bride from this world, but would have sought out provision for the next! Vīrū is alike my husband and brother, while worthy Shahrū is my mother; my heart is glad in the one, joyous at the other; why should I reck of Marv and Moubad? While I have Vīrū in my chamber, I need have no dealings with Marv! While I have in my embrace a fruitful cypress, why should I seek a dry and barren plane? "That person is patient in exile whose affairs are chaotic in his own house." My mother is seemly as the eyes, my brother meet as the soul; I shall sort with my brother like wine and milk; I do not wish old Moubad in a foreign land. Why should I reject a youth for an old man? I speak frankly, and do not keep this secret in my heart'."

17.

ZARD RETURNS FROM VĪS TO MOUBAD.   When Zard heard these words from Vīs, he twisted the reins of his horse black as night. On, on he went, unaware whether road lay before him or black pit: so merciless had he become in his thirst for vengeance that the world became in his eyes dark from discomfiture.[1]

The King's heart knew no rest from anxiety so long as Zard had still not come to Marv from Māh. He kept saying: "Where can Zard have gone now? Why is he so late in returning from Māh? He has no enemy in the land of Māh—who would dare to be hostile to me? Qārin, husband of Shahrū, would not dare—nor yet her eldest son whose name is Vīrū. What has befallen our Zard, pray, for his

1. Line of *Mb* transposed, following *I* and *G*.

36

journey has increased my travail! Is it the moody, willful Vīseh that has thus thrown us into grief—has firmly planted her heart in Māh and comes not at all to Marv?"

So spoke the King to himself, his eyes become sentries trained on the road, when suddenly a cloud of dust appeared; the renowned Zard prancing in it, like a wild elephant that has broken free from its bonds and is goaded to the heart by the mahouts: not knowing good from bad in its blind rage, plain and mountain as one in its sight.[2]

When Zard came disheveled as he was from the road, he went straight from the dust of the highway to the presence of the King. His face was still puckered from the tribulations of the ride; he had not so much as swung his leg from the back of his horse black as night.

The King said, "Hail, Zard, may you be remembered by your friends for nobility! Say how you have come from Māhābād; are you unhappy in your message or happy? Have you come successful or unsuccessful? Which of the two am I to call you?"[3] Zard answered him from horseback: "I am ever happy by the glory of the King! I have come unsuccessful from this journey; His Majesty now knows which he is to call me."

Then he dismounted from his steed, tongue girt for speech and lip parted; he laid that dust-covered face on the ground and called down blessings on the King with pure heart. He said to him, "Be ever victorious, ever questing for fame, and illustrious! In triumph, sovereignty, and beneficence rule the world as you deserve! May you have such eminence in your regime that you may fetter the demons like Jamshīd![4] May you have good fortune in your sovereignty, but may the land of Māh see suffering and trial! May the land of Māh be ruined from end to end, made the haunt of wolves and lions; may the land of Māh for a month[5] become the feeding ground of fire and sword! May all its wind be full of fire, its clouds waterless, its sun hot with pain, its moon cold with death!

"I saw the land of Māh like Farkhār,[6] full of decorations and royal

---

2. See n. 1, p. 36.   3. *G* makes the King say: "O Zard, art thou a lion or a fox?"
4. A king of the legendary Pīshdādī dynasty.   5. Persian *māh*.
6. Traditionally a city famed for the beauty of its inhabitants. See Minorsky, *Ḥudūd ul-ʿĀlam*, p. 263, re its location in Tibet.

arches; all over the city decorations were tied; it was like an idol-temple of China, so many decorations were there; men and women seated at the banquet, the meadows with beauties a sky full of moons. The ground was like a spring garden with color, blazing like the marsh tulip. Shahrū had richly prepared a wedding ceremony, the bride Vīseh and the bridegroom Vīrū. Of her marriage to the King one hears only the name—another has his desire of her! My face has gone the color of black cloth to think that you have dug a channel and another has drawn water from it. How can they take from you a wife who was given you? Maybe they do not realize your worth! Great and small are alike to them, as day and night to the eye of the blind. They have not perpetrated this unworthy action upon one who will fail to reckon retribution their due! But till the time of visiting an evil fate upon them we must look on this evil day. Vīrū is there, general of armies, grown proud in his ignorance at the feast. He has taken the title of Rūḥā;[7] he has allowed Ahriman to possess him. Everyone calls him King, they do not consider that there exists any king beside him. They do not count you among the kings; there is even a number that do not hold you to be a knight! Some call you 'Moubad and Dastūr';[8] some call you 'false Moubad.' I have told you their condition from start to finish, how self-obsessed have become these devotees of an odious faith."

18.

NEWS REACHES MOUBAD OF VĪRŪ'S TAKING VĪS IN MARRIAGE; HE GOES TO WAR. When Zard delivered this news to the King, the monarch's cheeks grew yellow. His face, that one would have taken for wine, so red was it, became such that one would have sworn it was fenugreek. From the teeming sweat that poured from his pure frame one would have thought his body was melting from very rage. In the extremity of his wrath he trembled like a willow tree: or like the reflection of the sun shimmering in water.

He asked his brother, "Did you witness this with your own eyes or

7. Minorsky, *Iranica*, p. 176 and footnote. Minorsky suggests reading Rūjā, "Serenissimus"; Professor W. B. Henning suggested Wrjā, "powerful."

8. *Moubad* and *Dastūr* are titles in the Zoroastrian religious hierarchy. On Moubad, see n. 6, p. 20.

hear it somewhere? Tell me of what you saw, not of what you may have heard from another. Report is never like the witness of the eye; nor heart's certainty the peer of supposition. Dispel supposition from my heart, tell me what you saw with your very eyes."

His brother said, "Majesty, I am not the man to tell you something of which I have no knowledge. With my own eyes I saw all I tell you, and I have concealed further much that I have heard. Vīrū was like a brother to me; before this Shahrū was as my mother. Now I never want to see them, for from love of you I am in feud with them. My body would not wish to have its dear life any longer should love of you decline in my soul. If you will, I shall swear a hundred times over by God and by your life, my liege, that I saw the banquet with my own eyes, but neither drank nor supped of it: for that feast and splendid banquet was in my eyes like prison and battle line, just as that palace of royal abode was in my eyes like dungeon and pit. I was restless at the song of the musicians; their notes sounded to my ears like curses. I have spoken what I know; now it rests with you, for it is yours to command and mine to be the slave of your command."

When Moubad heard these words, once more load upon load fell on his heart from grief. Now he writhed like a snake with wounded head, now boiled like a jar full of grape juice. The nobles who were in the presence of the King all ground their teeth, saying, "Why should Shahrū have done this, made over the wife of the King to another? What effrontery possessed Vīrū to seek the hand of a woman who is our King's wife?" They kept saying, "Now our King will wreak a foe's vengeance upon the land of Māh; now by means of the evil eye the enemy's will shall prevail in the house of Vīrū and Qārin. The world will take on such an aspect in the eyes of Shahrū that her worst enemy will be Vīrū, and it will not only be Vīs who will be bereft of Vīrū, or that city bereft of Shahrū, for many a spouse, many a famed city will be bereaved of spouse or of beloved king. A raging cloud with a torrent of death in its bosom will rain for a month upon the soil of Māh. Fate has sounded the knell of all that is there, for the property of one is now in the possession of another! Disaster hovers over that land; where is the army that shall fend it off? What streams of blood will boil in the limbs! How many souls will tremble and find no peace!"

When the King had been writhing inwardly for a time, with his heart scorching in the fire of thought, he summoned his scribe to his presence and scattered forth words like gold from his heart. He uttered a plaint to all kings about Shahrū, how she had become impious and broken oath. He sent a horseman by every road, to every city that had a lord. By letter he informed each one that he purposed to go to the land of Māh; he summoned some of them to his aid, from others he craved warriors; from Ṭabaristān, Gurgān, Kūhistān;[1] from Khvārazm, Khurāsān, Dehistān;[2] from the lands of Sind, Hind, Tibet, China; from Soghd and the Turanian marches, as far as Māchīn.[3] His court grew so full of armies that the plain of Marv became like the field of the Day of Judgment.

19.

VĪRŪ LEARNS OF MOUBAD'S COMING TO DO BATTLE. When news of the King reached Vīrū, how he was in feud against him and Shahrū, an army came from every city and every place to his court. It happened that at that time several princes, the elect and nobles of several lands, from Āzerbaijān, Reyy, and Gīlān, from Khūzistān, Istarkh,[1] and Isfahān, were all guests of Vīrū; their women and children were with Shahrū. At that bridal feast for five or six months they abode happy in the land of Māh.

When they became aware that Moubad Manīkān purposed to send an army in their direction, each one summoned an army by letter and put many more forces on the march from every land. Such a mighty army collected from every place that the plain, wide as it was, became too small to hold them. You would have sworn that Mount Damāvand was upon the plain of Nihāvand, so many warriors were there; all ready for battle, ready to lay down their lives for vengeance and justice; heroes and tried warriors to a man, whose strength matched the intrepidity of elephants and lions. So many

1. Minorsky, *Iranica*, p. 168.
2. In Gurgān. *Ibid.*, p. 178; Le Strange, *Lands of the Eastern Caliphate*, p. 377.
3. Southern China. Minorsky, *Iranica*, p. 168.

---

1. Istakhr.

footmen were there from the mountains of Dailamān[2] that you would have sworn they were a mountain of rocks drawn up in ranks! From the Arab deserts so many cavalry that they were more than drops of rain; then hoary champions, warriors versed in prowess and grown old in strategy, guarded the army in van and rear, one posted as commander at every point. The right and left flanks were entrusted to the Royal Guards, tried warriors all.[3]

On the other side Shāh Moubad in his turn drew up an army like an April garden. He drew up van and rear, left and right, a force of heroes and squires; when he came out of Marv with his army, you would have sworn the earth flowed like the Oxus! From the great clamor of drum and fife, you would have sworn the very world started from its place! The dust went right up from earth to heaven; you would have sworn the earth exchanged secrets with the moon! Or that the demons were rushing up to heaven and listening to the words of the angels! The army in the midst of the dust was like a brilliant star in a black cloud. Such a flood poured from Khurāsān that the very moon in the sky was frightened at it. It was no flood of water and rain from the sky, rather a cascade of fierce lions and dragons. On rolled the army in such multitude that it made the mountain a plain and the plain a mountain. A vast host came on like the ocean, its waves carrying away the mountains.

Thus they marched on to the land of Māh, the army enraged, the King wrathful. The two armies came face to face, like a sea lashed up by stormwinds. The center of one like a slashing sword; the flank of the other like a roaring lion.

20.

THE BATTLE BETWEEN MOUBAD AND VĪRŪ. When the monarch of the stars rose in the east, a monarch whose vizier is the moon, whose throne the stars, before him two lead-horses, black and white, the one of the night, the other of the Dawn that gilds the world, two war drums rolled out from two pavilions, two armies joined battle

2. South of the Caspian. Minorsky, *Iranica*, p. 174; Christensen, *L'Iran sous les Sassanides*, p. 209; Minorsky, "La Domination des Dailamites" (*Iranica*, pp. 12 ff.); *Encyclopaedia of Islam*, s.v. Dailam.

3. See Christensen, *L'Iran sous les Sassanides*, p. 208.

before two kings. No, not a war drum—a demon of wrath! Everyone who heard that din became full of rage. The shrill fife rivaled the Last Trump; its clangor raised the dead! As blossoms scatter from the boughs at the sound of spring thunder, so at the roll of the war drum the blossom of war spilled from the camp. In the center the kettledrum shrilled: "Forward, heroes, slayers of the foe!" In that din the cymbal played in duet with it, like singers performing to an accompaniment; the *santūr*[1] too rang with a hundred modes, like a nightingale in spring. The trumpet sounded together with it, like two minstrels in duet. Before one body was deprived of life the horn lamented in amazement. The flashing sword in the grasp of the warriors gloated over their lives; the ranks of mail and greaves on the plain were like a mountain in the midst of the waves of the sea.

The heroes were like crocodiles in the waves: on the mountains the cavalry like leopards. Men normally deliberate were like madmen on the field of battle—for he is a madman, by any reckoning, that shrinks neither from fire nor water, is not afraid of spear or sword, does not quail before elephant or lion! Thus were the champions on that field: sacrificing dear life for fame. They had no fear of dying in the battle; it was ill fame and disgrace they feared.

The sky was for all the world like a thicket with all its flags displaying tiger, lion, wolf, and boar; the plain had become like a cypress grove, so many flags waved on it; the moon gleaming from the brocade of the banners; on the crest of each a golden bird; eagle, falcon, peacock, Simurgh;[2] beneath the falcon, a gorgeously colored lion;[3] you would have sworn the falcon had the lion in his claws! The feet of the elephants and the hooves of the chargers struck sparks and crushed stones; the ground rose up from under their feet, went up to heaven, and descended again to earth; as there was no place for it to settle in the world, it went instead into mouths and eyes. Many were the black horses and young men who became white

1. A stringed instrument played with sticks after the manner of a xylophone.
2. Christensen, *L'Iran sous les Sassanides*, p. 211; *Shāhnāmeh*, paperback edition (Tehran, 1345 H.S.), II, 67. The Simurgh is a bird which figures in the Iranian epic.
3. The lion and the boar occur in descriptions of the coat of arms of Tristan. See *Tristan*, Appendix 3, p. 365.

42

and hoary because of the dust! The brave man stood out from the coward; for the one was joyful and the other full of care. The cheek of the one was the color of a *dīnār*; the face of the other like the pomegranate blossom.

When the armies faced each other at close quarters the heroes attacked each other furiously; you would have sworn two steel mountains clashed on that field. Messengers plied from one army to another; the javelin with four feathers, the black-feathered arrow; emissaries who found their way into the heart and settled in heart or eye. In every house wherein they took up their abode they turned out the master of the house.

The ranks of battle and the fear of death were so formidable that the Resurrection materialized before the warriors' eyes. Brother was estranged from brother: none had any friend other than their own prowess. They found no ally other than their right arm; no judge but the dagger; whosoever was aided by his right arm, the dagger gave judgment in his favor. You would have sworn the warriors had become sowers, but sowing steel in eye and heart! Speech makers fell silent, as men of sense were all senseless: no one heard any sound there but the roll of the drum and the shrilling of the fife.

Now the sword slipped into armor like water; now the arrow slid into the eyes like sleep; now the spearpoint glided into the heart like love; now the axe cracked into the head like wit. You would have sworn the bloodthirsty sword knew where the Creator had disposed the soul in the body! The soul escaped from men by the same road as the sword had entered. The Indian blade was like a lily; a flood the hue of Judas blossom raining from it; like a myrtle branch with pomegranate petals hanging from it; like pomegranate petals with seeds upon them. The javelin was like a tailor in the battle; it kept on sewing warriors to the saddle! When Fate triumphed over the lives of the warriors, one became a fleeing wild ass, the other a lion. As Fortune closed on the ranks of the warriors, one became a scuttling mountain sheep, the other a cheetah.

In that melee of champions and horsemen, in the midst of the sword thrusts and the rain of arrows, the dear father of Vīs, the hero Qārin, was laid low by the hand of the enemy, around him one hundred thirty of Vīrū's heroes. A yellow heap of dead was piled up, a purple river began to flow. You would have sworn the heavens rained golden hail, and round it tulip petals.

When Vīrū saw the champions laid low, and a great company slain round Qārin, all of whom had given up their lives for him but were wretchedly slain and laid low, he said in fury to his nobles, "It is base for warriors to be sluggards! Shame on you for what you have done; for these slain warriors fallen at your feet! See all these friends and kinsmen at whose death the enemy has become joyful! Does not anger well up within you for Qārin, that his grizzled beard should be dabbled in blood? They have laid a king so low in death; has he no avenger in the army? The sun of glory has set; the day of joy turned black; I fear that the heavenly sun will hide itself in the west without my having wrought vengeance on his enemy, or cursed his foes. You see that night has drawn on; the world is even now becoming close and dark. From dawn till now you have fought thus valiantly; but yonder sinister flag still stands; still the sorcerer Moubad is in his place! Now help me just for a time; be like dragons in prowess, for I shall wipe the stain from our escutcheon, and by vengeance make Qārin live again. I shall free the world from Moubad's affliction and gratify the soul of Qārin at his expense."

When Vīrū addressed the champions thus in his knightly courage, he hid nothing from the brave warriors.[4] Then with chosen cavalry-men, renowned nobles, and distinguished champions he rode forth from his own ranks like the wind and fell on the enemy army like fire. In his fury he was like a deluge that may not be stopped no matter with how much courage!

Speech was then carried on with sword and axe; the game the champions played was with heads! Son had no mercy at all on father, nor warriors on relatives and kin; brother was in feud against brother; in feud friend was worse than enemy! A darkness came up from the world, so that night came on before nightfall. At that moment men became blind as bats; the fount of light of the sun was choked with dust. Once eyes had been clogged up with dust, brother wounded brother: father failed to recognize son, and severed his

4. Reading *bar dilīrān* (conjecture).

head with the sword. You would have sworn the spearpoint was a spit, the bird upon it a spitted champion! Four-feathered arrows sprouted like trees from the eyes of the luckless. The tree of life sprouted from the body, over it the screen of helmet and mail; once the dagger ripped the screen, it cut the tree of life. The sky had become like a reedbed from spears; the earth like a winepress from men's blood. So much dust was there, so many swords dripping blood, that the whole world was full of smoke and fire. You would have sworn death had become a rushing wind, scattering the warriors' heads like so many leaves. The heads of the warriors were like polo balls, the legs of their horses like polo sticks. Death laid the warriors low on the soil, like a garden cypress cut off by the root. When the heavenly sun sank in the west, it became gold like the faces of lovers. You would have sworn the sun was the fortune of Moubad, and that the world was giving up hope of his glory. On the one hand the sun in distress in the heaven because of night, on the other Moubad in distress because of the enemy; the one disappearing from the sight of the eyes, the other deserting the striving warriors. When the King abandoned the field of battle, the world had fallen about the ears of his host.

21.

SHĀH MOUBAD IS ROUTED BY VĪRŪ. One luckless protagonist escaped ignominiously; the other became victorious by God's grace; had not the night intervened in that battle, the King's soul would not have survived that ignominy; dark night showed him the way of escape; darkness was as light to him.

He twisted his reins from the Khurāsān road and made for the direction of Isfahān from Dēnavar.[1] Neither Vīrū nor any of his champions or commanders pursued him; he supposed that the King had fled and was in the toils of shame and humiliation; that he would not again bring an army to Kūhistān, no more dare to injure him.

Vīrū's supposition was one thing but the decree of Heaven quite another! When Vīrū defeated the King of Kings and enjoyed the desire of the lucky from Fortune, an army came from the mountains

1. Minorsky, *Iranica*, p. 173.

of Dailam;[2] that host occupied all the land up to the plain of Tārum.[3] The general who was there fled and did not grapple with the enemy in prowess; for his enemy was a formidable figure and had behind him a vast army from that land. When Vīrū received news of that enemy, he was astounded at the workings of the malevolent Sphere whose will and pleasure go hand in hand with care even as bright day is the peer of dark night. The Sphere has no joy without grief, no life without death. Care is more copious in it than happiness; the heart of the sage is helpless in its hands. No sooner had it given him joy of Moubad than it snatched away his happiness by producing another enemy.

An army left him, galloping from this side; from the other, an army advanced. His dagger was still bloodstained; his flag still covered in dust; once more he disposed himself to fight the foe; once more raised the battle ensign; once more drew his bloody dagger, and spurred on his army to do battle with the King of Dailam.

As Vīrū marched by that route with his army, news of his action reached the King. He at once turned back on the road; you would have sworn he grew wings on the march. He marched his army so rapidly that the very wind in the sky was left standing by him. He came to Gūrāb[4] and brought his army there, for Vīs of the moonlike form was there.

22.

MOUBAD SENDS AN ENVOY TO VĪS.[1] When the Sun of beauties, charming Vīs, saw her body like a bird in a snare, she uprooted musk from silver with hazelnuts[2] and rained jewels from narcissi upon jasmine.

Crying in agony she said to the Nurse, "I have no equal in the world in distress! I do not know to whom to tell my plaint, from whom to seek remedy. To whom am I to appeal at this moment, from whom crave redress for the injustice of the world? How am I to

2. *G*: "Delamis and Gelanis and Kiamanis" (var. Kirmanis). See n. 2, p. 340.
3. Minorsky, *Iranica*, p. 174.
4. *Ibid*., pp. 173, 193, for discussion and photographs of the site.

1. See p. 47. This heading, which occurs at § 23, is inappropriate in *Mb*.
2. I.e., tore the hair from her head with her fingernails.

go to Vīrū's side, how deliver my soul from Moubad? With what fate, under what ascendant was I born, for since my birth I have fallen into tribulation. Why did I not give up the ghost at Qārin's side, before I saw the will of my enemy triumph? Father slain, brother departed, thus I am left forlorn and heartbroken. I scarce know what misfortunes I have suffered through ill luck; what more shall I suffer if I survive after this? What greater evil can befall me than that I should fall against my will into the hands of Moubad? When I cry no one heeds my cry; nor have I any helper in my distress. I shall be bewildered and in agony as long as I live, far from friends, at the mercy of enemies!"

Thus said that beauty to the Nurse, and rained tears of agony on her breast.

23.[1]

A messenger came from the King and brought a message from him for that moonlike beauty; words as sweet as sugar, in beauty worthy of that face.

This was the message the King sent her: "Be of happy heart, Moon of Moons! do not strike your face with those ivory hands; do not pluck out your ambergris-scented hair from that gleaming moon. You cannot extricate yourself from the fetter of the Sphere nor escape the destiny laid on you by God. See that you do not in your heart indulge in any fancy that you can wrestle with the decree of Heaven! If Fortune wills that you should be given to me, what use is frantic striving to you? Fate has issued its fiat, the Pen has writ the decree, and you now have no remedy but patience. I have come here for your sake, for I have become crazed with love for you. If you will become my true lover, many a desire will be fulfilled for you at my hand. I shall swear you a lover's oath today that henceforth we shall be two heads with but a single soul. I shall follow every ambition with an eye to your pleasure, say all I have to say at your command. I shall bring you the key of the treasures, make over to your hand all, great and small. I shall keep you supplied with such wealth of gold and ornaments that moon and sun will envy you. You shall be the elixir of my heart and soul, the queen of my seraglio. Since I have wholly

1. No heading in *I* here; see p. 46.

surrendered my heart and soul to you, what if I give you coins and jewels? My ambition will be realized in yours, my name be magnified in yours. I shall conclude with you many binding clauses to this treaty, asseverations with sign and seal and oath. As long as life inhabits my body, I shall hold you equal to my very soul."

24.

VĪS REPLIES TO KING MOUBAD'S MESSENGER. When the charming Vīs heard this message, it was as if she heard in it many curses: she rent the silken garments on her body and relentlessly beat her crystal breast.

When she rent the silk on her body, from neck to waist came into view a tantalizing, thrilling vision of love's enchantment: a fell captivation melting the very frame: silken, ermine-soft, smooth as beaver pelt and wild silk, burning the very patience of Reason and spiriting away sleep. When that moon two weeks old rent her garments, she brought into view a blossoming eglantine; with her sweet lips she gave an answer like stone and thrust the sword of war into the face of love.

She said to the messenger, "I have heard this evil message, and tasted from it searing poison. Now go, say to doddering Moubad, 'Do not cast a ball of disaster into the field. Do not suffer distress further than this in hopes of me: do not cast your treasure to the flippant wind. Beware of supposing that you will ever bear me alive from this castle, or that you will ever have joy of me, even were you a past master of sorcerers. Vīrū is my lord and king, a cypress in stature and a moon in aspect. He is my liege and glorious brother; I his mate and good sister. Whom am I to regard in this world in his stead? How am I to choose another in preference to him? You will never gain your desire of me, even should you encamp here forever; I have united myself to my brother, divorced myself from love of all others. While I have my own cypress and boxtree, why should I reck of the willow tree[1] of others?

"'But even if Vīrū were not at my side, your love would not even then be worthy of me. You slew Qārin so pitifully and did not have

1. G: "As long as I have a straight cedar I shall seek no bent willow."

48

mercy on that saintly old man; my brave father is dead, from whom is my stock and lineage. How can your suit be a worthy one? How long will you send futile messages? I am weary of my very life's thread because of this pain, which must torture me as long as I live. No one in the world is as Vīrū is to me; henceforth you shall not enjoy union with me. Since his position is thus firmly based, how should another have joy of me? If I break faith with him in love, what excuse shall I make on the other side before the Creator? I, young as I am, fear the Creator; are you not afraid who are an impotent old man? If you are wise, fear the doom of the Creator: for this fear is nothing if not appropriate to old men! The Lord of the world has vouchsafed to me ornaments and brocade and coin in plenty; do not seek to subvert me with ornaments—God has granted me ornaments without number. So long as I bear the scar of Qārin's memory, how can my heart find pleasure in ornaments? If I so much as glance at brocade and coin again, queenship will not be my due. If I rejoice in all these ornaments, I shall not be my father's daughter. I neither fear this army of yours nor covet your throne. You too, then, refrain from hoping for union with me, for your hope will not be fruitful. When you covet the property of others, wretchedness will visit you in desperation. How long will you course after a sight of me? for you will never set so much as a hand upon me. And even should the world visit tribulation upon me and surrender me one day into your hands, you will not enjoy union with me nor ever sit a single instant with me in delight.

"'Not even my brother, who is my chosen spouse, has thus far gained his desire of me. How are you, an outsider, to gain your desire of me, even were you Sun and Moon? I have not given my silvery body to my brother, with whom I was born of one and the same mother. How, then, shall I give it to you, simpleton, at whose hand my homestead has been ruined? I tremble when I think on your name; how can I grant you your desire with a heart in this state? Now that this feud lies between us, our hearts may not have joy of each other. Even though you are a powerful king, how can one make a friend of an enemy? "Love and rancor do not sort well together; rancor is iron, love glass." "A bitter tree bears bitter fruit, even though we may water it with sugared water." On the day when the falcon pairs with the mountain partridge[2] shall I sort with you in love. For one in whom wisdom is allied to royalty, how could a mate so wretched be fitting? What is the difference between practicing love in this fashion and drinking pure poison for a mere whim?

" 'When you hear this advice it will be bitter for you: but when you see its fruit, it will be sweeter than sugar. If you are wise, ponder well; what I say will soon come to pass for you. When evil nature brings you ill fortune, you will be overcome by regret—to no avail!' "

25.

SHĀH MOUBAD'S ENVOY RETURNS FROM VĪS. When the King's man heard these words, he saw no glimmer of friendship in that beauty; he went away and gave the King news of her, recounting to him all that he had heard. The King's heart became fuller still of love—it was as if sugar rained upon his heart. The words of the beloved when she declared that her brother had not had his will of her delighted his heart.

Vīseh was speaking the truth in all this and the King rejoiced at her words, for upon the night when Vīrū was bridegroom, and all were happy and rejoicing at his bridegroom's state, a condition overtook the bride which brought ill omen for the bridegroom. The decree of Heaven came down, tying their hands from realization of their desires. Indisposition broke from the body of the beauty of silvery frame; the wild lily became dabbled with blood. That Moon of two weeks became for one week as if a mine of rubies was aflow. When a Magian woman is in this state, her husband is bound to abstain from association with her, and if the wife hides her condition from him, she is forever forbidden him.[1] As long as Vīs of the idol form was in this state, the world was full of Vīrū's complaint; let the bride be as delicate and faithful as she was, the marriage was cursed with dread and affliction, for the bridegroom had been thwarted of his one desire and the world had set two hundred snares on his road. With all the lamentation that descended upon him, all thought of

2. Cf. Rāmīn's song, §55. For the symbolism of boar and falcon in Tristan, cf. *Tristan*, p. 29 (Introduction).

1. Modi, *Religious Ceremonies and Customs of the Parsees*, p. 162; Avesta, Vidēvdāt XVI, 17.

50

being a bridegroom left the groom's mind; with all the lamentation that descended upon the army, all thought of rejoicing deserted everyone's heart. It was just as if Vīrū's feast were a lamp upon which a sudden gust of wind had blown.

26.

MOUBAD CONSULTS HIS BROTHERS ABOUT VĪS. When the King heard of the condition of Vīs, desire for her increased in his soul. He had two dear brothers, one Rāmīn and the other the renowned Zard. The monarch summoned both to his presence and recounted the tale to them.[1]

From childhood, Rāmīn's heart had kept the secret of desire for Vīseh; he ever treasured love for Vīs in his soul, but kept his feelings hidden from others. His love was like a tended plot, all hope of water and rain abandoned. When he came with his brother to Gūrāb, water once more flowed into his field. Hope for Vīs revivified his love, the old desire in his soul became young again. Harshness sounded from his tongue when love was renewed in his soul; it came to his aid at that moment and lent his words a terse tone. When love lights its fire in the heart of a person his tongue waxes spirited in talk. The tongue, ungoverned by the heart, breaks its bonds and blabbers secrets without its owner's volition. Surely the heart is the guardian of the tongue; one cannot speak wisely if the heart is ignored. Perish the one who would decry the heart! Many the fault that besets this course!

When Rāmīn was thrown into confusion by the desire in his heart, he said to the King in kindly wise, "Your Majesty, do not lay yourself open to such tribulation in this affair! Do not suffer distress on account of Vīs and her beauty; much woe will befall you through so doing; you will throw to the winds abundant treasure. By sowing such seed in brackish soil you will be left empty-handed both of seed and of fruit. Vīs will never be your lover nor follow righteousness in dealing with you. If you seek rich ore and cast about endlessly you shall not find it so long as you do not seek it from the vein. How can you seek love and support from a child whose father you have killed? She will not shrink from flag and army, nor yet be taken in by coin

1. Cf. Mark's taking advice, *Tristan*, p. 50.

and jewels. Only through much disaster will you attain her; and once you have attained her you will not support the disaster she brings in her train. When you have an enemy as companion in your house it will be as if you had a snake in your sleeve. An even graver problem which confronts you where Vīs is concerned is the fact that you are old, while that charming maid is young. If you must take a mate, take one other than her; youth to youth, old age to old age. Just as someone young is your aim, she too should have just such a one. You are December, that sweetheart spring; a hard matter indeed to unite the two! And if you consort with her against her will, disabuse your heart of any notion that you will have joy of her! You will ever be sorry for what you have done, nor will you find any remedy for your agony. Separating yourself from her will be as rending a veil; your heart will never bear to do so; nor will you find deliverance from the travail she entails for you, nor again find peace in separation. Love of the fair is like the sea: shore and deep alike are inscrutable. Dive in it you may and that with ease; but however much you desire you will with difficulty escape from it. You are now seeking a desire which even tomorrow will turn into an affliction for you. You may leap into it now with ease—but you will not be able to jump out of it again. If you know that I speak truly, and am seeking your welfare by these words, listen to friendly advice from me; if you do not, it will entail damage for you."

When Moubad heard these words from Rāmīn this sweet advice seemed bitter to him. His soul in its love was like a sick man in whose mouth even sugar is bitter; had the writ of pain not run in his body, sugar would have tasted sweet in his mouth. Although Rāmīn's advice was designed to dissipate love, the King's love increased thereby. A heart full of love is not susceptible of health; blame but increases its fervor. When a heart is corroded with love, reproach only fans its fire. Blame is to the heart like a sharp sword; to administer it to lovers entails strife. Strife is the root of man's love; his heart, cold though it may be, becomes heated by it. Even should a cloud rise from the world and stones rain from it instead of reproaches, the lover would not fear the stony rain, even were spears to replace the stones. Everything which provokes blame is a fault, save the pursuit of love, which is a virtue. A critic by his remonstrance will not wash desire from the heart of a lover. Desire is like fire, remonstrance the wind; and what does the wind do when it blows on fire? Fire blazes every moment at the blast of wind—a whole world burns at its every flame. See how wind deals with fire; advice does likewise to the lover's heart. What is the foul-mouthed man as far as love is concerned? No less than a scorpion. "He who is not a lover is no man."[2]

As love, then, increased in the King's heart, Rāmīn's advice became yet more of a goad to it. He secretly said to his other brother, "See what may be my remedy in dealing with Vīs; what am I to contrive to gain my desire and increase the repute of my name? If I turn from this castle in desperation, I shall become a byword for disgrace in the world."

His brother said, "Your Majesty, present much wealth to Shahrū and subvert her with coin. Foster in her hope of favor, then inspire in her fear of God. Say, 'There is another world beyond this: visitation of the soul is eternal. What excuse is your soul to offer before the Creator when it is caught in the fetters of sin? When they say to you, "Why did you break your oath, why did you break the contract you concluded?" you will be left helpless and ashamed before the Creator, you will in no wise find a support or helper.' Devise speeches like this: embellish them with coin and brocade. Kings are seduced by these two things: well may beauties fair as the moon be so seduced! It is by these two means that the cunning man deceives his every victim: coin and speeches."

27.

MOUBAD WRITES A LETTER TO SHAHRŪ AND SUBVERTS HER WITH RICHES. The King was pleased by Zard's message and straightway wrote a letter to Shahrū. In it he expressed sweet words, studded it with jewels.

"Shahrū, do not forget the path to heaven! Hear my words with the ear of justice! Remember the eternal shame your soul will witness at the hand of the Judge! Remember the Judgment seat of the great

2. *Tristan*, p. 276: "Hearts and eyes often go ranging along the path that has always brought them joy. And if anyone tries to spoil their sport, God knows, he will make them more enamored of it."

53

Judge, the horror of Hell and the Reckoning. You know that this world will come to an end, and when it is quitted another world come. Merely for the sake of this world's desire, which lasts but a day, do not purchase distress and eternal torment! Do not turn your back on God, but fear God, the Creator and Judge! Do not be of the number of the oath breakers, for God is with those who keep their oath. You well know how we made our treaty, how we swore oaths upon it; you gave me your daughter when thirty years were to pass before you bore a daughter.[1] Your pearl was still in its shell when she was betrothed in my name. Why have you gone back on that compact and treaty? Why have you become the associate of Ahriman? I am not now at the mercy of enemies; I have the approval of friends; I represent not shame upon your head, but fame. Why have you become thus estranged from me and in league with my enemies? You bore this daughter through the medium of my aura of fortune; why have you now given her to another spouse? Know that it was my fortune that decreed that the bridegroom should not have joy of Vīs and his marriage bond. How has another attained to my spouse? How was this in accord with the decree of the Creator? If you ponder well you will know that this was heaven's work; since the title of union with me has lit on Vīs, no groom will have joy of her. Consider this fresh bond to be as empty air and divorce your heart from it accordingly. Give me your daughter with form like the moon; deliver your land from my vengeance. You will be accountable for every drop of blood that we shed here. If you are not the ally of the Demon of Wrath,[2] if there is any fear of God in your heart, it will be better for you to make an end of this feud and ransom an entire world with one woman. Otherwise the land of Māh shall be brought low in vengeance; how then will you escape blame for this offense? Do not in imprudence consider this feud to be trifling; no one would reckon such a feud as of small account. Should you turn from feud to love toward me, I shall endow Vīrū with sovereignty; I shall make over all my resources to him, he shall be the senior

1. *G:* "she came forth from thee in thy thirtieth year."
2. *G* has Eshma (Avestan Aēshma, Pahlavī Ēshm, the Asmodaeus of the Book of Tobit [New English Bible, Apocrypha (Oxford and Cambridge University Presses, 1970), p. 76]).

general over my army. When Vīs is Queen of Khurāsān you in your turn shall be Queen of Kūhistān. If some space of life be left us we shall pass it merrily and happily. The world shall be at peace under our rule, cleansed of strife and tyranny. When you have the chance of enjoying the world in ease, why must you be hostile to all?"

28.

DESCRIPTION OF THE GOODS SENT BY MOUBAD TO SHAHRŪ. When the King had finished this letter he made ready a treasure of jewels and riches. He sent so much finery to Shahrū that it cannot be registered in a scroll. There were a hundred camels with litter and sedan, then five hundred pack-camels; also five hundred mules[1] fully loaded, upon them loads of royal pearls. A hundred Arab horses, three hundred horses of Tukhāristān,[2] jewels like the star-studded sky. Two hundred gliding cypresses from China and Khallukh,[3] with locks like violets, curls like hyacinths, and cheeks like roses. Each one in stature like a silver cypress, with the Great Bear and the Pleiades raining on it; belts on their waists of pure jewels, on their heads gold and radiant diamonds. Each charming maid was a spring in herself, her face a garden in its midst. In point of tresses each one was a musky lasso; in point of stature each one a lofty cypress. In face each one was like ten moons fourteen days old, the sun was as the moon by the side of their faces; all with bracelet and necklace of gold, studded over-all like their mouths with jewels.[4] There were two hundred gold crowns and banners, likewise a hundred golden caskets full of gems; pure musk and ambergris scattered on them, in color and scent like a sweetheart's hair. There were seven hundred wine bowls, crystal and gold; like the moon and Venus at dawn. Then twenty assloads of Byzantine brocade, in color like a newly bloomed rose plot. There were many other things of various kinds besides, beyond description and measure. It was as if no jewels remained in the world that Moubad had not showered upon Shahrū.

1. *I.*
2. Minorsky, *Iranica*, p. 175, n. 2, quoting H. W. Bailey, *BSOAS*, XIII, No. 2 (1950), 403. The reading of *I* here confirms Professor Bailey's restoration. See pp. 134, 163, 278.
3. Minorsky, *Ḥudūd ul-'Ālam*, p. 97. Khallukh = Qarluq.
4. *G* omits the passage about the "gliding cypresses."

29.

HOW SHAHRŪ SURRENDERED VĪS TO SHĀH MOUBAD; THE
SINISTER ASPECT OF THAT NIGHT.[1]   When Shahrū saw all these
loads of varied sort, of gems, brocade, and coin, she became senseless
like the drunken in the face of the multitude of wealth and forgot her
son and daughter. Fear of God, too, descended on her heart, which
clove in two at her impatience. When the Sphere loosed the fetters of
the demon of night, then roused the gleaming moon with the news,
up in the castle Shahrū did likewise, and took a lesson from what the
signs of the Zodiac had done; for she opened the hall of the castle
to the King, then roused the gleaming moon with the tidings. It
was a night dark and thick with pitch, black and dreadful like the
day of separation; like a heap of indigo over the sky, like a Rājah on
an elephant over the earth; black as sorrow, blotted out like hope;
let down like a curtain in front of the sun; you would have sworn that
night had dug a pit in the west and that the sun had suddenly fallen
from the sky into the pit; that the sky had put on black garments in
mourning for it, and the heaven mustered armies from every quarter;
it ever wheeled its armies to the west, for there the general lay fallen
in the pit; the armies of the sky were on the march, the night serene
as the will of a monarch; a canopy over it like a blue wheel, all
picked out with jewels; at rest and securely set, its tent ropes fixed on
the mountains; moon and sun had both hidden their faces, sleeping
like lover and beloved. The stars were stayed, each in his place, like
pearls set in enamel; the sky like an iron wall, the stars indifferent
to motion; the Ram facing the Bull, scenting the Lion of the sky;
both stopped in their tracks from fear of the Lion, strength drained
from fore and hind legs; the Twins like two lovers asleep, twined
together like buckets on a waterwheel; the Crab lying at their feet;
you would have sworn it had become lifeless and pincerless; the Lion
standing before the Crab, arching its tail to its head like a bow; its
eyes bloodshot like a lover's; its mouth open like a split pomegranate;
a Virgin with two bunches of vines in her hands, rooted to the spot
like one drunk; a Scales with all its connections severed, the two pans
left but the beam broken; the Scorpion with head and tail brought

1. Heading as in *I*.

꒰ 56

together; languid as men afflicted with a chill; the Archer with the bow stuck in his hands, his legs frail and his hands *hors de combat*, the Lamb sleeping secure from him, hidden in grass and tulips; then the Lamb, on an arrow being suddenly shot at it, falling wounded thereby; the Water Carrier's bucket fallen down the well, the Water Carrier left astonished like a lost soul; the Fish stuck motionless against its will;[2] you would have sworn it was a fish fallen in the net.

The heaven disposed itself every hour and brought up some new wonder; from the Sphere's tricks with beads you would have sworn that with its dark ways it was a conjurer with full bag of tricks; it was skilled in sleight of hand like a juggler, and performed a repertoire of feats. So many shapes did the heaven create and display that you would have sworn it was a magician!

In its northern part it showed the Dragon, its tail round the Pole like a hedge; the Great Bear sleeping behind it, the Little Bear by it like a cub; another woman bound with a chain, a man kneeling before her; opposite them an Eagle with spread wings, its feet grasping an arrow; a Youth standing like a guard, in his hands a goblet and tray of gold; two Fish for all the world like two bags full of wind; a Duck with neck like a lofty cypress; a man without horse but still holding reins; another like a snake charmer with a snake; a man sitting on a silver throne, before him a horse broken from its halter; a man with a demon's head in his palm, a crown-bearer standing before him.

In its southern part appeared a dark stream, like ringlets of hair in its manifold twists and curls; near the stream a bounding Hare, two hounds coursing after it, unleashed by a man with a belt standing like a king; a Ship full of radiant gems, its anchor made of rubies; a Snake thin as a cane stem, a Crow in a meadow; a gold Cup before it, hailstones cast in it in place of wine; a silver Censer full of embers, a royal Crown full of jewels; a sign like a spotted fish, scales upon it like silver stars; a horse like a human, beautiful flowers blooming on its body; you would swear it was confused like a drunken man and had taken a lion's paw in its hands; a sign like a bird without wings, with a fine tail like a peacock's.

2. The account of the heavens in *G* ends here.

From the east was stretched a sinister ascendant, so that Moubad's marriage might be inauspicious; the sun was in conjunction with the moon, like a vizier whispering secrets to a king. Old Saturn accompanied them, the fourth house of the ascendant was their position.[3] Opposite the ascendant in the seventh house Deneb was the companion of aggressive Bahrām;[4] Venus left between them, desperate of propitious advent. None of the influences militating for justice, whose conjunction might have been propitious for that enterprise, were favorable.

It was under this ascendant that the King saw Vīs and did not experience of his mate the lot he fancied in his heart!

30.

MOUBAD ENTERS THE CASTLE AND BRINGS OUT VĪS. When Shāh Moubad entered the castle at such a moment and under such a sinister ascendant, he searched high and low for the captivating Vīs but could not see that freshly bloomed garden; but the radiance of her forehead and face, the scent of her musk-imbued hair, gave the King a clue to that sweetheart, for the very earth was scented with musk and the air tinged with ambergris. On went the King till he came to her side, and instantly took her crystal hand. He drew her out of the castle and led her to the camp,[1] where he handed her over to his attendants and bodyguard. Straightway they seated her in a litter; the very litter became like a profusion of blossoms at her presence. Around her were servitors and nobles, the pick of trusty lifeguards.[2] On the instant they sounded the brazen trumpets and raised the points of the flags to Gemini.

There and then did the monarch set out, and rivaled the fleet wind in his march; hasting on day and night, pressing along the road, delighted at the face of his beloved, like a lion which comes upon a teeming herd of asses, or a man who lights on a royal treasure. Rightly enough did he rejoice in his sweetheart, for he had in her a

3. See p. 63.   4. Mars.

1. *G* adds "for she would not go willingly, and he could not leave her."
2. Persian *jānsipār* (cf. p. 41). This term in Pahlavī denoted the royal bodyguard. Christensen, *L'Iran sous les Sassanides*, p. 208 (note by courtesy of Professor Mīnovī).

lover superior to the moon in the heavens. Right enough that he should take pains on her behalf, for he had all in a moment discovered a veritable treasure of beauty; pearls and ruby laughing and loquacious, bright as pure silver and scented like jasmine.

31.

VĪRŪ RECEIVES TIDINGS THAT THE KING HAS CARRIED OFF VĪS.
When Vīrū received tidings of the King he returned from Tārum[1] and made haste: by the time he arrived, the King had gone, and taken his beauty of moonlike face by stratagem; left him thousands of gems, and taken in exchange a single jewel. Shahrū had broken faith with her son, leaving fire in the heart of Vīrū. Vīrū's heart was full of rancor and distress, hurt as he was by both mother and sister. The blossom of the branch of loyalty was lost for him, the crowning beauty of his palace of splendor was gone. His castle was like a casket, but from the casket the pearl had fallen; his embrace like the heaven, but from the heaven the moon had set. His soul had been like a mine of silver; Fate had worked his vein of silver till it was no more. Although his silver mine was without ore, his eyes became a mine of another sort of ore.

Vīrū's heart wept at separation, Moubad's preened itself on his beloved. Now his eyes rained tears on yellow roses, now his soul cried out in pain and agony. Agony so drained the color from his cheeks that it was as if life had deserted his body. Separation rent the veil of his patience, sense flew from his brain like a bird. He rained curses on the revolution of Fate for making him the target of the arrow of separation; had it not robbed him of his sweetheart, the darling of all, and flung his star suddenly to the ground?

But though Fate was cruel to Vīrū, by the same token it kept faith with Moubad. It robbed one of a darling and gave her to the other; one met with injustice from Fate, the other justice. The abode of joy was set in confusion for one, the garden of triumph blossomed for the other. One had stones struck on his heart and dust and ashes on his head; the other the wine bowl in his hand and the lover in his embrace.

1. See n. 3, p. 46.

32.

RĀMĪN SEES VĪS AND FALLS IN LOVE WITH HER. When the eye of the King's hope had lit up, he bore that Sun back to Khurāsān.[1] On the way he became happy and joyful, the cruelties of this world forgotten. From the beauty of Vīs's face the litter had become the gorgeous palace of Mānī the painter.[2] Whenever a breeze blew on the litter the world became sweetly scented by her perfume. With its radiant solitary pearl it was like a casket; with its gleaming full moon like a mansion of heaven. It was as if the litter were a cupola, perfumed throughout by the tresses of Vīs; the sun traced on it, a golden veil drawn over it. Now Venus and the moon shone from it, now freshly rubbed musk scattered from it on the road. Now beauty scattered flowers in it, now fell captivating charm swung the polo stick. The litter was like God's Paradise, its postilion glorious Rizvān.[3]

Thus ran the decree of Providence, that Rāmīn's days of happiness were to come to an end. The fire of love was to blaze in his heart, reason and patience to burn on the fire.

A fresh spring breeze arose and stirred the curtains on the litter one by one; it was as if a sword had been drawn from the scabbard, or as if the sun had come out from behind a cloud. The face of Vīs came out from behind the veil and Rāmīn's heart became its slave at one glance. It was as if a sorceress[4] had shown her face to him and robbed his body of life with one look. Even had this been a poisoned arrow, its wound could not have been thus catastrophic; for no sooner had Rāmīn seen the face of that moonlike beauty than he was as one in whose heart an arrow had suddenly lodged.

He fell from his horse as mighty as a mountain, like a leaf that the wind rips from the tree. The brain in his head had begun to boil from the fire in his heart; heart had fled from body and sense from head.

1. Cf. p. 118. The sun rises from Khurāsān in the east.
2. Cf. n. 3, p. 29, and p. 264. Mānī (Manes) is celebrated as an inspired painter in Persian tradition. Widengren, *Mani and Manichaeism*, p. 107.
3. See n. 5, p. 29.
4. Persian *jādū*. In Persian folklore the *parī* possesses this power (Christensen, "Essai sur la Démonologie Iranienne," pp. 14, 62). The vogue for the latter word in Britain in Victorian times receives a dig from W. S. Gilbert in *Iolanthe*, subtitled "The Peer and the Peri."

Love penetrated his heart by way of the eye, and thus stole his heart through a single glance. The tree of loverhood grew from his frame, but his eyes planted it;[5] perhaps his sight had planted that tree in his soul so that it might quickly bear fruit of coral: for a time he remained thus fallen, like a man utterly drunk on copious draughts of wine. His rosy cheeks had turned the color of saffron; his wine-colored lips blue as the sky. The hue of life had deserted his face, the insignia of love appeared there in its stead.

From the ranks the champions, cavalry and foot soldiers, stood round Rāmīn; their eyes gone bloodshot at his pain, hope of his dear life abandoned. No one knew what had befallen him, what an ill fate he had suffered, what tribulation he had undergone. Everyone was cut to the heart by his agony, everyone who saw him was even more wretched than he; tongue dumb, eyes like a bleeding vein, the dread hand of loverhood heavy upon his heart.

When some little consciousness crept back into his soul, his eyes became like oyster shells, so full were they of pearls. He rubbed his eyes and wept no more from very shame before his fellow men. Every sage person supposed that the cyclone of epilepsy had blown him down. When noble Rāmīn mounted his horse, his precious soul was bitter from copious pain. He went on his way like a lost soul, like a madman unaware of his own state; his heart in the hollow of the devil's hand, his eyes fixed on the litter of Vīs, like a thief who keeps his eye fixed upon a place where there is a casket of jewels.

He would say, "How if fair fortune once more showed me the face of that Moon? How if again a wind came and snatched the veil from the face of Vīs? How if she heard one of my sighs and covertly showed that cheek out of the veil? If she saw my yellow cheek, and heard my agonized moans and sighs? If mercy invaded her heart for my yellow face, and she pitied my distress and pain? How if on the rest of this journey I alone were her postilion? If someone under-took a knightly quest and carried my greeting to that idol-faced beauty? If she saw me in a dream, saw my eyes full of blood and tears? If her stony heart became a trifle softened, and grew warm with the heat of love? If she, like me, came to be at the mercy of enemies through passion for a lover? Perhaps once she had

5. Persian *veirā* (conjecture; *I* has *veirān*).

tasted the sorrow of love she would no longer be so tyrannical and proud!"

Now Rāmīn would ponder thus, now try patience with his heart. Now he fell into the pit of temptation, now admonished his heart with sage counsel: "My heart, what has befallen you? How long will you speak thus? What is your aim in this vain fancy? You have begun to writhe for love of that Moon who is all unaware of your plight. Why do you nourish hopes of union with Vīs—no one attains to union with the Sun! Why do you live in hope as fools do, of something beyond hoping? You are like thirsty mortals seeking water—but you are in a desert groping after a mirage. May God your Creator have mercy on you! Your plight is sore and sorry!"

When Rāmīn became fettered by the shackle of love, hope shattered in his broken heart, neither could he seek his desire, nor again did he know any course but patience. He went his way in company with his heart's delight, his heart set hopelessly on comradeship with her. He snatched but this much benefit from being in her company, that at least he smelled the perfume of that jasmine cheek! As his soul lay day and night in chains, his heart rejoiced in her scent.

What more wretched wight than a lover? What plight worse than his? People go to inquire after one afflicted with fever and feel anxious about his grave attack, but the heart of a lover may be in the fire year in, year out and no one inquires about his malady! I ask you, all who are wise, is there any crueler fate than that which love visits on the lover? Enough in itself for the lover is the malady of living with the pain of love and in bitter lamentation. Rightly should our hearts burn for those in whose hearts love lights a fire! Ever to hide the pain of one's heart, never to dare divulge one's secret to any!

Rāmīn, every moment more in love, was like a partridge wounded to the heart in the talons of a falcon. He was at one and the same moment neither dead nor alive, but a figure haunting a no man's land in between. Only a glimmer remained of what had been a mountain of silver; only a bent bow remained of what had been a cypresslike figure. He went on his way thus forlorn, as I have related, thinking every step of his road a pitfall.

33.

MOUBAD BRINGS VĪS TO MARV THE ROYAL ABODE. When the King of Kings entered the choice city of Marv, the Moon of Moons matching the King of Kings as traveling companion, a thousand festive stands were set up in Marv; the beauties of fairy face sat thereon. The great scattered garments and jewels; the lesser scattered hazelnuts and sugar. The city's dust rising into the air was pure ambergris, just as the sand of its soil was jeweled. People counted the whole world as being that very day; they trod very silver and gold in place of earth. That day Marv the royal abode was Paradise; in it there was a garden dropping jewels. So many rose-hued faces were to be seen from roof upon roof that a hundred Venuses shone therefrom. So many musicians and lute players were there, so many silver-breasted charming beauties, that the heart was fatally overcome at the sight, the soul delighted and overjoyed at the sound. As this diverse celebration filled the town, see how the King's palace appeared: it was like a magnificent treasure, so many decorations decked it; it was like the mansions of heaven, so many stars graced it. A palace in grandeur like a world; its high vault like a whole sky. The roof of its hall was for all the world like a steed whose rider was ancient Saturn.[1] Portal, wall, floor, threshold were gay with decoration in Chinese fashion, in beauty like the luck of the fortunate; in prettiness like the faces of beauties inflaming men's hearts; the garden of the palace blossoming like the King's fortune, its flower plot smiling like the face of Vīs, the King of Kings seated therein in triumph, his heart cleansed outright of grief, like silver.

The commanders and heroes of the army were showering silver and gold upon him like rain. One after another they came forward to scatter their offering, recalling a mountain with a mound of jewels set before it.

The King disposed, took his fill, gave largesse; dispose, take your fill, and give, that justice may be done! Princess Vīs sat in the seraglio, which became like a garden by her presence. The King of

1. Saturn occurs repeatedly in connection with Moubad; compare his sinister horoscope at the end of §29. Minorsky, *Iranica*, p. 192. Here loftiness is the main point.

Kings sat joyful and happy, but Vīs sat sorrowful; weeping like a cloud day and night in her wretchedness, all hearts fallen to weeping at her distress. Now she wept at the memory of Shahrū, now lamented in grief for Vīrū. Now she wept tears of agony in silence, now wailed like those who have lost their hearts. She did not open her lips to speak, nor did she answer any who addressed her. It was as if a caravan of care reached her soul every instant. Her body had become like a bamboo tree; in color and hue like saffron.

When the proud and noble ladies saw her raining tears upon her cheeks, they entreated and implored her sorely—but her lamentation and agony declined not a whit. Whenever she saw Moubad she rent her body in place of her garments: she would not hear the words he spoke nor show him her fair face. She turned her beautiful face to the wall and sent a flood of tears of agony from her eyes down her cheeks.

Thus she was, both on the journey and in Marv; the King had no joy of her even for a day; the face of Vīs was glorious like a garden—but a garden whose gate is shut tight.

34.

THE NURSE LEARNS OF THE PLIGHT OF VĪS AND GOES TO MARV. When the Nurse heard of the plight of Vīs, how the King had abducted her, the world became dark to her eyes; it was as if her soul had instantly taken flight afar. She could do nothing but weep, she had no resource but lamentation. She made the plain into a river Oxus by her weeping, leveled mountains to the steppe by her lament.

She said, "Gleaming Moon, but two weeks old! other beauties have become as the moon; you as the Moon of Moons; what feud does Fate nurse against your soul that it should have made you a legend in the entire world? Your mouth is not yet cleansed of your mother's milk and yet your story is on every lip. The pomegranates of your breasts are not swollen from your bosom, and yet desire for you has swelled out of the seven climes. You are but tiny—why is your fame great? You are a gazelle—why is love for you a wolf? Your years are tender, but your suitors substantial in number; you are innocent of treachery, but your devotees traitors. They have driven you abroad from house and home, left me daughterless and helpless. They have exiled you from your family and left me without daughter and home. They have driven you abroad from your city and left me to suffer exile for your sake. They have exiled you for their own sake—and driven me mad for yours! God made the sight of you like my very soul; how may one live without a soul? May no trace of me remain in the world if for one moment I should wish time to pass without you! I make the plains like the River Oxus by my weeping, I level mountains to the plain by my lamentation."

Then she prepared thirty camels for the road, many kinds of royal panoply upon them. She brought for her daughter everything she might need, each and every thing such as was proper for a royal personage. In a week she traveled to Marv the royal abode; it was as if her soulless body traveled to its soul.

When the Nurse saw Vīs brokenhearted, her soul grew full of happiness; but she was sitting in dust and ashes, the tulip rent and the hyacinth snapped; weeping bitterly for her youth, her heart forswearing soul and life. She had taken to moaning and weeping over her body, her head hung low like a heron. Sometimes she cast dust on her head, sometimes poured tears of agony from her eyelashes down on her breast. Her cheeks were like a rusty sword, scored all over by her nails. Her heart had become as straitened as her mouth was narrow; her body as slim as her waist. When the Nurse saw her wretched and weeping, her heart burned on the fire of grief.

She said to her, "Precious darling, why melt your soul in annihilation? Why distill from the body blood which is its very life? Why shed what does harm to the soul? You are the light of the very eyes in my head, the co-mate of my good fortune. I wish you nothing but good and happiness; I am not desirous of injustice falling on you by your own hand. Do not so, fair Moon! Do not kick against the pricks of Fortune! and if you must do so, do not kick so fiercely; for all that will come of this sorrowing and misery will be yellowness for your face and wasting for your body. Your mother gave you into the hands of Moubad; your brother did not afterwards follow in your tracks. Now you are in the hands of a puissant monarch, his spouse, his very soul and world. Reconcile yourself to him and forbear to hurt him; no man of sense offends kings.

"Although Vīrū is a king of kingly descent, he is not Moubad's

65

like in eminence and sovereignty. In place of the farthing that has fallen from your hand God has given you a jewel. Though your brother has not been your stay and support, God is yet sufficient as your stay, Fortune as your support. If Vīrū has broken the contract with you, a lord such as this has united himself to you. Destiny has robbed you of a silver apple and given you in its place a golden orange! It has closed a door, but opened another instantly: taken away a lamp, but put a candle in its place. Fate has not done you so much wrong that you should thus seek pretexts for weeping. You should not be thus ungrateful: for you will quickly repent of your behavior. Today is a day of enjoyment for you—no day of moaning and crying and misery!

"If you will obey, you will rise from the dust, put on clean royal raiment, place on the crown of your musky head the gold coronet, deck the moon of your face with the Pleiades; by your stature you will cause a cypress to grow from the throne; by your face you will cause a garden to blossom from the palace; bring forth the rose of beauty from your rosy face, serve sweet wine with your wine-colored lip; take lives and steal hearts with your glance, enrich the soul and charm the heart with your kiss, make the night appear as day by your tulip-hued face, even as you make day night with your amber-gris-scented tresses. You will put the sun in confusion by your face, chain sorcerers with your locks, reduce the value of sugar by your laugh, ruin the market of ambergris with your curl, make men's hearts cold toward the fair, make the faces of the lionhearted look yellowly on the gazelles. If you don your finery you will be as I have said and more. You will invade every heart as a gem of beauty, and enter every soul more sweetly than sweetness itself! Deck your jewel in gems: make your stature a figured garment: for when a beauty is resplendent in finery her very fairness is increased by ornaments. You possess youth, beauty, and majesty: what more do you wish than what you have? Do not disapprove of the command of God: do not cause pain where none exists; the decree of God does not fear your cry; the wheeling sphere will not turn backwards! Why then do you have need of this senseless lamentation; why do you pour from your eyes these vain tears?"

As the Nurse recited all these words of advice, they were as mere empty air; it was as if she were throwing walnuts on a dome, or sailing a ship in the desert!

35.

VĪS REPLIES TO THE NURSE. Vīs of the moonlike form replied to her, "Your words are like fruitless seed; my heart is sated of scent and color; I shall not don raiment nor sit on a throne. Sackcloth is my raiment, dust my throne, and pain and sad sighs my courtiers: neither will Moubad have joy of me nor I renown of him. As I was a palm without a thorn with Vīrū, now I am a thorn that will not bear dates. If I must have a husband for the sake of desire, it suits me better to be free of desire. Since in the event he missed his desire, may no one else enjoy desire of me!"

36.

THE NURSE REPLIES TO VĪS. The Nurse began to speak again— for she had a wondrous store of words. She said to her, "Light of your mother's eyes, it is right that you should mourn for your brother; he was both brother and sweetheart to you, and you had known no joy of each other. What can be worse than that two faithful lovers should be together many a month and year, dwell together in joy day and night, yet not experience their heart's desire of each other; then remain far from each other and know no device whereby to be united? The one's sorrow matches the other's regret: their pain is everlasting; like a man who is humble and poor and suddenly stumbles on a treasure: but he is slothful and does not pick it up: thinking of it instead as already taken and spent. When he returns he does not find the treasure where it was: he remains forever the prey of regret and lamentation.

"Vīrū's lot with you has been thus: his luck has now turned evil and dark. That day and that fortunate time are gone when a bishop could take two castles! 'A departed lover is like the days gone by'; do not, if you are wise, cry over time that is gone! Do not indulge unwisely in fury or be fractious; obey me and rise from the dust! Wash your head and hair in rose water, then seek fair garments from the master of the robes. Don that raiment, sit on the throne, place on your head the gold crown encrusted with jewels! for noblewomen will come here, sprung from lords of gentle birth; I do not want them to see you thus wretched, sit thus with you in the dust.[1]

"In any event, you have the sense to know that you are today in the city of others: a hundred offices must needs be performed for strangers for propriety's sake; to observe propriety is the best of all courses: so that the tongues of strangers may thereby be stopped. Everyone who sees you thus will straightway talk of you in these words: one group will interpret your behavior as pertness; another as ill will; now they will say, 'She has failed to do us honor since she did not approve of us!'; now, 'Who is she, pray, that we should have to endure trouble on her behalf?' The right course, if you are sagely inclined, is to stop their tongues wagging about you. Know that everyone who holds others of little account has many enemies. Everyone who is proud and haughty will miss pleasure in his life. I tell you, eschew this evil habit; for others' sake, albeit not Moubad's. For your very fault is a virtue in his eyes, since he loves you with heart and soul."

When the charming Vīs heard these words, for a time peace returned to her heart. The words of the Nurse appealed to her and she in no wise sought to hurt her. There and then she rose from the dust, bathed her silvery body, and then arrayed it; the Nurse arrayed her face and hair, covered her with color and scent.

The eyes of Vīs wept on the finery, she writhed inwardly like a snake from grief, saying, "Alas for sinister fortune that has so abruptly deserted me! What soaring bird, what wind up in the air will witness my woe upon woe? People have mercy on outcasts and bring physicians for the sick; have mercy on an outcast such as I am, bring me a physician, for I am in sore need of one! I am torn from house and home, outcast, wretched, the arrow lodged in my heart; far from my worthy companions, exiled from my sincere friends. For grief for my mother and glorious brother my body is in the ocean wave, my heart in the fire. The world is in feud with me; Fortune at war with me; the sphere is most furious against me, the age most savage. Fate has rained upon me a flood of injustice, Providence has drawn upon me a blade of steel. If there were justice and an arbiter in the world, the very plants and pebbles would come to my defense!"

1. *G:* "from deference they, too, will sit down on cinders at thy side."

37.

THE NURSE ARRAYS VĪS; HER DESCRIPTION. When the Nurse arrayed the Moon of the fair, she arranged violets on mallow flower; Sirius and Venus shone from her forehead; moon and sun blazed from her cheek. Her bewitching eye was like warlike Mars; her jet lock like Saturn of malevolent aspect;[1] her lips propitious in activity like Jupiter, yielding sugar and raining jewels year in, year out. Her two curls were musk, her face camphor and vermilion, like a crow fallen slain upon snow. You would have sworn her cheeks were a bouquet of roses, her lips drops of wine. In both rise and swell that silvery bosom was over-all a matching pair of sweethearts. Her arms long and round and plump, each an enchanting tree; branches upon them of pure silver, but the fruit of the branches was jujube. Mouth like a rosebud not yet open, thirty-two pearls hidden in it; like thirty-two sparkling gems hidden under two rubies of Badakhshān.[2]

Seated, she was like a moon endowed with soul; when she rose she was a gliding cypress. Reason gazed spellbound at her, not knowing what to call that idol, never having seen any idol flawless like her, tall, graceful, sweet, and fair; in beauty like fortune and success, in sweetness like life and soul. From abundance of ornaments like a blossoming garden in spring; from wealth of jewels like a royal treasury. Had a sage seen that idol he would have scoured over plain and mountain like a madman. Had Rizvān passed by that idol, the faces of the Hūrīs would have seemed ugly to him. Had that beauty called the dead, they would have answered her from the grave. Had she washed her face in brackish water, sugar cane would have sprung up around it. Had she rubbed her lip on amber, that amber would have been upon the instant ruby.

Thus was that beauty of cypress figure, thus that idol of sunlike face. The beauties of China and the moonlike maidens of Barbary were before her like stars around the moon. Her face shining on the golden throne was like Byzantine embellishment or a Chinese figurine;[3] like a moon in a spring garden, thousands of stars clustering about the moon. Who can recount in words what the King sent

1. Cf. n. 1, p. 63.   2. Minorsky, Ḥudūd ul-ʿĀlam, p. 112.
3. G: "a porcelain face in gold."

her in the way of bales of material and jewel caskets; trays of attar and decorated bowls; moonlike beauties Chinese and Byzantine,[4] all camphor-pale of face and musky of hair, each one like a deer of the riverside who has never so much as looked on the lion of the plain, in beauty like peacocks strutting innocent of the hawk's talon.

Princess Vīseh sat on the throne, Fortune now her beauty's dresser, the seraglio before her become a reedbed, like some cypress grove planted next to a garden. The world rejoiced in her, but she was melancholy for love; blessings sounded like curses to her ears.

For a whole week Shāh Moubad now drank wine, now swung the polo stick; then he went for a week to the chase; no arrow from his bow fell upon the ground. There was no dearth of silver and gold on the day of wine drinking, nor of game on the day of the chase. When he wielded the polo stick he did so with such mastery that he drove the ball from earth to heaven. The polo stick ever kissed his palm, his horse's hoof the field. When he drank wine with his nobles he quaffed so mightily that he consumed the revenue of an entire world in a single day. His palm was like a cloud dropping rain, the goblet flashing in the cloud like lightning.

Thus was his drinking, his prowess, and his generosity; for he was ever generous and happy.

38.

THE NURSE PUTS A SPELL ON SHĀH MOUBAD TO RENDER HIM IMPOTENT WITH VĪS. When the Nurse so arrayed Vīs that the sun craved light from her face, the eyes of Vīs did not rest from weeping; it was as if her agony increased momently.

Away from everyone she would secretly say to the Nurse, "My chaotic fortune has fallen about my ears, made my heart weary of life, pulled up the very root of its happiness. I know no remedy but taking my own life; it may be that by killing myself I may escape from this wounded heart. If you do not cast about for some remedy for me and cleanse my soul of this anxiety, I shall speedily have recourse to the remedy of which I have spoken, and cut short by it my long travail; for each time I see Moubad it is as if I sat on the fire. As well death approach me as he! May his fortunes be as ill as mine!

4. *G* adds "and Balkhians."

Though he has washed his heart with the water of patience, and not so far sought his heart's desire of me, I yet fear that he will one day seek it, one day speak the hidden secret of his heart.

"Before he seeks his desire of me, you must lay a trap in his way, whereby I may not yield my body to him for a year, nor shrink from retribution or taking life. The mourning for Qārin will not be less than a year; for a year, then, you shall see me in this fashion; Moubad will not spare me for a year—for he feels neither fear of me nor shame before me. Contrive some enchantment by your cunning; perhaps you might cast a spell upon him to render him impotent with me. Once a year had passed you could once more release it; he would become your thrall; how could he find release? Perhaps by the time a year has passed from now, my days of ill fortune may come to an end. If you do not contrive the stratagem of which I have spoken, you will never have cause to rejoice at my fortune. May you have your desire of this world! Have your joy of Moubad! for I have no desire to gain good fortune in frustration; no desire for joy coupled with ill repute. Leave Moubad's desire to come to nothing; even should my life be lost, it would be worth while! Forbear to say, 'Give him his desire frigidly.' To lose my life is better to me than to be frigid."

When she told this secret of her heart to the old Nurse, it was as if she shot the arrow's point into her heart. The Nurse's eyes stared at her fixedly; the world had gone dark to them.

She said to her, "Light of your nurse's eyes, I descry no jot of justice anywhere in you. You have become black of heart from so much suffering; 'one cannot wash an Ethiopian of his blackness.' A legion of demon sorcerers has invaded you; seduced you from the road of justice and love. But since you have become adamant, and rolled up the scroll of Reason outright, I know no remedy but to humor your desire and cast a spell on the King to protect you, for the demon that has entered into you has blocked your way to all desire."

Then she brought brass and copper, described the talisman of each party;[1] then tied them together with iron, sealed the fastening of both with a spell. So long as the iron clasp should be fastened would

1. *G* describes the talisman as "two in the likeness of Moubad, and one of Vīs."

a man remain spellbound and impotent with a woman. But should anyone break its clasp, there and then the spellbound male would be released.

Once the King had become spellbound and impotent with that Moon, the Nurse took their clasped talisman into the open country, marked a piece of ground by the bank of a river, and hid it under the ground.

When she returned, she told Vīs exactly where she had hidden the talisman. She said to her, "I have done as you commanded, although I am distressed by your order; I have sought your pleasure in the matter of the order and have bound so noble a man with a spell, with a codicil on this wise, that once a month has passed your spell of ill luck will come to an end. By God's decree you will become happy, forswear strife and wrath in your heart. You should not say that it should be so for one year; reason does not countenance your being in such circumstances. When you reconcile your heart to my monarch, I shall bring the hidden talisman, lay it on the fire, burn it outright, and inflame your heart with happiness. For so long as the thing is in water and moisture, the King's fetters will ever be fast. Water has in essence a cold nature; manly strength remains cut off by cold; the moment fire burns the clasp of the talisman, the candle of manhood burns again."

When the Nurse rejoiced the heart of Vīs with the news that the King's toils would not be released for a month, evil Fate exhibited its contentiousness; see how it fouled sugar with poison!

A cloud of indigo hue came up from the sea, made the plain an ocean by its tears; from the floodwater a river like the Oxus appeared on every plain. The waters of the Marv River so swelled that half the city of Marv was ruined thereby. The flood obliterated the sign and the ground, and carried away the talisman of the blest King. Fate rendered that ground a river; the talisman bound the King forever. His sweetheart appeared in his eyes like people's coin in the eye of a poor man; he was like some hungry lion tied to a chain, its prey grazing fearlessly in front of it. He was still alive by the decree of willful Fortune but it was as if a member had died to his body. He lost his way on the road of joy; the hand of his desire fell short of delight; united to his love, the laughingstock of his enemies; the skin on his body was for all the world like a prison. At night he clasped his lover close, but it was as if she was sixty parasangs away.

Vīs had experienced two husbands; but she had remained intact like a spinster. Neither Moubad nor Vīrū had had joy of her; see how the world sported with her! It nursed her amid gentleness and enjoyment, led her on to high degree and fame, but when her stature became the doom of the lofty cypress, when the moon two weeks old became the slave of her face, a tulip bed bloomed on her cheek, twin pomegranates ripened from her bosom, the world deserted her and withdrew from the road of affection; all her fortunes were transformed; I shall recount to you all the adventures of that Moon, whether with the Nurse, with Rāmīn, or with the King, in words such that when a lover reads them he will shed tears of agony from the pain of his heart. I shall recite a romance in which love shall play many a part.

39.

RĀMĪN WALKS IN THE GARDEN AND LAMENTS HIS LOVE FOR VĪS. When the plight of the brokenhearted Rāmīn grew more, his fortunes in love declined. He always sought out lonely places, to sit and weep alone: at night he did not lay himself on his bed, but counted stars all night till daybreak. By day he rested not at all, fleeing from men like wild ass or deer. So strong was the memory of the figure of his love in his mind that whenever he saw a cypress he bowed to it; in the garden he sought out the red rose and wept over it at the memory of her face. Each dawn he picked violets and placed them on his heart as a memento of her locks. He did not drink wine from fear of losing patience, for wine would have robbed him once and for all of peace. The lute was his constant friend, his companions forlorn lovers; on every road he sang a sad song, all of separation from the sweetheart. When he brought up sad sighs from his heart the December wind blew in April. He so tore his heart from his body in lamentation that he dislodged the nightingale from the branch. He shed so many blood-stained tears on his cheeks that his foot was stuck in the mire from blood. The bright day was dark in his eyes, silk and brocade thorns under him.

He lived thus in wretchedness and sickness; no one asked him what was the cause of his malady. He burned and melted like a candle, his heart surrendered to the tender mercies of the fair; life had become worthless in his eyes; his heart had bid farewell to happiness. His clothes were pitifully drenched with tears; his soul was poised to escape from his lips from the pain of love, all hope for life and the beloved abandoned. The vision of the lover haunted his eyes and drove sweet sleep therefrom. He was sunk in the sea of separation, the world become a noose in his eyes; he had become as senseless as a drunken man from all his anxiety; the world was forgotten in his eyes. Now he told lots using his lover's name, to see how his fortunes would end with her; now he went into the King's garden and took witnesses to his plight from every side. He would say, "Bear me witness, see me thus at the mercy of enemies. When Vīs comes tell her my plight, cleanse her heart of its cruelty." Sometimes he wrangled with the nightingales and admonished them at length; he would say,

"Why do you sing these plaints? What in the world have you lost? You are up in the branches with your mate, not, like me, wretched and mourning! You have gardens of a thousand kinds, I have a thousand kinds of brands on my heart. Fortune has granted you a mate and a garden, but has visited on me in love pain and brand. You sing your plaint before the garden: why, then, must there be pain and brand? You sing your plaint in the presence of your lover: why are your hearts thus wounded by plaint? It is meet that I should moan early and late, for my love is not aware of my pain. Such crying and lamentation is proper for me, for I am far from that rose of the spring garden. This heart-rending sigh is suitable for me, for I am far from that delightful rose plot. It is right for me to be thus beside myself, wounded in heart by separation from my cypress. It is meet for me to give up the ghost in wretchedness, and fail to survive in the pain I suffer for my sweetheart."

So saying he wandered in that garden, his eyes full of blood and his heart of brands.

74

40.

RĀMĪN MEETS THE NURSE IN THE GARDEN AND TELLS HER HIS
PLIGHT. It happened that the Nurse came out one day, walking,
like Rāmīn, in that delightful garden. When Rāmīn saw the Nurse,
worthy as the soul, meet as the eyes, the blood coursed in his cheeks
from happiness; you would have said his cheeks clothed themselves
in tulip red. His face showed beads of sweat from bashfulness before
the Nurse, like pearls scattered on wine.

However passing fair and luxuriant a rose might be, Rāmīn's
cheek was a hundred times fairer;[1] his cheeks by the lobes of his ears
were still silvery, their silver as yet undarkened by budding hyacinth,
his chin was as yet camphorlike, his twin locks were like two musky
polo sticks; his cheek was as yet splendid as the tulip, his lip like
honey and wine mixed; his smile still like sugar, with jewels raining
from it; in stature he resembled the graceful boxtree, but the fruit
of the boxtree was Judas blossom. In form he was like a living moon,
but with crown and belt; the robe upon him was a hundred times
fairer than the adornments of the Chinese on the idol of Farkhār.[2]
The crown upon him was fairer on his head than the diadem on the
heads of kings of the world; a renowned king with pedigree back to
Adam, in form a silver-breasted moon abroad in the world. In
aspect fatal to the soul of a sage, everyone longing for such a fate!
Two kinds of sovereignty his meed, in beauty and in worldly sway.
He was at once brother and son to Moubad, moreover King and
Lord of Māh. As soon as a sorcerer saw his eye he would swear that
no better sorcerer than this could ever be found. Only for Rizvān to
see his face and he would acknowledge that none other than this
personage was fit to be commander of the Hūrīs!

This was the face, so fair and noble, that was become desperate
and frustrated on account of Vīs.

When he saw the Nurse alone in the garden it was as if he had seen
the face of everlasting Fortune. He greeted her and pronounced
many salutations; the Nurse did likewise to him. They inquired of
each other's health like two fond lovers, dearly devoted to each other.

1. Cf. the description of Tristan, *Tristan*, p. 85.
2. See n. 6, p. 37.

75

Then they took hands and went to a meadow of wild lilies; they spoke together of everything under the sun; their talk was ointment to the wounded heart. Rāmīn rent the veil of shame, for his dear soul was hot within him.

He said to her, "You who are worthier than life itself to me, I lowlier than a slave before you, you are sweet and your speech too; you are delicious and your aspect too; I crave from fortune radiance for you and for myself intimacy with your fortune; you are my mother, Vīseh my lady; I ever swear by her life that there has never been in the world, nor ever shall be, one like her with face like the sun and form like the moon, descended from queens, of high lineage. You would swear she had been born of her mother to raise fire from the seven climes—especially from this unlucky heart of Rāmīn, which is a very Khurrād and Burzīn fire![3] Though I burn constantly through injustice, may her heart never burn on such a fire! Though Fortune has broken faith with me, may glorious fortune be afoot for her! I constantly say, as I lament from love of her, 'Grant that her plight may never be like mine!' I constantly say as I burn from passion for her, 'Grant that her fortune may never be like mine!' For every single pain I experience through love for her I offer up a hundred blessings upon her fair face. Thus would I have it ever: I suffering torment at her hand, she enjoying felicity."[4]

Rāmīn's words pleased the Nurse: she brought the Pleiades into view from behind garnets[5] and said laughingly, "Rām, live forever, to the delight of your friends, far from evil men; may you enjoy greatness and health, may injustice not light upon your soul at Fate's behest; it is by your aura of fortune that I enjoy health and happiness, by your desire that I enjoy luck and good name; my daughter, too, is more radiant than the moon—may the evil eye be closed in her direction! May her months and years be fair as her face, may her well-wishers smile like her ruby mouth! May those who wish her ill writhe like her hair, those who wish her well be as radiant as her face!

3. Two of the principal sacred fires. See Duchesne-Guillemin, *La Religion de l'Iran Ancien*, p. 88; Stig Wikander, *Feuerpriester in Kleinasien und Iran* (Lund, 1946), p. 106.
4. Cf. *Tristan*, p. 206: "If my adorable Isolde were to go on being the death of me in this fashion I would woo death everlasting!"
5. Persian *bījādeh*: Minorsky, *Ḥudūd ul'Ālam*, p. 112; also "amber."

I see all your words as faultless, like your face food for the soul and fair, all except your saying that she has made you unfortunate and has hardened her heart to the injustice done you. I do not believe these words of yours—for she is not your queen or judge."

Rāmīn again replied to her, "None is so wretched as a lover! His heart is an enemy within the gates, seeking every day some pretext against him. Now he moans in the agony and grief his lover brings him, now weeps because of the brand of separation from his love. Although he becomes wretched at love's hand, he becomes reckless of his very life for its sake. Even though he experiences much calamity by it, he prefers it above all other aims. Love keeps his eyes now sleepless and now moist with tears because of his hopeless desire. He ever longs for the unattainable, and turns from what he attains. He gives his body over to love's catastrophe, and thereafter counts pain as pleasure. If a man could but enjoy sleep together with love, passion for the beloved would be even as pure wine, for its sweetness is the companion of its bitterness, as its delight matches its aftereffect.[6] A lover is in love like a drunken man, for good appears as abominable in his eyes. He is disturbed in love like a drunken man; from sleeplessness he is like one asleep. It is reason that tells bad from good; once love comes on the scene, reason does not remain in the body. A demon holds him ever in its thrall and keeps his eyes ever blind. How can reason ever sort with love? for the one keeps attacking the other, like wine. Reason would never direct the choice of something which constantly caused the veil to be rent. The veil is torn for me, alas, by the hand of love; patience is cut off from my heart, reason from my body. One day a wind suddenly arose and showed me the face of a daughter of the Hūrīs. When I looked, Vīs was that moonlike beauty; she made me distant as the moon from sleep and food. From the moment my eyes fell on that glorious paradise my heart fell a prisoner in Hell. It was as if that was no wind, but a cataclysm; it unveiled to me all of a sudden the face of disaster.

"You nursed me in my childhood and have seen me constantly since then; but you have never seen me in such a condition as this: betwixt life and death from agony of heart. It is as if the lion of my soul is become a fox and my cheeks become like straw from this

6. *G:* "his merriment is wretched as an owl's."

suffering. My body is transformed, my color turned; the one you would suppose a hair, the other, gold. The very eyelashes on my eyes have become as nails, the hairs on my body like snakes. If any day I hold a feast with my friends it is as if I were in battle against my enemies. In times of recreation I am so mournful and wretched that you would say I was doing battle with disaster; if I wander in the garden to take my ease I am like a man lost in a reedbed.

"At night on my bed and cushion of brocade it is as if I am drowned in the deeps of the ocean. In the daytime, in the midst of confidants and friends, I am like a polo ball before the polo sticks of the players. I lament as pathetically at dawn as the nightingale amid the spring blossoms. In the early morning I weep as copiously in my distress as the December cloud on the mountain crag. From those arresting eyes thousands of arrowheads have rained on my heart. From those captivating locks thousands of chains of every kind have looped around my heart. I am like a wounded wild ass in the waste, in whose heart has lodged the poisoned dart. I am like a lion scouring far and wide as it roars, seeking its lost cub. I am like a small child, brokenhearted, cut off from mother and nurse—or like a myrtle bough grown delicate which the decree of Heaven has snapped. Now I crave your mercy, implore the aid of your chivalry; show what chivalry you have—have mercy on this your helpless child! Save me from this burning fire, rescue me from this man-eating lion! Your heart has mercy on strangers and likewise pities madmen; well may you consider me a stranger, mad and lost to sense! By any standard I am worthy of mercy, caught as I am in the jaws of a fierce dragon! You, too, if you are human, have mercy on me, increase love for me in your heart by your goodness.

"Tell my message to that gliding cypress, that smiling idol, that living Moon, black-haired idol of ruby lip, spring of splendor, garden of delight, fairylike of face, the Sun of the earth, sweet of speech, a perfect Hūrī: say, 'You who are compounded all of excellence, nurtured by fondness and humoring of desire, the fair have sworn to your beauty and toed the line before you. The host of sorcerers have fled before you, Chinese beauties shied off at the sight of you. The moon two weeks old has prostrated itself in front of you, yielding its beauty to your face. Your cheeks have enslaved

78

sovereigns, your lips raised the dead. Beauties of Barbary have been laid low by your face, the very idol-carver himself renouncing idols!

"'My body has begun to melt in fear and hope, like mountain snow in the heat of the sun. My heart has fallen into love for you despite itself, struggling like a wild ass in a trap—reason banished, sense drained away, the very heart in my body neither awake nor asleep. I am unaware of peace and pain, my heart rejoices neither in music nor yet in treasure. I do not urge my steed to the polo ground with my companions, neither grasp the polo stick nor play the ball. I do not unleash the cheetahs after the wild ass, nor fly the falcons after the partridge. I neither drink wine nor consort with the fair; nor do I prefer any in the world to my sweetheart. I am not free of pain for a single moment, nor rejoice in anything for so much as a day. So captive am I in my plight that I can find no friend to be my helper. I writhe and moan from nightfall till morning; I am like a snake with a stake stuck in its belly.

"'My body will glean a cure from your words, my eyes find a potion in the sight of you. Only then shall I rediscover my patience and my sense when your sweet words reach my ears! Although year in, year out, month in, month out, I am in agony because of you, though I am left with red tears and yellow face, love for you is in my soul dearer than life itself, even though my soul has been filled with distress by it. I do not wish life without desire for you; I seek no happiness short of your good faith. If my soul ever wearies of passion for you, let the hairs of my head become sword blades! I know that so long as I live I shall be the slave of your slaves; the brightness of my day be from your face, the blackness of my night from your hair, your face of gay color be my early spring, your sweet lip my comforter; your face be as my sun, your tress be as pure musk for me, your eyes as jasmine, your words as blessings; I shall see eternal Paradise on the day when I behold that soul-inflaming face. Only then shall I gain my desire from fortune when I find my way to union with your face.

"'This is my constant plea to God day and night, that my luck may become triumphant by virtue of your face, that your heart may be kind to me, not seek haughtiness and ill will. Why must you shed the blood of a youth from whom you have never suffered harm? By reason of his great love for you, you are sweeter to him than life itself. He will cast the heart out of his body before he breaks with you, will buy the dust on which you tread at the price of his eyes. It is you he seeks out of the whole world—helpless as he is!—for you have cruelly stolen away his heart. If you but seek him out, he will surrender his body to you; if not, he will sacrifice his soul on top of his heart. I have told you the whole of my sorry plight—if indeed you can believe these words! If your kindness does not come to my rescue, I shall fall to earth bewildered and die. If you fan the feud and contend with me I swear that you will end by shedding my blood!'"

THE NURSE REPLIES TO RĀMĪN. When the old Nurse heard these words it was as if her heart were transfixed by an arrowhead. She raged like a lioness at the words, it was as if she had suddenly been struck by a whizzing arrow. Secretly her heart had mercy on Rāmīn, but she gave no sign of it to outward view. She said, "Rām! Noble one! Vīs will not become 'tame'[7] like your name! A thousand blessings on your soul; may weal a thousandfold be your remedy! I hold you dearer than my own soul, but your pain is far from cure. See, you have no hope of that radiant Sun ever shining on you; you must not so much as imagine that artifice will serve you with that cypress of the garden. Never allow your heart to hope that you will be able to deploy force against Shahrū's child! Better for you not to attach your heart to her, for by so doing you will cause yourself to be overtaken by misery. Do not recklessly throw yourself into a formidable task—this escapade will not turn out well for you! Do not torture your heart in this distress: do not vainly lay a load of grief on your soul!

"You have no guide in this wilderness: you will die with parched lips in the waste. You will experience nothing from this longing but harm; come, leave it be, if you seek to save your life! You should not tread with your heart the road of destruction, for no traveler has ever escaped from it: sagacity, shame, wisdom, and counsel are the soul's helpers in such straits, so that you may know bad from good

7. Persian *rām*.

꽃 80

and right from wrong, and may ponder in your heart a task that lies within your prowess.

"If indeed you are a reasonable man, set your hand to a branch whence your heart may glean fruit; walk on the road which is at your feet, go to a place that may be your dwelling. You will never pick flowers from this garden; never see fruit from the palm of success. The tulip will not smile on your face from the garden: hailstones will rain from your eyes as you weep. This garden is out of the reach of all: none may aspire to pick a rose from this bed. You will not see shade from the cypress of this grove, nor smell a whiff of the scent of this jasmine. This Moon will not display affection for you even should you pour forth your life in a hundred ways; if you give up the ghost in the midst of this agony no one will care about you, no one's heart bleed for you; you will not be victorious as is your ambition.

"If you traverse the sky, if you stop up the ocean by your valor, cause the Oxus to flow over the desert, make tulips blossom from the face of rock, bring another world into being from *hyle*, balance its globe on the end of a hair, if even you are a wily sorcerer, you will still be left stupefied by the problem of Vīs. Only when the branch of the Judas tree[8] bears dates will Vīs bow to your love!

"It is proper for you to turn your heart aside from union with her; she is the Moon; you can never be united with her. See that you never set your heart upon her condescending to be your mate! Who would dare to speak of this to her? who presume thus to provoke her vexation? You do not know how self-willed she is, how ill-natured by temperament. Though I had the nerve of a hundred lions I should not dare to recite your message to her. At all events you surely would not wish an enemy's words to be hurled at me in improper fashion.

"You well know what Vīs is today—the fairest of the fair; the moment I say these words to her she will humiliate me shamefully; among princesses she is like a monarch among fortunate nobles; in her haughtiness her pride reaches the sky; she does not consort pleasantly with people; her lineage is all noble stock; her treasury royal gems; in stock she is loftier than kings; in gems she need beg

8. *G:* "fir tree."

of no man. She has no dread of formidable enterprise; she is not to be subverted by sumptuous treasure; one cannot seduce her by jewels; what is the difference, to her, between jewels and the dust of the portal? Nothing has any value in her eyes; she does not reck the world as worth a farthing. One cannot bring her into the snare by spells, for she is a sorceress with bewitching eye.

"Now her heart is a trifle low; she is mournful in solitude and exile; far from house and home, she spurns entertainment and company. Now she sheds water from her eyelashes, now blood; now laments at fortune, now at the heavenly sphere. When she remembers her mother and brother she simmers like fresh aloeswood on fire. She curses the unlucky month and year that caused her to be separated from her birthplace and native land.

"Thus is this princess of the line of Jamshīd, famed over the seven climes for her beauty, whom her mother craved of God with entreaty, brought up amid tenderness and obsequiousness; now lamenting, racked with pain and distress, cut off from her nearest and dearest, far from relatives and friends, exiled from old comrades; her nights and days nothing but crying and wretchedness; in her weeping like a spring cloud. Her pistachio mouth does not laugh in joy; she has ever a frown of pain on her brow. Who dares mention your name to her? who dares recite this empty message? Do not command me to carry out this vain task, 'Can a man walk on his head?'

"I shall never contrive to carry out this task; such an enterprise is unworthy of a reasonable being. Even were my tongue more prolific than drops of vapor, it would still be a shame to court disaster by saying these words."

When the desperate Rāmīn heard these words he made the dust into mud with his tears. Weeping broke the heart in his breast at his tribulation; the torture of weeping stopped up his speech; he was impotent both of tears and of speech. Mercy on him, wretched as he was! The fire of love mounted into his brain from his heart; saffron bloomed from his tulip-hued face.

When his tongue had been tied for a time, heart broken in breast, breath caught, he again spoke fair words about his grievous pain and impatient soul; no matter how sorely he lamented and proffered entreaties and pleas, the Nurse's thrawnness did not melt a whit.

She was as stonyhearted and cold as ever; still as before witch-hearted and murderous. When Rāmīn redoubled his lamentations nothing emerged from her but hopelessness.

In the end Rāmīn caught her in his embrace, raining tears of agony upon her from his eyes; he said, "Mercy, Nurse of immortal soul! Do not lay my soul waste at one blow! Do not cut off my hope of life and youth, do not render my life like poison. Of all my friends you are my stay and refuge, you my rescuer and deliverer. What matter if you act as a rescuer, deliver me from the clutch of ill fortune? open the closed door before me, show me a way to the face of Vīs? If now I glean only despair from you, I shall die a sudden death before you. Do not so! Forbear to cast an innocent man into the dungeon; sprinkle salt sparingly on the victim of burns! I have made myself your slave; accept your slave; take my hand but once and rescue me from this tribulation! You and you alone in the world are the remedy for my pain; come to my rescue in my helplessness. I know none other than you in the world to whom to tell the secret of my heart.

"Recite my message to that beauty of jasmine-scented bosom; do not make excuses to me any further; as long as I live, my Nurse, I shall not let my hand fall from the hem of your garment. Even if you cut me to pieces with the sword I shall not seek remedy from any besides you. Even if you drive me away a hundred times my hope in you will only increase. You know how to remedy my pain, how to feel for this wounded, helpless creature! How, after all, can you consider me worthy of this fate? for a mother's heart will bleed for her child.

"You must march forward in my cause; you must not so much as draw breath to deny me. My plight is gone beyond my powers; I am left with a heart bathed in blood from this torment. It is vain to frighten me with talk of visitation; I reck no more either of head or of life. My head and my life are my sacrifice before her feet; I shall not abandon her as long as both are in place. In love I do not fear yielding my life; a hundred lives of mine are fit to be sacrificed before that beauty of fairylike face.

"Do not after this seek pretexts about my plight, do not make my soul the target for the arrow of grief. Do not be so malevolent and timid in the enterprise, for the task will be easy for you. By contriving men adapt mills to the wind; uproot the bed of a river; bring down birds from the heaven, bring fish out of the sea; lure raging lions to the trap, tie up wild elephants in chains; tempt snakes out of their holes, make them tame and playful by spells; cut a passage out through adamantine rock; level Mount Qāf[9] to the plain. Now you know more spells than any; you can likewise contrive remedies; you have a store of more than a thousand spells; all your thoughts are ordered and collected; nothing emanates from you that is not worthy of approbation; there is none so clever as you. At the moment of speech you have great lore in words; at the moment of action you have much store of talent. Match words skillfully to action; and by their twofold use cast a spell on Vīs. Had my fortune not been kindly disposed it would not have led you to me here. Since luck has been fit to aid me today it has made me victorious by the sight of you. As you are my comrade in this enterprise, even so may God be your helper in every task!"

So saying, he clasped her close to his breast and kissed her head again and again; then he kissed her lips and face.[10] A demon came and entered into his body; he quickly gained his desire of the Nurse, it was as if he sowed the seeds of love in her heart; when one has once gained one's heart's desire of a woman, it is for all the world as if one has placed a bridle on her head.

When Rāmīn rose from the Nurse's embrace her heart was exercised on his behalf; there and then the veil of bashfulness was rent, her former cold words grew warm.

She said to him, "Winning speaker that you are! you have carried off the prize from all in oratory. Your heart seeks its desire from everyone; every woman you see is called Vīs! Till today you were dear to me; but I am become dearer to you from this day forth. Barriers are down between us; for the arrow of desire has found the target; henceforth command all you will; I shall not draw foot away from your command. I shall make your fortune victorious over Vīs and exact justice for your love from that captivating beauty."

When the brokenhearted Rāmīn heard these words he said to her, "Light of my eyes! see how henceforward I shall worship you, how

9. The great mountain range supposed to surround the earth.
10. Cf. *Tristan*, p. 231; *Tristan* (*B*), pp. 58, 59. *G* has a gap here.

make my heart attend on you in service; you see how I writhe like a snake, how formidable and chaotic my plight! I am like one sailing the sea who suffers the wind and wave of the ocean; at night I say, 'I shall not survive till morning'; when morning comes I have no heart to live till evening! See how one passes his time who never for a moment entertains hope of life! Thus am I in distress on account of Vīs; I do not know night from day or day from night. Now I have fixed my hopes on your action; perhaps you will take my hand in this disaster. Now that I have heard these kind words from you, you have given me the key to the lock of happiness. Press chivalry into service, for words without deeds are not meet. Tell me when you will show me your fortunate face, when come again to see me; for I shall count the days and hours, and ever live in expectation of seeing you. Until I descry that you are joyous I shall sleep and rest on fire. I am so breathless to see you that I do not enjoy peace of body for a single moment. Like one beside himself I cannot keep my mind on one thought; like a madman I cannot stop in one place."

The Nurse of sorcerer's faith said to him laughingly, "You are versatile in speech! With these dainty phrases and sweet wheedlings you would bring consciousness back to the brain of the senseless! You have wounded my heart with these words, now that you have bound this appeal on my soul; you have loosed the bond from your own soul and have brought it and tied it on mine! Be sure not to grieve in any way, for deliverance from this distress will come to you. You shall see how I shall gain your desire, how paint the face of your enterprise with propitiousness, how I shall mount you on a fleet steed, how set you galloping into your enemies' eyes. Once every day at this time pass by this glorious garden; for I shall bring you news of everything I undertake and perform." When they both set their hearts to this compact, they kissed each other's cheeks. They took hands on the treaty with these words and then departed.

41.

THE NURSE WINS VĪS OVER TO RĀMĪN BY STRATAGEM. When the Nurse went to charming Vīs she became evil-minded and base-natured like a witch. She wove beguiling words and embellished them with wiles and spells. When she saw the charming Vīs down-cast, her pillow wet with her tears, a string of pearls loosed upon her breast from grief for her mother and glorious brother, she said to her, "You who are to me as my precious life, you are not sick. Why then lay your head on the pillow? What demon is this that haunts your soul, closing the door of every happiness upon you? You have bent the straight cypress of your form in grief, you must think you are in some dungeon, not in Marv! Lighten the heavy load from your heart, for grievous hurt will befall the soul at its hand. Is it not more than enough to suffer hardship, to remember the past and endure pain? There is no torment worse than suffering grief; no remedy is better for it than contentment. If you will obey, you shall spend your time in happiness; choose contentment by your fortune's aid. Contentment is a staunch friend to your soul; sadness means warring with the soul."

When Vīs, the heart's repose, heard these words, it was as if she gained peace for a time in her heart; she raised her head from the pillow like a sun, and spread a chain of ambergris over roses. The earth became a Chinese pattern from the color of her face; the air became ambergris-scented at the perfume of her tress. The palace vault and the face of the delightful beauty matched each other, gorgeously patterned alike; like some gaudily colored garden in April, decked out like Paradise with Vīs its angel. You would have sworn her cheeks were blossoms, with rain on them from her eyes. Her cheeks, blue and scored, were like a water lily in its tank; in the water of her tears her sleepless eyes were more beautiful than a narcissus in water.

She said weeping to the Nurse, "What kind of fortune is this? You would rather say it was a fire consuming all repose. With every day that dawns from the heaven my distress is renewed in a different guise. Am I to count the fault as lying with Marv, or the stars, or this self-willed, cruel Sphere? It is as if seventy mountains like Alburz had suddenly been toppled and fallen on my head. This is not Marv, but a land that melts the very body; this is no city, but a dungeon sixty fathoms deep. The pleasure dome, the garden, the royal palace, are like Hell-fire to me. My body has become the playground of pain; you would swear my soul was a fire temple. My heart from the fire of grief is for all the world like a fish quivering on a pan; now I burn from grief for my mother; now I become senseless from sorrow for my brother; night is for me like my hair, dark and long; in the daytime the door of tribulation is opened upon me. I rest not by day nor sleep by night; day and night I experience nothing but fever and torment. I suffer affliction from the night and distress from the day; the load on my heart is made ever heavier by the two; I swear that if ever consciousness returns to me it will be sweet as life itself to my heart!

"I have now abandoned hope of the world; for I have seen Vīrū in a dream; sitting on a horse mighty as a mountain, spear in hand, sword on breast, returning happy from the hunt, having performed many exploits in the field. He joyfully cantered his horse up to me, and for a little while caressed me with pleasant words, saying, in a voice sweet as sugar, 'How is it with you, my life, darling of your brother? in a foreign land as you are, and in the hands of enemies, say how it is with you parted from me.' Then I saw him lying by me, clasping my silvery bosom to his breast. He planted many kisses on my lips, bright as a parrot's plume, and on my eyes like the doe's, and by so doing but opened my scar: I can still hear in my ears and heart the words he pronounced to me last night; the sweet scent of that delicate form has remained in my nostrils and brain. How can Fate visit me with a more evil lot than that I should see Vīrū in dreams? Now that the Sphere portends such fortune for me, of what avail is my dear life henceforth? As long as I live this is sufficient grief for me, that my soul is dead and my limbs alive. You, my Nurse, have seen that in abominable Marv there is not one of God's creatures like Vīrū."

She said these pathetic words, her bleeding eyes sprinkling pearls. The Nurse put her hand on her head and breast and said, "Light of your mother's eyes, may your nurse be your sacrifice to ward off every pain! May she never hear of your grief and witness evil befall you! I have heard all your words, beauty with fairylike face, they have fallen on my heart like iron and brass. Though your pain may be infinite, the pain it affords my heart is even greater. Do not suffer distress that it is not proper for you to bear; do not pass your sweet life in bitterness.

87

"Keep your heart in peace while you may, for our life is but a span of two days. The world is like a caravanserai for men; our stay in it is but for a space. Its joy is at one and the same time tainted with distress; it does not last long, like the shadow of a cloud. The world is called 'Jahān' since to the sage it is as a 'leaping' charger.[1] Why do you suffer distress on its account? The world will be here when you pass on! Even if Fate robs you of one desire, you have pretexts for a hundred more. You are young, full of success, and a princess; your writ runs over the world in sovereignty. Do not say farewell once and for all to the world; do not involve your soul in eternal bondage. In this world, the young who are men all quest after desire, prowess, and enjoyment, each one delighting his soul with some ploy, passing his days in entertainment; some pursue the hunt with cheetah and falcon; some pursue music with harp and lute; some have retainers and seraglios, slave boys and beauties with pomegranate breasts! Women of the seraglio, too, all take pleasure in some pursuit; but you only sit sorrowing for Vīrū. You have no desire to seek anyone but him in the world. Though Vīrū is a puissant being, he is no angel nurtured in heaven!

"You said to me, 'In abominable Marv there is not one of God's creatures like Vīrū.' I have seen many youths in Marv, champions of the world, conquerors of lands, in stature like the cypress of the stream, in face like a blossoming garden, compounded of excellence and bravery, chosen out of the whole world as a champion; any wise men who were to see them would choose them each and every one above Vīrū. Among them is a puissant hero whom you would call an entire world in point of accomplishment.[2] If they are the stars, he is the sun; if they are ambergris, he pure musk. In lineage a king and noble back to the time of Adam, in birth brother to Moubad: Rāmīn of fortunate name and glorious fortune, an angel on earth, a demon in the saddle; his fair face much resembles that of Vīrū; all hearts are pledged to his love. The valiant of the world praise him, for they do not prevail over him on the day of battle. None quests after prowess in Iran like him; he can split a hair with a javelin and

1. Persian *jehān*: "leaping." Rakhsh, here translated "charger," is the name of the horse of Rustam.
2. Cf. the description of Rāmīn in *G* (p. 9).

spearpoint. There is no archer like him in Tūrān; at his command death[3] flies feathered; he sheds more blood than other knights on the day of battle; he drinks more wine than his comrades on the day of feasting. In prowess he is like a furious lion; in generosity like a spring cloud; for all the heroism that he may have, he has the same brand on his heart as you. He is like you in love, you that are as a silver cupola: you would swear an apple had been cut in two halves; see how you yourself are, he is even so, like a myrtle branch coated with gold. He has seen you, fallen in love with you, and pinned on you hopes of affection; his eye like a blossoming narcissus is in full flood like spring clouds. His face, like the gleaming moon, is the color of straw from being forlorn. He has a heart that has borne much affliction and suffered much dread in loverhood. Hardly having seen the world, he fell headlong into love for you, surrendered heart and soul at the sight of you. I forgive you and him in your love, for 'it is meet to forgive a pretty face.' I see you without peer in love, two lovers with lost hearts, luckless in this plight."

When Vīs with face fair as the moon, beautiful to behold, heard this devious speech from the Nurse, she did not answer her for some time, her eyes dropping tears on her fair face. Bashful before the Nurse, she hung her head on her breast, her tongue tied from replying, her lip frozen from smiling.

Then she raised her head and said, "Shame is the best mate for the soul. How well said Khusrou[4] to the soldier, 'If you have no shame, go and do[5] what you will!' If you had had shame and wisdom behind you, you would not have set your tongue to these words. Shame on you for Vīrū's sake and mine, for having taken thought for Rāmīn in our despite! Had hair grown on my very nails I should never have thought this of you! If you are mother, I am your daughter; if you are senior, I am your junior. Do not teach me flippancy and shamelessness, for shamelessness brings down on women evil days! What desire, what dread is there in my heart to prompt me to deceit? What renders me helpless, what causes me pain, that I should set aside my finer feelings and shame? I should be tainted with eternal disgrace, and have to wash my hands of hope for heaven.

3. Reading of *I*, adopted by Professor Mīnovī.   4. Cf. n. 1, p. 29.
5. *G:* "say."

89

"Even if Rāmīn be lofty as a cypress, in heroism and prowess the ornament of Marv, then may the good God be his helper! And as for me, may I have pursuits other than love for Rāmīn! He is not worthy of me, even be he fair; he is no brother, even were he like Vīrū. He shall never deceive me by his looks, nor you by words. You should not have listened to his words, and having done so should not have brought them to me. Why did you not give the worst imaginable reply, such as his message deserved?

"How well did the Moubad[6] say to Hūshang:[7] 'Women have more desire than shame and propriety.' Women are created incomplete; thus they are self-obsessed and of ill repute. They lose this world and the next simply for one desire; when desire comes on them they do not seek a good name by virtue of reason. If you possess reason, ponder in your heart; see what shame desire brings about!

"Though women have many wiles, they swallow empty words and speeches from men. A man frustrated of his desire casts about for a thousand snares to catch his desire from them. Woman is the prey of man in every way; man takes her all too easily. He brings her into his toils by a thousand devices, by hope, fair words, and solemn oaths: he proffers a thousand kinds of entreaty, all sweet nothings and pretty flattery. Once he has thrown her in the net and wrought his desire, become free from fear, his longing assuaged, in love his entreaty becomes caprice; he becomes a byword for capriciousness; it is as if the spirited colt of love becomes broken in; even as burning fire turns to ashes. The wretched woman becomes low in his eyes; the man of many wiles becomes wary of her.

"Unlucky woman, fallen in the snare! Cursed with shame and her good name sacrificed! The wretched woman laid low, the man riding high, the bow of arrogance drawn against the woman! The faithless man does not bear her mercy nor feel compunction about her, so inhuman is he. He does not practice love, feels no regret; does not speak fair or reckon with her shame. The woman, in her hope, melts at the sting of hope like snow in the heat of the sun. In love she is like a wounded wild ass, heart and soul bound by seal and fetter; now

6. Here in the sense of "priest."
7. Of the legendary Pīshdādī dynasty.

90

she is afraid of her husband, now of her family; now wastes in fear and shame before God; on the one hand, shame and humiliation without end; on the other, Hell-fire before her!

"At the place where they ask about good and evil, they do not dread kings and potentates! How can I find it in my heart to do something which will cause shame before mortals and dread of the Creator? If I perform an action welcome to the demon in me, Almighty God will burn me. If people discover my secret, everyone will seek to be my lover. Some will desire my body and sacrifice their souls in the quest of their desire; others will seek to shame and humiliate me, and address me only odiously. When everyone has obtained his desire of me, no place will be fit for me but Hell.

"Why, then, should I open to my soul a gate from which will come eternal dread for me? May reason be my refuge in every action, reason that seeks the Right and cultivates justice. May my hope be ever in God, for none but he is worthy of hope!"

When the Nurse heard these words from that moonlike beauty, the hand of her desire fell short of Vīs. She answered her on yet another tack, "Favorable events stem from propitious fortune." She said, "Fate springs from the heavenly sphere, not from man's ambition; thus it is that man is called 'slave.' Do you fancy that one can wean lions of their lion's nature by championship and courage; or by mere force of loftiness invest partridges with the nature of a hawk? Everything comes written from the sphere of heaven; this writ is in the very clay of our souls. The eternal writ does not alter, does not turn away from us by any amount of travail and effort. Once Fortune entered the lists it took you away from Vīrū; separated you from your city and from the sight of Shahrū. Now again what Fate wills for you shall come to pass: Fate shall neither increase nor decrease at your desire."

Vīs of the moonlike form replied to her: "Fortune brings both good and evil but everyone who does evil suffers evil; many a man has done one evil deed and suffered a hundred.

"The first evil deed was Shahrū's when she gave Moubad's bride to Vīrū. She it was who committed an evil deed, we did not. See how much pain and distress we have suffered! My name is besmirched and so is that of Vīrū; I am robbed of my desire and Vīrū likewise. What I have experienced is sufficient as a caution to me; now I have cut myself off from evildoing and from evildoers. Why should I fancy evil as my course and fasten the pretext for it upon Fortune? I shall be laid low by an exemplary fate should I be a partner to a notorious deed."[8]

Again the Nurse said, "Silvery cypress, noble Rāmīn is not my son, that I should help my child to wrest him from the fetter of love. If the Creator aids him, he will in no way witness cruelty at the hand of the Sphere. Perhaps you have heard the saying of the sage, 'God is able to do all.' He has created the world under his command, has laid down every affair according to due measure. I have seen many a wonder in the world whose secret is not to be found.[9] Many a one of evil faith becomes of true faith; many a Korah[10] becomes humble and poor. Many a ruin becomes palace and hall, many an open space becomes plot and garden; many a noble becomes lowly and common; many a commoner becomes a king or a noble. If it is to be that you are to taste bitterness from love, you cannot draw your head out of the hoop! If Providence treats you kindly, it will be none other than the decree of Heaven.

"Of no avail are wisdom, chivalry, wit, abstemiousness, rage, brawn, riches, jewels, fame, greatness, counsel, talent, kingship, fasting, mettle, or saintliness, neither sight of Shahrū nor of your relatives and kin, neither good advice nor true counsel. Once love has come, one must manage willy-nilly; suffer at the hands of others what may or may not be one's desire. My words will be revealed to you soon, for you have as yet seen but smoke from this fire. When you experience love farther than this you will then praise my words; you will see clearly and I too whether I am moved by love for you or spite; whether pretext came from Fortune or not, whether Fate be gentle to you or otherwise."

42.

THE NURSE RETURNS TO RĀMĪN IN THE GARDEN.   When next day the shining sun like the face of charming Vīs rose in the east, the

8. This rendering (based on a reading of *I*) is suggested by Professor Mīnovī.
9. *I. Mb:* "surpassing which none is to be seen."
10. Qārūn, the Korah of the Bible.

Nurse returned to the tryst; she and Rāmīn sat in the shade. Rāmīn saw her and became[1] happy, like a thirsty plot that has become watered.

He said to her, "You who are worthy of preferment, will you not say how you are since yesterday? You are happy, for you have seen the face of Vīs, heard sweet speech from her sweet lips; happy the eye that sees the face of that Moon, happy the brain that receives her scent! Happy your eye and heart in the company of that face, happy the neighbors in that lane!" Then he said, "How is that beauty, before whom may Rāmīn's soul be lowly? Did you convey to her my sad message? Did you tell her of my plight?"

The Nurse replied, "Warrior hero, be patient in love and in delay; one cannot remove drunkenness from the drunken, loose the bond of cold from winter, wash the earth of rose water and rose, stop up wind and sea on it, draw the heart of Vīs into the net, wean her from love of her mother and of Vīrū, release her from that ancient bond, set another bond on her anew. I conveyed to her whatever message you gave me; she rose in wrath and abused my name; she gave no answer and was angry with me, and said such and such and such."[2]

When Rāmīn heard all the Nurse said, bright day became dark to his eyes. He said to her, "Men the world over are not one and all faithless and shameless; not everyone has a flawless body, not everyone has a heart of identical nature. One ought not to drive every ass with one stick, nor yet name everyone with the same name. Even though she has seen the ways of people of evil faith, I too should not be counted as one of them.[3] Why blame wildly a sin which I never even committed, never even conceived in my heart? Blame lies ill on innocence!

"Give my message to that one of silvery frame, that twines locks of many a twist; say, 'You Moon, you beauty, you with eyes like a Hūrī, face like an enchantress, fair as spring, quick to anger! Form acquaintance with love, do not conceive suspicion of faithlessness in me! I swear to you a hundred oaths, compact those oaths with you,

1. *I. Mb:* "saw her very happy."
2. In *G* (pp. 82–83) the Nurse delivers the substance of the message of Vīs.
3. Lacuna in *I* here.

that as long as I live I will keep the contract of love for you, will not withdraw my head from the treaty of your love. As long as my soul graces my body, love for you will remain in its place by my soul. I shall not forget the thought of you in my heart either on the day of peace or on the day of commotion'."

He said these words and dropped tears like wine from his eyes on those two bouquets of roses. You would have said his eyes were shedding pearls from the love hidden in his heart!

The Nurse's heart had mercy on that desperate one, for he was worthy of mercy, having lost his heart. She said to him, "You who are to me like my bright eyes, in love clothe yourself with the armor of patience. Humiliation has visited love as a result of crying; craziness has come upon you because of humiliation. If you desire my soul in Vīs's stead I shall give it to you, and not delay in the giving. I shall go and strive better with that idol, wear a jerkin of shamelessness. As long as my soul lives I shall not turn from her, for I have devoted my soul to your cause. I see no more upright heart than is ours; heart's desire is fulfilled when the heart is true."

Again she went to Vīs of the face as fair as the moon, with speech contrived in her heart in tenfoldwise. She saw her like a moon two weeks old caught in the toils of separation; her heart smoldering and her eyes weeping, like an oven from which a holocaust rises; bright day dark in her eyes, silk and brocade become under her like black snakes.

The Nurse gave tongue once more, for she had a store of pearls like the sea. She said, "May the one who has caused you to writhe vanish from the world and lose his life! May distress and pain lie heavy on his soul who has made your distress and pain heavy, separated you from house and home, kith and kin; from sweet mother and glorious brother, one the equal of the soul, the other of the heart. You have ever in this world been in distress, weak, restless; your soul does not find escape from pain and agony, your heart become cleansed from brand and pang [4] What is the point of the reason God gave you, since there is to be no cure for your pain? I burn when I see you

4. *G* adds: "But now in this strange land why dost thou continually act like one mad?"

94

aflame, I writhe when I see you twist. A reasonable being seeks remedy from reason, transacts every task by the means afforded thereby; God has given you reason and knowledge—but has not granted you peace by virtue of that knowledge! You are like an ass carrying a load of swords; it is of little avail to it when a lion comes near! How long, now, will you suffer this distress, scatter garnets thus on *dīnārs*? Do not so! Spare the days of your youth! Do not thus pile distress upon agony! Do not wail so bitterly on an alien soil, do not curse Fortune and the Sphere.

"Your angel is at your side year in, year out, month in, month out, always listening to your words.[5] Do not vex your angel and Fortune thus by words which are unworthy! You are the queen of Iran, the Moon of Tūrān;[6] peer of beauties, Sun of the Hūrīs. Do not cast your youth to the waves; do not melt your silvery frame with the heat of distress! This life of ours is short; the life of this world does not last long. The soul is priceless and precious. Why is it no more to you than half a farthing? People do not treat their dear ones so by keeping them wounded and distressed. Your soul is your devoted friend, bound to you in eternal comradeship; are you to do nothing month in, year out but treat a kind friend as naught? for Rāmīn, who has become devoted to you, is no more in your eyes than the dust of the road.

"Do not act so! Be kinder than this to your friends; be to the world as a fruitful tree; have mercy on that brokenhearted youth and forbear to wear both him and your own frame to naught. Do not be a stranger to that noble one; cherish love for him who has cherished love. So long as no one realizes joy and desire of you, what more is your face than a talisman on a roof?"

When Vīseh heard these words she grew angry and spoke many hard words to the Nurse in rage: she said to her, "You of ill will and many curses! May neither you nor Vīs nor Rāmīn remain alive!

5. In Zoroastrian belief the *daēnā*, a heavenly counterpart to every mortal, is promoted in heaven in proportion to the good deeds a person performs on earth. After death the soul of the mortal is united to its *daēnā*, who, in the case of a man, appears as a beautiful maiden if his deeds have been good, but a hideous hag if otherwise. See Avesta, Hādokht Nask, II, 7; R. C. Zaehner, *The Teachings of the Magi* (London, 1956), p. 134.

6. *G:* "queen of Eraq and Khurasan."

May Khūzān,[7] your cursed homeland, perish, and with it your words and evil eye! May none but Jonahs emerge from your city, may none but wizards be born of your womb. If there be born of it thousands upon thousands may they all be demons and monsters,[8] whose deeds may be insufferable, whose words unfit to hear! May there be not one among the wise who gives his child an evil nurse like this! When he draws impure milk from the nurse, of tainted lineage and unclean nature, she will make his pure escutcheon of spotless tincture baser than the mettle she herself boasts. If the very child of the sun were to drink her milk there would be slender hope of its giving light! Shame before God upon my mother, who debased my pure mettle! gave me into the arms of a witch like you, innocent of shame, wisdom, and justice! You are a curse to me, not a nurse! You would rob me of reputation and worth! Teach me wisdom, nobility, and right! Protect me from evil night and day!

"You praised yourself so much for high repute but were after all of ill fame. With your violent nature and shameless eye, your merciless words and deeds, you have ground your good name into the earth, you have wrested all love for you from men's hearts. No one grants you quarter and mercy but those who are like you frivolous and without shame. What more is your speech to me than a death knell? I fall to the ground at it like the leaf in autumn.

"You say to me, 'In this short life why do you not enjoy pleasure and heart's desire?' If I do good as long as I live it is better than indulging my own desires. One cannot gain glorious Paradise and the sight of God through the desire of this world. To the wise, the world is but a game; no game lasts for long. So, Nurse, do not distress your soul; do not break faith with your soul on my account. For I shall not heed your silly words, shall never fall into your trap. I am no child to be taken in by any gaudy color—nor yet a bird to be flushed by a single stone! The words you have heard from the senseless Rāmīn are like a spell in my ears, not a message. Take care not to recite them to me, nor seek of me satisfaction for the demons. I have mortified my soul to this world—and made Reason the captain of my soul. The God of wisdom and faith is in any wise better than

7. Minorsky, *Iranica*, p. 169. *G* has "Khuzistan."
8. Cf. the curse in Avesta, Yasna XI, 6.

demons of Khūzān and Rāmīn; I shall not offend the God of Heaven, nor gamble away eternal Paradise for a shameless heathen Nurse who has sacrificed this world and the next for Rāmīn!"

When the Nurse saw the anger of the charming Vīs, heard her words about the God of Heaven, she reflected in her heart for a time, how to find a cure for this pain. Her evil-natured demon did not rest, her self-centered nature was the same as ever, till the fates of Vīs and Rāmīn should intermingle like oil and sweet juice. When she had collected countless spells, of every hue, origin, and class, she once more loosed her tongue and spoke words like the decoration of Noushād;[9] she said to her, "You who are dearer than my very life, beyond my ken in beauty and goodness, be ever truthful and upright, ever of fair name and happy fortune; what desire and dread do I have that should lead me to deceive one of pure birth like you? Why should I speak deceitfully to you? I have no desire to obtain men's property! Rāmīn is no relative or connection of mine; not of my kin or birth or progeny.

"Will you not tell me what good he has done me that I should become his friend and your enemy? All I ask of both worlds is your desire and thereby your good name. I shall tell you this secret openly, for now I have no recourse other than this: you are born of man, surely, you are no demon or sprite or daughter of a Hūrī; you have broken with a pure spouse like Vīrū and have bound Moubad in his turn with a spell; no man has enjoyed you, for till this very day you have given your body to none. Neither have you had joy of anybody nor experienced the fullness of joy with men. Twice husbanded, you have bid farewell to both; what more are they to you than a bridge on the far side of a river? If you are to have a man at all in the world you will never find a noble champion like Rāmīn. What does it profit you to be as the sun in face if you are to enjoy no desire by virtue of this beauty of yours? You have not tasted this pleasure; you do not know that life without him is not sweet.

9. Dāūd ibn ul-'Abbās, descendant of the local Persian rulers of the Vakhsh Valley in the upper Oxus, built in the third century A.H. a palace and estate outside Balkh, called Noushād. They were destroyed by Ya'qūb ibn Laith the Saffārid in 870–71. The poets of Khurāsān referred to the place as an earthly paradise. (Note by courtesy of Professor Mīnovī.)

"God has created woman for man—and you, too, are a woman born of man. Royal and noble ladies, the great ones of the world who dictate their pleasure, all have husbands and are of happy heart, youthful like cypress and myrtle and boxtree. Although they have famed husbands, they have a lover besides in secret; now they have their fine husbands in their embrace, to their heart's desire, now a charming lover. Even should you have the riches of all kings on earth, you will not gain your desire so long as you are without husband and lover. What are royal trinkets, brocade, gloriously tinted fair jewels? These things a woman needs only for the man, for they increase the joy of a man's heart. Since no man rejoices in you nor you in any man, why are you always in red and yellow? If you know that I have spoken these words truly, abuse and curses from you are not my deserts: I have spoken this in affection, from a motherly and nursely love, for I see Rāmīn fit for you; you his sweetheart, he your lover. You are the sun, he a moon two weeks old; he is a cypress, you a blossoming bough. You will sort together in love like milk and wine; sort together and have joy of each other! When I see the two of you together I shall have no more care in the world."

When the Nurse spoke thus to Vīs the Devil came to her aid with his host. She set thousands of traps in the path of Vīs, opened thousands of doors before her heart. She said to her, "These noble women, sitting in happiness with sweetheart and lover, have each and every one the means of joy; your lot is constant pain and lamentation and sighing. Your days of youth have come to old age; you have never for so much as an instant experienced happiness. Surely you are not made of stone or brass; how can you bear to be so long in distress?"

At these thoughts the love of Vīs waxed warmer; her stony heart softened a fraction; all her body fell into the trap save her tongue, which kept her secret hidden.

With words sweet as sugar she said to the Nurse, "No woman can avoid a mate; all the words you have spoken are true; you have not been mean to me in affection. Women, even though they be frail and weak, and be the apple of the eye of the heroes of the world, have thousands of bad points in their nature. Better not to attach oneself to them: my very words stem from the fact that vehemence is of the very nature of women. That speech was to my ears as a poisoned arrowhead sunk into the heart. I showed a trifle of vehemence since I listened to words smacking of vehemence. I turned my tongue to abuse but now I repent wholeheartedly. I should not have spoken hard words to you, nor you hidden your secret from me. When I am not disposed to have anything to do with a person, my distress is sufficient reply for him.

"Now I crave from the generous Creator that he may deliver me from evil; that he may not stain me with the vice of women, may preserve my soul from their stain. May he keep my body glorious whilst I live, as my friends desire and in despite of my enemies. May he keep me far from evil counselors like you, for your pupils are ill-fated."

When next day the world became like a flower garden, the radiance of the sun like a rosebud, noble Rāmīn went to the trysting place; then the Nurse came distressed and sorrowful; she said to him, "Rāmīn, how long will you talk and seek bright water in the midst of the fire? One cannot embrace the wind, nor grasp the ocean in the hollow of the hand, nor yet inspire love in stonyhearted Vīs, nor lay the head with her on one pillow; the water of love will exude from adamantine rock before it will from her; a mountain of hard rock is her superior in love! When you shout in a mountain gully it echoes your voice; the heart of Vīs is much harder than a crag; she is like the scorpion in ill nature. That lofty cypress gave you no reply; rather abused me in hundredfoldwise. I was left amazed at the abuse of that beauty; my spells find no path into her. Deceit, trickery, spells, and charms are to her like wisdom to the drunken. She will never accept my entreaty, as iron will never be melted by water."

When noble Rāmīn heard these words, he became like a wounded partridge in the talons of a hawk. The world grew straitened and dark to his eyes, hope far away and fear of Death at hand; his body become the abode of the cloud of disaster, moisture upon his eye and lightning in his heart. Twin arrows were lodged in his soul and heart, from anger and from the words of his love.

He cried out in his distress once more, some hundred times he said,

"Nurse, have mercy on me! Come to my rescue yet once more; I have no other friend like you. I shall never let my hand drop from the hem of your garment; I hang upon your neck for dear life. If I have to despair of my hope in you, I shall roll up the carpet of life. I shall go and tear the veil from my secret, desert my life and the world. If you will deign to persevere once more, tell that one of the jasmine-scented breast of my plight. I shall be eternally grateful to you that Ahriman shall not have found his way into me. Perhaps her heart of stone will burn for me, perhaps she will light the lamp of love. She may repent of her evil-naturedness, forbear to shed my blood and take my life. Give her loverlike greetings, say, 'Desire of the old and the young, you hold my heart, and rightly so: for you are a jouster adept at the art of keeping hearts in thrall. You shed my blood: and it is meet that you should, for you are the resurrection of lovers' souls. You are queen over my soul and heart, and deserve such sovereignty; if you spare my life, I shall spend it adoring you. You know I am capable of adoring you, and am not the one to abduct people; though you may have many lovers, none shall adore you like me. If you consort with me you shall find how great are my constancy and love. You are the sun; if you shine on me you shall find me a very ruby in love for you. If I am worthy of love and affection, relieve me of the burden of gloom and wretchedness! Spare my life, so that I may devote it to the pursuit of your love! Then, if you desire to take it, you may do so any day you choose.[10] And if I fail to wrestle with your nature, I shall become indifferent to my life. I shall throw myself from a high mountain, leap into the waves of the deep sea. My life shall be upon your head and in the next world I shall require it of you before the Judge who purposes justice, who shall mete out all justice to the world. For my part, I have said what I have to say; the rest is for you; may God be sufficient witness for us both!'"

With all his lamentation and agonized tears Rāmīn distressed the heart of the Nurse. She left him with wounded heart, the pain within her greater than his. When she came to Vīs she sat silent, her heart troubled with care and anxiety. Once more she strung together fair words like pearls for Rāmīn's sake.

10. *I* resumes here.

She said, "Sovereign of the fair, Moon among Hūrīs, near and far alike die before you;[11] I wish to say one more thing to you:[12] shame before you has stifled my voice. I fear King Moubad—with good cause, for all fear evil men: I shrink from shame and retribution, lest my fortunes grow dark by their means. I fear Hell, too, at the latter end, lest in Hell I become damned and disgraced. But when I think of Rāmīn, of his sallow cheek and heartfelt tears, and his cry, 'Nurse, have mercy! Life and the very world have shrunk to naught in my eyes!' he closes the eye of Reason in my heart, and my heart melts for him again. I feel such compunction for the poor youth that at his lamentation I set my life at nought.

"I have seen many lovers in this world, eyelashes moist with tears of blood, heart tortured with pain, but never have I seen anyone as helpless as this; one jot of his distress would be enough for a hundred lovers. You might think his words were swords, his eyes mist: my composure is cut through by that sword: the dwelling of my patience is ruined by that mist: I fear lest he may suddenly die and God visit his death upon me. Do not so, Moon of beauty! Have mercy on that wretched youth, do not stain your soul with his blood; what increase will you gain if you shed his blood? who will be worthy of you should you desert him? Not now, not for a hundred years to come will there be a youth with that might and stature! Young and swift, generous, eloquent: signs of the Divine Glory evident upon him. When God gave you this fair face, I swear that it was for none other than he. He fashioned you like a Hūrī, with face like brocade, then guarded you in sun and shade in order to bestow your love upon Rāmīn; he would then be our Khusrou and you Shīrīn.[13] I swear that it shall not be otherwise—that you shall have no lord but Rāmīn."

As the Nurse swore oaths one after another she gradually convinced Vīs, forgiveness for Rām increased in her heart; she began, loverlike, to beguile him; her contentiousness waned and her love waxed; a puff of smoke rose from the fire. Loyalty arose in her heart

11. *G:* "for thy sake die alike . . ."
12. Cf. the thoughts and advice of Brangane, *Tristan*, pp. 200–1.
13. Khusrou Parvīz, the Sassanian king who came to the throne near the end of the sixth century A.D., is celebrated in Persian tradition along with his queen, Shīrīn. Christensen, *L'Iran sous les Sassanides*, Chapter IX.

like the morning,[14] then the day of her love dawned. She kept turning her head to seek excuse: now looked at the ground, now up at the sky. She did not rush to answer haughtily, for silence was her guide. Her face from very shame burned in two colors: it became now wine-red, now yellow. Her body in shame was like a spring of water, beads of sweat dripping from it like lustrous pearls.

Thus is the wont of the souls of lovers who forgive their dear loves! A heart full of love draws the heart out of the body, as the magnet stone iron. Love is not to be practiced one-sidedly, like an ass whose load will not balance on one flank. The old witch of a nurse knew that this time the arrow had sped straight from her bow; the fleeing wild ass had fallen into her trap, the wind had bowed its head to the fetter through her spell.

43.

VĪS SEES RĀMĪN AND FALLS IN LOVE WITH HIM. On the day of Rām[1] the King of the land sat at court with the champions of the army. His palace became full of stars and moons from the number of beauties and generals of the court. The nature of everyone enjoyed its desire as the monarch did, everyone's hand sprouted a wine bowl like a narcissus. Joy rained from the bowl of wine, even as chivalry and generosity blossomed from drunkenness. The generals and commanders of the army were each and every one like moon and stars.

Rāmīn was the sun in their midst, his eyes narcissuslike and his cheek like wild rose. His locks like grapes, his cheek like grape juice, musk and camphor fit to be the slave of both. In stature he was like a cypress of the stream towering above the cypress of the blossoming garden. His heart in straits, his mouth tiny, his waist slim; in his distress of heart the world had grown straitened in his eyes.

He sat at the feast amid wine and song, like a drowning man fallen in a river. He enjoyed a double drunkenness—from love and from wine; he suffered a double weakness—from drunkenness and from separation. His face from drunkenness was like molten gold; his heart from weakness like a sleeping dreamer. The face of the beloved

14. Cf. Isolde's feelings, *Tristan*, p. 196.

1. The twenty-first day of the Zoroastrian month. A. V. Williams Jackson, *Zoroastrian Studies* (New York, 1928), p. 126. Rām was a genius of pastures.

hung before his eyes like wine, the scent of the beloved was like sweet basil in his brain.

Vīs sat above the garden; the very garden became glorious by her face. The Nurse had brought her secretly, with many a deceit, wile, and trick; she had sat her on the roof of the gazebo, with her eye to a chink in the window. She kept saying, "Look, apple of your mother's eyes, when have you seen one fairer than Rāmīn?[2] See if your lover and spouse Vīrū, son of Shahrū, is like him in beauty! This is no face, it is a masterpiece divine; the King's palace is like fresh spring by virtue of it. It is right that you should enter the lists of love with such a face, that you should be in harmony with such a charming lover."

When Vīs set eyes on Rāmīn, it was as if she beheld her own dear soul.[3] When she looked closely at Rāmīn's face, she laid waste her loyalty and love toward Vīrū. Then thoughtfully she said in her heart, "How, indeed, if Rāmīn became my mate? What, say, shall I suffer at the hands of this heart-ravisher who has thus dissipated the stock of Vīrū? Now that I am separated from mother and glorious brother, why should I burn in fire? Why should I sit so long in loneliness? How long am I to suffer tribulation? I am not made of iron! I shall find no heart's treasure better than this; I shall not turn my head from his covenant and command."

Thus she thought to herself and regretted the days gone by. But she did not reveal her love to the Nurse, although she was crazed with love. She said to her, "Rāmīn is as you have said, and of most glorious soul. He is master of great and good arts, and is much like Vīrū of auspicious fortune; but he shall fail to obtain his desire; even were my face the moon, it would not shine on him! I do not wish myself to be thus afflicted with sickness, nor would I wish this distress upon him. I do not deserve shame and deprecation, he distress and wretchedness. For my part, may God grant him weal, with my name and his love for me lost from his memory!"

When Vīs came down from the gazebo the bright sun became dark from her eyes; the foul fiend of love came to grapple with her and clutched her heart in his poisoned claws: snatched her away,

2. I. Mb: "could any be fairer than he?"
3. See n. 5, p. 95, on the daēnā, and §104, p. 351.

103

bore her off, and scoured away with his claws strength from her body, patience from her heart, color from her cheek. Vīs, brokenhearted, was like a coward, peace riven from her soul, blood stopped from her heart; now fancy ruled her, desire blinded the eye of reason;[4] now she would say, "What may befall me other than that the desire of my enemy should prevail over me? It is not as if no one has ever practiced love; or as if a heart's desire has never been worth trouble; if one be someone as noble as Rāmīn, why should one shrink so much from an ill-wisher?"

Now her shame would drive her desire far away, Reason command her thought. She feared eternal shame, dreaded too the requital for this world's deeds. As she dreaded God and Hell, Reason preferred chastity to love. She repented of love and romance, she chose in their stead freedom and fear of God. She set her heart on becoming in no wise involved in a notorious deed; on preferring Reason to Rāmīn, on not laying her head on an improper pillow. When she made righteousness the captain of her heart, fear of God made her soul saintly.

The Nurse was unaware of what Vīs was about and that through righteousness she had lent succor to her soul. She went to Rāmīn and gave him this good news: "The bough of fortune has risen skywards: the timid Vīs has become a trifle more tame, reformed of her former impetuousness and awkwardness. I know that she will come to your side, the tree of your woe will bear happy fruit."

Brokenhearted Rāmīn became as happy as a dead man recovering his dear life. He kissed the ground in front of the Nurse and said to her, "You who are rich in wisdom, gratitude to you is greater on my head than a crown, for you have freed me from fear of death. May God reward you in Heaven for this trouble and these fair words! I know no reward worthy of you, even were I to pour forth my life before you! You are as my mother, I as a son before you; I shall always own you my lady. I shall not turn my head from your command or grudge you my body or soul. I shall seek to meet any wish you cherish, through my deeds, treasure, and reputation."

Saying much in this strain, he laid before her three purses of coin, further a royal jewel-box of pure gold, in it six clasps of radiant

4. Cf. *Tristan*, p. 196, where Isolde is similarly affected.

pearls; many rings of gold and jewels, much musk and camphor and ambergris. The Nurse did not accept what Rām offered her, but said to him, "You who are the most glorious desire I could cherish, it is not for baubles that I adore you, for I have many valuables; in my eyes you are the bright sun, I would have the sight of you, not a reward." But she picked out a golden ring as a keepsake from Prince Rāmīn.

44.

THE NURSE GOES ONCE MORE TO VĪS WITH NEWS. When she came to Vīs she found her downcast and saw the waters as of a river on her lap from weeping. Again Vīs grew angry with the Nurse and spoke to her of shame before God and fear of Him.

"Since I fear God, neither Rāmīn nor worldly shame befit me. Why should I act disgracefully, ponder disgrace? My fortune will be disastrous through disgrace. On the one hand, when my family know of this, what will they then say to me, what call me? On the other hand, when I appear before my God, what excuse shall I proffer, what pardon crave? What shall I say about having lowered my head and my reputation to a hundred disgraces for a single desire? Fine and loving as Rāmīn may be, eternal Paradise is better than he. If Rāmīn be brokenhearted for me, what is that so long as the Creator be pleased? Should I descend to Hell for his sake, what will love of Rāmīn profit me? I have never indulged in corrupt practice, nor ever shall, even should blackness overtake my day like night."

When the Nurse heard these words from that beauty she assumed the nature of a fox in devising cunning ploys. She said to her, "Desire of your nurse's soul, you have no resources save fury! Why do you never hold to one saying, but switch around like a mill wheel? The mill turns, and you turn likewise; you are like the dice on a backgammon board. Like turquoise you constantly turn color; like iron you ceaselessly display rust. How shall you run from the command of God, how contest with the revolving sphere? If you remain thus ill-natured, it will be impossible to live in your company. Keep the land of Marv and Moubad with it, leave me the land of Māh and Shahrū! I have no one in Marv other than you; you well know that even the Devil cannot stand your ways! You treat me as nought, like those of ill will; you bring me to book several times a day. I shall go and dwell happily with your mother and forbear to behold you and all your tantrums. As for you, I wish you joy of God and whomsoever else you please; I have had my fill of Marv and of your ways!"

Vīs answered her, "Why have you conceived such love for Rāmīn in your heart? You constantly befriend a stranger and desert me for him. How can you find it in your heart to cut yourself off from me and go and find ease with another? How can I stay here without you, for you are as a mother to me? How disastrous are my fortune and my fate! How ill-starred and intractable my lot! I am separated from home and mother, and from my noble family and my brother. You were all that was left to me in the world, saving me from the brand of loneliness. Now you too have deserted me and gone over to the camp of the oath breakers. Thus have you said farewell to me once and for all, and cast your name and honor to the waves. Many a day will you suffer the pangs of regret, nor find any remedy for your pain."

Again the Nurse said, "Moon and Hūrī, do not stray! You are far from the road. Destiny has laid its hand on your fate and made an end; of what avail now are these pointless words? Lay aside pretty speeches and tell me when you will see the face of Rāmīn. When will you receive him in refuge, how rescue him in his plight? These numberless speeches have dragged on all too long; protraction is utterly meaningless and unfruitful. Temper your speech with chivalry, wake youth from its sweet slumber. Bring to life the spring of joy, make the sapling of chivalry blossom! Take your share of royalty and youth, spend your days in triumph and happiness. You are not of divine or angelic clay but compounded of mortal clay such as we are: always desire-ridden and obsessed with ambitions: many a bond of desire and ambition lies upon you. Our God so compounded our clay that the desire of woman is no higher than that of man. You have not experienced joy of men and thus do not know what delight they afford. Should you but once commingle with a man, I swear that you will not have the patience to abstain from this deed!"

Vīs of the moonlike form replied, "Eternal Paradise is finer than man. If you advise and deceive me less, I shall abstain from joy and from men. The pain you inflict lies heavy on my heart; but as it is, my heart is innocent of desire. Even did I not fear the harm you might do me, how much suffering would Rāmīn undergo! Not even were he to become a falcon would he attain to me, not even were he to be made wind would he blow on me. Now strive as you may that this secret may remain hidden from the world. You well know how powerful is Moubad, how formidable when he is seized by rage. Even when he suffers no offense he is like a slashing sword; even when he undergoes no injustice he is like a roaring lion. Should the day ever come when he suspects me, he will do a damage to my life. So long as this secret remains hidden the eye of disaster will be closed in my direction."

45.

VĪS AND RĀMĪN COME TOGETHER. When a tree is to be of straight trunk, so much is clear from the beginning as soon as it sprouts. Similarly when there is to be a delightful year, its fineness becomes evident right from Nourūz. Thus it was with the story of Vīs and Rāmīn: it was fated to come to splendor from its beginning. Though they suffered much distress of heart, they experienced great pleasure in the midst of pain. When Vīs became kindly disposed and had mercy on Rāmīn, Fate scoured the rust of spite from her heart; that week they came together in such wise that they were troubled by no one.

The King made ready for a journey from Khurāsān, pitched his pavilion on the road to Gurgān. From there he traveled toward Kūhistān; when he arrived there he traversed Reyy and Sārī. Rāmīn remained at his ease in Khurāsān, protesting himself ailing. His brother gave over to him his throne and state, and ordered him to mete out justice to the people. Thus the King was gone from splendid Marv, Vīs and Rāmīn left there.

The first day that beauty of fairylike face sat, all charm, color, and scent, in the midst of a pleasure dome whose top touched Gemini; decorated with gold designs and jewels: its foundation firm as the love of Rāmīn, its decoration gorgeous as the face of Vīs. Three doors opened off it to the garden, three more to the hall and seraglio. Vīs sat like the sun on the throne, with no care in her heart about beauty or fortune. Amid the jewels and ornaments that decked her from head to foot, she made idols seem ugly even to their sculptor. A thousand roses blooming in her cheeks, thirty stars hidden in her mouth. A heavenly scent wafted from Vīs of the face of an idol like a delightful perfume from a glorious garden. The garden breeze and the perfume of Vīs were together salve for the wounded soul. The rose bloomed in beauty like the cheek of Vīs, musk gave forth perfume as if in reply to her. The smoke of musk and ambergris hung like a cloud; who ever saw a cloud coming up from a censer?

The palace's show of blooms consisted of the faces of beauties; its raindrops of rose water. You would have sworn palace and hall were Paradise; its Hūrī Vīs, and its Rizvān the Nurse. Now she decked the captivating Vīs, now the hall and glorious garden.

When she had cleared the dome of strangers, she admitted Rāmīn by the roof. When Rāmīn entered the King's pleasure dome he saw no dome, rather Heaven with its Moon. Though he saw the face of the charming Vīs, his heart could not credit the sight. His sick heart became so full of happiness that it was as if he were an old man who had found his youth. His ailing body was transformed by joy; it was like a corpse restored to life. His soul like a parched field, despairing of water and rain, drank up the water of life from the perfume of Vīs and became ennobled forever. When he sat by that Moon illumining the world the smoke that would singe even fire settled in his soul.

He said to her, "Paradise of bliss, in your glance you are eternal sorcery. Heaven of desire and joy, God has wrought a masterpiece in you. You are the princess of all princesses in lineage, the enchantress of enchantresses with your bewitching looks. You are a rose the color of camphor, scented like musk; an idol of stature like the boxtree, face like the tulip. In beauty you are even now like the sun; happy the man upon whom you shine! Only cypress and boxtree can match your figure, and then only if they match the decoration of Noushād.[1] In loveliness you are the gleaming moon that makes dark and dolefulness fade. Fortune has granted you such beauty that you scour the rust from the souls of the unfortunate. If I may be among your attendants I shall be prince of puissant lords. If I be worthy to attend you I shall rub shoulders with none less than Jupiter."

1. See n. 9, p. 97.

When Vīs of fairy birth heard these words, she answered him primly, teasingly, and haughtily: she said to him, "Chivalrous, fortunate youth! I have seen much grievous woe in the world; but never have even I seen such as this, whereby my eyes are inured to disgrace; I have soiled my pure body, negated faith and shame; this ill portion has been served me by two people—one Fortune, the other the Nurse. She it is who has cast me into this humiliation, by sorcery and spells and oaths: she has brought into play all her repertoire of entreaty and sympathy. Tell me what you would do with me, whether it be a friend's or an enemy's will. In love you are like the rose, of one day's permanence; or like cornelian and turquoise. Month and year come round in turn, and you turn likewise. You shall regret what you have done. If your bond is to be like this, why indulge in all this lamentation? for the sake of satiating the desire of a day, why suffer eternal shame? A single jot of shame is not worth the desire of a hundred years, for corrosion will eternally remain upon your soul therefrom. When a desire lasts, then, but for a day, it is meet for the soul to abstain from it."

Rāmīn gave tongue once more[2] and said to her, "Gliding silvery cypress! I know no land like the land of Māh, wherein there has grown a cypress such as you crowned with a moon. I know no mother like pure Shahrū, whose daughter is Vīs, whose son Vīrū. A thousand blessings on your land and on your noble lineage! A thousand blessings on your mother from whom was born your heavenly form! Happy she who is your mother so fine, happy he who is your brother! Happy again the one that has been with you for a day, seen you and heard your name! Happy again the one who has nursed you or been your friend! This fame alone suffices Marv the royal abode,[3] that it is the abode of a captivating beauty like you. This pride and crown alone suffices the King, that he has a Moon like you in his seraglio. This splendor will suffice me to eternity, that I have become ennobled by union with the Sun. With this ear which hears your voice, these eyes that have seen your face, I shall henceforth hear nothing but good repute, see nothing but heart's desire and success."

2. *G:* "Anew Rāmīn began a eulogy."
3. Minorsky, *Iranica*, p. 170.

Then Vīs and Rāmīn made a solemn treaty together to their loyalty.[4] First noble Rāmīn swore oath, by God who is Lord of the world; by the bright moon and shining sun; by propitious Jupiter and pure Venus; by bread and salt and the religion of God; by bright Fire and the Spirit skilled in speech: "So long as the wind blows on the mountain range, or water flows along the riverbeds, so long as the dark of night does not last, or fish fail to rot in the stream, so long as the stars wheel in the sky, and the body has love in its soul, Rāmīn will not repent of his faith, nor break his oath and treaty, nor will he love other than the face of Vīseh, nor take any other as lover, nor delight in them." When Rāmīn swore loyalty and made binding contracts by love and affection, Vīs swore an oath to him that she would never break treaty with her lover. She gave Rāmīn a nosegay of violets[5] and said, "Keep this always in memory of me. Whenever you see violets freshly blooming, remember this treaty and oath. May any who causes his treaty with me to break be thus blue and crookbacked! For when I see the rose in the garden I shall remember this oath and covenant.[6] May the life of any who breaks this bond between us be of but a day like the rose!"[7] When they both swore oaths thus, they made a treaty by love and affection, called to witness the God of the World and the stars of the sky; then they lay down side by side, and talked together of their adventures in days gone by.

In joy Vīs had her king in her embrace; Rāmīn a moon two weeks old in his arms. Rāmīn's arm encircled Vīs like a golden band around a silvery cypress. Had the eye of Rizvān beheld them he would not have been able to say which was the fairer. Their bed was all set with pearls and jewels; their pillow full of musk and sugar; the sugar became the confidant of their words; the jewels shared in their happiness. They pressed lip on lip, face upon face; the ball of joy was thrown onto the field; from clasping the lover close to the breast their two bodies became on the bed like one. Had the rain fallen on those two jasmine-breasted lovers, their breasts would not have

4. Cf. *Tristan*, p. 282, where Tristan and Isolde swear to love each other and Isolde gives Tristan a ring. Cf. the violets given by Vīs, below.

5. See p. 268.

6. *G* adds: "I will take a rose as a token."

7. Dramatic irony, as the person who is guilty of the offense is Gul ("Rose"), the couterpart of Isolde of the White Hands.

become moist. Rāmīn's heart was all wounded with pain; Vīs pressed her heart to it like a salve. If he had suffered copious loss from his eyes he now claimed compensation for it in sugar. For every arrow Vīs had shot at his heart Rāmīn pressed thousands of kisses on her rosy cheek. As he pranced in the lists of happiness he put the key of desire in the lock of happiness: his delight in the lover grew the more when he saw the seal of God was as yet intact upon her. He pierced that soft pearl of great price; seduced a saint from her virginity. When he drew the arrow from the wound, target and arrow alike were covered in blood. Vīs of the rosy limbs was wounded by the arrow, her heart's desire was realized in that wounding. When both had slaked their desire their love grew apace; they remained on this wise for two months, enjoying only happiness and their hearts' desire.[8]

46.

VĪS AND RĀMĪN GO TO KŪHISTĀN TO JOIN MOUBAD. When news reached the King that the sick Rāmīn had raised his head from the pillow, he straightway sent a letter to him, saying, "We are sore at heart and unhappy without you; be it wine drinking or polo or the hunt, all is doleful in our eyes without you. Come so that we may for a time hunt game, take our ease, and wash the rust from our hearts; for the land of Māh is green with spring verdure: Venus and the Moon shine from its soil. Mount Arvand[1] has drawn on a sheen of Byzantine linen; it has thrown off the ermine cap from the crown of its head; its mountain sheep now lies among the tulips; its mountain goat has hidden its body among the flowers; so much floodwater of spring lies on the plain that the cheetah cannot catch the deer without a raft. When you read this letter, make haste; enjoy spring to your heart's desire. Bring Vīs with you, too, for her mother desires of me that she see her."

When Moubad's letter reached Rāmīn, the brazen trumpet sounded through his hall. He set out with his sweetheart, his journey sweetened by the face of his lover. When he arrived rejoicing in the land of Māh, the King and the royal army came to receive him. Vīs

8. Cf. *Tristan*, p. 201.

1. Southwest of Hamedān. Le Strange, *Lands of the Eastern Caliphate*, p. 195.

went straight from the road to her mother, shamed before her brother's face. She rejoiced at seeing each and every one, but then her joy turned all to distress: for she was cut off from the face of Rāmīn, sight of him was veiled from her. She now and then looked at his face secretly, saw him by the King or on the road. She was not satisfied with this much sight of him and, seeking more, suffered distress thereby. Desire had so seduced her that she could not abstain even for a moment from Rāmīn. Love of Rāmīn was dearer to her than her very life; how dear to the heart is the first love!

47.

MOUBAD DISCOVERS THE SECRET OF VĪS AND RĀMĪN. When Rāmīn had been a month with the monarch, hunting and feasting early and late, he then desired to go to Mūqān[1] and engage in fishing there; the King was asleep with Vīs in his embrace, his heart burnt by the brand of that sunlike beauty; for he had in his embrace so delightful a beauty, but not for so much as a day did he have joy of union with her. The Nurse came secretly and said to Vīs, "Vīs, how can you sleep on such a day? Rāmīn purposes to go to Armenia, to hunt game and fight the foe. They have informed the army of his departure, moved the pavilion to the plain of Māh. Even now the roll of drums and the blare of brazen trumpets rises from his hall to the moon and the Pleiades. If you wish to see his face, far fairer than Chinese brocade, slip to the roof and look from there; your heart's desire is about to vanish suddenly! With arrow and cheetah, francolin, hawk, and falcon, Rāmīn will hunt your heart. He purposes to depart and go far away, steal peace from you and my soul from me."

It happened that the King was awake and heard these devious words of the Nurse. He leapt from his bed and sat raging, angry and wild as a furious elephant; he set his tongue to abusing the Nurse, saying, "Filthy, low creature! there is none more impure than you in the world; you are more disgraceful than a dog, and of less price! Bring me this filthy, sinful creature, whore, hag, with mind of a bitch! I shall give her her deserts, pay her back for her nursing! If nothing but stones rained from the sky on the city of Khūzān forever,

1. On the Caspian Sea. Minorsky, *Iranica*, p. 174; idem, *Ḥudūd ul-ʿĀlam*, p. 142.

crystal arms and hands on her breast; she said to him, "Puissant king! Why do you frighten us with retribution? All you have said is true; you have done right not to conceal fault. Now if you will, kill me; if you will, banish me; if you so desire, gouge out my eyes; manacle me forever in chains; drive me naked into the bazaar; Rāmīn is my choice in the two worlds, soul of my body, soul of my very life; he is the light of my eyes, my heart's ease; my lord, lover, sweetheart, friend. What if I give up the ghost for love of him? I have life only for the sake of love. I shall not relinquish loyalty and love for Rāmīn till I lose my life. That face on that cypress stature is sweeter to me than Māh and Marv alike. His face is sun and moon to me; sight of him is at once my desire and my hope. Rāmīn is dearer to me than Shahrū, dearer to me than Vīrū. I have told you my secret openly; be wrathful or merciful as you please. Kill me if you will, or hang me; I neither have abstained from Rāmīn nor ever shall. You and Vīrū are sovereigns over me, both kings whose writ runs; if Vīrū burns me or imprisons me, I shall approve whatever may be his will for me, and if your sword robs me of my life, my fame will thus live on in the world: 'Vīs laid down her life for Rāmīn.' I would purchase such fame at the price of a hundred lives! But so long as this hunting lion, murderous and raging, survives, who dares breach his den? who dares take his cubs? If Rāmīn lives a thousand years, who will dare take my life? When I have in my hand a proud ocean, why should I shrink from burning fire? You will only then be able to separate me from him when you are able to breed men! I fear neither death nor pain; see what resource you must put into play!"

When Vīrū heard these words from his sister, the situation grew worse for him than death itself. He took Vīs away into a room and said, "This was no trifling mishap that you should have spoken with the King in my presence, and ruined both your own reputation and mine; are you not ashamed before the King and me, that you would consort with Rāmīn and not Moubad? You do not say what you have seen in Rāmīn that you have chosen him before all others. What does the treasurer guard in his treasury, other than music and song, harp and lute? This is the sum total of his knowledge: to play the lute, to strum on it some mode or melody; people never see him otherwise than drunk and shouting, with his clothes in pawn at the taverner's; Jews are his companions and friends; they always dun him for the price of wine. I cannot think how you came to fall in with him, how you should have surrendered your heart to him in love. Now you should dread shame and Heaven and forbear to perform an action which will mean shame for you. Why do you consider a mother like Shahrū and a brother like me worthy of humiliation through you? Nothing remains of your forebears but the souls; do not stain them with disgrace. Do not become all at once broken in by the desire of the demon; do not squander repute in both worlds simply for Rāmīn's sake. Even though Rāmīn be all nectar and sugar, eternal Paradise is sweeter still than he. I have told you what I have come to know heretofore; now I leave you with God and your husband."

Vīrū spoke thus to his sister; Vīs shed pearls from her eyes; she said to him, "My brother, you have spoken the truth and gleaned the fruit of the very tree of truth. But my soul has fallen into the fire in such manner that no advice can rescue it; my heart is so broken in love that no man knows how to mend it. Destiny has decreed my fate; thus it was to be: what use is all this advice and talk? What is the use of closing the door of the house now, when the thief has carried off all the contents of my house? Rāmīn has so fettered me in love that I can never any more escape from his bonds. If you tell me, 'Choose one of these two: eternal Paradise or the face of Rāmīn,' I swear that I choose Rāmīn, for I see his face as my Paradise." When Vīrū heard these words from his sister he no more shed pearls on the ground;[4] sore at heart he left them, entrusting their affairs to the Divine Judge.

When the sun of the world ascended in the revolving heaven like a golden ball on the polo field, the King played polo with his nobles; horsemen swarmed onto the field. On one side King Moubad was captain, having chosen twenty teammates from the champions: on the other side King Vīrū, having picked twenty colleagues from their number. Rafīdā was one of the King's team, with Rāmīn, as Arghish was Vīrū's teammate, with Sharvīn;[5] and there were other nobles and celebrities, lords, champions, and cavaliers. Then they

4. *G:* "pearls before a sow."
5. Minorsky, *Iranica*, p. 167 and note.

threw the ball on the field, hit it up to Saturn with the stick. Vīrū and Rāmīn showed prowess that day; sometimes one took possession of the ball from the other, sometimes the other way round. Of all the famed champions none struck the ball better than Rāmīn and Vīrū.

Vīs with form of moonlike beauty was watching with the beauties of the camp from the roof of the pleasure dome. She saw her brother and Rāmīn, and fancied them even out of such an array of manhood. From her anxiety she became sad at heart, her face pale and her brow furrowed. Trembling seized her silvery body; it was for all the world like a cypress swaying in the wind. She filled her langorous eyes with tears and shed lustrous pearls on roses.

The Nurse said to Vīs with sweet coaxing, "Vīs, why has the Devil gained the upper hand over you? Why do you struggle so much with your soul, why vainly shed so many tears? Is not Qārin your father, Shahrū your mother, Moubad your King, and Vīrū your support? Are you not this day Vīs of the fair face, like a sun among the moon-like beauties? Are you not queen and princess of Iran, are you not lady and sweetheart of Tūrān?[6] You are famed in Iran and Tūrān,[7] for you are all-powerful in both. In face you are all roses, in hair pure musk; rival of the moon, envy of the sun. You enjoy fame in sovereignty and beauty; you have a lover enjoying his every desire like Rāmīn. Even if you have a hundred kinds of woe in your heart, they vanish when you behold the face of the beloved. The heaven longs to have a moon like you, the world to have such a queen.

"Why do you cry wildly to God, who has vouchsafed his Paradise to you here on earth? Do not scowl so upon Fortune, for displeasure brings wretchedness in its train. What better can you ask of the generous God than he has given you on earth? majesty, beauty, youth, luxury, ease, success; should you hanker after more than you have, you will suffer catastrophe from hankering after excess. Do not so, moonlike beauty! Be satisfied with your lot, rest content with what God has given you! Do not hurt the King so by your fury, do not leave your brother sore at heart on your account, for these wounds like drops of rain shall make up a day of Flood when they collect together."

6. *G:* "Eraq."
7. *G:* "Thurket'h and Khuazasan."

The eloquent Sun, the beauty with cypress stature and scent of jasmine, answered her and said, "My nurse, how long will you utter vain words: seek in your folly water in the Fire? Have you not heard from the sages learned in the world's ways, 'War is easy for the by-stander,' or heard this saying from the old,[8] 'People's pain is of little account in other people's eyes.' I am like one on foot, you on horse-back; you have no inkling of the tribulation of walking. I am sick and ailing, you healthy; you do not know what pain and weakness cost me. The King of the World is my lord and master; but he is ill-willed and contentious; he may be a husband, but he is far from being a heart's desire; for he is evil-minded and of evil ways and old. Let Shahrū be who she may, she is ill-disposed to me; she is to my eyes like others' coin; let Vīrū be like the very moon of heaven; what good is that to me, seeing that he is not for me? Even if Rāmīn be all beauty and grace, you yourself know how apt a seducer he is; he has no stock save of sweet oratory; he does not seek righteousness in love. His tongue has all the appearance of sugar; but his nature is colocynth at the time of trial. I am involved with my lover in a hundred ploys, all in vain; at the time of love, surrounded by a hundred lovers and without a lover. I have lover, husband, and brother; at the hand of all three I burn in fire. I have become famous for taking husbands: I have suffered pain in the pursuit of love. My husband is not as other women's husbands; nor my lover like the lovers of the fair. Why must I have a husband and lover who cause my soul pain and distress? A golden bowl into which my enemy pours my blood is hardly the one for me. Had my fortune aided me, my sweetheart would have been none but Vīrū. Neither Moubad nor Rāmīn would have been my mate; nor would friends with enemies' ways have been my portion. One in feud against my life, like grief, another like stone and glass; the tongue of one does not bear out his heart; both tongue and heart of the other are cruel."

48.

SHĀH MOUBAD RETURNS FROM KŪHISTĀN TO KHURĀSĀN.
How fair a place is Marv! How fair is glorious Khūrāsān! Stay there and enjoy the world at your ease; everyone who knows the Pahlavī

8. *I. Mb:* "this golden saying."

language knows that Khurāsān means "that from which the sun comes." "Khor āsad" in Pahlavī means "the sun comes." The sun rises from Khurāsān on Irāq and Fārs. Khurāsān means "The sun coming," for the sun comes thence to Iran. What a beautiful name, and what beautiful water and soil! Her land, water, and soil are all three pure. Especially is the city of Marv in Khurāsān for all the world like April of the year. The soul rejoices in its air, its water and breeze suit the body. You would swear its Marv River was Kousar;[1] that its soil, too, was a second Paradise.

When the fortunate, exalted King returned to the city of Marv from Kūhistān, he went onto the roof of the pleasure dome with Vīs of the silvery frame, sitting like Solomon with Bilqīs. He looked and saw those verdant plains and hills, and saw the world like the face of the charming Vīs. He said with winning smile to that beauty of idol face: "See the world, verdant as your face. Look at the plain of Marv and its meadows; its gardens and streams; vine upon vine blossoming, garden upon garden; its mountains and foothills all beauty and pleasantness; will you not say, moonlike beauty, which is fairer, in your narcissuslike eye, Marv or Māh? In my eyes the land of Marv is fairer; you would swear it was the heaven full of stars. You would think the land of Marv was Paradise, that God had compounded it out of his blessing. Even as Marv the royal abode is fairer than Māh, I am superior to Vīrū in every point. I have many lands like Māh, many servitors like Vīrū."

See how Vīs threw modesty to the winds; how in love she had a heart like a lion; she said to him, "Your Majesty, whether prosperous Marv is good or bad, I leave it to you. I have stationed my heart here against my will; for I am fallen into a trap like a wild ass. If I had not had the sight of Rāmīn, you would have heard the name of Vīs from the other world. As long as I see Rāmīn's face early and late, what is the difference to me between Marv and Māh as places? Without him the garden is a desert to me; with him the desert is to me a garden. Had not my heart gained its peace in him you would not have seen me alive to this day. I obey you for Rāmīn's sake, for I have attached my heart to love of that disloyal youth. I am like a gardener tending a rose; I care for the rose thorn for the rose's sake."

1. A river in Paradise, according to Muslim belief.

When the King heard this reply from Vīs the color of anger sprang to his cheek. His eye became red as Judas blossom, his cheek as yellow as saffron. The heart in his body became as burning fire, his body like a trembling willow from anger. When in his wrath he purposed to kill her, reason and love gained the upper hand over anger. When rage dissipated sense, reason pacified his rage. When the fire of his anger grew recalcitrant, the hand of Fate threw water on the fire. Since God purposed good to her, how could the King have disgracefully taken her life? Arrow and dagger know of God; they do not wound him whom God assists. No ill-wisher overcomes him; he springs from under the foot of the elephant and from the jaws of the lion, just as Vīs of the idol form sprang away. Destiny tied the hand of disaster from her. She was like a treasure locked away, closed to all; but open to Rāmīn. When the King had been moody for a time, he bowed to reason in his rage. He did not carry out any retribution on her but loosed his tongue in devious words.

He said to her: "You whose descent is from dogs; who have had a demon as teacher in Babylon! May the thread of Shahrū's life be cut off; Vīrū's house and home be annihilated; for none but heretics are born of that mother, none produced by that stock but sorcerers. 'A snake will have no progeny but serpents; a rotten branch will bear none but rotten fruit.' Shahrū has had more than thirty children; she has not borne two children to one single husband! children such as Īzadyār and Īrānshāh and Rūīn, such as Nār and Ābnāz and Vīs and Shīrīn:[2] each one born of a disgraceful mother, suckled by a harlot nurse; among them you too are sprung of Jamshīd,[3] and you too have flung your pedigree to the winds! Now three ways are open to you; the road is open to whichever place you wish; one is Gurgān, the other the road to Damāvand, the third the road to Hamedān and Nihāvand. Out you go, on whichever road you choose, your companion hardship and your guide disaster, the wind ever behind you, a pit in front, all your road bereft of bread and water; now the plain you traverse covered in snow, now in snakes, its plants colocynth and its water pitch; lions your companions by day, ghouls

2. *G:* "Adrabad, P'harakhzad, Viprond, Abanoz, Vis, and Shirin."
3. A king of the legendary Pīshdādī dynasty who lost his throne through a misdemeanor, variously described in the sources.

119

by night; no ferry for you across water, no bridges for you over rivers."

49.

VĪS GOES FROM MARV THE ROYAL ABODE TO KŪHISTĀN. When the lofty boxtree heard these words she became happy and delighted at what Moubad said; she made obeisance to him and bloomed like a pomegranate blossom; then withdrew from his presence and said to the Nurse: "Go, Nurse, and take the good news to Shahrū and also ask a present from Vīrū for good news. Say, 'Your darling sister has come, your dear lover and sweetheart. The shining sun has risen upon you from a direction you little suspected. A good omen has come for your hope; two suns have risen upon you from Khurā-sān.' Ask a present from my mother also for good news: say that the moon has escaped from the claw of the dragon, the date been cut from the sharp thorn, the fresh foliage become secure from cold; propitious Fortune has woken from sleep, the radiant pearl come up from the sea. Now that God has delivered me from Moubad, I know that he has saved me from every ill."

Then she said, "Majesty, live forever, live according to your friends' desire far from evil men. I wish you blessing and prosperity; may your soul be a sun to men. Marry a wife hereafter such as may be fit for you and have a hundred servitors like Vīs. Choose from among the idol-faced beauties such a substitute for me that enemies may become blind from seeing her; in lineage brilliant as a lamp, in pedigree like the sun; renowned both for purity and for beauty; as much a byword as the moon, dear as the soul to every heart. May you be endowed with greatness and beneficence without me, may I have health and happiness without you! May we two enjoy such fortune hereafter that our luck may gain our every desire. May we traverse the world in such joy that we forget each other." Then she freed her slaves and gave the King the keys of the treasury. She said to him, "Give this to another treasurer, who shall be better than I in the seraglio. May you have no distress without me, I suffer no harm without you."

So saying, she did him obeisance and left; the King's palace was thrown into confusion by her. Wailing arose from every corner, a river of tears flowed from every eye. The King's minions and the women of his household made his soul burn with lamentations. They made a river of blood with their tears, and one and all bade farewell to Vīs. Many the eye that wept for her, many the heart that burned at separation from her. Everyone cast his heart into that storm of lamentation; it was as if the Flood of separation carried everyone's heart away! That moonlike beauty was not alone on her journey; thousands of hearts were her companions. Everyone was broken-hearted at being separated from her; Rāmīn was wounded even more sorely than the others. He could not rest by day or by night in his distress, and again fell sick from his heart's pain. Though weeping was of no avail to his soul, he did not rest from weeping for a single moment. Now he wept for his heart, now for his mate; day and night he clamored to his heart:

"What do you want of my soul, my heart? for its suffers nothing but ruin from you. You have blackened my days with the brand of love, you have bent my young cypress graceful as a pine; now you may know the bitterness of love, for your life is all frustration of desire; you knew no peace even for a day in separation: what will your days be like now? Much bitterness will you have to taste, many the tribulations you will have to suffer; now prepare yourself to suffer care, to experience separation like the bite of the snake. Now that you have suddenly suffered separation from your love, your date has vanished and the turn of the thorn has come! Writhe, my heart, for you deserve pain; the evil you have done has come home to roost. Shed heart's blood, my eyes! for the darling lover has left you. You shall find a ready market for your tears now, for you will be peddling them in the bazaar of separation. As many tears as you may rain will be worthy of this grief; pour out all the heart's blood you contain! You espied the fair face of that sweetheart and drew me to the line of her love. Now it is yours to strain blood through the eyes, never to rest from weeping in the day of separation: polish out the color of my cheeks with blood, wash blackness from my eyes. It is meet that you should no longer see the world, for you shall not see another sweetheart like Vīs.

121

Why should you possess sight hereafter, for your sight is refreshed by none but her? If I must give up hope of seeing her, I shall never again look on moon and sun. I shall gouge out my eyes, for if I am to be separated from her I prefer blindness. When I am denied sight of my darling, it is meet that I should have no eyes. My sinister fortune, gone black as night, you are a furious lion, I a wounded wild ass. I had before me a pleasant meadow, a fine sweetheart in it too; you sprang an ambush and stole away my sweetheart, and left me bereft of companion and lover. Now take my life, for I have no need of it; it is only proper for one as unfortunate as I to have no life. Cruel, mean Fate, that could not bear to see us together! For once it granted me one desire in the world, then snatched it away from me again! If its way is not cruelty and injustice, why is it happy in my pain?"

Thus sang brokenhearted Rāmīn, his body innocent of peace and his head laid on the pillow. In his forlornness he pondered much how to find deliverance from his distress. He fashioned a trap by the hand of subterfuge and sent a message to the King: "It is now six months that I am afflicted, tied fast with illness my bond. Now some little strength has returned to my body, the bloom of health has been restored to me. I have inspected all my horses and accouterments; all like me have lain six months idle. My steeds and chargers, my cheetahs and hounds, have all lain rested from coursing; my cheetahs have not coursed after the mountain sheep, nor my hawks flown after the partridge. My heart is weary of this sloth, for sloth is the start of baseness. If the King grant me permission, I shall go to the hunt for a space. I shall go from here to Gurgān and Sārī,[1] and fly the hunting falcon there. I shall flush the pheasant with my hawks and unleash my hounds on the boar. Now I shall make the thicket the prison of the boar, now the air the prison of the winging bird. From there I shall go to Kūhistān and hunt wild ass and deer a while. I shall bring down the mountain stag from the hill, unmuzzle the leaping cheetah on his track on the plain. I have looked for six months on nothing but this doleful palace; let me see the hunt for

1. *G:* "Amul, Gurgan, and Kharav."

the next six; when six months have passed I shall come one day and join the King from Kūhistān." When the King heard this hollow message, he replied to Rāmīn in foul words. He knew that his words were lies; that he had contrived by artifice an abortive stratagem; it was love that was wearisome to him, not the palace; it was Vīs his heart craved, not hunting. He set his tongue to abuse and curses and said, "May Rāmīn disappear from the world! May he go on a journey but not return; death will be better for him than return! Tell him: 'Go now wheresoever you will, ill omen and sinister fortune your companion; your road full of snakes and the mountains you traverse full of leopards; their grass and stones stained with your blood! You have sacrificed your life to Vīs; she too dies of longing for you. This evil nature will only leave you at death; but by its means Hell will materialize before you. My words are today by way of advice to you; bitter, like wine, but for your good. If you give ear to my advice, you will glean much sense therefrom; you will seek a noble woman of Kūhistān, endowed both with nobility and with beauty; tie yourself to her under auspicious omens; be happy and satisfied with that bond and haunt Vīs no more, for you will hereafter be slain in her embrace. I shall strike fire from the dagger blade, burn on it both the woman and my brother. When disgrace comes upon me from a brother, he is better under the stones! See that you do not count these words as sport; one does not sport with a marauding lion! When a cloud comes, do not fight with its rain, but with all speed arise from the track of the flood.'"

When noble Rāmīn heard these words he cursed the heretics roundly;[2] swore by moon and sun, by the King's soul and his own and the covenant, that he would never traverse the land of Māh nor transgress the bounds of the King's warning; never see the face of Vīs nor consort with her retinue or kin. Then he said, "Your Majesty, you do not know that I am otherwise disposed to you. In one way you are king over me; in another you are as God. If I turn aside from your command even by so much as a hair, may I find my severed head before me! I fear you as I do pure God; I consider you both the same at the time of command." He sent this sugar-sweet

2. Cf. Avesta, Yasna XII.

message, but this was the secret hidden in his heart: he was in haste to set off, and on his way hunt a moonlike beauty.

50.

RĀMĪN GOES TO KŪHISTĀN AFTER VĪS. When Rāmīn came happily out of the gate half his distress at separation disappeared; when a breeze wafted to him from Kūhistān a sweet heavenly scent reached him; what a happy road is theirs whose route leads them to their beloved! Though they have a hard road before them, they count it a garden and a palace. The more endless one's road seems, the more one rejoices at the face of the lover. Even though the road be bare, it becomes a path of roses when it has a happy end. Thus it was with the road of Rāmīn, whose love increased every moment; like a bitter task whose end is sweet.

Because of him Vīs of the moonlike form was, despite herself, withered like a leaf in Āzar;[1] the land of Māh had become like a dungeon to her, the roses of her cheeks had become the color of straw. She had cast off all ornaments from her body, laid on one side all finery. She had abandoned sleep, food, and happiness; the desire of her heart had rent the veil upon her; all desires of the world were broken in her heart; her heart was stopped from desire and her lips from laughter. Her mother's face had become a snake in her sight; love for Vīrū likewise become as naught. By day love was her daylong companion, shining and delightful as the face of Rāmīn; dark night was her confidant, her souvenir of the musky hair of Rāmīn. Day and night she sat on the palace roof, her eyes fixed on the Khurāsān road. She kept saying, "How would it be if one day a delectable wind blew from this road, a pleasant breeze wafted at dawn, at daybreak came Rāmīn! rising from his horse like a straight cypress, his face toward me, his back to Marv. His prancing horse multicolored like a peacock, the very illuminations of the Artang[2] mounted upon it." Vīs was ever lost in such thoughts, abandoning her body to pain and her heart to distress. One day she was sitting on the roof, at the time when the sun cast the light of dawn; two suns appeared from the

1. Now the ninth month of the Persian year, November–December. See Minorsky, *Iranica*, p. 192.
2. Or Arzhang. See n. 3, p. 29.

quarter of Khurāsān, which rubbed two kinds of rust from the world; one was the rust of night, rubbed from the earth; the other the rust of grief scoured from the heart of the lover. He hastened to Princess Vīs as a sick man makes for medicine. Myrtle and boxtree entwined together, both wept for happiness. Both kissed Judas blossom, then sweet coral lips. Both bloomed in happiness like roses, and hand in hand went into the house.

Vīs with face like the moon said to Rāmīn, "Your heart has gained its desire, your mine yielded ore; let this royal house be yours; dwell therein in joy and happiness. Now grasp the curl and the cup in the house, now capture birds and game on the plain. You came hunting from Khurāsān; your quarry fell easily into your hands![3] I am your deer and pheasant, your boxtree and lofty cypress; now sit at the foot of cypress and box, rejoice your heart in a quarry like me! You and I shall pass our days in joy and never reck of tomorrow. Whilst golden days are with us we shall dwell in happiness, for we shall have no task but rejoicing. In bright day we shall take the cup of nectar, at night take the sweetheart in our embrace. We shall never turn our hearts away from joy for an instant, we shall seek our every desire only to gain it. We shall triumphantly follow every whim of our hearts, for are we not alike blest with victorious fortune and young?"

Then both slaked their hearts' desire and remained together for seven months; it was winter and the cold season in Kūhistān; the two lovers were drunk and happy in the seraglio. Amidst wealth and absolute sovereignty, enjoyment, love, and royal state, see how marvelously they slaked their hearts' desire; they left not a morsel of happiness unsavored.

51.

MOUBAD DISCOVERS RĀMĪN'S VISIT TO VĪS, COMPLAINS TO HIS MOTHER, AND WRITES A LETTER TO VĪRŪ. When King Moubad learned that Rāmīn had grown evil in nature, had once more gone and joined Vīs, again mended his broken love—Rāmīn's heart would only then be patient for Vīs when the Devil was patient in evil works; if a hare one day became a lion, Rāmīn's heart might

3. See Introduction, p. xvii.

125

become weary of Vīs; if a sparrow one day became a hawk, Rāmīn's heart might be weaned of this nature—he straightway went to his mother and lamented miserably about his brother; he said to her, "Can this deed be right? See if any sage would countenance it! that Rāmīn should court disaster with my wife, disgrace my royal throne. What worse shame could there be in the world than that one woman should consort with two brothers? My heart has altogether forsworn mercy; this is why I divulge this secret openly; I have for long hidden this shame from you; now that I have no other course I tell it to you. Know it, so that you may know what Rāmīn is about and may not vainly call down curses on me; I shall so lay him low that your eye will become as a spring cloud. You are Hell and Heaven to me; do not tolerate this ill fame attaching to me; only then will my face be cleansed of shame when I wash it in his blood."

His mother answered him and said, "No clever man ever cuts off his own hands; do not kill him, for he is your brother; you have no other brother like him. Is he not your comrade and ally in the battle? Is he not a shining sun at your feast? Once you are without Rāmīn you will be friendless; your life will be sad without him. When you sit he will not be your companion, nor your partner and sure support. God has given you no son to be one day lord of the world. Leave him alone to be your support and refuge, so that your house may survive by his hand. Man's life is not eternal; life ends for him one day. Once God's order comes for your soul, your house and home will fall into enemy hands. Better that he should be ready in his place; perhaps he may become like you a glorious ruler; perhaps the crown will remain in this line, our house endure in this land. Do not kill your brother: renounce your wife, give the keys of the treasury into another's hand. There are numberless beauties and fair ones who have hair like musk and faces like silver. Choose one and settle your heart on her; give the keys of the treasury into her hand. Perhaps a pearl will come out of that shell for you, worthy of kingship and happiness; what hope can you have of the stock of Vīs other than that she is of the line of Jamshīd? Though her stock is royal and noble, a hundred faults lurk behind this nobility.[1] Do not so,

---

1. Cf. n. 3, p. 119.

Majesty! Exercise reason; do not stain your soul with this feud; you will find a thousand mates like Vīs; why do you not turn from that whore? I have heard another thing; and I know that I have heard it aright; I have heard that that faithless lover of ill nature has once again become a thrall to Vīrū, has been sitting feasting with him day and night, in her cups now sober and now drunk; this is what Vīs has always craved of fortune; now that she has gained it sorrow has left her heart.

"What do you want with poor Rāmīn? It is from Vīrū that your destruction threatens. If Rāmīn is in Hamedān it is because he, like you, is in love with Vīs; this is the fault of evil-natured Vīs: that she gives herself every day to new lovers. Why have such prettiness and beauty if her love for any one person does not last long? She is like a rose which although it is prettily colored does not last long; its love is of short stay."

When Moubad heard these words from his mother his heart relented a shade toward his brother. He was so enraged with Vīs and Vīrū that his cheeks went yellow from the anger in his heart.

He straightway sent a letter to Vīrū, making his pen a sword, so angry was he. He said to him, "Who has directed you, pray, to seek preeminence and perpetrate injustice at my expense? Who is your protector, who your support? for your aims are exceeding high and selfish! Who, pray, vouchsafed you this courage: you are a fox with a lion's nature! What are you doing facing up lionlike to lions, you who cannot hold your ground before a braying wild ass? How do you presume to take my wife, helpless and weak as you are? Although Vīseh is your sister, how can my wife sit as your spouse? Why do you hold her in your house? I shall listen to no excuse for this deed. Where have you ever seen a wife mated to two husbands? or two fierce elephants tied on a hair?

"It may be that since I saw your abode your support and refuge have become rather more substantial than before! In all the time you have been stalwart and champion I have never seen any renown gained by you in the world. Never on any one day have you imprisoned a king, nor defeated an enemy, nor levied tribute on a land, nor conquered a city in triumph. I have never witnessed your prowess nor heard of it from friend or enemy. You know what your line is like—its members fall from grace at the moment of exalta-tion![2] In point of lineage you are like a mule who when he is questioned takes pride in his mother. I see you shoot arrows in every pursuit such as hunting and archery—not, however, in battle. On the polo field you gallop, and gallop well; you play the ball and wield the stick excellently; so long as you are in the palace seraglio you finely display the accomplishments of heroes: but once you enter the battlefield and face your opponents, you run as women do before men! When in the land of Māh you swagger like a lion; but when you leave it even a fox considers you feeble! Perhaps you have for-gotten my blow which robbed your soul of reason, your body of sense, the blows, too, of the famed warriors, renowned champions of Marv, skilled horsemen; in rage like the lion of the plain, in prowess like fighting elephants. Still over the march of the land of Māh shrieks and lamentation come up. That same sword and arm of mine stand ready that have wiped enemies from the face of the earth! When you read this letter, heed my words, for my sword is hungry for your blood.

"I have heard all that you have said before this; how you have boasted of your heroism to people, saying, 'The King came on suddenly like a fierce lion leaping from the ambush; it was because I was slumbering and sleeping that he snatched my Vīs from Gūrāb; had I been in the land of Māh the King would never have carried her off.' Now at any rate you are not drunk but sober; you are a glorious monarch on your own ground; I have acquainted you of my dispositions; I have dedicated my heart to combat with you; put out a scout on every road, a margrave on every march; collect an army from the land of Iran, from Āzerbaijān and the plain of Gīlān. Dispose your army till I come; for I shall quickly undo your defenses; you may as well cast your treasure to the flippant wind, for all your vain trouble will be as wind! I shall not come to battle this time in such wise that you will find quarter for your life in war. I shall make your land a plain from the numbers of the dead; I shall cause a Tigris of blood to flow over the plain. I shall bring Vīs, barefooted and unveiled, on foot in front of the army like a dog. I shall so

2. No doubt a reference to Jamshīd. See n. 3, p. 119.

humiliate her that henceforth no one shall dare to make an enemy of the great!"

When the King sent this message to Vīrū he straightway warned the nobles; they made good their preparations for the march to Māh and for battle with Vīrū.

52.

MOUBAD GOES FROM KHURĀSĀN TO HAMEDĀN. At dawn the blare of trumpets rose; the army moved off like a sea. It was as if the Oxus were coming with a roar toward Kūhistān; everywhere the King pitched camp the moon could not venture to pass over the top of the camp. The earth labored under the load of the army; for they moved along like a mountain of iron. You would have sworn the army was the rampart of Gog; and they were infinite in number like Magog.[1] The messenger hastened on in front of the King; the King marching on behind the messenger. When the messenger reached King Vīrū, strength left Vīrū's limbs; the world grew dark to his eyes; at the King's anger his eyes became like blood. He said, "This is strange; what words are these? against whom is all his strife directed? He has settled my sister in his seraglio, then expelled her in midwinter December; he has struck himself the blow, now he is crying out: so that two injustices are perpetrated. My choice sister is now his wife: but you would swear she was his ill-wisher and enemy. He has driven her from his presence with a hundred humiliations; nor has he summoned her back by so much as a single letter. He it was who committed the sin; now he has grown angry with us; this is the conduct of one who has turned his back on justice! The King is not made of stone or brass; what was his need for speaking such wild words? He brought an army once and saw me; I know that he was satisfied with the sight he had of me! He left me in such ill fortune that he became a byword for humiliation in the world. The contest of us two generals was not hidden, that one might distort it

1. In Muslim tradition Gog and Magog are two peoples who in the last days shall be so numerous that they will drink all the water of the Tigris and Euphrates and kill the inhabitants of the earth. Alexander the Great built a rampart behind which they are to be shut up till the last days. Qur'ān, Suras xviii, xxi; *Encyclopaedia of Islam*, *s.v.* Yādjūj.

by words. Now that he has fallen by my hand, why does he build all these castles in the air before me? I have never witnessed a stranger tale than this: 'Two men fear a broken bow.' How can he frighten me? He it was who was frightened; no reasonable man holds battle with me to be easy."

53.

VĪRŪ SENDS A REPLY TO MOUBAD. Then he sent him a due reply, bitter at its end and sweet at the beginning; he said to him, "King, renowned monarch! Great one, avenger, doer of your own pleasure! What has befallen you from seeking your own pleasure but distress and disgrace? You are a king, sovereign and monarch; your writ runs according to your every desire; it is meet that you should be deliberate; that you should have thorough knowledge of every affair. You are my senior; it is improper for you to speak other than in due manner and as befits your station. Wise men speak in line with justice; they seek repute through justice. You possess more wisdom than any; why do you wound your heart with feud? There should be no feud between us; feud is not meet for friends. Even though you speak wildly, I shall not; even if you pursue feud, I shall not do so. You have expelled your wife from your home; why do you fasten pretexts on another? There is no need here for letters or messengers; here is your wife; take her wherever you wish. If you issue a command, I am your obedient servant; I shall send her to you instantly. I swear by my life that since I have come here I have not seen her more than three times. And what if I have? What shame is there in seeing her? I cannot be cut off from my sister. Since your wife is my sister, what harm is there in her sitting by me? See that you do not fasten this suspicion upon me; no untoward act shall ever emanate from me. If your reason weighs me well, it will know that I am not susceptible of such a notion. The answer respecting Vīs is what I have related; I have given a full exposition of how matters stand in regard to her.

"Now let us speak of our reputation, for we are both questing for reputation in the field of prowess. 'Say to enemy and friend alike what everyone who hears may approve.' In this letter you have sent to a junior you have come before the judge all on your own; you have made sundry boasts and uttered remarkable words; you have prided yourself on the battle of Dēnavar;[1] I gained knightly distinction in it. You said to me: 'That same sword of mine is ready that has wiped enemies off the face of the earth.' If they have beaten your sword out of steel, they have not beaten mine out of boxwood! Your sword may well cleave helmet and coat of mail; mine cleaves rock and anvil. Then you said: 'Perhaps you have forgotten how my blow robbed your soul of reason.' Perhaps you saw my blow in a dream: for whilst awake you found it beyond your powers. In this letter you have written from end to end words that I should have spoken in my own name, to the exclusion of yours; you have put on a cap instead of a crown. 'Two cheeky eyes are better than two treasures.' 'A cheeky person says all he wishes without difficulty.' If you read this letter to the army, much hidden disgrace will come out.

"Then you abused my lineage, saying that my mother was better than my father. Warriors acquire nobility from their fame according as they evince their valor.[2] How do they seek nobility on the battlefield? They gain grandeur by the mace, the dagger, and the javelin. If you come to meet me on the field of battle, you shall soon learn how I shall set about you. I shall cleanse my escutcheon by the temper[3] of my sword; I shall do knightly deeds on the battlefield, but say nothing of them. On the field where heroes vent their anger, what is lineage, what empty words? Not worth a farthing. Leave words on one side; show your heroism: for heroism is our helper this day. Let us vie each one in fame and prowess and see how the Creator gives his judgment!"

When the letter came to the end of its content, he set a seal of red gold on its superscription. He said to the messenger, "Take this and go quickly; convey this letter to the King as swift as smoke." When the messenger came from Vīrū to the King he found him with his army on the road. He saw the sky like a jungle, so full of spears and lances was it; the pebbles on the road had become like collyrium. When the King read that winning letter he was stopped in his tracks by this reply; for he had conceived the idea that Vīrū was contending with him for Vīs; when he saw such words in the letter he repented of his cruelty and fury.

1. See n. 1, p. 45.   2. *I.*   3. Persian *āb*, which also means "water."

He straightway sent a minion to Vīrū to say, "You have freed us from anxiety; they represented you to me in a disgraceful light; now I realize that they did so unjustly. Now I have dismounted from the bay horse of wrath and mounted the gray of friendliness. I shall be your guest in Māh for a month, we shall be as well-disposed friends. Make ready the appurtenances of hospitality in your palace and royal garden; I am your guest for a month; then I shall be your host for a year. See that you do not nurse rancor toward me in your heart; bring Vīseh to me straightway, for Vīs is now my sister, you my brother; the world-illumining Shahrū my mother."

When Moubad's reply reached Vīrū, and innumerable greetings and presents reached Shahrū, the Demon of Wrath hid his face once more, the rose of happiness bloomed in the garden of love. The eyes of peace opened from their sleep, water flowed again down her channel. They again brought Princess Vīs and handed her over to the King, like a sun. The hearts of all were happy for them, you would have sworn that it was a wedding occasion. For a month they enjoyed happiness and hunting; they now played polo, now drank wine. After a month they took the homeward road and went from the land of Māh to Marv.

54.

MOUBAD CHASTISES VĪS. When the King reached choice Marv his heart rejoiced in the face of the Moon of Moons. His sun was the face of Vīs, his pure musk her hair. One day he was sitting with his sweetheart and spoke of the desire of Vīs for Rām. He said, "You dwelt so long in the land of Māh since Rāmīn was your companion. Had Rāmīn not been your confidant your stay there would not have lasted half a day." The Sun of jasmine bosom answered him, "Do not have such grave suspicions of me; now you say, 'Vīrū was with you,' and count my so much as having seen Vīrū a fault; now you say, 'Rāmīn was with you.' Why do you slander me so? 'Do not assume that Hell is as hot as men say—nor that Ahriman is as evil as people would make out.' 'Theft may be the robber's trade; people tell numerous lies about him besides.'

"You well know that Vīrū is young: he hunts on plain and mountain; the only occupation he knows is hunting and sitting with the nobles drinking wine. Rāmīn is the same in habits; he is a stout friend to him. They were together, in brotherly fashion, sitting day and night with music and goblet. The young are sweet companions for the young; for youth is the sweetest of all desires. God created youth out of the very heaven; its scent is that of Paradise. When Rāmīn came to the land of Māh he was for six months Vīrū's companion in entertainment, in the palace, on the polo field, in the chase: in sadness, joy, and counsel. As for Vīrū, he was a brother to him; as for Shahrū, a mother. Not everyone who displays love in some direction has some sin underlying his love! Not everyone who somewhere lavishes love has ill designs in his heart! Not every heart is as impure as yours, not every man as barefaced as you!" The King said, "Very fine, if it be so; Rāmīn's heart deserves a blessing! Can you swear on oath that Rāmīn has had no connection with you? If you can swear to this there will be none as chivalrous as you in the world." Vīseh answered him and said, "I shall swear a hundred oaths on this nonexistent connection. Why should I fear an offense I have not committed? I shall proclaim my innocence by oaths. A soul that is innocent of offense does not writhe; 'uneaten garlic does not make a mouth stink.' Do not frighten me with bonds and oaths: an innocent person treats this lightly. When no unrighteousness underlies it, what is the difference between taking an oath[1] and taking cold water?"

The King said, "What better than this? what more worthy of your purity? Take the oath, and if you escape from suspicion you shall have cleansed your soul of blame. Now I shall light a fire and burn on it much musk and aloeswood; there before the religious dignitaries of the world swear a mighty oath by the fire; as soon as you have sworn the oath you shall have cleared your soul of sin. I shall have no words for you, no contention or strife or cruelty. Thenceforward you shall be my soul and world, I shall hold you as dear as my life. When purity is made manifest in you, I shall confer all sovereignty on you. What better than that sovereignty which purity approves?" Vīseh said to him, "Do thus: make yourself and

---

1. Persian *sougand khordan* ("to take an oath") originally meant "to drink sulphur" and has its origin in the ordeal. Christensen, *L'Iran sous les Sassanides*, pp. 304–5. Cf. the ordeal of Isolde in *Tristan* (Chapter 23).

me of pure faith; so long as you nurse suspicion of me you will suffer harm thereby. It is far easier to hide a past sin from men than to deny it."

The King at once summoned the moubads, and from the camp the officers and paymasters.[2]

55.

MOUBAD GOES TO THE FIRE TEMPLE; VĪS AND RĀMĪN FLEE TO REYY. He presented innumerable gifts to the fire temple, such that one cannot number them one by one. Coin, royal gems, land, mills, and numerous gardens: fleet steeds of Tukhār,[1] uncountable sheep and oxen. He brought some fire from the temple and heaped up a fire like a mountain on the field. He fed it generously with sandalwood and aloe, nursed it with camphor and musk. A fire like a mountain rose from the courtyard, which rubbed shoulders with the whirling heaven; like a golden dome, stretching to the sky, trembling and shedding all its gold like a beauty in fine crimson silk,[2] leaping, roaring, drunken, and joyous. Its brilliance was like the day of union, it moaned like the day of separation. It shed light over the world from its face, darkness fled from its light. No one in the world, man or woman, knew why the King had lit that fire. When the King's fire rose up from the courtyard, its head rose above the moon, it was so high.

From the pleasure-dome roof Moubad and Vīs and Rāmīn watched the fire leaping up to the Pleiades. The nobles of Khurāsān stood, all facing the fire. Of all those nobles not one knew what the King purposed to burn with that fire. Then Vīs looked at Rāmīn and said to him, "See what this man is about: how he has lit a great fire for us; he means to burn us in this fire. Come, let us two flee from here and cause him in turn to burn on fire. Moubad tricked me yesterday about oaths, spoke words as sweet as sugar. I in my turn have set a trap for him; it is not I who have fallen into the trap. I said to him, 'I shall swear a hundred oaths that Rāmīn has not

2. Minorsky, *Iranica*, p. 177.

1. *I*. See n. 2, p. 55. Minorsky, *Iranica*, p. 175. *Mb*: "swift mares."
2. Persian *mulḥam*. Arthur Upham Pope, *Survey of Persian Art* (London and New York, 1938—), III, 2002.

consorted with Vīs.' Besides this I spoke many words to him, deceived his heart on a sudden with wiles. Now in the presence of the whole city and army he means to demonstrate my innocence. He will say to me, 'Pass through the fire, acquaint the world with your body's innocence, that all, great and small, may know, for they are suspicious of Vīs and Rāmīn.' Come, so that before he summons us his belief in this righteousness may remain in his heart."

Then she said to the Nurse, "What do you say, and what remedy can you seek for us against this fire? You know that this is no moment for contention: this is a moment for flight. You are skilled in remedies and practice spells; see what remedy you can contrive for our plight! For in such a situation a remedy must needs be found; one cannot linger here a moment.

The Nurse skilled in talismans said to her, "This is no trivial event that has befallen; how can I apply a remedy to it? how loose the end of this chain? Perhaps the Creator will help me and light the lamp of good fortune. The knell has sounded. Do not linger here! Come with me where I am bound."

Then she made her way into the seraglio by the roof. See how she thence contrived a trick! They took abundant gold and jewels, then all three went into the baths. There was a way through the furnace into the garden, a way unknown to all. The three made their way by this route into the garden, fled Moubad with burning hearts; Rāmīn scaled the wall nimbly and let down his turban from its top. He contrived to haul up the other two and to let first one and then the other down on the other side. He secured his turban to the top of the wall, then slipped down from it himself. Like demons they hid their faces from men; the three went off in the guise of women.

Rāmīn knew of a garden where there was a sage gardener; he went straightway to the gardener and rested when he was within the garden. He secretly sent the man to his dwelling and summoned thence a squire whom he directed thus: "Go and bring horses, choice and as fleet as may be; also such food as you have, my arms, and all my hunting gear." They brought everything he desired; at the time of evening prayer he made ready to depart.

From Marv he went like the wind into the desert, no mortal having glimpsed his face—a desert that was the abode of affliction, as dreadful as the jaws of a dragon. It became like Farkhār[3] by the presence of the faces of Vīs and Rāmīn, like a perfumer's tray from their scent. Desert, salt waste, and shifting sand, the murderous simoom, and ravening lions seemed to the two lovers like some glorious garden, so happy were they to be together! The waste became beautifully colored from their faces, the simoom became as the morning breeze from their scent. They were unaware of heat and desert, it was as if they spent not a single night on the journey.

It is inscribed on a stone in China: "Hell is like Heaven to lovers." When a lover is in his loved one's embrace all evil is passing fair in his eyes; desert and mountain as a garden to him, snowy slopes like a rose plot. For the lover is like a drunken man who in his drunkenness knows no distress or tribulation.

They crossed the desert in ten days and came from Marv the royal abode to Reyy. In Reyy dwelt a friend of Rāmīn's, in the time of chivalry his twin soul. Chivalrous, virtuous, faultless; the possessor of fine estate. Fortune had granted him his will in felicity; his name was Bihrūz[4] son of Shīrū. His house and home were pleasant as Paradise; his friends ever rejoiced in him. It was a dark night, the moon in conjunction with the sun; the stars had hidden their faces from the eye. The world had become like the pit of Bēzhan;[5] the sky had become the co-mate of darkness. Rām went on to the house of Bihrūz, attended in his every desire by propitious fortune and success.

When the kindly man saw Rāmīn his eyes could not credit the sight. He said, "What a wonderful moment; who could hope to receive a guest like Rāmīn!" Rāmīn said to him, "My brother, keep our arrival concealed under the veil of secrecy: do not tell any one that Rāmīn has come from the highroad; tell no one of your guests." The knightly Bihrūz answered him, "My lucky star has brought you as my guest; you are my lord, I your servant—nay, lower than a servant. I shall carry out your commands as long as I live; I shall be but a slave before your slaves. If you so order me, I shall leave

3. See n. 6, p. 37.
4. "Felicitous."
5. In the Persian epic Bēzhan was cast into a pit by Afrāsiyāb. *Shāhnāmeh*, paperback ed. (Tehran, 1345 H.S.), III, 166.

the house with the servants. My house, and more, is yours: my soul desires only your pleasure."

Then Rāmīn, Vīs, and Bihrūz dwelt a hundred days at their pleasure; their hearts relaxed in enjoyment and the door fast; the dust washed from the face of their desires by wine; by day enjoying happiness and bliss; spending their nights in pleasure and fulfillment of desire. Now they had wine in the hand, now the lover in their embrace; drinking wine to the cheeks of the sweetheart. The lamp of the fair, Vīs of rosy limbs, dwelt with her sweetheart in joy and ease. At the night's end when toward morning Venus rose, she awoke to the sound of the minstrels; though she was still drunk and drowsy from the wine, they placed pure wine in her hand. Her sweetheart Rāmīn sat by her side, with now the lute and now the harp in his lap. He sang:

"We are two fond lovers, ready to lay down our lives in love. At the time of constancy we are treasures of loyalty; in our enemies' eyes we are arrows of cruelty. Even as we savor joy and delight, our enemies suffer tribulation and wretchedness. We never become sated of love through mere distress, nor do we turn our faces away from the highroad of love. In love we are like two bright lamps, in joy like two blossoming gardens. We glean nothing but joy of our love, for so triumphant are we that no less is our due. Happy Vīs, sitting by Rāmīn! like mountain partridge by the side of hawk! Happy Vīs, sitting cup in hand, drunk both on wine and on beauty! Happy Vīs, sitting enjoying your heart's desire, whilst hope lies shattered in Moubad's heart! Happy Vīs, opening your lips to smile, then laying them on Rāmīn's! Happy Vīs, drunken by Rāmīn's side, his co-religionist in love! Bravo, Rāmīn! How neatly have you planned things to hunt a prey like Vīs![6] Bravo! Rejoice in your heart's desire, for you have a fair companion with whom to enjoy it! Bravo! In the Paradise garden you are ever with an April rose! Bravo! You are the companion of the sun, and will gain all you desire by its glory! A thousand blessings on the soul of Shahrū, whose daughter is Vīs, whose son is Vīrū! Blessings

6. See Introduction, p. xvii.

on the land of Māh, which gave birth to a Moon like Vīs! Blessings on the soul of Qārin, from whose loins sprang this gleaming Moon! Blessings on the laughter of Vīs, which has enslaved the world! Bring, Vīs, the royal cup, filled with wine as crimson as your cheek; if I take the cup of drunkenness from your hand, drunkenness brings me no languor. I do not know how I have become drunk in desire of you, whether by your face or passion or the cup! Even were I to take a cup of poison[7] from your hand, I know that it would be a cup of nectar! My joy finds peace in you, my cares melt away before you. My heart is a casket, you its jewel; my embrace is the heaven, you its star. May this casket never be bereft of its jewel, or this heaven of its star! May the garden of your cheek ever be in bloom, may my hands ever be its gardener. Many a day shall they read our names, wise men shall be amazed at us; it is meet that such beauty and love should earn eternal fame. My heart, you have suffered sore pain and wounds; now you have gained your desire of your lover. You have found a heart as brimful of love as yourself, and with it a beauty of rosy cheeks more radiant than the sun. Take your joy in this face day and night, and plot the struggle against your enemies. For in the world date goes with thorn, love's joy with care. Even if you now squander your soul in the quest for her love, it will not merit so much as one glimpse of her face. The be-all and end-all of the soul is such enterprise, the be-all and end-all of the world such a lover! Now drink wine and let tomorrow be; you will be visited by nothing other than God's decree. Who knows but your lot in the quest of love may be better even than you dare to hope?"

Whenever Rāmīn drank wine, he recited such poetry; on the one hand, Vīs rejoiced in her every wish and desire; on the other, the King suffered pain and affliction. If they enjoyed happiness in the

7. *Mb, I*: *hūsh*; Persian *hūsh,*[1] "intelligence" (Pahlavi *ōsh, id.*), is to be distinguished from *hūsh*[2], "death" (Pahlavi *ōsh, id.*). The word here appears to be *hūsh*[2], which is contrasted with *nūsh*, "nectar," in this poem; *nūsh* is frequently opposed in the sense of "antidote" to *zahr*, "poison": *hūsh*[2] is tentatively translated as "poison". *Mi* reads *nūsh* for *hūsh* in this passage. See *Burhān-i Qāteʿ* (Tehran, 1334–35 H.S.), *s.v.* hūsh.

midst of their desires, the King suffered longing and misery. For he desired to administer the ordeal to Vīs and free his heart from the chains of suspicion.

56.

SHĀH MOUBAD WANDERS THE WORLD IN SEARCH OF VĪS. When the King sought Vīs, Fate made his day like a dark night. He looked for her everywhere for a day and a night, a fire like to consume the world smoldering in his heart. When he despaired of seeing Vīs the bright sun became dark to his eyes. He handed over all the kingly power to Zard, who was both his minister and his brother. He chose out of all his accouterments a sword, a fleet horse like a rushing cloud, a bow stout as a heathen's heart, a quiver full of flying diamonds. He went off into the world alone seeking Vīs, his tongue calling her name from the pain of his heart. All over the face of the earth—Rome, India, Iran, Tūrān[1]—everywhere he asked for some clue to Vīs, but neither saw her himself nor heard of her from others. Now he was on the mountains like the wild goat; now on the plain like the lion; now like the demon in the wilderness; now like the snake in the swamp. Over mountain, jungle, plain, and river he wandered for five months like a madman. Now cold wounded him with its sword, now heat tormented his soul. Now he broke his fast with travelers, now ate burnt bread,[2] now drank shepherds' milk. He hardly slept; and if ever the poor King slept the earth was his carpet, his hand his pillow.

Thus for five months over plain and mountain the road was his companion, distress his fellow traveler. His ill fortune was Rāmīn's good luck, all his bitterness had become sweet for his rival. How many stones his hand dashed on his head! How many tears his eyes shed on his breast! On, on he went like a lost soul, always wandering along some road, or left solitary in some lone spot. He wept so much at his lot that his tears were more copious than rain.

He said, "Alas for my fate! I have squandered army, treasure, and chattels without number, all for the sake of my heart; now I am bereft of sovereignty and heart. I am far from both heart and lover;

1. *G* adds "Greece, China."
2. Lit. "charcoal."

far better to die on such a day! As soon as I take one step to seek her it is as if a limb drops from me. My distress has become manifold since my very soul has deserted me. You would swear the wind was fiery before me, the ground iron under my feet. Everything delightful I see in the world appears to my eyes like a dragon. What does my heart resemble? A straining packhorse. What is the air like to me? Fatal poison. Let love be unsuitable for old age—but why must I have this love together with all this pain? This pain would make a child a doleful old man; see, then, to what an old man will be reduced. I chose an angel of Paradise out of all the world and came face to face with Hell in separation from her. The more I recall her cruelty and tyranny in my heart, the more love and devotion for her increase in me. The more I count her faults, the worse I become; you would swear I love her faults. Before I became a lover I was powerful, keen-sighted, and knowing in my own affairs. Now in love I am weak as water; I have grown to be unable to know even when I see! Alas, my reputation for sagacity! Alas, my tribulation in the ways of love! The wind has suddenly blown away all my endeavors; fire has forthwith fallen upon my soul. My heart has become blind from love and sees none of this world's desires.

"What will they say of me now in the world? All will wash their hearts of love for me; they will count me mad and crazed, for is not a madman indeed as I am? bereft of happiness and kingship, sleeping thus with the wild ass and the deer. Why, when my charming sweetheart was by my side, did I listen to the vain words of my enemy? Since I cannot endure separation from her, why not obey her commands? If some day I see her cheeks again, I shall present her with all my treasure and signets. I shall be at her command as long as I live; she shall be my lady, I her slave. Now that I am the slave of love, whatever is her pleasure is mine."

When the King had wandered in the world five or six months his body became all languid and weak. He was ever in fear of the blow of Fate, in terror lest it should one day seek a pretext for his death, lest he die in his ill fortune and alone and then an enemy take his place. He saw fit to return from his journey, abandon the desire of searching for Vīs; spend his life in hope of her; it might be that one day he would find a clue to her. Straightway he went to Marv the

royal abode; once more the whole world rejoiced in him; you would
have sworn that a waterless field had found moisture, or a poor and
needy man a hoard of coins! Happiness descended on noble Marv;
everyone gave presents for good news in his joy. People decked all
the bazaar with festive stands and sat among them making music;
they showered down so much gold and so many jewels that the poor
of that land became rich.

57·

RĀMĪN WRITES A LETTER TO HIS MOTHER. When King Moubad
departed from the gorgeous palace and dome, turned his heart aside
from kingship and his city, preferred the desert and abandoned the
palace, wandered in his wretchedness and ill fortune and returned
when five or six months had passed, Rāmīn wrote a letter to his
mother from Reyy and clad her soul in a garment of joy: for the two
brothers, Rāmīn and the King, were both born of this pure mother;
Zard was of a different mother from theirs; I have heard that she
was of Indian lineage.

The messenger came to Marv in secret, more speedy in his haste
than the autumn wind. Ever since the King and Rāmīn had departed, their mother's tears had been bitter. Now she dropped blood
from her eyes on her face, now cried out at the pain of her heart;
for two sons like the King and Rāmīn had severed themselves from
her at once; had chosen a woman out of both worlds and cut themselves off from both mother and kingship. When she received tidings
of Rāmīn she became happy; that news was to her body as the very
soul.

He had said in the letter: "Excellent mother, the world has cut me
off from my brother; for he is in feud against my life; he threatens me
month in, year out like a sharp sword. He is offended at both Vīs and
me and ever seeks to make an enemy's will prevail over us. One hair
of Vīs of the moonlike form is dearer to me than a hundred brothers
like him. I derive nothing but pleasure from Vīs, but suffer nothing
from him but haughtiness and pride. Whenever I dwell far from
him I enjoy nothing but felicity and my heart's desire. Whenever I
am at court it is as if I were in a dungeon, such is my fear of him. He
is not the heaven, the moon, or the sun, for he is of the same mother

and father as I. Take any matter of repute you choose—I am no less than he; I am worth fifty like him on the battlefield. Since I have left detestable Marv I have not rested from sport and laughter. In Marv I was by day and night for all the world like a deer in the claws of a cheetah. Was it not enough to endure that affliction against my will? Does there have to be fire in its train? Why does he presume to burn me in fire? He is not God, who metes out Fire and deals out retribution.

"Now I am safe and sound where I am; I rejoice in Vīseh and grow drunk on wine. I have sent this letter to you in secret so that you may know how I am and what I do. See that you do not allow yourself to grieve in any way, for this world's distress is fleeting. I have set forth my situation, my fortune and whereabouts, and will inform you henceforth of what befalls. I purpose to wander in the world till the time when the King's throne is without a king. Once Moubad's throne is empty, Fortune will surely set me thereon. His soul is not anchored to a mountain, nor yet washed in the Water of Life; and should he survive yet awhile, I swear that I shall collect an army, drag him off his throne, and sit thereon myself with my sweetheart. This shall be soon, not late; keep my words in your heart. When my words are borne out, say 'Bravo! There is no sage better than you.' Accept the greetings of Vīs who is food for the soul; sweeter far than the scent of the rose at dawn."

When his mother read her son's letter, she poured forth her soul in happiness over it. The King returned from his journey the day after the letter was delivered from the road. Their mother's heart was delivered from the pain it had suffered, it was as if she would take wing from very joy. The ways of the world are thus marvelous; lucky the man who takes warning from them. It executes a few tricks in miraculous wise, then neither joy nor distress remains. Beware of bemoaning the world's afflictions, for if you do you moan in vain; beware of taking pleasure in its desires, for if you do you rejoice in empty air.

58.

MOUBAD'S MOTHER GIVES HIM NEWS OF VĪS AND RĀMĪN AND WRITES A LETTER TO RĀMĪN. When the King had rested for a week he was ever sad from loneliness; when his minister left his presence the demon of thought overtook him. One night his mother said to him, "Why, my darling, do you melt in pain and distress? Why are you so mournful and downcast: are you not King of Iran and Tūrān? Do the kings of the world not pay you tribute? hold their very hearts and sight by your grace? You hold the world from Qairuvān[1] to China: you can satisfy any whim. Why are you thus ever wretched, why do you countenance this dolefulness for your soul? Everyone increases in excellence with old age, for then one emerges from the dream of youth. One no more treads the road of evil, does not seek from old age the desires of youth, for old age is the strongest chain with which to bind them, white hair their best counsel. But since you have become old your desire has increased; my heart is much wounded by this desire that you manifest."

The King said, "My mother, thus it is: you would swear my heart was in feud against me. I have chosen a woman out of all the world; I cannot rest a moment without her. She neither accepts advice when I tender it nor becomes tamed by happiness and gentle ways. She sent me wandering through the world for six months. How much suffering did she visit on my soul! Now I am melancholy and disturbed at the thought that I must live in the world without sight of my beloved. As long as the heart lives within my body I shall not prosecute war against any enemy; if my soul only found some clue to Vīs, my long distress would come to an end. I have sworn that if I see her face I shall give over to her crown and signet. I shall never again turn aside from her command, but hold it as the command of my God. I shall draw the veil over past sin and never confront her with it; I wish Rāmīn, too, nothing but good; let him be my brother, support, and stay."

When his mother heard these words from him it was as if fire fell on her heart. She shed tears of agony on her cheeks; you would have sworn she shed pomegranate seeds on saffron! She took the hand of her noble son and said, "Swear an oath to these words, that you will not shed the blood of my Vīs and Rāmīn, nor yet engage in strife against them; that you will fulfill the words you have spoken in such a

1. South of Tunis. Minorsky, *Iranica*, p. 168.

way that you do not grudge good faith; for I have news of them, which I shall divulge when you bind yourself by a true covenant."

When his mother spoke these words to the King, his face bloomed like a tulip from happiness; he fell down before his mother in supplication and kissed her feet a thousand times. He said, "You who are the peer of my soul, deliver me from burning Hell! Perform yet one more noble office for me, revive my soul for me yet once more! I shall treasure your command in my heart and never turn my head from it."

Then he swore an oath before his mother by the glorious religion and the Spirit of Wisdom, by the God of the world and the faith of the holy, by the bright souls of the righteous and of the ancestors; by pure Water, Earth, Fire, and Air, by culture, loyalty, wisdom, and justice: "Henceforth I shall not seek to wrong Rāmīn but shall cleanse my heart of his injuries and works. I wish no harm to his body or soul; from my heart I shall only show him love. Vīs shall be the queen of my seraglio, the salve of my heart and soul. I shall pass over her past sins and never tax her with them again."

When the King thus swore an oath and contented his heart about Vīs, his mother thereupon sent a letter to Rāmīn and recounted all that had passed. She used words more radiant than jewels, sweeter than sugar when heard. She said in the letter, "Soul of your mother, a mother's command is Heaven and Hell. When you read this letter, make haste: rescue my life this once more, for my eyes are blind from much weeping; my body is like to sever from my soul. The lamp of my soul has died in my body, the spring of desire is withered in my heart. Thus I remain till I see your face; I am prostrate on the ground before the Judge; it is you I would see in the world and none other; no one else is as glorious to me as you. The King, too, is doleful like me; from missing you, you would swear his body was bereft of soul! Once he was without you he realized your worth, he wandered in the world to the limit of his powers. How much trouble and affliction he suffered throughout the world! How many hard days he endured! Now he has returned and become full of regret; there is no cure for him but seeing you. He has duly sworn a holy oath that he will never break his covenant in affection; he will hold you as dear as soul and eyes; and more, as a favorite brother. Outside you shall have jurisdiction and command, as Vīs shall have within the seraglio. She shall be queen, you general; noble Moubad like a father to you both. There will never be any anger or offense; he will seek to please your heart in word and deed. Do you in your turn forswear in your heart fear and estrangement; do not give way to fury and forbear to be thus belligerent. 'Even if you have substantial capital you see no profit from foreigners.' Since you have a margrave's charge in Khurāsān, why seek asylum elsewhere? For Khurāsān is paradise; God has compounded you of its clay and has granted you sovereignty over it. Why do you ever seek to be separated from it? In all your exile and infinite pains, what aim can you hope to pursue greater than kingship? What have you in your nature better than hope? What will you find in the sky better than the sun? When there lies at your feet a mine of jewels, why do you painfully seek another mine?"

When the reply to Rāmīn's letter had come to its end, they conveyed it by fleet coursers. Rāmīn's heart warmed at the letter; he inquired after his mother and Moubad. Once he learned of the covenant and oath, he took rein for Marv from Reyy. He sat his sweetheart in the litter, like a royal pearl in a crown; the dust of every road grew like musk and tulips from the scent of the locks and the color of the face of that Moon; though hidden in the veil, she yet shone like a moon two weeks old; though she was a caravan-traveler on the road, she was yet like a cypress grown to royal stature; the sky had washed her with the water of love, the Pleiades broken a thousand strings of pearls. She had been established at her own devices for six months, neither sunlight nor moonlight had shone upon her; she had become as delicate as a drop of water, as fresh as a green and verdant cypress. For each beauty she had possessed a hundred had been multiplied upon her; none had seen her like nor yet heard of it. When King Moubad's eyes fell on her he forgot all the affairs of the world. The love in his heart increased in the same measure as the beauty of Vīs had grown. He forgot all the hurt of the past; it was as if Moubad's demon had become an angel. Once more they set their hand to pleasure and counted the world but a laughingstock and sport; they rejoiced in fulfillment of their desire and watered the field of desire with wine.

59.

MOUBAD SITS AT THE BANQUET WITH VĪS AND RĀMĪN AND
RĀMĪN SINGS OF HIS PLIGHT. When the King, Vīs, and Rāmīn
all together became once more free of sorrow through love, they
forgave the sin of the past and scoured rancor from their hearts with
forgiveness. The King of Kings one day held court in triumph, sitting
joyfully with Vīs, the delight of all hearts, the crystal wine bowl in
hand, filled with ruby-red wine like the face of Vīs. He summoned
noble Rāmīn, bade him be seated, and took his pleasure in the face
of both; the portion of his ear was the harp of Rāmīn, that of his eye
the face of the beauty. When ever and anon Rāmīn played the harp,
stones would have come to the surface of water in very joy! He sang
a sweet song of his own plight, and the face of Vīs flushed like a
rose:

"My wounded heart, do not live thus in care! You are not all
rock or brass! Do not be so displeased with your love or so
wretched in heart. Cheer your heart awhile with music and
wine, lay the dust of care with the wine bowl. If some short
space of life is left, this world's cares will come to an end. The
selfsame sphere that has done you injustice will seek pardon and
one day treat you fair. Many the day that you will be happy and
free of these cares; though the world has altered your state, its
complexion will not always be the same."

When wine wreathed in the King's head reason quarreled therein
with wine; he begged another sweet song of Rāmīn, prettier even
than the last in telling the tale of love. Once more Rāmīn sang a song
that soothed the care of old in the heart:

"I saw a blossoming spring garden, worthy to have love
planted in it. I saw a gliding garden cypress, I saw a talking
heavenly moon, I saw there an April rose, its scent and color
both of Paradise; fit to be a comforter in the hour of grief, a
joy in the hour of happiness; I surrendered my heart to its love
forever and preferred the gardener's trade to all else. I ever
stray amongst its tulip beds and gaze on its blossoming spring

glory. Day and night I am a denizen of the garden, while my enemy is left like a knocker on its gate. Why should the jealous bear envy? 'God gives everyone his due.' The wheeling sphere is worthy of the moon, thus it is that God has vouchsafed the moon to it."

When the noble King heard this song, love was renewed in his heart through joy. The grief of separation from Vīs departed from his heart; he asked Vīs of the face like the moon for a cup of wine, so that he might become wholly drunk on wine and scour the corrosion of existence from his heart.

Jasmine-bosomed Vīs said, "King of Kings, live in happiness to the desire of your well-wishers; may all your days be thus triumphant, all your deeds worthy of blessing; it is meet that we should drink wine this day and call down blessings on the King. It is meet too that the Nurse should see our good fortune and sit with us in happiness for a time. If the victorious King pleases, we shall inform her of what we do and summon her to the King's banquet for a time; for there is no one who loves the King more than she."

Then they summoned the Nurse to the presence of the King and sat her on a throne before Vīs. The King said to Rāmīn, "You hand round the wine; for it is better to drink wine at the hand of friends!" Rāmīn, light of the world, complied; he joyfully poured and drank wine. The wine showed its mettle in his brain and joined forces with his heart full of love. As he was handing wine to Vīs of the tulip cheeks, he whispered to her, unknown to the King, "Beauty of fairy descent, drink pure wine in joy and pleasure, so that we may water the field of our love with wine!"[1]

The heart of Vīs thrilled at this sweet speech; unknown to the King she smiled at Rāmīn; she said to him, "May Fortune be your guide, may your field be fruitful in the land of Love! So long as life inhabits our bodies may both our hearts increase in love! Forbear to choose others before me in your heart; for my part, I shall choose not even my soul before you. You shall rejoice in me, as I do in you; you ever in my thoughts, I in yours. May both our hearts be mines of happiness, the heart of Moubad a fire of torment!"

1. Cf. with this passage the motif of the love-potion in *Tristan*.

147

The words they whispered secretly reached the ears of the King but he affected not to hear what he heard and chivalrously kept his heart in control.

He said to the Nurse, "Now you pour wine," and said to Rāmīn, "Take up the harp; sing a lover's song to the harp, and with few words make our joy abundant." Then the Nurse poured wine for them; Rāmīn could not restrain himself from crying out in the love of his heart. He sang a sweet appealing song; you, too, if you drink wine, drink to it:

"My face has grown yellow from the pain of separation; wash the yellow from my face with wine. Rosy wine will make my cheeks of rosy hue and scour the corrosion of care from my soul. Once the color of my cheek is crimson, my enemy will have no clue to my inner pain. I try every device I know to hide my pain from my enemy. This is why I am lost in drunkenness day and night; I can find no device other than drunkenness. How joyful the wine drinking which cures helplessness! I am ever drunk and sipping wine, so that I may not know care. You would swear my beauty with moonlike face knows that I am thus at the mercy of the brand of her love. Though I may slay heroes, love robs me of my life! O God, you are the savior of the helpless; you know the remedy for me and more besides. Even as you bring bright day out of night, bring joy for me out of this tribulation!"

When Rāmīn sang to the harp for a time, even rocks would have grown soft at his melody. Though he hid the love in his heart, some little sign of what was hidden glinted through. How could a heart lost against its will in the white heat of fire find rest in the furnace? As drunkenness joined forces with love and youth fanned both fires, how could Rāmīn's heart have practiced patience? how have kept its place in such circumstances? He was young, drunk, and in love; the harp in his arms; his lover sitting by another lover; hardly surprising that some clue should have shown in him of his lover's plight! Just as water when in flood will ooze willy-nilly under any barrier, even so when love waxes strong advice and wisdom are as nothing in its eyes.

When the victorious King became drunk on wine, he went joyfully into the seraglio with that moonlike beauty. Rāmīn went to his own place, his bed of thorns and his pillow sunless. The King's heart was full of vexation at Vīs and he rebuked her in his drunkenness. He said to her, "Alas that all this beauty is not accompanied by any inclination to love! You are like a fair and gorgeous tree, blooming delightfully in a spring garden; its flowers and leaves fair to see but bitter to taste; your words and aspect like sugar, your ways and deeds like colocynth. I have seen many flippant and shameless women, but never seen or heard of one like you. I have seen many lovers in the world who have taken all kinds of sweethearts; never have I seen a shameful love like yours, nor yet a sweetheart like yours! As you sit right in front of me it is as if the two of you were alone! The fortunes of the lover are ever in chaos; his eyes go blind from his chaotic fortunes! He is obvious and fancies otherwise; even in the company of a hundred he fancies himself alone. The mere clod of earth behind which he sits appears to him like Mount Alburz! You in your love are both thus: seeing your love but failing to see the shame.

"Do not be so bold with me, idol-like beauty, for 'boldness makes a friend an enemy.' 'Even though a King becomes an ass one day in front of you do not be bold and mount him!' 'Kings are like fire,' and fire always by nature raises its head in refractoriness. Even though you may possess the strength of an elephant or the nature of a lion, do not try conclusions with burning fire! 'Do not look upon the sea only when it is calm; look at it when it is stormy!' Even though its water be calm, once it boils up you will not be able to withstand its boiling! Do not be so bold with me, for you have not the power to withstand my wrath. Do not lay the foundations of this high wall, for it shall all at once collapse on top of you! I have suffered much tribulation because of love for you, tasted much bitterness in separation from you; how long will you keep me in this plight, how long keep my heart wounded by the sword of anger? Forbear to treat me thus unkindly, for you shall thereby cause damage to yourself! If one day you release me from your bonds, abandon contentiousness, and show me love, I shall inscribe loyalty and love toward you on my very soul, and in my joy confer on you all I possess. I shall give you Khurāsān and Kūhistān; you shall be the sun of my seraglio. I shall

like a javelin. From his love for Vīs the snow seemed to him a shower of roses, the dark night was to him like brilliant day. The edge of the roof was to him like cupola and pleasure dome, the ground sodden in mire like silk pure and of sumptuous weave.[2] Though he was far from the face of his love, her perfume still came to his senses. As he had no way of being united with his love, he was content with her perfume, the elixir of the soul. What do you know sweeter than love where the lover is fearful of an enemy? He dreads that one day an ill-wisher will suddenly learn of his affair with his love; then the sweetheart will be blamed, and a veritable Judgment Day come about his ears.

When Rāmīn had sat on the roof for some time, cold joined forces with the dark night. He was not harmed by snow and rain, for there was a burning fire in his soul. Even had every drop become a hundred rivers, it would not have damped so much as one ember of that fire. The world that night was in peril of a Flood, for the tears of his eyes joined forces with the rain, his heart was in torment, his soul lost in desire for his mate!

Sighing he said with grieving heart,

"My fair one, do you consider it right for you to be indoors whilst I am in the midst of snow and rain? You now have your love in your embrace, sleeping on ermine and squirrel fur; here am I all alone, without my love; my feet caught in the mire of distress. You are asleep and do not know how your lover weeps bitterly. Fall, snow, on my soul full of fire! for all suffering is sweet to the desperate! If I so much as heave a sigh I shall burn your snowflakes and set fire to the whole wide world. Wind, blow fiercely for a moment; ruin the whole world with your blustering; stir her tresses from the pillow, drive sleep away from her eyes. Carry the sound of my moans to her ear, tell her how brokenhearted I am. Tell her of my plight as I sit alone amid the snow, at the mercy of my enemies. Maybe her heart may burn for me a little; for even my enemies' hearts burn for me. If a star came out from behind this cloud, it would weep more copiously than I at my pain."

2. Persian *mulham*. See *Survey of Persian Art*, III, 2002.

As Vīs became aware[3] of the movement on the roof, Rāmīn's moans came to her ears. The desire of love invaded her soul; she there and then sent the Nurse to him. By the time the Nurse came back Vīs was in such a state that you would have sworn she was bereft alike of patience and of soul.

The Nurse descended quickly from the roof and gave a message from Rāmīn to Vīs. "Sweetheart, moonlike beauty, quick to tire of love, bold in drinking the blood of lovers! Why have you quite grown presumptuous toward me? What have you eaten that makes you sated of love for me? I am the same in loyalty and love as you saw before; why, then, are you not the same? I am amid snow, you amid silk and brocade. I cannot wait to see you; you possess your soul in patience. You are surrounded by happiness, I by pain and distress; you are attended by pleasure, I by pain and torture. Perhaps the Creator decreed our fortunes thus: ease for you but pain for me. If God has granted your every desire, I count it right; may it ever be thus! I pray to him that you may obtain your every desire; for you are delicate of heart and cannot bear grief. It is meet that it should be mine ever to be a slave, ever suffer cares. Be happy, for it is your desert; follow your desire, for you are my queen.

"You know how wretched I am, bound in heart by that musky lasso; the night is dark, and I am bereft of patience and denied my desire; sleep has deserted my eyes and patience my heart. Like a madman I clamber over roof and wall; my very life and the whole world have become as nought in my eyes. I ever nourish hope of seeing you; do not burn this hopeful heart of mine. Make the dark night day for me, make your embrace my refuge: in bitter cold like this that bites the very soul, there is no fit refuge other than the embrace of a lover! Show me your face, that elixir of the soul, stroke me with your tresses that rub musk! Press your silvery bosom on my gold breast, for silver and gold are best together. My heart has lost its way in love for you; separation has become a pit yawning in my path. Do not be altogether content in face of my pain; do not countenance my having fallen into the pit of distress! If you cut off my hope of seeing you you will even now rend the veil of my patience. Do not set the sword of your cruelty to my soul; do not cut off my

3. *G* adds· "again."

152

hope in your love and loyalty, for so long as I live I shall be but the slave of your slave!"

When charming Vīs heard this message, her heart boiled like juice simmering on fire. She said to the Nurse, "What remedy do you know for me? How shall you deliver me from the hand of Moubad? For he is asleep; should he wake, our plight will be a sorry one. If he remains alone in this room he will wake and discover what we do; there is nothing for it but for you to sleep with him as lover with lover;[4] turn your back to him and your face away from him, for he is drunk and a drunken man knows nothing. Your body is much like mine; should he caress you, how will he tell the difference? In his drunkenness and unconsciousness how will he tell one skin from another?"

So saying she took the lamp from the room and by this subterfuge left the Nurse with her husband. Then delirious with happiness she went off to her lover and cured his wounds with a kiss. She drew the squirrel fur off his silvery breast, laid in it for him dewy roses. From her figure she took off the garment of black fox fur; stripped the garments from her body and care from her heart. You have seen rose and narcissus together at Nourūz—thus were those two charming sweethearts; like Jupiter in conjunction with the sun, or a fire ever fed with straw. Their faces filled the earth with tulips, their perfume made the air redolent of musk.

The clouds cleared, and the stars came out and seemed to watch their play. When the sky saw those two royal jewels it removed the jewel-raining clouds from very shame! The two lovers exchanged secrets in joy and became partners in bliss. Sometimes the pillow was the hand of Vīs, sometimes the hand of Rāmīn, elixir of love. You would have sworn they were milk and wine mixed, or silk and gorgeously woven cloth[5] thrown on each other, twined together like snake on snake; how sweet it is for lover to twine on lover! Laying lip on lip, face on face; not even a hair would have been able to part them. All night they exchanged secrets; sometimes busy at secrets, sometimes making love. They tasted abundant sugar in their kissing and had much joy of their play.

4. Cf. *Tristan*, p. 207, where Brangane sleeps with King Mark.
5. See §55, n. 2, p. 134.

153

When the King woke from his drunken sleep the Moon of Moons was not in his embrace. He caressed the limbs of his bedfellow—but in place of a silvery cypress a dry reed met his touch! How could the old Nurse resemble Vīseh? How may a bow resemble an arrow? To his touch the Nurse was plain to tell from Vīs—gorgeous woven cloth is easy to tell from thornbushes! The King leapt from sleep like a tiger, thundering like a cloud from the rage in his heart. He grabbed the hand of that witch and said, "What demon are you that are clasped in my embrace? Who threw you into my arms? How have I become benighted by a succubus?" He repeatedly called to the palace servants for lamps, candles, and light and asked her over and over again, "Who are you? What thing are you? What is your name?" The Nurse gave him no answer; no one heard all that noise and shouting save Rāmīn, lying in his lover's arms; she was asleep but he awake. He ever kissed garnets with sugar and rained pearls upon pomegranate blossom. He was dreading the dawn of day, for at dawn he must suffer distress. He sang a sweet song to his heart, bemoaning his imminent separation from his love:

"Night, you are very fair and delightful; to all you are night, to me like day. When bright day rises for all, my night appears from darkness. Now early dawn approaches; prepare yourself, my heart, to receive the fatal arrow! What a fair ploy love would be if it were not accompanied by separation! World, you know no way but evildoing; you give happiness only to snatch it away again. If you one moment grant me my desire of nectar, you follow it with a cup of poison.[6] A curse on the first day love became sweet in my heart! Bracing my heart to meet any ill, I launched my ship on the waves; ill fortune threw me into a love more than love of possessions and children. What pain is this that cannot be told to any? To whom am I to say 'Rescue me!' When I am near I dread separation; when I am separated I have no patience to endure pain. I know no captive like myself, nor any standby but God. God, rescue my suppliant heart! for I have none but you in the world."

6. See n. 7, p. 138.

Rāmīn bemoaned his wounded heart and only increased his distress by anxiety. Sweet sleep had carried off his lover and filled the pillow with pomegranate blossom and hyacinths. Rāmīn heard the King's shout from the seraglio, for he had become aware of that stratagem and ploy. You would have sworn fire had suddenly poured into his heart; he roused his sweetheart from her sweet sleep.

He said to her, "My fair-faced love, arise! The disaster we sought to avoid is upon us! You fell into sweet sleep from drunkenness; but thank heaven for the wakefulness and anxiety of Rāmīn! I was lost in grief at the thought of being parted far from you; my heart had cut off hope from my very soul; there was I thus fearful and trembling on account of one disaster; but yet another even worse has befallen us! The shouting and commotion the King is setting up has reached my ears and quite severed sense from my heart. My heart tells me at this moment: 'Draw your foot once and for all out of the mire! Go down and sever his head from his body, and free the world from this wretch!' I swear that this brother's blood is of as little consequence to me as the blood of a gnat!"[7]

Vīs answered him and said, "Do not be overhasty! Pour on the fire a dash of the water of reason! When your distress comes to an end on the appointed day, your desire will be attained without bloodshed."

Then like a wild ass leaping from the lion she quickly came down from the roof of the pavilion. See what a fine artifice she practiced! She quickly slipped into the seraglio; the King was still drunk from wine; the jasmine-bosomed beauty went to his bedside and sat down.

She said to him, "You have hurt my hand from clutching it and pressing it so; take the other hand for a time and then take it where you will." When the King heard the voice of the idol-faced beauty he was unaware of her redoubtable ruse; he let fall the Nurse's hand from his and released that harlot from the net of shame.

The King said to jasmine-bosomed Vīs, "My fair one, why were you silent so long? Why did you not answer when I called you, but instead flippantly placed my heart on the fire?" Once the Nurse had escaped from the trap of distress, Vīs of the face like the moon became emboldened. She began crying out, "Alas for me! Year in,

7. *G:* "of a cat."

year out I am in the hands of enemies! Even though I go on the straight path I am like a twisting snake; the stamp of crookedness is on all my goings. I wish a jealous husband on no woman, for a jealous husband is ever on the lookout for trouble! I do no more than lie in bed with my husband, who enjoys his every desire, and he blackens my name with disgrace!"

Shāh Moubad said to her by way of excuse, "Do not suspect me of being lacking in love, for you are my soul, and more than my soul, since you guide my soul to joy. What I did was done in drunkenness; why did I drink wine and not spearpoints? You served me overmuch wine at the banquet and by this generosity brought disaster on your own head. May I not live in prosperity if I have so much as a trace of suspicion of you! If I have done wrong, I crave excuse; have the grace to pardon a suppliant like me! Offenses emanate from the drunken in their foolishness; but when they seek pardon do not exact harsh justice from them! 'Wine stops up reason, as sleep closes the eye; excuse cleanses sin, as water garments!'"

When the King craved humble pardon, Vīs, the guilty one, deigned to become reconciled to him. It is ever thus in love, for the lover is ever the prey of humiliation. He craves excuse for his lover's sin; when it is not accepted his excuses are redoubled. Many a time have I seen a deer of the plain with a hunting lion groaning in front of it, or a brokenhearted master with his heart in the toils of love for a slave! Even though the lover may become a fierce lion, in love he assumes the nature of a fox. From the love in his heart his fury is damped; he does not dare to be furious with his lover. Everyone who does not know love well calls its captive a madman. Let none plant the sapling of love in their heart, for that crop will all too soon bear fruit in the form of disaster for them!

60.

MOUBAD RECEIVES TIDINGS OF THE ROMAN EMPEROR AND GOES TO WAR. Thus is the nature and way of the world; it is in feud with those of its own clay; it rejects the same person it summons and takes away everything it gives. Its bitter is ever partnered by its sweet, its blessing ever accompanied by curse; its night goes hand in hand with day, its ease with pain; its disaster with prosperity, odious fortune with riches; there is no happiness in it without grief, no triumph without wretchedness. Read this story of Vīs and Rāmīn and see the devious ways of the world therein! Sometimes it brought into play care, sometimes joy; now it was their friend, now their enemy.

No sooner had the King reconciled himself to Vīs than the Devil[1] fell into the midst, put out the lamp of love, and felled the tree of happiness by the root. King Moubad received tidings of the Emperor of Rome, how he had turned his heart away from the path of affection. Embarked on evil ways, he had assumed a new nature and raised his head above the sky in self-seeking, broken all established treaties, and imprisoned many subjects of Moubad. He had brought an army from Rome to Iran which had laid waste many prosperous localities. A mob of people invaded the King's hall, casting its dust on their heads; shouting and crying for help one and all, seeking redress for the injustice of fate.

The King resolved to go to war and root out every thorn from the garden of his realm. He sent letters to the kings and nobles and raised an army from every city. A host gathered in Marv so mighty that the plain of Marv was too narrow to hold it. The blare of the trumpet rose in his hall; the King, turned strategist, marched forth. The expedition became the autumn wind, Marv the garden; once the wind arose, neither garden nor blossoms remained.

As the King marched his army out, he remembered the matter of charming Vīs; how she adored Rāmīn, how her heart harmonized with his. He said to himself, "She has foolishly run away from me once and left me bereft of heart, patience, and lover; if she again flees thus she will shed my blood with the sword of separation. Better, then, to keep her fast this time, for I then suffered sore grief from searching for her. I cannot bear to face separation hereafter; the once I faced it was enough for me. 'Where a man is sagacious, how may a snake glide twice upon him out of its hole?' 'It is surely much easier to tie the knee of a camel than to seek the camel once it is lost!'"

1. Iblīs. *G* has Eshma (see n. 2, p. 54).

When he had thus pondered much in his heart he summoned Zard of glorious lineage and said to him, "Noble brother, equal of my soul and eyes! See, have you ever witnessed such deeds—or yet heard them of any man of experience—as Rāmīn has done me these many times, so as to render my heart weary of dear life? Year in, year out I burn on fire by the hand of Vīs, the Nurse, and my brother. They do not fear fetters or prison, they dread neither Hell nor God. I am helpless in the hands of this trio of sorcerers; no remedy for this pain is forthcoming. What may one do with these three demons, who know neither shame nor fear? Who shamelessly do everything they please, without fear of losing reputation; because of these three my fortunes are in ruins, my days black; distress upon my soul, visitation upon my house and home; because of them I am sore at heart and racked with pain, prostrate and wretched. Although I am King of Kings of the world, I know of none more helpless than I; what is the point of lordship and kingship if my fortunes are black as pitch? I mete out justice to all in the world, but suffer a hundred varieties of injustice from my own fortune! Warriors who have broken the ranks of the enemy[2] have been put in their place by me—and now one woman puts me in my place!

"All the injustice I suffer arises from my heart, which throws its lot in with my enemy because of being a lover. The world seeks to denigrate me since it lusts after blood to fill its cup! The face of my reputation has gone black with a hundred shames; not even the water of a hundred rivers will wash the corrosion from it. On the one hand, my wife treats with my enemy; the sun of my reputation is clouded by her; on the other, my brother has sprung an ambush on me; he has drawn the dagger in feud against my life; he is ever watching an opportunity to step in like an enemy and murder me. I do not know what will be the end of my affairs, or what Fate purposes to do with me. I ponder so much on this day and night that you would swear I had no soul left in me. Why seek an enemy a hundred parasangs away when the enemy is right under my nose in my own house? Why seek a pretext for shutting the door when the water rises from within my own house? I have fallen in old age into affliction such as to banish the world from my thoughts. Now I have

2. *G:* "Goliath heroes."

to go to war and leave Vīs here whether I like it or not; she will penetrate even iron walls and brass bars to gain sight of Rāmīn.

"I know of only one recourse, to take Rāmīn with me to war and leave Vīs sorrowing here imprisoned in the castle of Ishkaft e Dīvān.[3] Once Rāmīn is on the march and Vīs imprisoned, they will find no way of coming together. But I shall entrust the castle to you; you must exercise constant vigilance; my heart relies on you, for you are vigilant in every task. There is no need for me to tell you what to do; but above all, be on your guard; guard these two witches in that castle from the wiles and stratagems of ingenious Rāmīn! I shall travel two hundred stages and increase my fame by glorious exploits; should Rāmīn find his way to Vīs by stratagem, all the fame I am questing after will be turned to shame. Even though two hundred people build houses, it only takes one to crack them asunder! I have in my house three sorcerers, who are as good as three armies in devising stratagems! If a thousand armies of demons confronted them, these three sorcerers would get the better of them by their spells! They have bound me, as you see, and broken the hope of happiness in my heart. They have torn by trickery the garment of patience on my body and disgracefully rent the veil of my good name. No drowning man in the raging sea suffers a third of the evil I have suffered at their hands!"

When Zard heard these words, he said to him, "You who are in wisdom higher than the moon! Do not lay this burden of care on your heart, for care makes a man sick. What is a mere woman, after all, that you should lament about her with bloodstained tears? Even though she be as accomplished in sorcery as Ahriman, no one is more feeble than she in my hand. Not so much as a breeze shall find its way to her, nor sun and moon shine on her cheeks. She shall not see in that fortress so much as a human soul till you return from the war. I shall guard that idol sorceress as a miser his coins. I shall ever count her as precious as noble men their guests."

Then the King straightway departed with seven hundred heroes and took Princess Vīs to the fortress.

3. See n. 1, p. 160.

61.

KING MOUBAD TAKES VĪS TO THE CASTLE OF ISHKAFT E DĪVĀN.[1]

The castle of Ishkaft stood on a great mountain; no mountain, but rather a mansion of the heavens! Its rock was hard as anvils; no storm made the slightest impression upon it. So wide was it that it was half the world; so high that it was a pillar of the heavens. At night its bluff was like a candle; moon and stars the fire at its top. Up on its top men rubbed shoulders with the moon and shared the secrets of the heavens.

When the King brought captivating Vīs to the castle he added a second moon[2] to the sky. The castle took the form of a stone censer. See what a wonderful picture it made! In the censer the cheeks of Vīs were the fire; her charming mole the ambergris thereon. The castle was made as blooming as a spring garden by that Moon worthy to be a prize in castle walls! Jasmine-bosomed Vīs sat with the Nurse: five doors locked upon her by the King. He sealed all the doors with his own seal and entrusted the seals to his brother. The doors of a hundred treasures were open to Vīs; provision for two hundred years was laid up therein. In the castle was every desire her fortunes might require, save union with her lover and sight of Rām.

When the King had completed the dispositions at the castle he came to Marv and made preparation for the march. The army he had was like a mountain of iron; even its least distinguished knight was better than Bēzhan.[3] Every man marched laughing and merrymaking save Rāmīn who was weeping and lamenting. From the torment of burning love he had fallen into a fever, like a partridge that a hawk has clutched in its talons; the dust of grief settled on his cheek, the hope of union broken in his heart. His dear soul itself had become as nothing to his body; silk and brocade become like thorns under him. He knew no peace by day nor rest by night, laid low as

1. "Devils' Gully." Minorsky, *Iranica*, p. 168, points out that some artificial grottoes (of supposed Buddhist origin) in the hilly reaches of the Murghāb River are now known as *dīvkan*, "dug by the demons." The dramatic landscape of this area fits well the description here.
2. *G:* "another sun."
3. See n. 5, p. 136.

he was at the mercy of his enemies and frustrated of his desire. His vitals were full of barbs, his heart of wounds.

He said secretly to his heart: "What love is this that will never grow less? My heart does not have pleasure in it for so much as a day! Since I have made acquaintance of love, the eye of my fortune does not see light. Bad enough that at other times it jabbed thorns into my heart; this time it has shot an arrow with poisoned barb! The sweetheart, without whom there is neither patience nor peace in my body, has vanished from my eyes. I have been guilty of faithlessness in love, for when I witnessed the day of separation from her I did not die! I must indeed have a heart of stone and be made of very iron, that I can bear to see the world without her! If my body is to be deprived of the face of my love, it is better that it should be deprived of life too! What plight, my friend, do you know worse than that death should be sweeter to me than life? If my love may not be with me, far preferable for there to be no life in my body! I desire dear life for the sake of my love, just as I desire my eyes only for seeing her. Now that I have become deprived of my love through my fate I have no further call for life and eyes!" As he thus lamented his inharmonious fate, he began another song to his heart:

"My heart, if you are a lover, heave a sigh; for there is no judge for the injustice of desire. Who in the world has mercy on lovers? Who has mercy on others' pain? If I moan, I moan with justice—for they have cut off the sapling of my happiness. They have taken my sun away from me and rubbed my wound with salt through separation from her. Now shed your bloodstained flood, my eyes; for what day is it that you husband your blood? I shall never again see woe like this: right enough that my tears should be only of blood! If you have rained blood before in grief, it is right that this time you should rain my life forth! The face of the world is renewed by rain; why is my face withered through rain? The fire of tribulation has melted my heart, brought it to my eyes, and run it down my golden cheeks. Though weeping is not fit for men, it is for me, in separation from such a lover."

161

When the King made his way back from the castle, Rāmīn learned of the plight of Vīs: grief was added to his grief, pain to his pain, the dust of separation settled on his yellow cheek. Rain fell from his eyelashes like the Flood and washed the dust of separation from his sallow face. He sang moving words such as are appealing to a lover:

"I am he who is brokenhearted, far from his love: wounded by fortune and abhorring his heart. Since a beauty fit to be guarded in a castle became my lover, I have become like one imprisoned in a brazen castle. Take my message to the sweetheart, breeze, say, 'I have a hundred brands upon my heart because of you; your vision remains in my sight, as your speech remains in my memory. The one has erased sleep from my eyes, the other torn the world from my memory.

"'Though I were made of iron, I could not persevere in this affliction so as to see your face again. If my pain could be divided, not a single soul would remain in the world without pain. The pain of helplessness has so reduced me that death is better for me than life. When shall I be released from this pain, for you are my cure, and you are cut off from me?'"

When Rāmīn fell into such a sore plight he became like a thread from threnody and like a cane from complaining.[4] Even his sworn enemy had mercy on him when he saw his face. Within a week he was so altered by his sickness that his silver arrow had become a golden bow. Fallen prostrate and ailing in his litter, he came with the King as far as Gurgān. Such was his sorry state that he had abandoned hope of this world; you would have sworn he had the poison of arrowheads in his vitals!

The nobles went before the King and told him all his plight. They said to him in entreaty: "Lord, Rāmīn is your brother and son; you will not find a knight like him in the world, nor another so renowned in every art; everyone stands in need of a younger brother such as he: for many a heart's desire may be secured by his hand. You may know that a brother like him beside you is better than a host of

4. Wordplay in the Persian here.

armies! Your enemies' teeth are blunted by his hand, for he is a raging lion and a furious elephant.[5] Let it be that you were hurt by him one day: you have now pardoned him and reconciled yourself to him; do not now irritate old sores anew; forbear to snap this blossoming branch through rancor! For he is within an inch of death; of his mountain hardly so much as a wisp of straw remains. Spare his life this once more, and do not command him to perform this journey. Travel is unpleasant at the best of times even in health; just think how it must be in pain and weakness! Leave him to rest for a month, for he is much tired by the trials of the march. Once his pain has subsided a little, let him go to Khurāsān, by your leave. Perhaps that climate and city will restore him, for this country is as poison, that as antidote!"

When the King heard these words from the nobles, he left noble Rāmīn in Gurgān. Once the King departed, Rāmīn rested and purged all pain from his members. His saffron became once again Judas blossom, his stature which had been like a bow became like a swaying cypress. Desire of the sight of his love fell upon him, like fire in his heart and an arrow in his breast. He left the city of Gurgān riding alone, mounted on a fleet horse of Tukhār[6] swift as the wind. All the way he sang like a nightingale, trilling manifold songs and divers modes:

"My love, I do not wish life without you, nor ease, nor this world's desire; as I seek you I shall fear no enemy, though the whole world be my enemy. Even if all my road be snakes, if there be a hundred iron walls on it, all its water be the haunt of crocodiles, all its mountains the lair of leopards, the grass on its plains swords, their sand like tigers and lions, its wind a simoom, its cloud a thunderbolt, nothing but swords raining on my head from the cloud, the dust of its wind arrowheads, the rain of its clouds stones, I swear by your life that I shall not turn back from the road; if I do so, I am no knight. If sight of you is to be had in fire, I shall put my seeing eyes into fire. If union with you is to be had in the jaws of a lion, I shall engage him in dialogue

5. *G:* also "a strong castle."
6. *I.* See n. 2, p. 55, and p. 278.

with my sword. The way to union with you will be short for me, a three months' journey will be only a step. What though there be a sword in the path and Venus and the moon turn to spear-point and arrow?"

62.

VĪS LAMENTS RĀMĪN'S DEPARTURE. When Vīs learned of Rāmīn's departure, the morning became as night in her eyes. Separation poured saffron on her Judas blossom, her eyelids scattered jewels on amber. Parting practiced the goldsmith's craft on her cheeks, but the jeweler's in her eye. Smiting her patterned hands on her face, she turned her fresh pomegranate blossom to violets. Her garments were blue like those in mourning; her cheeks ruby-red like tulip beds. So cruelly did she smite her patterned hands on her cheek, so many bloodstained tears did she shed on her garments, that separation robbed her of her gorgeous coloring, making her cheeks like her garments, and them like her cheeks.

She ever bemoaned her loneliness away from her mate, and said to the Nurse as she moaned bitterly, "I have sacrificed my youth to loverhood, my life to love for my sweetheart. I fancied that we would always be together and enjoy every desire the heart might cherish; destiny has broken the bonds between us, separation has rent the veil upon us: my sweetheart, whilst you were in my embrace my bed was sweet with delicious sleep; now that you have filled my bed with thorns and woken me from that sweet sleep, since you have made my eye sleepless from grief and filled my breast with running blood, my heart is afraid early and late that you will perforce undertake war against the foe; that the sun will blaze upon your face like the moon, dust settle on your black locks; in place of a crown you will put on helmet and mail; and take up the bow in place of the lute and cup; you will put on armor in place of silk and brocade; and it will chafe those fair limbs of yours; even as you have shed my blood with your onyx eye you will spill the blood of enemies with the dagger. Why did I not listen to all you said? Why did I not go with you when you departed? Perhaps the dust of your road might have settled on me, made musky by those black locks. My heart is your companion on the road, wounded by separation and bathed in blood. Guard your companion on the road, forbear to wound it more than you have already done; fair actions are meet from the fair; it is proper to treat lovers with affection. Treat me, you with the bloodthirsty face, as befits the sun of your countenance; remember me and ponder my plight; shall not a rich man take thought for a beggar? You saw how it was with me in the smoke of love; now fire has arisen from the smoke. After this separation, so dread and long, any pain seems mere play in my eyes. What Flood is this, pray, that has overtaken my soul whereby the Oxus itself flows from my eyes? My heart is like a letter full of distress and pain, whose superscription is this yellow face! See how much lamentation the letter contains, for there is a river of blood across its superscription!"

When Vīs lamented sorely in her pain and writhed in great distress like a snake, the Nurse's heart burned for the beauty; she counseled her nothing but patience and said to her, "Be patient, for in the end he who is patient will attain his desire. All your care and distress will come to an end and happiness grow from the seed of patience. Although for the desperate it is much more difficult to be patient than to drink poison, yet be patient, and hearken to your nurse's counsel: for bitter patience[1] shall bear you sweet fruit. Who but God knows your remedy? He can deliver you from these toils. Keep calling the Creator to your aid, persevere in noble action toward all. It may be that God will take your hand to help you, and the fire of your enemy suddenly go out. I can tell you only this by way of advice, for I know no remedy but patience." Captivating Vīs replied to her. "How can one be patient in the fire? Treat me more charitably than this; do not tender me advice; your walnut will not balance on this dome! My lover has departed without so much as bidding me farewell; what is the difference between this advice and a bridge on the farther side of a river? My heart and yours are not alike: only the hem of your garment blazes—but my very soul! What is it to you that I writhe in anguish? 'People's pain is of no account to others!' You tell me, 'Patience is your remedy.' How very easy it is for the onlooker to put his best foot forward! You are exempt, for you are like one on horseback who has no inkling of the tribulations of those on foot! You are a veritable Korah in patience, and I indigent; in the eye of

1. Persian ṣabr, which also means "aloe."

the replete, the hungry are like the drunken; thus are you, Nurse, in relation to me: well may you choose patience on my behalf! But once abandon you desperate, as I am, and you would lament even more than I throughout the world! You sit on the sidelines and require patience of me; but will you kindly tell me how I am to be patient without heart? If a ravening lion has no heart, even the fox will worst him on the plain! Surely you cannot think it right that such a bloodstained flood should rain from my eyes? No one seeks his own ill fortune; no wise man courts suffering for himself! You have dug this pit of ill fortune before me and have pitchforked me into it with a hundred wiles; now here you are sitting at your ease at the edge of the pit, babbling 'Call on God for help!' It is easy enough to fling a rug into water—but not quite so easy to fetch it out again!''

63.

RĀMĪN COMES TO VĪS AT THE CASTLE OF ISHKAFT E DĪVĀN. When Rāmīn came from Gurgān to Marv, the garden of happiness was empty of rose and cypress. In the seraglio he failed to find the figure of Vīs, that heavenly cypress with the blooms of a garden about it. He did not see the pavilion of the palace rosy from her face, nor the hall musky from her hair. The place, for all its glory and beauty, was like a dungeon to his eyes without his sweetheart. You would have sworn that garden and hall, like Rāmīn, were weeping for that idol. When Rāmīn saw the abode of the lover bereft of the lover, he became like a pomegranate with its husk split. His eyes rained down pomegranate seeds like drops of wine trickling from a cup. He mourned over that garden and hall, and rubbed his fair face in its soil:

"Palace, you are the same happy palace where that idol was the pet partridge; you were the heaven and the fair your stars; even the East gazed spellbound at them. A lute sounded in your every chamber, a beauty singing a song to it. In your throne room were tried champions, in your hall wild asses fit to grace a banquet. Now I miss in you that chatelaine from whom moon and stars rose: your champions and wild asses are gone from their places, you have lost all those men at arms and horses white and bay. You are not the palace I saw, you resemble nothing so much in the world as Rāmīn; the world is a sorcerer, plying its own devices and following its own will; it has robbed you of your happy days, and Rāmīn of the days of success. Alas for those days that are gone when I had my fill of desire and joy! Never again, I fear, shall I see you happy and myself seated upon your throne!"

When he had sung much in this strain and become desperate of seeing the face of that world-illumining sun, he came out of the gate sighing and set his face to Ishkaft e Dīvān. The desert, salt waste, and weary road were in his eyes like rose plot and jasmine bed; it was night when he reached the castle; night, however, became the means of his seeing his lover.

Cunning Rāmīn knew whereabouts his love would be in that castle; he made for the spot where she was and gave a signal of his presence in the dark night. There was no archer like him in the wide world; no warrior as courageous; he put a four-feathered arrow to the bowstring and let it fly from the thumbstall like a flash of lightning. He said to it, "Fortunate flying bird, you are my messenger to the beloved! You carry elsewhere the message of separation; this once carry from me the message of union!"

The arrow sped just as he desired and landed on the roof of the sun of the fair. It descended through the roof into her chamber and settled on her lion-footed couch. When the Nurse saw that propitious arrow settled on the couch of Vīseh, she quickly leapt to her feet and picked it up; in her joy she thought the dark night day.

She took it to captivating Vīs and said to her, 'See this fortunate arrow! It is a messenger from noble Rāmīn, sprung from his brazen bow! for it bears the glorious badge of Rāmīn and gains its good fortune therefrom. An angel has visited Ishkaft e Dīvān;[1] this dark hall has become bright from its radiance! The sun of good fortune has risen and has taken away from us the night of distress and suffering. Hereafter you will dwell amid the very desire of your heart and experience nothing but joy and your heart's dearest wish." When

1. Ishkaft e Dīvān being in Persian "Devils' Gully" (see n. 1, p. 160).

Vīseh saw the arrow of her lover, his name inscribed on it as badge,[2] she kissed her lover's name a thousand times; laid it now on her cheek, now on her heart. Now she said, "Fortunate arrow of Rāmīn, more precious to me than my very eyes! You are a greeting from that hand and generous palm; may they encircle my neck forever! I shall set your point in ground ruby, and your notch in unground pearls; I have a heart wounded by separation from Rāmīn; I have in it a hundred arrows like you, and more: but from the moment you have reached me, you have plucked all the arrowpoints from my heart. I have seen no barbed arrow like you; nor ever message so welcome as the one you bear."

When Rāmīn shot his flying arrow the host of the demon of anxiety attacked him; he said, "O Lord, where has my arrow gone now? Has my desire been fulfilled or not? Had Vīs become apprised of my plight she would have found a way to me by a hundred devices." Then he said to his heart,

"Risk your life, my heart, and fear no enemy! By the God of the world, the moon and sun, by the heaven in which we place our hopes, I shall not retreat from this castle till the moment when I attain to my desire. Even were its wall of iron, forged in fire like my heart, around it venomous fatal scorpions full of poison, ever leaping at men like arrows, the garrison all sorcerers, with claws of lightning and arms like mountains, even though its battlements were crawling with snakes spelling hurt to mortals, my heart would still in valor seek a way into it, and break down its doors and walls. My heart would not fear even those magic snakes, through the fortune of God and the strength of my right arm. I should rescue my sweetheart therefrom, Fate would prostrate itself before my dagger. Courage would kiss my hands, so much prowess and championhood would it witness in me. So long as dear life inhabits my body, keeping faith with Vīs shall be my quest. I shall not fear, even though I confront a whole world of warriors, enemies one and all like the King and Zard. I am Saturn,[3] even though they be proud;

2. Cf. *Tristan*, p. 235.
3. See n. 1, p. 63.

I am the sea, even though they be fire. Save at the time of showing mettle we are of one clay; everyone knows good from inferior!"

Here was Rāmīn lost in anxiety, there Vīs caught in the trap. Her tongue from love repeating, "Rām, Rām!"; her soul in passion seeking Rām.

The cunning Nurse said, "Soul of your mother! Fortune is your mate, the Sphere your helper; as your good fortune will have it, it is now the month of cold; the world is all like a frozen river. Now because of the winter cold the guard sits trembling in his sentry box;[4] there will be no sentry now on the roof; your desire will be triumphantly realized. Since there is no sentry on the roof to trouble you, your cause will triumph at last; for Rāmīn is close by us, although in the dark he cannot be seen. He knows where we are in the castle and that we sit in the King's apartments. He has often been in this castle with the King and knows two hundred ways up every stone in it. Now there is a hothouse with hollow interior, with a door in it facing the castle wall; open its door and light its fire; show a day to Rāmīn in the midst of night; for as soon as he glimpses the light his heart will be freed from anxiety. He will come speeding from the plain up the wall, and I shall then contrive some means of hoisting him up."

The Nurse spoke thus and then did accordingly; by artifice she placed a demon in thrall to her ring. When Rāmīn saw the light and fire, a captivating Moon by the fire, he realized where the room was and what his sweetheart meant by the fire; when he saw the crest of the mountain golden from the fire, he came rushing from the plain up onto the mountain. No mountain sheep would have ventured onto that spot; you would have said a winging bird had grown legs!

Thus is the heart in love; it cries out neither at tribulation nor at loss! When it takes the road to union with its love, it is ready to take the cares of the whole world upon its soul! It counts the length of a journey as short and a fierce lion as a fox. The desert is like a palace and rose plot to it; the palace like a field of lilies; what is it to it

4. *G:* "twice only the sentinels have made their rounds."

whether it beholds a swamp swarming with lions or a garden full of peacocks? What does it matter whether a river comes before it or a stream? a mountain range or a hair? Desire lends it such courage that you would swear it were weary of the world! There is no readier customer for desire than the heart; thus it is that there is no controlling anyone's heart; it purchases desire at the price of peace of heart and soul and prides itself on having found a bargain! Desire does not know bad from good; thus it is that reason terms desire "blind." Had desire had the illumination of sight, it would not have jumped at buying any evil.

When Rāmīn approached the wall closely Vīseh saw him from the top; they let down to brokenhearted Rāmīn forty pieces of Chinese brocade tied together, folded in double thickness very firmly; he scaled it like a falcon. When he climbed up into the castle its roof looked as if the moon and Venus were in conjunction; milk and wine mingled in a single cup; lily and rose came into the same garden. Gold and gems were mixed together; musk and ambergris compounded in one. The world mixed together nectar and rose water; you would have sworn love and beauty embraced. The dark night grew radiant and bright; the month of December became like the season of the rose garden. The hearts of two lovers rested from lamentation; the lips of two desperate ones were rubbed by kisses; two lovers with faces like brocade, fair as Farkhār and Noushād,[5] entwined together like cypress and boxtree. The two went happily into the pavilion[6] and took the golden wine bowl in their silvery hands. They threw the load of separation from their backs and, with wine, watered the field of love with nectar. Now they delighted coral with kisses; now recalled the events of the past. Now Rāmīn would recount his wretchedness from the pain of love and his sickness; now Vīseh would recount all the evil done to her by Shāh Moubad.

It was a December night; the world wrapped in black, become

5. See n. 6, p. 37, and n. 9, p. 97.
6. Cf. the Cave of Lovers, *Tristan*, p. 261; with Devils' Gully, the name of the castle here, cf. *ibid.*: "the cavern had been hewn into the wild mountain in heathen times, when giants ruled there." The whole episode here resembles the passage in *Tristan*. See n. 1, p. 160.

like a demon from the moon down to the Fish.[7] Three kinds of fire burned from three places: roses were scattered in the pavilion by them: one from the fireplace of the room, with tongues of flame like a coral cypress; another blazing from the cup of wine, its cheerfulness like the fortunes of the lucky: the third fire blazed from the faces of Vīs and Rāmīn, their musky locks playing the part of the smoke of the fire. Three pure-hearted friends sat together, the door of the pavilion barred like rock. No fear of an enemy finding them out and the road to joy and pleasure being barred; no fear of being separated tomorrow and exiled from each other's face. One such night is better than a whole life otherwise. How joyous was their union on that night! When Rāmīn saw the face of charming Vīs and beheld such a moment corresponding with his dearest desire, he sang a sweet song to the lute with a voice that would have laid waste the heart of a Hūrī:

"What if you have suffered distress, lover? endured affliction and undergone frustration? You will not gain happiness by ease; ncr fame without tribulation. Though you have traversed the sea in separation from your lover, you have gained the pearl in union with her. My heart, though you have suffered distress in separation, you have now eaten the fruit of your distress. Did I not tell you 'Practice patience, for nearness is the upshot of of distance? The end of winter is Nourūz, as day is the end of dark night. The longer you wander in the desert of separation, the greater the joy of union. The more you contrive in your plight the greater your joy when you gain your desire.' I have escaped from the fire of Hell, have become an angel and sit with Hūrīs. Your face makes my dwelling a garden, flowers bud there in December by the presence of your cheeks. I planted constancy, and it has brought up joy for me; the gleaming moon has bowed in love toward me. I preferred constancy to every other course, thus it is that the world has been constant to me!"

When charming Vīs heard these words she filled the cup to toast her lover; like a narcissus she had the golden cup in hand; she rose

7. See n. 2, p. 17.

from her place like a gliding boxtree. She said, "This is full to toast the love of heroic Rāmīn, loyal, constant, rewarded with constancy: more than sovereignty to my hope, more than light to my eyes. My heart lives more in hope of him than the denizens of the earth in hope of the sun. Till I die I shall be in the thrall of his love and shall worship loyalty to him. Even though I were to toast him in fatal poison it would become nectar for my soul and medicine for my heart."

Then Vīs drank the bowl full of wine, a hundred kisses from Rāmīn in its train. Every time she drank a cup of wine she tasted the sugar of kisses as dessert! How sweet it is to drink wine alone with the sweetheart; to caress the musky locks of the darling with the lips! When Rāmīn drank wine he drew her lips to him and after the wine tasted wine-colored sugar. Now he slept drunken in the lover's embrace, amidst musk, silver, pomegranate, and pomegranate blossom. Thus for nine months Rāmīn had before him bitter cornelian wine with sweet rubies; the cornelian brought him the treasure of drunkenness, as the rubies smoothed away the pain of languor. The cornelian flashed from the golden bowl, the rubies smiled next the Pleiades. He took his pleasure every night till dawn; his arms full of roses and his pillow graced with the moon. At dawn they rose from rest and set their hands to the cup in wassailing. When Vīseh took up the cup of wine her lover sang a sweet song:

"Wine of fair hue scours corrosion from the heart; gorgeously tinted wine restores color to the cheek. Desire is pain, and wine its cure; cares are dust, and wine the rain to lay them. If there be care, wine steals it away; if happiness, wine increases it. Where care dwells, wine burns it away; where happiness, it illuminates it. Today my fortune is secure: my lover by my side, my lot as fair as herself. Now I am amid lily and rose, now drunk amid musk and hyacinth. My lip hunts wine-colored sugar, a wine-colored rose blooms in my garden.[8] Fortune has made my steed swift, mighty in coursing after desire. I am the hawk whose flight is high, my prey a charming sun; I do not

8. With this passage cf. Introduction, p. xvii.

172

care to capture pheasant and partridge, my prey is none other than the radiant full moon. My joy like a lion with brazen claws has captured a silver wild ass to its heart's desire. I have slipped from my head the halter of wisdom and stepped into the bazaar of pleasure. My cup is not idle for a moment, my desire never at peace for an instant. All year I glean from the cheek, locks, and lip of my love roses, musk, and sugar by the pannierload. Now that I have her radiant face, I have no need of the moon; now that I have the sweet scent of her locks, I have no need of musk. This place is the highest heaven for me: for a Hūrī is my companion therein. The sun has become my courtier, the moon my cupbearer; why then should I not take wine early and late?" Then he said to jasmine-bosomed Vīs, with words far sweeter than sugar, "Bring, my Moon, the cup of rosy nectar; red as your face and propitious as union with you; we shall never have a happier time than this nor see blossom fairer than this in your face; why should we not be carefree and rejoice in the day of happiness? Come, let us bide joyfully and see what may come on the morrow! Come, let us snatch this day, for never shall such a day return! Neither do you wish separation from my face, nor I deliverance from your love! Thus is constancy and love, thus happiness and life! If God has decreed it thus, we have no choice but to suffer his decree! They placed you in bonds and prison, left me sick in Gurgān; since God has wrought my destiny upon you, he has placed me in the heavens at your side. Who could do this but a Creator who needs no helper in any enterprise?"

Then they remained thus for nine months, in joy and pleasure early and late.[9] Now drunk, now full of languor; even so much as to rest was a trial. Provender for a hundred years and more was laid up for them; they needed nothing from outside. They enjoyed fulfillment of every desire and plucked the thorn of separation from their hearts. Rāmīn did not become weary of pleasuring, nor did Vīs become sated of enjoyment and desire. Two bodies in love like one; no task but eating, drinking, and sleeping! Now the wine cup in

9. Cf. *Tristan*, p. 267.

hand, now the sweetheart in the embrace; joy of love in the heart, wine in the head. In their pleasuring they carried off the ball of love and tended the branch of life with wine. The door of the castle was shut and with it the door of care; the lid of the wine jar was broken and with it repentance. The three became partners in joy; what they did was hid from the world.

No enemy knew their secret save, in Marv, Zarrīngīs, daughter of the Khāqān.[10] In lineage, daughter of the princely Khāqān; in form, princess of the beauties of the land. Her face had become the sun of Beauty, her heart past mistress of sorcery. So skilled was she in sorcery that she could cause a tulip to blossom out of steel. When Rāmīn came suddenly back to Marv and went round the King's palace and garden, seeking Vīs everywhere in lamentation, bathing his face in bloodstained tears, neither could his eyes descry her face that was manna to the soul, nor his brain detect her perfume that inspired love; weeping and lamenting for the memory of Vīs he rushed like a madman to every nook and cranny. Then he quickly departed from Marv, leaving a trail of blood like the wounded. He twisted his reins from the desert road and sped off on the mountain track; you would have sworn he was a leopard seeking its mate, careering over that mountain ridge on the prowl; such a wilderness that the plain was a garden by its side; such a mountain that Sinai was a knoll beside it. Its declivities stretched down to Korah in Hell; its heights raised their heads up to the sky. Rāmīn was now in the well like Joseph, now above the moon like Jesus.

The sorceress Zarrīngīs knew that Vīs was the cure for Rāmīn's pain; that he was weeping and lamenting for Vīs, rushing like a madman amid mountain and pass; that he had set off on a long and hard road, and would not return till he had found his cure.

64.

KING MOUBAD COMES FROM ROME AND GOES TO VĪS AT THE CASTLE OF ISHKAFT E DĪVĀN. When the King became victorious

10. Khāqān, a Turkish title meaning "supreme monarch," is used in later Persian terminology of Turkish rulers and of the Emperor of China. Minorsky (*Iranica*, p. 179) suggests that the title is here being used retrospectively with regard to some neighbor of Iran.

on his expedition, he returned in triumph having gained his ambition; he had traversed all Armenia and Arrān and exacted hostages and tribute from Caesar. Kings were his vassals, he the overlord; he had become drunk both on sovereignty and on joy; heaven was the cushion of his crown and the mast of his standard; earth was the dais of his throne and the camp of his army. The surface of heaven had been cracked by his crown; mountains had become flat as the plain from his accouterments. He had enjoyed brilliance of his fortune and carried off the ball of sovereignty from kings. From every king and ruler there was at his court either a contingent or a hostage; he had imprisoned the kings of the world in triumph, as who should say, "I am the King of Kings."

When the King came to glorious Marv, mourning set in in place of banqueting; for he heard the words of Zarrīngīs, and his heart began to writhe in torment, his brain to cloud with smoke. For a long time he boiled as he sat from the rage in his heart, then leapt to his feet, sent couriers to the generals, and acquainted each one of impending departure. Then the drums rolled out at the court, giving great and small alike marching orders. The kettledrum rattled at the monarch's gate, as if to say, "Your Majesty, how can we make this long march?" The brazen trumpet began to wail for those two lovers up in Ishkaft e Dīvān; you would have sworn it knew Rāmīn's plight, how sweet life was about to become bitter for him. The King of Kings became overcome by wrath; he had conceived a desire to put Rāmīn to death. Half his army was not yet returned from the march; they had followed a weary road for a year. The remaining half, not yet having loosed their belts or doffed their helmets from the march, set off with him against their will and took the road for Ishkaft e Dīvān. One soldier would say, "Our march is not yet done, and now all this route march is in aid of Rāmīn!" Another, "We are always on the road to keep Rāmīn from Vīs!" Another, "Rāmīn is more of a curse to the King in his house than a hundred Khāqāns and Caesars."[1]

The King hastened on with his army, like cloud and wind over mountain and plain. The dust of the marching army stretched its head from earth to sky like a demon. The watchman peered from

1. *G* adds: "They said a thousand things."

his watchtower in the castle and saw the black cloud raised by the army and its dust. General Zard was suddenly told, "The King approaches in triumph." Shouting, din, and commotion arose in the castle as when the wind falls upon the trees. Without the general having received him, King Moubad strode into the castle hall, moving more swiftly than the arrow of Ārish,[2] his eyes become like two fires from the anger in his heart. When he saw the face of Zard in the hall, you would have sworn a tulip looked on a cold wind. He scowled in his anger at Zard, and said to him, "You who are the worst pain to my heart, may the Judge and Creator deliver me in this world from you two brothers! At the time of loyalty a dog is better than you; at least a dog is endowed with loyalty; you are not. When they compounded your clay I do not know under what star they did it. One of you is the equal of a demon in sorcery; the other the equal of an ass in stupidity! You are fit only to stand guard over oxen; how are you up to guarding Vīs from Rāmīn? I deserve all the pain I suffer for having posted an ox as warden of a castle! Here you are sitting outside with the door shut; while inside sits Rāmīn enjoying his heart's desire. Are you pleased with your handiwork? I must say you have taken enormous pains about my affairs! So stupid are you that you little know Rāmīn is secretly laughing at you; here you are sitting outside bawling, whilst he lounges indoors taking his pleasure! The whole world knows it, but you are the last to know. It is a travesty that such a position should be disgraced by a creature like you."

General Zard said, "Fortunate King, welcome from your propitious journey. Do not distress yourself by wild words; do not encourage Ahriman to make an inroad into you; you are a king and can say what is your sweet will about things known to you or otherwise. It is a proverb on the tip of the tongue in the seven climes, 'Kings know male falcons from female.' For kings are in a privileged position in regard to the rest of the world; they need not fear to say just what they will. Even though what you say may not be certain, who may dare to gainsay you? You arraign my soul for a sin to which I have had no means of access. You took Rāmīn from me;

2. An archer in Persian legend who shot an arrow to mark the frontier of Iran; cf. p. 252 and Avesta, Yasht VIII, 38. Minorsky, *Iranica*, p. 172. *Mb*, notes, p. 458.

176

how do I know what either you or he may have done? He was no bird to fly away from you and traverse the whole world in his flight; he was no arrow: how did he mount up to this castle? How pass through these closed doors? See your seals impressed on these doors, with the dust of a year on them. When you have a castle mounted on solid rock, with a brazen wall, iron locks and gold seals on it, sentries on guard over its every approach, guards posted on its every roof, even had Rāmīn known a thousand stratagems, how could he have opened doors like these? Who could ever credit that Rāmīn could open locks fastened like these? And even supposing that these closed doors had been opened, how could intact seals have been replaced upon them? Do not believe such a report, Your Majesty; set reason as judge over this notion. Do not speak words inadmissible in wisdom, that reason would not count as worth so much as a single grain."

The King said, "Zard, how long will you talk in this strain and make the locks of the doors your excuse? What is the point in fast and firm locks when you have failed to exercise prudence besides? In castles, alert sentries are worth any amount of locks and bolts; lofty as the wheeling sky is, God has nevertheless stationed the meteor as its sentinel. I shut the house in front of the hall; but behind there were chinks and ways of entry in ten places! What is the point in these locks, delightful as they may be in themselves? Without the trousers, they are no more than a trouser cord! Why do you waste effort on tying your trouser cord? It will hardly clothe you without the trousers! What is the point of my closing the doors and sealing them only to entrust them to a dimwit like you? You have in a moment turned all the fame I have amassed in a year into shame! My fame was a palace colored like a garden; you have blackened its doors and walls with shame." When he had expostulated with Zard for a while he drew from his leggings the key of the hall; he threw it to him and said, "Open the locks; for neither locks nor redoubt have served any purpose." The Nurse was forewarned by the scraping of the doors and heard the King's voice as he spoke. She ran like the wind to Princess Vīs and gave her tidings of the King of Marv. She said to her, "Here is Shāh Moubad come; an evil star has risen from the east. The lightning of injury has flashed from the cloud of grief; the flood of care has descended from the mountain of anger; now you shall see a furious dragon beside whom a very sorcerer will be lackluster; now you shall see a world-consuming fire by whose smoke day will be turned to night in the world."

When Vīs and the Nurse were at a loss for a remedy they lowered Rāmīn down the wall; he ran over the mountain like a mountain sheep, his soul full of dread and his heart of distress. Crying, desperate, bereft of patience and of his love, as he dashed over the mountain he said to his heart,

"Whatever do you want of me, Destiny, that you visit my fortune with nothing but destruction? You are ever on the lookout for a chance to contend with my fortune and shed my blood with the sword of separation. Now you visit my soul with cruelty, now invest my happy life with bitterness. The revolution of fate has become like an archer; separation is its arrow and my soul the target! My peace is that of a shattered caravan; my soul like a tribe dispersed. Only yesterday I was on a throne like a king; now I have become a wild sheep on the mountain ridges. I wail till the very rocks split in front of me; I cry till the snow goes the color of Judas blossom. The partridge cries with me at dawn; you would think it was taking the high part and I the low! Even thunder is not the equal of my cries, for it arises from smoke, they from fire. Even clouds are not the peer of my eyes; for they are mere drops, whilst here is a raging ocean. My lot, once happy, has become reduced to this! You would swear my heaven had become earth! Those happy days were the spring; and spring does not last long in the world."

After Rāmīn had wandered on the mountain tops for a time, his eyes from weeping like clouds on the mountains, you would swear that the grief of separation from his charming love nailed his legs down. He had no remedy but to sit and weep for a time over his heart and sweetheart. Wherever that faithful lover sat he made a stream flow with the tears of his eyes, singing in his loneliness such songs as those who essay love are wont to sing:

"My love, you do not know my plight, how bitter is my life without you. My sweetheart, my plight away from you is so sad that even a partridge in a snare would weep for me. I am wretched and brokenhearted, for I have no news of you. I do not know what anguish may have overtaken you, what tribulation your loving soul may have suffered. It is meet that I should suffer pain and hurt; but may you never endure any care! May my life be the sacrifice of your fair face, all my enemies a sacrifice before me. If I were to enumerate your several beauties, my life would end before I had done. If I weep, I do so rightly, for such a fair face has been separated from me. I beseech God with a hundred entreaties that I may live till I see you again. But left thus forlorn away from you I hardly think that I may live to see tomorrow!"

When charming Vīs was left separated from Rāmīn, you would have sworn she was left in a dragon's jaws. She ran madly about the seraglio, smiting a rose plot with her silvery hands. Now she plucked roses from her gorgeously tinted face, now hyacinths from her black locks. The world became full of musk and ambergris from her hair, the air full of smoke and fire from her sighs. As she heaved burning sighs from her heart she rapidly tore ambergris-scented hair from her head. Round her the castle of Ishkaft became like a censer, a fire in it of musk and ambergris. She constantly beat her breast with her fists without mercy and made a hot flow of blood run from her eyelashes. Her heart was like molten iron and brass, which scatter sparks when they are hammered. Not only was a flood of jewels flowing from her eyes, but the necklace of jewels was snapped from her neck; the ground became like the sky from them, with jewels upon it like flashing stars. She tore from her body the gold-woven garments like spring blossom and put on instead the black garb of mourning. Heart full of pain, face covered in dust, she forgot both Moubad and Zard. All her distress was because of her sweetheart, for she had become parted from him all of a sudden against her will.

When Shāh Moubad entered the seraglio, he saw her face, like a garden, scored; but also forty pieces of embroidered woven cloth, tied tightly together like a rope, lay in front of Vīs, the knots not yet untied from them. The Nurse, the cause of the calamity, hid from the King. Princess Vīs sat in the dust, clothes rent and arms scored.

Her tresses like a lasso torn from her head, the silken garments cast from her breast, dust of the earth all thrown on her head, two rivers of blood flowing from her eyes.

The King said, "Vīs, spawn of the demons! Curses be upon you in both worlds! You fear neither men nor God; you shrink neither from fetters nor from prison; my counsel and advice are wasted on you, as my bonds and prison are as naught in your eyes.[3] Will you not tell me what I am to do with you? What is meet other than to put you to death? From the multitude of stratagems and spells that are in your head, what is the difference to you between mountain and castle, plain and steppe? Should you mount to the sky with these abominable ways, the stars themselves would become your accomplices. There is no point in wounds or admonition where you are concerned, nor in undertakings or covenants or oaths. I have tried you heretofore in many ways; how many rewards and retributions have I not meted out! You neither become cowed by my rewards nor do you shrink from my retributions. Perhaps you are a wolf noxious to all, or a demon that has turned its back upon good; to outward view a perfect jewel, inwardly like a broken potsherd! You resemble the soul in beauty and delicacy, but the world in treachery and faithlessness. What a tragedy that this fair face and form should be marred by such a legion of faults! I have practiced much consideration toward you in my heart, have spoken much in secret and openly; do not so, Vīs, do not hurt me thus: for this injury shall be the means of your destruction. You foolishly sowed the seed of ignominy, and now the seed you sowed has borne fruit; I shall not cherish hope of your love further, even were you the moon and sun themselves; I shall not henceforth seek to be considerate to you; for your faults have one and all become plain. In my eyes you were the moon, but you have become a snake; from the lowness you have practiced you have become low. I shall no further seek your love; I am not iron, stone, or brass. How does the day I spend with you differ from a picture I write on water? Or the advice I reel off to you from seed I scatter on salt ground? Should a wolf ever evince a talent for being a shepherd, loyalty and love might be evinced by you!

3. With this passage cf. *Tristan*, p. 259.

180

Even though you be nectar, I have become sated of you; I have planted the sapling of patience in my heart.

"Since I have not had joy of you and have tasted only bitterness from the sight of you, I shall repay you in the same coin and break oath with you as you have done with me. I shall make you so weary of dear life that you will not so much as think of Rāmīn. Neither will Rāmīn have joy of you nor will so much as the memory of him remain in your heart. He will not take up harp and lute before you, nor will you sit by him drunk or drowsy. Neither will he play the lute to you, nor will you titillate his heart with flirtation. I swear I shall bring such anguish upon your souls that even adamantine rock will weep for you both. So long as you engage in a love affair you are the worst of my enemies; every time you make love you do no less than plot against my life. Now I shall turn the tables on you and rid my heart of my enemy once and for all.

"If I am endowed with counsel and sage heart, why do I keep two enemies in my house? 'How does a man who has an enemy within his doors differ from one in whose path a lion sleeps?' 'What is the difference between a man whose watchman is an enemy and one who has a snake in his collar?'"

Then he approached Princess Vīs and took hold of both her musky locks; he dragged her from the lion-footed couch and trailed her through dust and ashes, twisted her crystal arms and hands and tied her hands behind her back like a thief, then he lashed her so fiercely with a whip on back, haunches, breast, and thighs that her limbs became like a split pomegranate, blood dripping from them like pomegranate seeds; the blood oozed from her silvery limbs like wine trickling from a crystal cup. Vermilion rose upon her camphor body like ruby and garnet out of a silver mountain; her body was in many places the color of indigo from bruises; blood like the source of the Nile[4] flowed from the indigo. The blue with red in its midst was for all the world like a tulip bed amid Judas blossom.

Then he chastised the Nurse even more sorely, for her wounds were all on the back and head. He struck her so savagely as to beat her to death, or at any rate teach her a lesson by those blows. Vīs and the Nurse fell senseless, their limbs covered in purple, like garnets

4. Persian *nīl* means both "Nile" and "indigo."

coating silver, or mallow flower sprinkled on lilies. No one knew whether they would survive to con again the book of fate.

Then he flung them both into a chamber and resigned himself to the death of both. He shut the chamber door fast upon them: all in the world were sore at heart at their pain. Then he removed Zard from within the gates and chose a successor for him from among the warriors.

Then in a week he traveled to Marv, the royal abode, and became sore in heart and soul from grief. He repented of torturing his wife, and said to his heart in secret day and night: "What smoke is this that has risen from my soul, that the world has suddenly come to an end thereby? What was all this rage and all this torture visited upon my lover who is dear to me as my own soul? Although I am King of Kings of the world, in this kingship I am at the mercy of enemies. Why did I behave with such fury toward a lover in love for whom I was so crazed? Why, my heart, have you become your own enemy? Why do you burn your own granary by your own hand? Truly, lover, you are in feud against your soul; for you do not consider the morrow by the side of today; you foolishly perform an action today whereby a snake shall bite your heart tomorrow."

Let no lover be furious and proud, for fury shall cast him in the fire. Should a lover lack patience, he will see no joy in the pursuit of love. Why should a lover exhibit fury who cannot possess his soul in patience for so much as a moment away from his sweetheart? A lover dotes upon the offense of his love, for the privilege of passing it over.

65.

SHAHRŪ LAMENTS BEFORE MOUBAD. When the King came away from the castle, the Moon of Moons was not with him. Shahrū went wailing before the King, scoring her shining moon with hazelnuts. She said, "My darling, soul of your mother, whose cheek was her cure in every pain, why has Moubad not brought you at this time? What evil have you suffered from this cruel demon? What has befallen you by inharmonious fortune, what distress and tribulation have you yet once more undergone?"

Then she said mournfully to Moubad: "What excuse do you

proffer for not bringing my Vīs? What have you done to that sun of sweethearts? Why have you deprived the stars of the moon? Your seraglio was a garden by virtue of her presence; now what is the difference between this seraglio and a desert? Now I see your house bereft of light, your Paradise of its Hūrī. Hand my daughter over to me, otherwise I shall make the sea full of blood by my lamentations. I shall cry till the very mountains cry with me and suffer distress eternally for my sake. I shall weep till the very age itself weeps with me and the whole world becomes your enemy. Show Vīs to me, otherwise you shall be cast down from your throne. The blood of Vīs shall be upon your head, your very toe become your shackle!"

When Shahrū wept sorely before Moubad, the King, too, cried bitterly. He said to her, "Whether you lament or not, whether you purpose ill or good to me, I have done something I have never done before, nor shall again: dissipated my majesty and your reputation. If you see the face of that idol-faced beauty you will find a Chinese pattern amid the dust; you will see a stately cypress lopped down, laid low amidst dust and blood. Youth itself wailing over her silvery body, Beauty itself weeping over her rosy cheeks; the cloud of mud hiding the sun of her face, the corrosion of blood eating into the chain of her locks." When Shahrū heard these words from Moubad, she cast herself on the ground like an avalanche: the earth became a mass of blooms from her limbs, the palace a cup of wine from her tears. The arrow of distress shot by the world had lodged in her heart; she writhed in the dust like a snake. She moaned, "Worthless Fate! You have stolen from me a peerless pearl; it is as if some sage had said to you, 'If you are to steal, you might as well steal a pearl!' Perhaps like me you are delighted with the pearl to have buried it in the earth like a treasure. Perhaps when you saw that heavenly cypress you planted it in the garden of Eternity! Why did you root up that cypress with jasmine blooms, and once having rooted it up, cast it down headlong? How can a pine that has been felled rise again? How can ambergris give scent under the soil? O Earth, you who swallow men, how long will you go on gulping down moon and beauty, Khusrou and Kai?[1] Was not the repast you have gobbled

1. Kai is the title of the rulers of the mythological Kayānī dynasty, one of whose kings was Kaikhusrou.

till today enough, that you have now had to swallow up such a captivating Moon? I fear that that silvery body will molder: for silver will assuredly molder in earth! My star must be black, for my jewel lies rotting in the clay. The cypress will no longer swagger in the garden, for my cypress has been laid low in Marv! The moon will no longer shine in the heavens, for my Moon has been hidden in a pit. Perhaps the Pleiades have witnessed my agony, for so many stars to gather together there!

"My beauty, cypress-figured, moon in face, my idol with locks like chains, scent like musk! You were the comforter of my days; from whom may I now gain comfort in my distress for you? To whom may I tell this heavy grief, from whom seek redress for this injustice? He who murdered you slew a whole world; but still worse, slew me. I shall summon physicians from Rome, India, and Iran; perhaps they may contrive to cure my pain. My beauty, for me the world held you alone; I saw none to equal you. Your heart grew weary of the world; so you departed and took a worthy mate in Paradise.[2] My idol, since death has taken your soul, my great hope has vanished along with you. Who now shall be worthy of your ornaments? Whom may I find of your worth and grace? Who shall be worthy of your patterned silks, your gown, necklace, crown, and earring? Who shall dare take the news to Vīrū that Shahrū has fallen to weeping over the death of Vīs? Vīs has gone, and robbed sun and moon of radiance, for she shone like sun and moon from the throne. Vīs the sun of moonlike beauties is gone; I am left calling, 'Vīs,' as I seek and seek her.

"Perish the mountains of Ghūr and its castle, for there the eye of my fortune became blind! They slew my Moon in the mountains of Ghūr, and left her slain in a mountain cleft. Today in the mountains of Ghūr at Ishkaft e Dīvān the demons are all rejoicing;[3] they all know what will come of this blood; how much blood of the nobles will be spilt. Even though I cause a veritable Oxus to flow for the shedding of the blood of Vīs, with the blood both of my own eyes and of my enemies, it will not be worth so much as one drop of the blood which has flowed from those tulip-hued cheeks of hers.

2. See n. 5, p. 95, on *daēnā*.
3. Since the name means "Devils' Gully."

"Marv, ornament of Khurāsān, beware of counting this bloodshed and calamity as light! Does not your water come from the mountains of Ghūr? Now instead of water it will appear blood! This year your streams shall run blood; disaster shall arise from your mountains and plains; you shall see spearpoints and swords of renowned warriors more numerous than the leaves on the branches. Before your army has had a breathing space, an army shall bring anew a Flood of destruction upon you. From the land of the West to the land of the East men shall gird themselves to avenge the blood of charming Vīs! When the knights come from the wide world they shall crush you beneath the hooves of their chargers. The world has been destroyed by the hand of Moubad now that my darling daughter has departed from it.

"Cypress and boxtree will swagger in the garden now that the graceful boxtree is no more. Musk and ambergris will be sweetly perfumed now that those twin captivating locks are no more. Sugar will be delicious and sweet now that that sweet ruby is no more. The tulip will bloom on the mountainside now that that moon among courtly damsels is no more. The day of Nourūz was envious of Vīs, for it had not the power she possessed to entrance the heart. Now this year beautiful roses will grow and bloom the more fair for not seeing her cheek; spring will smile the more beautifully this year for not being a prey to shame before Vīs.

"Alas, my Vīs, queen of Tūrān, princess of Iran, Sun of Khurāsān, Moon of Kūhistān, hope of kings, splendor of Moons, eloquent Moon, cypress of jasmine scent, sun of the land, hope of your Mother! Where, where are you, my fair one? Why do you ever seek to be separated from me? Where shall I seek you, gleaming Moon: in pleasure dome or garden or hall? Every day you sat in the pleasure dome, you were a gorgeous garden in its midst; when in the garden, did you not become a brilliant moon? when in the hall, were you not the very crown of Saturn?[4] If I see the tulip in the garden now you are gone, it sets a brand on this wounded heart; if I see the rose in the plot now you are gone, it becomes a halter round my neck. If I see the moon in the heaven, it is a snake to my eyes and the heavens a pit. I do not know how I can live without you; for

4. See n. 1, p. 63.

185

without you my eyes have wept a river of blood; I have had to live to see your death, taste the poison of separation from you in my old age; if this pain were to weigh even on a mountain of adamantine rock, it would pulverize the mountain in an instant! If this grief weighed on the deeps of the sea it would in an instant make them dry as stone.

"Why did I bear such a luckless child as her? Why did I conjoin so sinister a bond? I ought not to have borne a Moon in my old age, brought her up, and given her into the hand of a demon. I shall go and sit lamenting till I die, and weep over the castle of Ishkaft e Dīvān. I shall draw up a breath from my burning heart and cleave the rock of that castle quite in twain. Why did they take my Hūrī to a castle which was never other than the abode of demons? I shall go and cast myself down from that mountain, so that there may be a slaughter like a death-feast! I shall not realize the desire of my heart so long as I am parted from her; why am I alive frustrated thus of desire? I shall go there and surrender my pure soul, mingle my dust with the dust of Vīs. But I shall not give up the ghost till I have caused smoke to rise from the ruin of the King's soul; it is not proper that my Vīs should be sleeping under the soil whilst the King clasps another in his embrace; not proper that my Vīs should be falling to pieces in the earth whilst the King carouses in the fall of the year.

"I shall stir up commotion in the world and tell everyone the hidden secret; I shall go and say to the wind, 'You are the same wind that secretly carried the scent of my Vīs; I conjure you, inasmuch as you carried scent from her whenever you passed over her locks, be my aid in avenging the blood of that Moon, bring destruction down upon her enemies.' I shall go and say to the moon, 'You are the same moon that secretly envied my Vīs; I conjure you, inasmuch as that captivating beauty shared face and fame with you in the world, be my aid in avenging that Moon, for I demand the price of her blood from her enemies.' I shall go and say to the sun, 'Triumphant one, lend me your great name in aid; I conjure you, inasmuch as you were the crown of Vīs, or rather a jewel in her crown, I conjure you, inasmuch as you are like her; like her, fair and radiant in face, multiply your light on the city of her friends, do not show your face to the city of her enemies!'

"I shall go and say to the cloud: 'You are the same that scatter pearls like the words of my Vīs; the hands of Vīs were compeers of yours; ever like you raining gems. I conjure you, inasmuch as she was the cloud of bounty, who in place of lightning was all laughter and joy, rain down a deluge on the city of her enemy, flashing lightning leaping amidst the flood!' I shall go and offer up entreaties before the Creator, rub my cheeks in the dust; I shall piteously say before him, 'O God, you are great and all-powerful, O God, you are judicious and long-suffering that you do not rain death on Moubad! You have given the world into the hand of this tyrant, whose evil waxes greater with every day that passes. He does not show mercy to your creatures, but burns your world by his injustice. Like a sword, the only art he knows is cutting; like a wolf, his only purpose is to rend. God, exact justice from his soul for me! Rid his palace, house, and home of him! Even as this tyrant has brought up smoke from my ruins, do you bring up smoke from the ruins of his happiness and very soul!'"

66.

MOUBAD REPLIES TO SHAHRŪ AND SPEAKS OF THE BEATING OF VĪS AND THE NURSE. When Moubad witnessed Shahrū's lamentations, fear both of her and of Vīrū fell on him; he said to her, "You that are more precious than my eyes and have suffered many kinds of pain at my hand; you are my sister, Vīrū is my brother; jasmine-bosomed Vīs my queen and lady. Vīs is to me eyes and light, more even than life and possessions and sovereignty. I so adore that false lover that I hold her dearer than my very soul. Had she not acted wrongfully toward me, she would have enjoyed fruit of my love to her heart's desire.

"Just now I concealed her true circumstances from you; it was to this end that I spoke these wild words to you. How can I put to death someone I hold dearer than my own soul? Though I am a captive in her hands, my constant desire is to die before her. Though I am in this plight because of the brand of her love, my constant desire is to see her happy.[1] Do not lament so sorely for her; do not smite your silvery hands on golden face; for I am doleful as you;

1. Cf. *Tristan*, p. 258.

how should I countenance dolefulness in myself? I shall send and bring Vīs from the castle; for I cannot support the pain I suffer because of her; I do not know what my soul is to suffer at her hand; no, I should not say 'I do not know'—I *do* know, only too well! Much bitterness shall I taste, much distress shall I suffer; so long as Vīs is in my seraglio I shall see nothing from her but spells and stratagems. So long as she is my spouse and sweetheart my occupation will be none other than suffering care. I attribute all the pain that afflicts me because of Vīs to my wounded heart; I have a heart that is not under my own control; you would swear it was no heart of mine! Sitting here on the royal throne I am like a wild ass mauled in the claws of a lion. The door of my will is shut with a hundred locks; may no child be born with my fate! Hardly surprising that I who experience no joy at the hand of my heart for so much as a single day should gain no joy of Vīs!''

Then the monarch ordered Zard, "Go to the castle like the rushing wind; take with you two hundred warriors and bring Vīs back from the fortress.''

General Zard went with two hundred soldiers and brought Vīs to the King within a month; her limbs still bruised by the blows of the King, like a wounded wild ass struggling from the trap. For that month, brokenhearted Rāmīn dwelt hidden in Zard's house. Then Zard spoke much for Rāmīn before the King, who pardoned him once again and mended his tattered fortunes. Once more the demon of wrath hid his face, the flower of joy bloomed from the branch of love. Once more the face of the Moon of Moons shone in the palace of the King of Kings. The King's life became sweet with pleasuring; the hand of the Moon tinctured with wine. The hand of joy loosed the fetter of bounty; the falcon of bounty trapped the partridge of joy. Once more began a time when they had nothing to do but take their pleasure. They covered the ground in rose and eglantine, suffused the soul with sweet wine. A fair wind sprang up for them; those sufferings slipped from their memories.

Neither grief nor joy lasts in this world; extinction is the end of both. Keep your heart happy as far as you may, for life is made more by happiness. Since our span does not last long, where is the necessity for vainly suffering grief while it does?

67.

MOUBAD ENTRUSTS VĪS TO THE NURSE; RĀMĪN COMES INTO
THE GARDEN. On the eve of Monday on a spring day when the
King returned from Gurgān and Sārī he decreed a stockade for his
palace, an iron wall and brass bars, Byzantine keys and Alanian
locks, forged from Indian steel; wherever there was a casement or
window he decreed an iron grill to be placed over it. The King's
abode became so strong that not even the wind could penetrate it.
Then he locked all the doors; his gold seal was superimposed on the
locks.

He gave the Nurse the keys of the locks and said to her, "Necro-
mancer, mistress of demons, I have bitter experience of your unchivalrous ways; practice chivalry this once. I purpose to go to
Zāvul[1] for a time; my stay will last a month or thereabouts. Guard
my palace here till I return; for as I have fastened its locks so shall
I open them. I give you the keys of the doors as a trust; keep faith
just this once! You know as well as any that in the keeping of a trust
breach of faith is hardly glorious. I shall test you this time, and if you
behave well requite you with good. I know that I only increase my
vexation inasmuch as I try something already tried; however, I have
selected you since I have heard from the sages that 'when you entrust
your property to thieves you achieve rather more security from
them.'"

Once the King had admonished the Nurse at length he gave her
the keys of the abode, for he had no alternative.

On a fortunate day and at a propitious time he went joyfully
through the gate. One day he came down to the camp, the thought
of Vīs uppermost in his mind. The grief of parting and the care of
separation had made kingship bitter for him.

In the camp Rāmīn was with the King; unknown to him, he came
at night to the city; in the evening the King looked for Rāmīn, for
he wanted to drink two or three bowls of wine with him. When they
said, "He has only now gone to the city," he knew that this was a
stratagem and a spell. Rāmīn's departure from the army at night
was in order to see the face of his sweetheart. As soon as Rāmīn

1. In the southeast. Minorsky, *Ḥudūd ul-'Ālam*, p. 345; *idem, Iranica*, p. 168.

arrived he went into the King's garden, but found its gate shut fast on the Moon like a rock; he came melancholy into the garden, his heart full of brands from thought of Vīs. Crying and lamenting from desire of his mate, moved by impatience and melancholy, he sang:

"My sweetheart, since they separated me from you those who envy me have attained their dearest desire. Come for a moment to the edge of the roof and see me, one hand on my heart and one on the pillow in my grief. You would swear the dark night was a sea, its bounds invisible in the wide world. I am sunk in this dread sea, my tears its coral and pearls. Though I be in the midst of a garden, I struggle in raging waves because of my tears. I have watered the garden with my eyes, I have made the rose plot pomegranate-red with blood. What profit is there in my weeping sorely, for you do not care about my plight! I shall bring up a blast from my burning heart and burn up this castle and these stout bars; but how burn the castle which contains my sweetheart? If fire so much as singes the hem of her garment, that burning will be felt in my heart. Two archers ever sit in your eyes marking my soul; drawing the bow of your eyebrows on me, wounding my soul with the arrow of your glance. Though fortune has driven me from your side, your vision haunts me month in, year out. Now it drives sleep from my eyes, now makes blood flow over my cheeks. How may I sleep when you are not in my arms? How stay alive when you have left me?"

When Rāmīn had lamented over his heart for a while, he rained a bloodstained flood from his eyes over roses; there amid lily and box and eglantine, sweet sleep suddenly carried him off. That raining narcissus, beside which the very storm cloud was mild, went to sleep; the heart full of pain and grief, beside which Hell itself was a gorgeous garden, rested; his heart was only able to rest for a moment since the scent of the garden was the perfume of his sweetheart.

The desperate prince slept in the garden whilst his sweetheart, her moonlike face scored, rushed about the seraglio like a madwoman, shedding moisture on a garden from her narcissuslike eyes. She knew that her Rāmīn was in the garden, which without her was to his heart like a burning brand. She abjectly implored the

Nurse, "Nurse, deliver my heart from this agony! Open alike the lock of the door and of my soul; show me the sun in the dark night! The night is dark, and my fate dark, too; yet the way to my sweetheart is but short; but because of so many doors shut fast as rock you would swear the distance were sixty parasangs! Alas! If there were only a road, however hard, between us and not these manifold locks! Come, Nurse, have mercy on my soul! Bring the key of the door and open the lock! They engendered me with misfortune in my very clay; they clasped a thousand locks upon my soul. Are not the locks of my love enough? Why must I be faced with locked doors, too? When they locked the doors on an imprisoned heart they wounded a body already nursing wounds. Ever since my love has twisted his twin curls, he has imprisoned my soul in a musky chain. Ever since his fair face has left me, the arrow of his stature has remained lodged in my eye. See my eye wounded by a silver arrow! See my soul locked in a musky chain!"

The Nurse answered her and said, "After this none shall see anything but chivalry of me; when a lord like the King has departed hence and left so many instructions with me, how may I open his locks tonight? When he grows angry, how shall I get the better of him? Even though a thousand armies came to my aid I hardly think they would prevail over Moubad. He has thus required of me observance of my oath; you do not tell me how I may contrive to break it; even were you a hundred times more desirous of seeing Rāmīn than you are, you would not find it in me to be thus unchivalrous. The King is encamped by the city gate; he has not gone half a parasang from the city wall; how do you know that he is not simply carrying out a test and dissimulating the while? I well know that he will not stay there; this very night as morning approaches he will come; we must beware of perpetrating all this evil, for evil will be requited with evil at the hand of Moubad; what an excellent proverb this is for the sagacious: 'Evil will one day rebound upon the evil!'"

When the Nurse had spoken these words to the Moon she turned from her abruptly in the anger of her heart, saying, "My idol, you, too, arise: do not further provoke the King in his wrath. Possess your soul prudently in patience for this one night, then dispose your affairs as you may; for tonight I fear Moubad and dread some evil befalling you at his hand. Grant me the favor, Vīs, this one night, that the eye of the devil may tonight become blind."

The Nurse departed, but not so that beauty of moonlike form; she rushed round and struck stones on the wall. She could find neither casement nor any place where there was a chink; nor could she find any way onto the palace roof. But since the torment of love inflamed her soul, she ingeniously devised an artifice for herself; before the hall stood a pavilion, its foot touching the earth, its top Saturn; many ropes were tightly tied on it, each one a remedy and comfort for Vīs; the beauty like a silvery hill took off her shoes and mounted it like a flying falcon; when she gained its top, she leapt from the pavilion onto the roof; the wind carried off the rosy-red tiara from her head. She was left bareheaded and barefooted; her necklace snapped, its pearls scattered. The earrings were quite shattered on her ears; her fair face was left without ornament.

Then she hurried to the edge of the garden, her soul full of desire and her heart full of brands; she tied her linen *chadur*[2] in a cranny, gripped it, and then leapt from the wall. Its hem caught in the bricks of the wall; her gown was torn to pieces on her body. Although the spot was soft and yielding, her feet hurt from the leap. The loop of her girdle was snapped on her waist, and the trousers ripped on her thighs.

With neither garments nor ornaments remaining on her body, but either torn or fallen off altogether, wandering round the garden barefooted, running to every plot seeking her lover, both her eyes and feet shedding bloodstained teardrops, she said, "Alas for this sinister fate! Where shall I seek my gay lover, where seek the spring of charm? It is better that I should not run wildly about seeking the shining sun in the night! Wind of the dawn, I implore you by lover-hood, take pains for me for an instant! If you are kindly disposed to the desperate, I am desperate; have mercy on me for a moment! For even if your foot were to tread round the whole world it would not become as bloodstained as this soft foot! Not yours to traverse a long road or grapple with harsh unpleasant pain! Pass over two

2. A flowing garment of a single piece of material, worn over the head and capable of veiling the face.

blossoming eglantines; one visible, the other hid from me; see where you can find someone who has covered many a one like me in shame, who has made unchaste a thousand chaste maidens, abducted them and left them lying on the road; gouged a thousand hearts from the breast by his eye, and thrown them on the fire by abandoning them to exile. See my plight in the pursuit of love; lost in distress, shame, and humiliation! Senseless and frustrated by a hundred kinds of calamity, bereft of patience and peace by a hundred varieties of cruelty!

"Take my message to that fair face, in which all beauty is assembled; bring musk from it and mix it with my pomegranate blossom; take ambergris from me and rub it on his hyacinths; say to him, 'Spring blossom of the garden, worthy of joy and happiness!' Say, 'Sun of charm! who have won sway over beauty! You have thrown fire on my soul and sent me wandering over roof and wall in the dark night. You have not spared me sympathy in my desperation, nor shown me consideration in my wretchedness. Ill fortune has driven me from the world; the world is asleep but I remain awake. If I am human and of this world, why then am I not ever as its denizens? I lament my desperation and fate; perhaps my mother bore me bereft of good fortune and desperate!

"'You said to me, "Why do you not come here?" Well, I have come—but where are you? Why do you not come to me? Whom do you fear? Why do you not visit the poor patient sick of separation? If I must be hopeless of seeing you, the sharp pain will remain in my soul; if I gaze on the moon instead of at your face, it is as if I gazed on a dark pit. If I smell musk in place of your locks, the purest musk is to me like the dust of my lane. If I find nectar in place of your lips I swear that it is like pure poison to me. You are my lover, not musk and ambergris; you are my remedy, not nectar and sugar. The snake of your locks has bitten my heart, my wounded soul trembles on my very lips. Your lips are the antidote of my soul, your cheeks the sun of my fortune. Alas for my ill fortune! Where are you tonight? Why have you cut yourself off from association with me? Friend and enemy alike have mercy on me—why not you?'

"Where are you, gleaming moon? Why do you not rise on me from the east? Raise your head from the mountain like a silvery mirror and see how a hundred kinds of grief engulf my soul! The world is like iron eaten by rust; the sky has broken faith with my soul. My heart has departed and the sweetheart is far from me; two lovers are left desperate and forlorn! Help me by your aura of fortune, guide me by your light. You are the moon; my sweetheart, too, is the moon; the world without your face is black for me. O God, have mercy on me, wretched as I am. Show me the faces of those two moons! One endowed with glory and light, the other with grandeur and sovereignty; the station of the one the mansion of the wheeling sphere; of the other, throne, saddle, and field."

When the host of heaven had marched halfway, the gleaming moon came up from the east, like a silvery ship on the deeps of the sea, like a bracelet on the hand of a Hūrī. The sky washed its face of soot, and likewise washed the melancholy from the soul and heart of Vīs.[3] She found her sleeping lover blossoming in the midst of the garden like a rose. The violet locks and eglantine face of Rāmīn had made a pillow of violets and eglantine. The moon came up from the mountains and Vīs from the seraglio, a musk-laden spring wind from the garden. Musk and ambergris were mingled; the moon two weeks old joined with the sun. Rāmīn awoke at the scent of Vīs and found at his pillow a cypress with jasmine blossoms. He leapt up and clasped her to him, then took her two locks like ambergris. Now he scattered ambergris from her locks, now sugar from her rubies. Their lips pressed together were like *mīm* upon *mīm*;[4] their breasts like silver upon silver. The two jasmine-bosomed lovers twined on each other like two pieces of brocade laid face to face. You would have sworn that wine and milk were mixed, or pomegranate blossom and lily entwined; night was turned to day by their faces; their fortunes became like Nourūz from happiness; a thousand nightingales sang from the branches of the rose, celebrating their love all night. The tulip laughed at their happiness, the ruby cup in its hand. The rose drew fairness and beauty from them, as the new-blown narcissus caprice and charm. As they revealed lovers' secrets to each other they joyfully granted each other's desire. But Fate showed its evil face and reaped the field of joy with the sword of pain. In the dawn

3. *I. Mb*: "washed it from the soul and face of Vīs."
4. *mīm*: the *m* of the Persian script.

194

it brought their plight to such a pass that it made the garden a branding ground for both!

The nature of the world is, after all, evildoing; why do you listen to tales of its "kindness"? No one sees any mercy at its hand, for it is devoid of love, respect, and shame.

68.

THE KING RECEIVES NEWS OF RĀMĪN AND GOES INTO THE GARDEN. When the King received news of Rāmīn, once again wrath rose in his heart. He wrestled with his heart all night, saying to himself, "How long shall I be burdened with this wretch? So long as a single mortal remains in the world, he shall quote my name for ill repute. I have entrusted my good name to Ahriman, I have made myself a veritable figure of disgrace! Even were Vīs not Vīs but the sun, and were like Heaven the reward of the fortunate, it would still not be worth while enduring all this cruelty from her, or undergoing all this care for the sake of love for her. What profits it though her body be as sweetly scented as rose water? It is a torment like fire to my soul; though her lips be the elixir of the world, they are fatal poison to my soul; though she be in beauty like a Hūrī of Paradise, she is in feud against me like an evil demon; seeking love from her is a fruitless task for me; it is like washing a clay brick to get it clean! What is the difference between taking the heart and entrusting it to love of her, and eating bitter aloes for the sake of sweetness?

"Why have I tried something already tried, why vainly increased my own pain? Why have I sought love from a demon, why sought sight from the blind? Why have I sought charm from a bear, why asked the way of a ghoul? Why have I sought loverliness from Vīs, why trustworthiness from the Nurse? I have closed a thousand doors with lock and seal—and then handed over seal and lock to her! How confused in heart, how slow in thought must I be, to try thus far something already tried! I have thrown my musk to the fickle wind, handed my sheep to a ravening wolf. I have made the choice of fools, and am now placed no better than they. A fool chooses his way of action and is left thereafter blind and repentant. It is only right that I should be left in the worst possible case, for in my actions

I am both blind and deaf. I see and do not believe my eyes; for my soul is not helped by my reason. If reason were the teacher of my heart it would not ever be so unhappy.

"If I now once more retreat from this road, the whole army will become aware of my secret. I do not know what they will call me hereafter: for already they call me ignoble. My whole army, great and small, call me one and all less than a man. If they so call me, it is no more than I deserve; what kind of man am I that I cannot cope with a woman?"

All night till dawn the King of Kings traversed a hundred roads in thought; now he said, "I shall hide this disgrace, not struggle with ill repute and humiliation"; now, "I shall even now turn back: let me become notorious in the world, if I must." Sometimes reason made him content, at other times a demon made him wrathful. Now he became like water, bright and sweet; now like smoke, bitter and acrid. The more he pondered on his plight, the weaker reason became in the hand of anger and rancor.

When the gleaming moon rose in the east the King came hastening back to Marv.[1] He could not find his way into his own dwelling, for his hall was closed by lock and seal. The Nurse came up showing lock and seal, and by this artifice pacified his heart. He found every one of the locks even as he had closed them, untouched by hand. He saw the door of the cage fast as rock, but its tame partridge flown from captivity; the end of the thread sealed and unopened, but the jewel fallen from the necklace.

He said to the Nurse, "What have you done with my Vīs? How have you spirited her through these locked doors? Since Ahriman is your guide, how shall a mere locked door bar your way? My door is locked, but Vīs is flown; no doubt she has this night flown to Damāvand! Why flown? for she herself is of right glorious name; she has a thousand familiars like Zahhāk!"[2]

Then he lashed the Nurse so cruelly with a whip that she became as senseless as the dead. Then he ransacked palace, garden, and hall

1. Cf. *Tristan*, p. 271.
2. The monster king, Zahhāk, is imprisoned in Mount Damāvand, in the Elburz, according to Persian legend. See Minorsky, *Iranica*, p. 160, n. 1, on this passage.

through and through, inside and out, up and down, seeking Vīs everywhere, but could not find that fascinating and charming face. In one place he found her gown fallen, her golden shoes laid in another. Who would have dreamt that that Moon would make her way along the pavilion ropes?

When the King, ruler of the world, came into the garden, preceded by many lamps and torches, no sooner had fortunate Vīs seen the torches than the heart fled her body like a pigeon.

She said to Rāmīn, "Rise and flee, my love, for it is best to avoid enemies; beware of staying longer with me, for darkness accompanies this light! The King is coming to attack us, like a furious lion leaping from its ambush; you should escape; it is right I should suffer wounds; whatever pain you suffer, whatever bitterness you taste, be they what they may, let them fall on me; but may your lot be all happiness and triumph; now depart under the protection of holy God and leave me to this flood and holocaust; I am become a byword for ill fortune; for every one kiss I receive from you, I suffer a hundred lashes for it. I shall not eat a single date without a thorn; nor see happiness without pain and care."

The heart of wretched Rāmīn fell into such a plight that you would have sworn he was without a soul like a dead man. He was rooted to the spot like a statue; strength had ebbed from both his arms and his legs. Pain lay on his heart on account of Vīs; you would have sworn his heart had been transfixed by an arrow-point.

Then he rose from her embrace against his will; but no sooner had his soul leapt from a snare than it fell into a dungeon; for the King was like a trap laid for him, the dungeon of the pain of separation yawned before him. No sooner had he leapt out of the fatal trap than he jumped into a deadly pit. When a lover gains union, there is no enemy like separation. All troubles are a light matter to a lover when his soul dreads separation. Any affliction seems as nought to his heart when it comes upon him when he is with his love. May none have a love like this; and if they do, may they not suffer separation!

When Rāmīn left the embrace of Vīs, he shot forth like an arrow from the niche of the bow. He scaled the smooth wall like a swift mountain sheep climbing the folds of a crag. Once he had scaled it

197

he leapt down the other side; he had fallen nicely into the trap; now he leapt no less nimbly from it.

Jasmine-bosomed Vīs lay where she was, in prostration that was worse than death. In memory of the departed Rāmīn who had been her pillow, she laid her musky lock on her silvery hand. Under her locks, twisted loop on loop, her ten fingers were like a fish in a net. Her heart was the cupbearer, her eyes the cup; her face like one drinking wine on mallow flower and tulip; the patterns[3] on the hand of that beauty with gorgeously patterned face were, like her locks, black and fine and full of curls. The gorgeously figured face of that Moon, a prize to be guarded by castle walls, was like the garden of the King, full of spring color; the King stole up to her pillow and found the Moon fallen from the sky into the garden. He tried repeatedly to rouse her to her feet, but the Moon did not wake from her slumber. So senseless was she in the pain of separation that you would have sworn her soul had departed from her with her lover. The King sent trusty soldiers, foot- and horsemen, to every nook and cranny; they scoured high and low and set about searching the garden from end to end; they could not find any creature in the garden, save the birds that sang on the boughs. Now they ransacked the trees and peered into every one. They examined every tree two hundred times, but found no one but Vīs. They sought Rāmīn as if their lives depended on it, but little knew that he had leapt over the wall!

The king said to jasmine-bosomed Vīs, "Will you not tell me what you were doing here? I locked upon you fifty doors with nails and blocked the casements of a hundred roofs and walls. Once my back was turned you did not rest for a single night, but flew like a bird up from my house, like a demon that not even a sorcerer can control with spells, incantations, and bands of steel; reason is as far removed from you as the sky; desire as near to you as the very soul; inasmuch as you are cursed with sinister fortune, your eyes and ears are blind and deaf; even advice as precious as pearls is as pointless where you are concerned as slippers to a miser or a pot to a washerman! If I persist in admonishing you, reason will desert my soul; should I persevere in giving you endless advice, my tongue will do violence

3. *Mb*, notes, p. 459.

to words; from the abundant evil that has come upon me from you I count your faults not as one but as many hundred. Indeed you are an echo of Bīmesh[4] since you always become refractory when faced by good! If justice were to materialize before you, your soul would cry out at the sight! Only for you to see the head of goodness and you cut it off; only for you to find the heart of purity and you rend it. You are the sworn enemy of truth; give you a sight of its eyes and you will gouge them out. You are a demon, but visible; a ghoul, but in beauteous shape. You burn down the house of saintliness; you sew up the eyes of good name; I know of none more shameless than you, unless it be me, your lover. Perhaps some demon of evil has said to you, 'If you commit sin you will become an inmate of Paradise.' May you perish and with you he who adores you and she who is your nurse and he who is your lover. I swear that your blood is permissible to be shed, for your soul is an affliction to many souls. None knows your cure other than my sword, which will grant you death and relieve you of your life. I shall even now relieve you of that life, and rid you of yourself with my dagger." Then, grasping her lassolike tresses, that murderous dragon pulled her along; in one hand the tempered silk-fine blade, in the other twisted musk: whoever saw silk made from water[5] and iron? whoever saw a lasso made of musk and ambergris?

He was about to cut off her moon from her cypress and scatter her roses in the mud; the sword poised over her head was less to jasmine-bosomed Vīs than the pain of separation from her sweetheart. Zard the commander said, "King of Kings, live fortunate according to the desire of your well-wishers; stay your hand! If you shed the blood of this maiden you will spill the remedy for your own pain. A severed head will not grow again; this is why no wise man seeks bloodshed. Many days will pass in the world before a maid so fair of face will be born again! When you remember the moon of her face you will writhe more than the snakes of her hair; you will not find a Hūrī like this in heaven; you will not find any as beautiful as she on earth. You will be repentant but it shall avail you nothing; much blood

4. Professor Mīnovī compares with this name the demon's name *Danhash* in the *Fihrist*, ed. Flügel, p. 310; *G:* "thou art a devil . . ."
5. Persian *āb:* a play on *āb dādeh*, "tempered."

shall you shed from your eyes! You once essayed separation from her; I do not fancy that you will do so again! If that detestable dye appealed to you by all means thrust your other hand into it as well.

"When this fair face of hers was distant from you, I saw in what sore plight you were from love of her. Sometimes you were with the deer in the wilds, sometimes with the fish in the river. Sometimes you were with the wild asses in the desert, sometimes with the lion in the reedbed. Have you forgotten the pain and affliction which befell you—and us—during separation from her? You were hurt by her, I by you; how much care we suffered! Remember the covenant and oath you concluded and swore before God the Judge. Do not break your oath, Majesty, it does not befit you; forswearing thus will one day rack your soul with pain. Remember the respect due to Shahrū; recall the services of Vīrū; although Vīs offended against you one day, you know that she does not offend against you today; merely to lie down to sleep in the garden alone is hardly an astonishing action in anyone! Why do you impute to her a sin which she has no means of carrying out? When you have a garden like this, its wall stretching to the very Pleiades, steel nails fast on its gate, had there been an inamorato with her in the garden, how could he have vanished from here this instant? No bird could fly over this gate, no demon shatter these bars! Perhaps she was melancholy and wandered into the garden: you have now placed brand upon brand. Ask her how it was with her, then chastise her according to what she has to say; if you strike your dagger into charming Vīs the wound of your pain will thereby be aggravated."

At Zard's copious words and entreaties the King reconciled his heart to that beauty of idol face. He severed some ringlets from her locks and contented himself with cutting those curls; he took her hand and led her into the seraglio, which became like a garden from the beauty of her face.

He conjured her by the God of the world to answer, asking, "How did you extricate yourself tonight from all these barriers? You are not a bird, an arrow, nor yet the wind; how did you land in that garden from the seraglio? I have begun to suspect that you are learned in spells and sorcery! It would take someone thoroughly versed in incantations to do this: otherwise how could he achieve such a feat?"

Jasmine-bosomed Vīs said, "God my creator ever prospers my fortunes: what if you evince churlishness toward me if God purposes well for me? now rescues my soul from your sword, now exacts redress for me from your soul; you diminish me, God increases me; you bind me, God sets me free. Why do you call me enemy and foe? It is with God that you struggle, not with me; for he rends asunder all you sew up; cuts down all you plant; you set me now in fortress, now in seraglio; now treat me with fury, now ply me with artifice. God does not leave me afflicted by you but releases me from all these bars and prisons! You may be my enemy; he suffices as my savior; you may be a Khusrou;[6] he suffices as my friend; he it was who delivered me from your bonds tonight so that not so much as a hair of my head was harmed. When I was melancholy in your palace I cried out to him against your tyranny and cruelty; I rehearsed your acts of oppression before God, then fell asleep in my wretchedness and sorrow; an angel came to me in a dream, a handsome youth clad in green; he took me up out of the dome of the seraglio and laid me down in garden and rose plot; my bed was of eglantine and lily; Rāmīn, light of the world, was in my embrace; there we two stayed, joyous and happy, exchanging lovers' secrets; lying thus at our pleasure, rose and lily blooming around us; I opened my eyes from sweet sleep and fell out of that sweetness into bitterness; I saw you like a roaring lion, your sharp sword drawn like fire; whether you believe me or no, thus it was; an angel was my companion in a dream. If your treatment of me is not injustice, you know 'there is no jurisdiction over one who sleeps.'"[7]

The King believed these words, for she told him a lie in the guise of truth.[8] He sought much excuse for his sin and suffered regret for the events of the past; he bestowed uncountable chattels upon Vīs and the Nurse, choice garments and jewels. They counted the pain of the past as not having been, and took ruby-red wine at their ease.

6. See n. 1, p. 29.
7. Cf. *Qābūsnāmeh*, ed. Levy, p. 50.
8. *I. Mb:* "the moon-formed one told him a lie."

Such is the heart of the children of men; it does not remember past joy and grief. Why lament over the day that has passed you by, why ponder upon the day that is to be? Where is the necessity for suffering care over what has been, or feeling concern over what is yet to be? Yesterday will not come along with you because of your care, nor tomorrow hold off for all your concern! Better, then, to live happy and pass at least one day of your life in joy. Even though you live a hundred years joyful and triumphant, your life will never amount to more than one day. Whether you endure distress or quest for fame, you will have no more than the day wherein you are.

69.

MOUBAD HOLDS A BANQUET IN THE GARDEN AND THE SONGSTER MINSTREL SINGS A SONG. On the day of Khurdād[1] in the month of Urdībihisht[2] the world was as splendid as Karkh[3] by Baghdad. The desert was like a garden in beauty; the garden like an idol-temple, so many idols filled it! The tree by the stream scattered silver: the breeze from the spring blossom sifted musk. The garden was the court, the blossoms masters of ceremonies, its nightingales played the harp, its doves the flute. In it the narcissus stood like a cupbearer, cup in hand; the violet hung its head like a drunken man. From the abundance of their jewels, the branches were like the crown of Khusrou;[4] the gardens like the face of Leilā[5] with their fair aspect; the face of the plain was all emerald with greenery; the rocky mountain full of coral with its tulips; all the open plain like a Hūrī with its tulips, the meadow all fair curls with its violets; the earth was like Paradise in fairness and beauty; the world like a bride in charm and grace.

The King sat in the garden, the Moon of Moons by his side. On his right hand was noble Vīrū, on his left Shahrū, ornament of the world. Knightly Rāmīn sat before him, and in front of Rām the

1. The sixth day of the month.
2. The second month (April–May).
3. Minorsky, *Ḥudūd ul-ʿĀlam*, p. 140.
4. See n. 1, p. 29.
5. The romance of Leilā and Majnūn is one of the stock themes of Persian poetry.

songster minstrel.[6] He strung the modes of those whose taste is fine; the nobles took their pleasure; mild wine circulated round the company, the cheeks of the guests drinking wine blushed wine red. The brilliant minstrel sang a song which had concealed in it the story of Vīs and Rāmīn. Now, then, see how quick you are; can you solve the meaning hidden within it?[7]

"I saw a tree growing on top of a mountain, such as scours the corrosion of care from the heart; a tree stretching its head to Saturn, its shadow falling over the whole world. In beauty it is like the sun, the world fixes its hopes on its leaves and fruit; beneath it, a bright spring, whose water is nectar and whose sand radiant pearls. On its banks tulip and rose bloom, violets and mallow flower and hyacinth grow; a bull of Gīlān grazes by its bank, now drinking its water, now cropping its verdure. May the tree be ever shady, may its shadow be more grateful than the heaven! May the water of the spring ever flow, and the bull of Gīlān ever graze by it!"

The King leapt from his seat in anger and caught Rāmīn's throat with one hand, in the other his poisoned dagger; he said to him, "Evil-minded, ill-starred youth, swear to me by sun and moon that you will not have any connection with Vīs; otherwise I shall sever the head from your body, for my body has become headless because of the shame you have brought upon me."

Noble Rāmīn swore an oath by the creator of the world and the moon and the Pleiades: "So long as I live in both worlds, as I have not deserted my love, so I never shall; that rosy-cheeked face is the focal point of my worship, as the sun in the heavens is to others. She is my dear soul, and one cannot abandon one's own soul by one's own will!"

The King's wrath against Rāmīn increased, and he quite loosed his tongue in abuse; he threw him down to cut off his head and expunge the seat of love with his dagger. Rāmīn deftly caught the

6. Boyce, "The Parthian gōsān and Iranian Minstrel Tradition," *JRAS* (April, 1957), p. 10. *G:* "the court singing girls."
7. *I* has a further song by the minstrel explaining the double-entendre of the first. *G* explains the meaning in the text.

King's hands; you would have sworn a male lion caught a fox; he threw him down from the dais to the floor and snatched the Indian blade from his hand. The King was drunk and barely conscious from wine; his awareness impaired and his strength gone; he was unaware of what Rāmīn did; yet all this hurt remained in his heart. Thus do love and drunkenness induce various kinds of pain and languor in the reason; had the King not suffered from this double complaint, no sort of evil would have come upon him.

When next day the blazing sun rose and its radiant face lit up the world, the sky was like a burnished sword blade, the earth like rubbed saffron.

70.

BIHGŪ COUNSELS RĀMĪN. There was a sage in Khurāsān, the past master of the astrologers of that land; a soothsayer whose name was Bihgū; he had carried off the polo ball from everyone in eloquence. He sat with Rāmīn early and late and cleansed his soul with the water of advice.

He said to him, "You will be king one day and take in your grasp any desire you wish. The tree of your desire will become fruitful, you shall be the paramount lord of the world." When he came before Rāmīn in the morning he found him sad as could be and weeping bitterly; he asked him, "Why are you downcast? Why do you not redouble your joy and pleasure? You have youth and a royal throne; when these two are to hand, what more do you want? Forbear to distress your reason thus far in desire, nor cause your soul to writhe this much in affliction. Your soul will plead a suit against you before the Judge, on the ground that you constantly keep it full of care! During this brief span of life why do you busy yourself other than with merrymaking? If the decree of God is not to be altered, it will not be turned aside from us by grieving! Where is the necessity for vainly suffering grief, or suffering care for what is yet to be?"

When brokenhearted Rāmīn heard these words he said to him, "You who are my very seeing eyes, all you have said to me is well said indeed; but when the Sphere is mean, men's hearts are not of stone or steel, to rejoice should they become full of grief. How much power to accommodate itself has a body? How much long-suffering has a heart? The evildoing of the world is too much for the effort, patience, and strength we can summon. Destiny has showered rain on everyone else, but on my heart a deluge! It never fails to pass over me a single day without visiting on me a brand that burns the vitals. Should it one day dangle an ambition before my eyes, it produces a snare from the ambition. If the world scatters roses on my head, it jabs an arrow into my heart from each one. I have never drunk a cup of wine to my own desire without draining a cup of poison in its wake. Who may find joy welling up from his heart in such a plight and in the midst of such a life? Having just witnessed humiliation such as I did yesterday through the King's anger, it is right enough that I should hesitate to accept advice but bemoan my fate till I die."

Then he gave him a blow-by-blow account of what had lately befallen them, what humiliation the King had heaped upon him in the presence of Princess Vīs, the Moon of Moons. "Now that my eyes have witnessed such a disaster is it any wonder that I keep them full of blood? Better to die than suffer humiliation, possess the soul in patience and taste bitterness. I can stand any pain but humiliation; forbear to seek from me patience therein!"

When Rāmīn told his plight to Bihgū, his vitals wounded and his eyes red with weeping, see what reply Bihgū gave him; if you have to give a reply, do so thus: he said to him, "You who bemoan your fate, you are a lion; how long will you shrink from jackals? Fortune will one day answer your call, having visited so much injustice upon you: so long as desire is sweet to your heart, your body will thus suffer affliction. You ought not to have surrendered your heart to your lover when you were unable to suffer the distress she brought in her train. You sowed the seed of love in your heart, hoping that it would bear fruit in the form of a Hūrī of Paradise; you little knew that whenever you sow love every sort of affliction is your harvest! Whenever the task is picking roses it is meet that thorns should scratch the hand! You are, in love, like a trader; you experience from it now profit, now loss; you told yourself that you would experience fire without smoke, gain profit without loss; one whose work is planting seeds always treasures such anticipations in his heart. But there are many tribulations to be borne between seedtime, growth, and harvest. You little knew that before you saw the fruit of your seed you would reap many tribulations and much hurt. Desire in the heart is like a raging sea; to plunge into it is not the act of a wise man. What is the difference between love in your heart and fire? How can it be pleasant to pass one's life in fire? So long as the Moon of Moons is your lover the King of Kings shall be your enemy. Reconcile yourself to experiencing trouble and humiliation; and to possessing your soul in patience whether you like it or not; your body will ever be the seat of wounds; your heart the abode of distress. You are in the lists with a raging elephant; I do not know how you may escape; you are locked in battle with a wild lion; I do not know in what stead your heroism will stand you! You are travers-ing the sea without a ship, seeking from it a royal pearl; I do not know what the upshot of your enterprise will be; what good or evil Fortune will mete out to you. You are pitted month in, year out against a dragon from whom no enemy escapes; perhaps one day he will spring up in your path and seize you unawares in the wrath of his heart. You have built your house on a flood; you are slumbering in it like a sleeping man; perhaps a deluge will come one day and suddenly carry away the house and you with it. You have writhed a hundred times in the snare: since Fortune aided you, you sprang from it, but perhaps the day may come when you will not be able to spring out and your soul may not have any means of escape; then that humiliation will be worse than the present; for your blood will be upon your own head. What humiliation can you imagine worse for your soul than that you should remain forever in Hell? On the one hand, you will end regretful: on the other, your final fate will be catastrophic. If you will only obey, you will hearken to my advice: practice patience and strive in long-suffering. There is no heroism like patience, especially on the day of separation and at the time of exile. If you are heroic and seek patience, you shall thereby wipe this corrosion from your heart. If you avoid seeing Vīs for a year, seek someone else in her place, prefer another to her, you will not suffer distress on her account at the time of separation; you will in the end succeed in not even remembering her. When love for a sweet-heart overcomes the heart there is no better remedy than distance.

206

All love lessens from not seeing the adored one;[1] 'whom the eye does not see the heart does not grieve over!' Absence has erased many a love, so that you would swear it had never been. Many a day you will find your heart recalling Vīs only vaguely.

"Events confront man; he grasps at his desire without his own volition; by the sword, by coin, by science, by plan and stratagem and spell; the events which have confronted you in the world are such that you do not know what plan to apply, what cure to administer. You have become a byword in the seven climes, you are ever of low degree in your brother's eyes. When great and small take the bowl of wine at the banquet they number you among the shameless. They do not know anyone as rancorous as you in the world; they call you nothing but unchivalrous. They say, 'Why should someone like him live, a disgrace to his brother in mettle? Even had Vīseh been the moon and sun, desire of the reason, joy and hope of the soul, it would not have been right for sagacious Rāmīn to practice love and make a compact with Vīs; better that there should not be in the world that happiness and desire which brings disgrace upon the soul. For one like Rāmīn, champion and musician, to soil his nature with ill fame! Once the nature is soiled with a single shame, the water of a hundred rivers will not wash the corrosion from it. Like our soul, which subsists to eternity, ill fame survives so long as the soul inhabits the body. It seems Rāmīn has not so much as a single friend to restrain him from such enterprises. "A friend armed with good counsel is better than a jewel; a heart that takes life easily is more precious than a whole kingdom."'

"You have enjoyed the desire of your heart from Vīs; have plucked the fruit from the branch of love. Even if you see her for a hundred years she will be the same; she is no Hūrī of Paradise nor yet the moon in the sky. If you seek you shall find a thousand superior to her in beauty and purity. How can you dissipate life and youth with one woman in this profitless manner? If you take another lover, you will hold your bond to her as naught in your heart. You have known no sweetheart but her in the world; this is why you have chosen her before other beauties. You deal in stars, for you have not known the moon! Expel desire from your heart that has lost its way,

1. Cf. *Tristan*, p. 295.

try a road of your own: with your brother you hold in victorious sway the wide world from India and China to Byzantium and Barbary; it is not as if there is no other land but the march of Khurāsān, or no other sweetheart but Princess Vīs; seek out an abode for yourself in another quarter, seek out a silvery-bosomed beauty from every city.

"Review all the beauties till you find a sweetheart fairer than the moon; a beauty such that beside her fair face Vīs will slip from your memory. Enjoy fortune and life: ever slake your desire of this world.

"How long will you sit thus in misery? How long suffer anguish in your precious soul? The time has come for you to feel compunction before the nobles, and to treat your brother, too, with consideration. The time has come for you to seek your desire of youth; to quest for fame in banquet and battlefield; to bear in mind greatness and act upon an auspicious omen. You should now seek kingship, for you are worth no less: why do you haunt the Nurse and Vīs? You have dissipated your good name because of them; your contemporaries are questing after position and rank; you, month in, year out, are seeking out Vīs and the Nurse! Your companions seek sovereignty; you, sport and impurity. Your days of sport and play are past: how long will you go on galloping over the field of play? What demon is this that has cast a spell on your soul and thus made you quite feeble? You are in thrall to a sinister demon, not in obedience to the lord of the world.

"I fear that in the end your affairs will take such a turn that your enemies shall gain their desire; if you act on my humble advice, you will escape from all this misery;[2] your grief will turn to happiness; your tribulation to ease; disaster will turn to joy, folly to wisdom. If you have not had more than your fill of the events you have witnessed, well, then, I may as well not have spoken, nor you heard my words! Go on acting as you are doing and see what befalls! The world will make a move to counter your every gambit. You are at the center, I on the sidelines; 'the onlooker sees most of the game!'"

When desperate Rāmīn heard these words, you would have sworn he became like a donkey stuck in the mire. From confusion his face now became like a tulip, now like saffron, now pitch. He said to him,

2. *I. Mb:* "you will not further seek to act rudely toward the King."

"What you say is true, my heart is in feud with my soul. I have hearkened to your good advice, I assure you, and cut myself off from this silly heart, I swear. You will no more see me questing after desires; desire will not cause a river to run over my face.[3] Tomorrow I take the road to Māhābād; I shall wander about the world free as a wild ass; I shall not cultivate the society of lovers nor practice love with the fair; why should I in vain hope perform an action that causes my soul eternal shame?"

71.

MOUBAD COUNSELS VĪS. As Bihgū spoke to Rāmīn, the King, too, addressed to Vīs of the fairylike face fair words so sage that the stony heart of his spouse softened toward him. He pressed into service phrases of every kind; came to an end and began once more from the beginning. He said to her, "Spring of those who seek love; in face sun of moonlike beauties: how much suffering have I undergone for desire of you, what pain have I suffered from your cruelty! For long I have had to do with love, for you have thrown the days of my life to the wind! I know no beauty that you do not possess; no excellence that is not mine. There is no ruler in the world today better than I; you are queen of the fair, I King of Kings. Come, let us two be lovers: and rule the world in joy. In the seraglio be queen and lady; I shall be King of Kings to the outside world; I shall have the name of sovereignty, true, but you all power of command. Wherever there is a city and famous place, wherever there is a mountain meadow bright with gaudy blooms, I shall surrender all sovereignty to you, for now you deserve a hundred such. My viziers shall be yours, my secretaries yours. Give them commands in every affair, for you are worthy to issue commands. Since I am enslaved by love for you, and am in soul and heart devoted to desire for you, who in the world may dare to strive against you, or wrest his heart from your covenant and behest?

"My sweetheart, accept my advice; for even as I am good I wish you well. Unlike you I am not ill-disposed, nor all untruthfulness at heart; my soul is devoted to love; my tongue the very dragoman of truth; all that my soul seeks is love and love alone; all that my tongue

3. *I.*

209

speaks, truth and the whole truth. Set the seal on my speech in purity; for there is no speech as good for you as mine. If you will sort with me with loving heart and no more play the backgammon of discord, you will become such that the kings of the age will kiss the threshold of your audience hall. But if you persist in acting in the same old way toward me, there will be no worse enemy than myself! Do not do so, my Moon; abhor my wrath, for even fierce fire shrinks before my anger. My fair one, feel shame before Vīrū; for none has a brother like him; how can you reconcile yourself to that champion always having his face blackened by shame on your account? Had you felt shame before your brother I should have treated you with great gentleness. But since you are innocent of love for your brother, how can I credit talk of love from your lips? Since you do not guard the good name of your ancestors, and are unworthy both of brother and of mother, how then can I aspire to love from you, even had I the moon and sun for crown? Now once and for all give me an answer; do not kick against the pricks of fate and play into the hands of your enemies! Tell me what you have in your stony heart—the sapling of enmity or of friendship? For I have become weary of life from love of you; henceforth I shall cross-question you only with the sword! It is not meet to exercise consideration further: for my secret has become notorious throughout the world."

72.

VĪS REPLIES TO MOUBAD. When charming Vīs heard these words, she rose from her place like a garden cypress; she said to him, "Noble lord, more massive in clemency than Mount Damāvand, your heart has practiced the way of endurance; your hand the custom of scattering pearls; God has vouchsafed to you all that is proper; talents calculated to prosper your throne; your talents are more evident than the sun; your actions fairer than hope itself. You are the glorious king of the age: live in the age forever! In nobility you are the sky of fame; in sway, the sun of success; your propitious fame is like the blazing sun; your writ runs like the decree of God. Your Majesty, you know that the Sphere is about a different task every moment; all its actions we continually witness are according to the order and decree of the Creator. God has set it in motion by design; and thereby has settled all things great and small in it by so disposing. From the beginning of the world till the last day it marches round us in but one way. It turns as the Creator has commanded it; he has guided its way according to his desire. He has compounded better and worse in us even as he has written on our heads the decree of right and wrong. The compounded clay will not be transmuted by wisdom; nor will the decree be amended by heroism; be it the foolish or the cunning of this world, all are perplexed and impotent in their affairs. Whether my nature be pure or adulterated, it is even as God has created it. Having once been created in the beginning, I was brought up according to that same design. Even as God has made you victorious, may he not conversely have made my soul unlucky? I am innocent of good and evil; for I do not wish evil for myself. I did not say, 'I do not accept safety, but pain, suffering, and blame.' They created me for suffering, even as they brought me up for wretchedness. I did not say, 'I would have my cheeks yellow and desire my soul and heart to be constantly full of pain.' Any day I have called myself happy, that happiness has turned to torture for my soul. What remedy have I, since my luck is thus? You would swear that the Sphere was in feud against my soul! From losing its way my heart is the color of indigo; it seems some ghoul is the guide of my fate! I have now become so weary of my soul that I wish myself the prey of the lion. I shall tear the veil of my heart with my nails and sever the thread of my soul with my teeth. I have no further need of heart and soul; for from them arise my suffering and pain. Not so much as a breeze blows on my heart for a single day; on no one day is the soul happy in my body. Since my fortunes have collapsed in such chaos, and the eye of my fortune is always slumbering, why should I pursue a love whose fruit is pain and eternal shame? A lord such as you has become my enemy; kith and kin have deserted me. My enemies have come to know my secret; the world has become like a dungeon in my eyes. What is the point of the pursuit of love in the midst of this tribulation, of affection in this wretchedness? So much blame has come to my ears that I have become nothing less than a notorious figure in the world.

"They have opened a door on my dark soul and placed a lamp in the porch there; light has fallen on my heart; reason has sought

every moment into a new trap, hearing reproach from every tongue, he sent a message to the King to say, "I purpose to go to the land of Māhābād; pain melts my body; maybe that climate will restore me; I beg King Moubad that I may be general in that land; perhaps I shall find some clue to health, my body become free of pain and languor.

"For a time on mountain and plain I shall seek the pleasantest hunting, sometimes trap mountain sheep and deer with the cheetah, sometimes capture partridge brown and gray with the hawk. Then at any time the King may command I swear by head and eyes that I shall come speeding to the court."

Rāmīn's message pleased the King; he granted him his desire in his majesty. He bestowed on him Reyy, Gurgān, and Kūhistān[2] and enjoined him to mete out justice to the people. As Rāmīn moved his camp forth in kingship, the reveler of the banquet suddenly became the traveler on the road. He went to see Vīs, intending to mount once he had visited her.

When he came before her he sat on the throne, but that smiling idol waved him away and said to him, "Arise from the King's place! Since you are of lesser state, avoid the place of the great! For you to presume to sit in the King's place is as much as to seek his position. It is premature for you to seek this position; perhaps your demon has tempted you along this road!"

Rāmīn departed downcast from her, cursing his fortune under his breath. He said, "My foolish and unrighteous heart! See from whence anguish has arisen for you! You experienced all that former tribulation because of passion for Vīs; now see what you have heard from her lips! Let none seek love from women, for the rose will not bloom from the salt desert. Love of women is like the tail of the ass— it never grows longer for all you measure it; I have for some time measured this ass's tail and taken my way seduced by the tempting of the demon; I thank God the Creator that now my eyes and heart are awake; I have distinguished virtue from vice, the fine and good from evil. Why have I vainly dissipated my youth and thrown my life to the winds? Alas for the days that are past and gone, alas for

2. *G* adds "Hamian and all Eraq."

my hopeful heart! 'Better to rend one's throat with one's own hand than to hear abuse from one of low degree!' 'Leave a house which turns out to be cursed by an ill omen to fall in ruins as quickly as may be!' This cold abuse has come at the proper moment, for it has only made my heart more sated of her than before. Since I am to cut my heart off from her, why lament at hearing abuse? I have obtained a pretext for separation; the limit of my woe has come into view. I might have bought such abuse for a hundred jewels in order to attain separation! Now that she has granted me fortune free of charge, flee, my heart, from tribulation while you may! Flee, my heart, from the blow of fate! Flee from eternal shame! Flee, that you may not shed my blood; if you do not flee now, when will you?"

Rāmīn's heart remained pondering thus: it was for all the world like a wound crammed with pepper.

When jasmine-bosomed Vīs saw him downcast, she found her heart full of the arrowpoints of grief. She repented of her hasty speech, since Rāmīn was hurt by it. She brought out from the royal treasury one hundred thirty chests of tanned leather embossed with gold; in them beautiful colored garments, all silk weave of Rome, Shushtar,[3] and China;[4] each one like spring blossom in ornamentation, different kinds of embroidery worked upon it. Each one was in fairness like the fortune of Rāmīn; she sent them one and all to his couch; then clothed him in royal garments, a tulip-colored robe and a crimson turban in whose crimson pattern gold was interwoven, like the face of a desperate lover and the cheek of his love.

Then they took hands and went on their own into the garden. For a time they enjoyed happiness and play, two sweethearts entwined together; the garden was gorgeously colored by the hue of their faces, the breeze blew musk-laden from the perfume of their locks. Now the two would laugh as they embraced and played, now both weep from the pain of separation. The eyes of jasmine-bosomed Vīs were filled with bloodstained tears, her cheeks the color of a *dīnār* spattered with blood. The cornelian of her two lips was turned to turquoise; the heart of the very world bled for her plight. One eye, but a thousand clouds raining pearls; one soul, but a thousand

3. In Khūzistān. See n. 12, p. 220.
4. *G:* "Chinese, Baghdad cloth of gold."

214

kinds of distress. The rose of her cheeks was scored by hazelnuts dipped in musk; pearls shone from her bloodstained narcissus.

She said, "My sweet faithless lover! Why do you make my day dark night? This is not what you told me on the first day, nor this the old compact you concluded with me! How much must our love have declined for your heart to become sated of love for me! I am the same Vīs, the same beauty with face like the sun; now as ever of cypress stature and jasmine bosom! What have you experienced from me other than love and loyalty, that you have cut your heart quite off from love of me? If you have found some new love, forbear to cast the old love for me into the sea! Rāmīn, do not visit the cruelty of separation upon me; Rāmīn, forbear to expose me to the tender mercies of my enemies! Do not so, Rāmīn, for you will return repentant, the bond of amity snapped, the treaty torn! Once you turn your face away from me, though you seek sight of me at the price of your life, you shall not find it. You will not be able to face in your heart separation from me; when you return you will with difficulty find me. Now you are a wolf; but then you shall be a sheep and shall be bankrupt of all this pride and self-seeking! You shall mourn before me like the high notes of the harp, rubbing your cheeks in the dust of my feet.[5] You shall experience from me the selfsame suffering that I have experienced from you; taste from me what I have tasted from you. I shall practice toward you this same haughtiness and capriciousness; I shall requite you good for good and evil for evil."

Eloquent Rāmīn replied to her, "God has knowledge of my secret; he knows that I cannot bear to be without you, but that I am tormented by fear of enemies; it is on your account that the world has become my enemy and my very shirt is wary of me. The deer on the plain has become a leopard to me, the fish in the sea a crocodile.[6] The sun does not shine on me other than in wretchedness; the cloud does not rain on me other than in misery; from the abundance of abuse that I have heard from men I have witnessed the Judgment Day in this world. I fear well-wishers and friends as much as enemies

5. Vīs recalls her prophecy later.
6. *G:* "even mice overcome me like panthers, and fishes affright me like dragons."

and those who wish me ill. Whenever I drink a draught of water from the hand of anyone I fear lest it be pure poison. In my dreams I see swords, leopards, dragons, and lions;[7] I am afraid that the King may do away with my life unawares by some stratagem. The moment I no longer possess life, I shall not have in the world a sweetheart like you. As soon as they take my life, I shall not be able to lift a finger either in my own cause or yours. What better than that there should be a soul in my body, and with it in my breast a sweetheart like you?

"It is better, then, that I should preserve my soul and keep love for you grounded in it. In the world, too, the night is pregnant; who knows what shall be born of it on the morrow? What if there be separation for a year, if after it come eternal intimacy? The world has many wiles and spells; who knows how many spells it maneuvers? Who knows how much light will shine after black separation? Although I am ever full of pain, wretched and prostrate, I am nevertheless hopeful of a remedy for it all. Although wretched for years and months, I do not fail in hope of the day of triumph. Our God, full of mercy and equity, has given everyone such hope: hope that one day we shall survive the day of trouble and affliction and follow it with delight and happiness. So long as I have life, I have hope that one day the sun shall be my mate. You are the sun, and so long as you are not by me the world is to me like those dark locks of yours. I have experienced much suffering from Fate, and it is love for you alone that has provoked it. I know that this suffering is passing, and my heart is certain of joy hereafter. 'When trouble most multiplies fetters and nails all trials are resolved.' 'The breeze opens the eye of the spring blossom when snow closes the mountain passes.'"

Jasmine-bosomed Vīs said, "It is even so; but Fortune is in feud against me; I do not imagine that once it has stolen my lover away it will again suffer me to see his face. I am afraid you may one day see in Gūrāb a maiden like a resplendent pearl; a cypress in stature, the cypress jasmine-bosomed; a Moon in face, the moon secreting musk. Then you will have no consideration for loyalty to me; but will surrender your faithless heart to her. Beware of passing through Gūrāb, for there the heart turns like a waterwheel.[8] From the

7. Cf. note 6.
8. Persian dūlāb.

216

abundance of beauties and maids fair as the moon that you will see, you will scarce know which one to choose, for in that land all women are like the moon in the heavens. When they show their faces to men they steal the heart with their fair countenances and tresses, as the wind in spring snatches the rose petal from the boughs. They will ensnare you with their bewitching tresses and sorceresses' eyes; as the lion traps the wild ass and the cheetah the deer. Even though you have a thousand hearts like anvils, you will be left helpless in desperation at the sight of them. Even if you are adept at binding demons, you will not know how to escape them."

Rāmīn, light of the world, said, "Even if a Moon were to come and revolve round me for a month, Canopus her bracelet, her crown the sun, Pisces her waistband, and Venus her necklace, all her words enlightenment and all her actions enchantment, lips nectar, kiss a wondrous cure, cheeks all charm, and eye bewitching: her aspect making the old young, her lips bringing the dead to life, I swear I would not fail in love for you, nor choose any love above yours; in my devotion to you, even the Nurse would be more to me than a moon with such a throne and jewels."

Then they kissed and pressed their cheeks together a thousand times and made their eyes rivers of blood as they bade each other farewell. As they heaved sighs of grief from their hearts they threw burning embers up to the heavens. As they shed the flood of tears of grief at separation they scattered jewels all over the plain. From the multitude of their sighs the sky became Hell; from their tears the earth became the sea of Oman. The two desperate lovers were poised like crazed things betwixt Hell and ocean.

When Rāmīn mounted, took up his accouterments, and lifted the veil from the face of his sweetheart's patience, Destiny fashioned a bow from the figure of Vīs, to shoot Rāmīn from it like an arrow. Rāmīn sped like an arrow flying afar, but the bow stayed where it was dabbled in blood.

Vīs cried in her loneliness, "Patience is lost to me till you return; an ill fate has started you on the road; the desire of my heart has flung me into a dungeon; my love, so long as you remain on the road she who ever desires you will languish in a dungeon. What fortune is this? A curse on such fate! Sometimes throwing me on the ground, sometimes setting me on a throne! My sad heart contains more pain than could be contained even in sixty parasangs of plain. It has made my eye like the sea in abundance of moisture, my soul like Hell from abundance of grief; right enough that sleep should not visit my eyes, nor patience remain in my soul; who would stand dwelling continually in the ocean, who bear to rest in Hell? What could be worse than that when mentioning my enemies I should say, 'May my enemy be even as myself!' I do not say, 'May he suffer such and such!' Instead I say, 'May he be wretched and lamenting like me!'"

As Rāmīn set off from the hall, the clamor of brazen trumpets rose to the Pleiades. The dust that rose from the cavalry was like a black cloud, whose rain was the tears of Rāmīn. Although he was hurt by his sweetheart, for the brand of cruelty lay upon his heart, he yet writhed in the pain of separation, the dust of separation settled on his cheeks.

No lover has patience, least of all on the day of separation and at the time of parting! When a heart is patient in separation, love of the fair is not its way!

74.

RĀMĪN GOES TO GŪRĀB, SEES GUL, AND FALLS IN LOVE WITH HER. Although Rāmīn attained to lordship of a march and championship at the court of his brother, yet for all his command and sovereignty his heart without Vīs was like a fish without water. He traveled the marches of his kingdom, the will of his command ran current. He traveled to every city and place and toppled evil men the world through. He made Gurgān so free from fear and so secure that the wolves[1] acted as shepherds to the sheep. In the bounds of Sārī eagle and partridge were friend and mate of the mountain[2] partridge. From the plenteous carousing and joy in Āmul you would have sworn that the water of its river was wine.[3] By virtue of his justice all in Kūmish spent their days and nights in enjoyment of desire.[4] From fear of his sword the wild ass[5] in Gūrāb drank water

1. Persian gurgān.   2. Persian kūhsārī.   3. Persian mul.
4. Persian kām: "desire." I reads "Kāmish" for the place-name.
5. Persian gūr: "wild ass." Persian āb: "water."

with the lion of the forest. He encamped in Isfahān with an army that was the best army[6] in the world. From Gurgān to Reyy, Ahvāz, and Baghdad the carpet of peace and justice was spread. The world was like a sleeper resting from tribulation; everyone rejoiced in good fortune. The very age itself became relieved of all need; the kingdom became as prosperous as Paradise. The envious detached their hearts from the world; the trees bore the fruit of felicity. The nobles took the wine bowl in hand day and night, having at last caught fortune in their grasp.

As Rāmīn traversed his marches, it so befell that he passed through Gūrāb. Nobles such as Shāpūr and Rafīdā,[7] glorious as moon and sun in that land, one and all prepared entertainments and illustrious royal banquets for him; in the early morning they all went to the chase and took wine at their ease as fortunate men will; now on the hunting ground with arrow and dagger, now in the banqueting hall with music and wine bowl. Sometimes they trapped lions in the reedbed, sometimes grasped the wine bowl in the gardens. They passed their days in the fine manner I have described, all in pleasure and hunting. Whether in sobriety or drunkenness Rāmīn's heart was like a pomegranate stuffed with pain and languor. For every arrow he shot at the game the desire of his heart shot one at him. At night when he remained alone away from his friends he caused a river to flow with the bloodstained tears of his eyes.

Thus fared his fortunes till one day he saw on the road a captivating sun. A beauty, a fresh spring, heart's ease, a tyrant, horsed to steal hearts, in beauty a sovereign, a robber of hearts, in kisses a rich fortune for the soul, delight for the heart; in cheeks a garden and rose plot, a sugar plantation in the midst of the plot! Her twin locks had conned the recipe of every spell, copied the curve of every *jīm*[8] and *nun*.[9] Her lips had become the cure of every hurt, had robbed all honey and sugar of glory; her mouth narrow like a *mīm*[10] of cornelian; her twin teeth peeping from it like the glittering Pleiades. In her eye she affected an archer from Abkhāz;[11] in her locks

6. Persian *sipāh*: "army." Persian *ān*: "that." Isfahān is here spelled *sipāhān*.
7. See Minorsky, *Iranica*, p. 167.   8. The Persian letter *j*.   9. The letter *n*.
10. The letter *m*.   11. In the Caucasus. Minorsky, *Ḥudūd ul-ʿĀlam*, p. 456.

a scorpion of Ahvāz; her cheeks were a bale of Shushtar[12] brocade; her lips a bale of 'Askarī[13] sugar cane; the one like roses on which musk has been scattered, the other like pearls over which wine has been poured. Her hyacinth[14] had become an armorer working upon roses;[15] her narcissus[16] a bowman working upon the moon;[17] the Pleiades were cast among chain-mail, musky bark was fitted to her bow.[18] Her cheek earned the name of "pomegranate blossom of Barbary"; her locks merited the byname of "sweetheart's chain." One had been watered by the spring of the elixir of life, the other twisted by the hand of captivation. Her cheeks all snow and blood, milk and wine; her mouth all sugar, nectar, honey, and pearls. Round the one twisted a musky scorpion; round the other, flashing stars. Stone and steel had become slaves to her heart; as the cypress and boxtree to her figure. She had veiled her silvery limbs in half-transparent silk; like a dappled fish in bright water. On her head a crown of musk and ambergris; above it, a diadem of gold and gems. Her hair fell from her head to her feet, scented like musk and colored like a witch's soul; like night depending from the morning star, or a throne of musk set about the moon. The corner of her cheek was like brocade full of roses; the brocade worked with hyacinths.

Such was this beauty, fit to melt the frame and delight the heart; sweet of voice, haughty in caprice; like a garden, its blossoms moon and Pleiades; like a mass of spring blooms with rose and lily its pride; a beauty whom the Creator had fashioned prettily and the dresser decked out anew. Her body brocade, but brocade set with pearls; her face fair, but gorgeously painted. In the profusion of her ornaments she was like a treasury full of ornaments; in the abundance of her jewels like a mine rich in gems. Ambergris rained from her curls as pearls and jewels from the embroidery of her garments. For a whole parasang radiance accompanied her together with the zephyr of love. The moon shone from her crown, the sun from her shining face, Canopus from her neck, and the Pleiades from her teeth. In beauty she was like sovereignty and youth; in sweetness like desire

12. In Khūzistān. *Ibid.*, pp. 130–31.
13. *Ibid.*, p. 130, *s.v.* 'Askar-i Mukram.
14. Her curls.   15. Her cheeks.   16. Her eye.   17. Her face.
18. Order of lines here as in *I*.

and life. In fairness like a garden in spring bloom; in grace and charm like the deer of the meadow. Eighty beautiful maidens, picked from the fairest of the fair, attended her; idols of China, Rome, India, and Barbary, around her like eglantine around cypress; before her like the Pleiades before the moon.

When Rāmīn saw that gliding cypress, a living idol, a Moon come to life, you would have sworn it was the earth-illumining sun he saw, for his eye was filled with splendor at the sight. His legs grew weak, and he stared, rooted to the spot; so feeble did he become that the arrows dropped from his grasp. His eyes did not believe what they saw; was it an idol, the moon, or the sun?

He said, "Is this Paradise I see or spring, a Hūrī of Paradise or a Chinese figurine? A lofty cypress in the garden of charm, a pheasant strutting in the garden of joy? The idol-like beauties are an army, she their queen; or like stars, and she their Moon!"

Noble Rāmīn was pondering thus when that silvery cypress approached him. You would have sworn she was an old friend of his, for she came up, embraced him,[19] and said to him, "Illustrious king of the world, the land of Māh is made bright as the moon by your presence.[20] Stay with us this one night; you have become grieved; rest this one hour! Accept entertainment of us this one night, for we shall keep you in comfort and happiness; I shall bring you rose-colored wine bright and sweet that has the scent of musk and the color of fire. I shall bring you wild fenugreek from the woods, violets sweetly scented as yourself; fowl and spring francolin from the glade, mountain partridge from the hill. I shall bring you rose and white lily from the garden and make your banquet like many-colored brocade. I shall hold you precious as my dear soul, for thus do we treat our guests."

Rāmīn, light of the world, said, "Moonlike maiden, tell me your name and lineage; from what lineage are you sprung in Gūrāb? Have you plighted your silvery body, or not? What is your name, from what place are you? Do you desire me as spouse, or not? Should anyone become your suitor, what dowry would your mother

19. Cf. *Tristan*, p. 294, where Isolde of the White Hands, to whom the character of Gul corresponds, displays a similar familiarity toward Tristan.
20. *Māh*: "moon," also "Media."

require of him? Your sweet lip is full of honey and sugar; will you not tell me what is the price of a cane of that sugar? Even if the price of your sugar were life itself, I swear by your life that it would be cheap at the price!"

The eloquent Sun, a charming angel, a Hūrī of fairy face, replied to him, "I am not one whose name is hidden; do I have to tell anyone who I am? For the sun is not hidden from any man; everyone knows the shining sun! My mother is Gouhar and my father Rafīdā; distinguished for good name throughout the land. My glorious brother is lord of a march, the knightly ruler of Āzerbaijān. My mother bore me under a rose tree and named me sweet-smelling Gul:[21] I am of renowned lineage both on mother's and on father's side; the former is from Hamedān, the latter from Gūrāb. I am rose-petaled, rose-scented, of rosy limbs; rose my face and cheeks; my name is Gul; all in Gūrāb swear that I am now Princess of Gūrāb. My beauty has descended to me from my mother; my nurse has brought me up with love and tender care. In face I am moon-visaged like my mother; in figure, cypress-statured like my brother. My neck is crystal, my breast silvery; soft as ermine and perfumed with eglantine.

"Why do you inquire about me and my family? for I know your name and lineage well; you are Rāmīn, the King's brother, to whom love for Vīs is as precious as the soul. Here you are possessing your soul in patience in Gūrāb away from the sight of her; that is, if a fish can ever be patient out of water! You are staying apart from that graceful boxtree; that is, if the Tigris may be parted from Baghdad! This calamity may be washed from your soul as soon as blackness from the skin of the Ethiopian! The old nurse has attached your heart to Vīs, contriving nails and chains by her spells: never to abandon Vīs or become attached to another lover. Since you cannot bear to abstain from her, devote yourself to her alone; you shamed by her, she by you. The King has become enraged by you; God displeased with both of you!"

When noble Rāmīn heard these words, he cursed his desperation in his heart; for he had become a byword for desperation and had heard blame from everyone in the world. Again he spoke gently to that Moon words that seduced her heart: he said to her, "Beauty of

21. Persian *gul*: "rose."

cypress form, idol with face like the sun, countenance like the moon; Gūrāb is like the sphere of the sun from your presence: your palace a mine of pure silver from being graced by you; your shift is made a treasure of beauty when you wear it: no one knows what wealth is in your treasury!

"Do not blame the victim of disaster; rather pray to God that he may obtain deliverance. All the works of the world are a mystery to its denizens; the hand of Providence overreaches humankind! Forbear to upbraid me with my evildoing; perhaps Destiny has written this fate upon me! Do not recall the past works of the world; for one cannot recover an action past and gone. If you will bear with me, moon two weeks old, you will not recall deeds that are in the past; you will not reck of yesterday but see today and choose me out before any you may see; become my true companion, my confidante in companionship; you shall be the sun in my castle, your face spring in my Chinese temple. If I obtain my desire of you, you in your turn shall obtain what desire you may cherish. You have no option but to choose a generous king; I none but to choose a gleaming moon. Be my moon with all your heart; for I shall be your king with all mine. I shall bestow on you all I possess in the world; even should you desire my life, I shall offer it to you. Other than you there shall be no queen of my palace, no remedy of my soul. The moment I am united with you, I shall swear before you by the Truth that so long as there be mountain and plain in the world, so long as Oxus and Tigris flow to the sea, water come from the spring, fish from the sea, the sun show its radiance and the night its blackness, sun and moon shine, the splendid cypress flaunt itself in the garden, the morning breeze waft over the mountains, the unbroken wild ass graze on the meadow, you shall dwell with me and I with you forever; we shall live in hope of each other's love. I shall take in my embrace no lover but you and shall forget all others I have seen. I had no lover fairer than Vīs; but I now abandon her in this world and the next."

The Sun of rosy limbs answered him, "Do not set a trap for me by sorcery, Rām! I am not the one to fall into your trap or accede to your desire as an easy conquest! I require of you no sovereignty, neither absolute sway nor authority; no field full of the commotion of armies, no vault full of coin and gems; this is my desire of you, if I may gain it, never to turn my head aside from your command and will. You shall be to me a king possessing the whole world; I to you a servant. If you can cherish my love and persevere in loyalty to me, you will find no lover like me in the world, respecting loyalty, seeking to be faithful, remaining true. The march of Khurāsān is no place for you; stay here happy and at your ease. Do not again frequent Vīs the witch; how may Moubad's wife be yours? Forget her, however dear she may be; men's property is their own. Swear on oath that you will not cherish love for her, nor send her a message or emissary. If you will swear such an oath to me, our bodies shall have two heads but one soul."

When Rāmīn heard these words from that Moon he forbore to set his tongue to a reply; he accepted this proposal from Gul, took her hand, and escorted her to the house. When Rāmīn entered the hall of Rafīdā hand in hand with that Moon of cypress stature, they scattered a hundred cupfuls of jewels at his feet and sat him on a gold-ornamented throne. They decorated door and wall with brocade and covered the ground with pure ambergris.

75.

RĀMĪN MARRIES GUL. Rāmīn, light of the world, made a compact, sworn with an oath according to their custom, "So long as life inhabits my body, Gul of the sunlike face shall be my wife. I shall no more seek malevolent Vīs nor any of the fair of the world besides Gul. Gul shall be my lover as long as I live, my heart shall be indifferent to all others. Gul of the rosy scent shall be my joy, the land and realm of Gūrāb my dwelling." Then they summoned the nobles and once more scattered pearls and gems. All threw their hearts open to pleasure, and set about gaiety and rejoicing. Then Gul sent a messenger to her family to apprise everyone of this event. From Gurgān, Reyy, Qumm, Isfahān, Khūzistān, Kūhistān, and Hamedān, from every city came a king, from every march a margrave. The seraglio became full of a concourse of Moons; the hall filled with a company of kings. They set up festive stands for forty miles; everywhere people sat drinking wine. So many cups full of wine were seen in the hands that you would have sworn the plain was all tulips.

When day broke, by every meadow and stream there came to the ear divers songs. When night fell, from every plain and upland meadow a lamp shone from every hand—its bowl of wine; the rock of the mountains was cornelian-hued; the streams in their turn ran nectar. The wild asses saw so much sport on the hillsides that they learned how to sport and play! The birds saw so much celebration on the mountains that they became connoisseurs of wine drinking! There were so many strains of melody in the gardens that all the birds became harpists and flautists; there was such abundance of musk on the face of the countryside that it all became Kharkhīz[1] and Shushtar;[2] so much wine was poured on the mountain ridges that a flood of wine ran down the streams, so much on the plain that Korah[3] was like to become drunk under the earth! The vapor of sweet scents hung like a cloud; dust was washed from the wide world by wine. Great and small, all, men and women alike, spent their time in the chase and in pleasure early and late. Now they flung the javelin, now played the lute, they were now drunk, now drowsy, with wine. They plied now the cup, now the polo stick; now performed songs, now jousted with the spearpoint. Now they chased the gazelle from the hill, now distress from their hearts. Now wild sheep, stag, and mountain goat descended willy-nilly to the plain, now deer and wild ass mounted from the plains to the heights pursued by cheetah and hound. The world is not free of woe in and out of season; in that land there was no care for a month. A world of lovers consorting with lovers; passing day and night innocent of distress and grief. Nobles opened their hearts in largesse; minstrels were in great demand. Each one sang in honor of Rāmīn a pretty song and well-tuned lay. They sang:

"Rāmīn, live forever happy and joyous, far from all care; you enjoy your every desire, you enjoy all fame for which you quest; your ambition has been granted in good measure through your victoriousness, your name has become renowned through fair fortune. You have come on a hunt[4]—what a wonder! You have seized a fine prey in Gul; in glory the sun has become your quarry, the Rose of beauty has bloomed in your embrace. Now

1. Minorsky, *Ḥudūd ul-ʿĀlam*, p. 96; *Encyclopaedia of Islam, s.v.* Kirgiz.
2. See n. 12, p. 220.   3. See note 10, p. 92.   4. See Introduction, p. xvii.

225

you ever have a rose by you, your constant religion is rose worship. The rose of Paradise is hardly like your Rose; for your heart has become this Rose's plot. What rose has, like this one, blossomed on the moon, its rose plot a moon two weeks old? You have a rose in your embrace in December, and better still, you have a rose without a thorn! Your rose has a live rose plot; do you know where there is anywhere such a plot? A rose plot that is by your side early and late, sometimes in the garden, sometimes on the throne. Take your pleasure with it, for it sheds its petals neither in summer nor in winter. A rose whose thorn is a curl that diffuses musk and, a greater wonder still, its musk enchants the heart; a rose whose gardeners are twin scorpions, whose guardians twin narcissi. A rose from whose color youth springs, even as life from its scent. A rose fit for you to pursue with your whole heart, to smell with your very soul. A rose with the scent of musk and the color of wine, planted by angels, watered by Rizvān. A rose which has become rare, all others ordinary; round which charm has set a snare of ambergris. A rose dispensing ambergris all around, dispensing sugar all along its path. May this rose live long in Rāmīn's hand, and with it the bowl of wine. So be it triumphantly; may the world be according to the desire of both!"

76.

GUL TAKES OFFENSE AT RĀMĪN'S WORDS. When they had spent a whole month in rejoicing, with polo stick, wine, song, and the chase, the spring of the wedding[1] came to its end, the renowned dignitaries departed; Gul and Rāmīn took their rest and departed joyfully to the castle of Gūrāb.

Again came the dresser and adorned that jasmine-bosomed beauty from head to foot; the Moon of Gūrāb became so gorgeously adorned that the eye gained splendor from the sight of her. You would have sworn her face was ornament upon ornament, the corner of her cheek blossom upon blossom of spring. Although her hair was jet black, as was her doelike eye, yet the dresser applied musk to her locks, even as she touched up her twin doelike eyes with collyrium.

1. _I._

She prinked up her twin curls and eyebrows, beautified her cheek at corner and side. Gul of the rosy scent became like a blossoming rose; like a cypress embellished with gold and gems. The bright dew of youth dropped from her cheeks; the water of life ran from her lips; her patterned face like a Chinese temple; her patterned hands as full of curls as her hair.

When Rāmīn beheld the face of the captivating sweetheart, her cheek like a blossoming garden; saw her tresses exuding musk like a cloud; her earrings a star in the cloud, her twin locks like loops of ambergris twined about, her cheeks like tulips piled one on another; as many pearls on her neck as the raindrops that spatter on the lily; could a star appear by day, it would be as the gems on her neck! her lip laughing like a ruby endowed with the power of speech, in color and scent like a night-scented mallow, he said to her, "You who are Moon of Gūrāb in beauty; the moon of your face has robbed the very moon of reputation; today you are the antidote of my soul; for you are very like charming Vīs; like her you have a lip of nectar and a bosom of silver; you would have sworn an apple had been cut in twain." Gul was annoyed at Rāmīn's words and said to him, "You of ill thought and evil ways, is the speech of the nobles thus? Is this how princes behave? May there be no other in the world like Vīs, accursed both in beginning and in end and ill-starred! May there be no sorceress in the world like the Nurse; from whom a wizard might derive his stock in trade! It is they who have made you self-seeking, and thereby of ill fame. You will never derive profit of yourself; nor will another lover glean fruit of you! The Nurse has rendered you senseless quite; you do not lend your ear to the advice of others."

77.

RĀMĪN WRITES A LETTER TO VĪS. Once Rāmīn saw that he had wounded her heart, see how he sought excuse for the wound. In Gul's presence he took up parchment and pen, and inscribed the parchment with musky ink. He drew the sword of cruelty and cut with it the bond of faith. That faithless lover penned a letter to a lover all constant and faithful.

He said in it, "Vīs, do you at all know how much harm has

befallen me from you? God and others besides have become offended at me, everyone in the world has upbraided me. I listen now to advice, now to blame; I have become a byword for love in the world. If only my eyes could have descried in the world a single person to approve my action! Here is a wonder indeed! You would have sworn my love was wrath, for men and women alike to curse it thus! Everyone in the world who heard my name baited me with opprobrium. The face of my good name became ugly thus, and even uglier the face of my desire. Now a sword hung over my head, now a lion stood in my path. Ever since I saw you I was not happy at heart; in my wretched heart no breeze stirred. My anguish increased by separation from you; for it was accompanied by a sea of blood in the shape of my eye. My affliction grew worse when I saw you; for it was then accompanied by fear for my very soul and head! Has there ever been a day when I have been separated from you without causing a River Oxus to flow from my eyes? Has there ever been a day when I have seen you without suffering a hundred kinds of pain in my heart? What of it, had there been fear for soul and head, had there not also been shame before men and dread of God? You saw me before I was in love and saw how fancy-free I was in my youth. Every leopard was like a deer in my eyes; every crocodile a mere fish to me. I did not boil up at every wind like the sea; you would have sworn the very sun paled before me. When I was angry even a lion was weak before me; when furious, arrow and sword were feeble; when my falcon mounted the air, the very moon in the heaven shrank from it. The steed of my desire galloped so swiftly, how could cares catch up with it? My hope was like a farseeing eye; my joy saddled like my charger. My cup was full of sweetness as I took my pleasure; my heart's desire was full of jewels from my joy; I was a boxtree in the garden of sport; I was steel on the battlefield; the rocks of the mountains were all gold to me, the pebbles of the rivers all pearls. Then you saw how my plight became after this: that selfsame fortune of mine became weakest of the weak; my youthful cypress figure became bent; my moon two weeks old became the peer of Suhā.[1] Desire made my back crooked as a hoop; you would have sworn Fate made another person of me;

1. The star Alcor.

when the hand of love poured fire on my heart, joy fled a hundred parasangs from me. I found reason exiled from my heart and helpless in the hand of love. Everyone in the world had become like an archer; the blame of everyone an arrow and my soul the target. I already had the brand of love on my breast: why did I need blame to be leveled at my head? As I was already drunk from the cup of desire, why did you have to lay hands upon a drunken man? Now I send you much greeting, although I have become wary of your love.

"Now I shall acquaint you with my adventures and tell you how fine and splendid are my fortunes. Know, Vīs, that since I have become separated from you I am king over every desire of my heart. I have washed my heart with the water of patience and sought out a fine mate according to my very own desire. I have planted a fragrant rose in my heart and am ever in Paradise with my Rose. Now there is ever a rose blossoming by me; now in my hand, now in my embrace, now in my bed, now on my pillow; as precious to me as soul and sight. Gul shall be my wife to all eternity; whilst I have her I have no need of moon and sun. With Gul, my palace is like a garden; with Gul, my castle is like a rose plot. From her I have experienced joy and satisfaction of desire three times the pain and wretchedness I experienced of you. My soul would have been like to fly from my body had it experienced such fortune of you! When I recall the years that are past I have mercy on my wounded soul, for how it practiced perforce all that patience! how it drank all that poison in distress through you! I was not aware of the world at that time, for I rejoiced even in tribulation. Now I have woken from that sleep and become sober after that drunkenness. Now I have snapped the bond of affliction in twain and escaped from that prison of ill fortune. I have sworn an oath to Gul of rosy fragrance, by the glorious Word and the wise Spirit; by the God of the world, by Moon and Sun, by Religion, Wisdom, Enlightenment, and Hope,[2] that so long as I live I shall be faithful to Gul and lay my face to hers in happiness. Hereafter Marv shall be yours, Māh mine; the King with you, my Moon with me. One hour in which I am the companion of this Moon, dwelling happily in the land of Māh, is better than a hundred years of that life which was no more to me than eternal imprisonment.

2. *G:* "Faith, fire, wisdom, and hope."

Hereafter do not count the years and months and days; do not inquire much into my days and ways. For the days and ways of my exile are long; and my heart has nothing to desire of you, hearts' desire! When such fortune and circumstances make their onset, patience is better than silver by the assload."

When Rāmīn had finished this letter he set on its superscription a golden seal. He gave it to his postilion and ordered him to take it speedily to his love. The postilion set off like the swift wind and reached Marv the royal abode in two weeks. They informed the King of this and brought the postilion straight from the road to his presence. The King took the letter from the man and read it, and was amazed at those words; he quickly gave the letter to charming Vīs, gave her glad tidings of Rām's fortunes,[3] and said to her, "May your eye be bright! For Rāmīn is now with the Rose in the rose plot! Rāmīn has gone and taken a wife in Gūrāb and speared you, branded as you are, upon the spit."

When the messenger arrived with the letter of Rāmīn, commotion arose in the heart of Vīseh: straightway her heart attested to her that Rāmīn had been disloyal to her.

When Moubad gave Rāmīn's letter to Vīs, a blaze of anguish overtook her soul; her blood boiled within her in distress; but she hid her secret from other people. To outward view her lip smiled like a tulip, but her heart within her was like a molten anvil. To outward view she was as bright as the heaven, whilst within she was like burning Hell. In her laughter she dissimulated the heaviness of her heart, by her swift step she concealed her lameness. Her cheek went yellow from reading the letter, as if it, too, had some little knowledge of the scribe's art.[4]

She said to him, "I have prayed to God to destroy one day the prosperity of the enemy. Perhaps Your Majesty will now no longer address odious words to me, or seek pretexts against me moment by moment. I shall present gifts to the poor to celebrate this joy, and also take many jewels to the fire temple. He has escaped from grief now, and so have I; the enemy's prosperity is shattered. Now I have no care in the world, for my soul has no fear of your cruelty. Even

3. *G:* "in derision asked something in return for his good tidings."
4. See p. 265.

in the midst of desire, fame, and triumphant fortune I neither ate nor slept for so much as a single day. Though the moon has deserted me, the sun remains; 'everyone has hopes of the sun.' Now I shall be happy in my youth and spend my life in ease. My eyes shall become radiant at the sight of you; what if I do not see the face of Rāmīn?"

She said these words but her heart was not at one with her tongue; the outer aspect of her words did not reflect the inner. When the King withdrew she burned in fever; her soul hovered on the brink of departure from the torment of love. Her heart began fluttering in her bosom like a pigeon whose head is caught in the talons of a hawk. Cold sweat dropped from her limbs like dew settling on a yellow rose. The straight cypress of her figure trembled like a willow in the wind; she shed rubies on jasmine from her narcissus eyes. She beat her silvery breast with her golden necklace and swept the dust of the earth with her musky tresses.

She writhed on the ground and said, "What is this arrow which has come to pierce my eye? What fortune is this that has made my days black? What fate is this that has ruined my days? Come, Nurse, and see this calamity which has suddenly come like a flood from its ambush! From the golden throne it has cast me on the ground and has scattered thorns on the path of my patience. Do you know, or must I tell you, what distress has come upon me from Rāmīn? He has gone and taken a wife in Gūrāb, then written a letter to give me this news! What will people say of me now in Marv? It is meet that men and women alike should lament over me! Seek a remedy for the sake of my very life; for how can I rescue my soul from this pain? Why have I had to hear this news? If Death itself had overtaken me before this it would have been preferable. Now I have no need of gold or gems; I need neither life nor mother nor brother. My joy in the world was made sweet by Rām; with joy gone, what is the point of these toils? He was like my dear soul; and the body does not find any joy in the world without a soul! I shall go and cleanse my soul of all sin and seek my recourse from God; I shall give all I possess to the poor; perhaps in the time of prayer they will help me. I shall earnestly beseech the Judge of the world that Rāmīn may become repentant of his deed. He will come in the darkness of night from Gūrāb, damp with rain and with moisture congealed upon him; his body, like mine, weak and trembling; his heart, like mine, wretched and burning; now from merciless cold, now from distress, he will crave quarter from Vīs and the Nurse; on that day he shall experience at my hand the same perfidy in love as we experience from him today. O God, exact justice for me from Rām; render him bereft of patience and peace even as I am!"

The Nurse answered her, "Do not suffer this much distress, for it is not proper for you so to do; do not suffer care; wipe the corrosion from your heart by resignation, silence, and enlightenment. Do not so wound your graceful body; do not cause your peaceful heart so to writhe; do not mete out injustice to your soul and your youth; for even death is better for your soul than this life. From thus much scoring your beautifully colored face, tearing out your musky hair, a face fairer than a garden of Paradise has been made by you as ugly as the face of Ahriman. You need the things of this world such as you have and more: but you need them for the sake of your own soul; once dear life no longer breathes in you, perish the Nurse, the King, and Rāmīn! Suppose I give up the ghost from thirst; there need then be no single drop of rain water in the world; once the world is rid of me, what do friends and enemies matter to me in the world? All men are bold to take up with women; but like Rāmīn they are quick to weary of love. If Rāmīn the false in love has become tired of you, before whose face the very sun bows down, he will likewise tire of the love of Gul, that very tongue soft as wax[5] will become like a sword; if he sees a thousand moons and stars, the light of a single sun will not shine upon him from them. Even though Gul of Gūrāb is in face like the moon, she is in low degree like the dust of the lane before you. The very sole of your foot is fairer than her face, as the very dust under your feet is sweeter than her perfume. Since Rāmīn was left lonely and forlorn, I forgive him for taking a wife; a man far from sweet wine may be excused should he drain dregs."

Jasmine-bosomed Vīs said, "My nurse, you know that I have wasted my youth in the practice of patience. Women have husbands and lovers besides: but now I have neither lover nor husband. Such

5. *I. Mb:* "your tongue will become a sword upon him."

husband as I have is suspicious of me; such lover as I have is ill-disposed toward me. I have dissipated my reputation and worth; I have lost my capital for the sake of profit. I have thrown away my *dirham* for the sake of a *dīnār* and am now left in distress without either. Do not counsel me contentment, Nurse! for no one may sleep content on fire! My pillow and bed are fiery; the demon of love is my companion on the fire. How may I be patient on the fire, even were my soul made of stone and brass? Forbear to counsel me contentment further; do not measure the wind before me; no wise man knows my cure, no sage my remedy. A hundred poisoned arrows have been shot into my heart up to the feathers by this courier and his letter. What do you say, Nurse, of this fatal messenger who has suddenly shot all these arrows into my heart? He has brought a musk-scented letter from Rām; he will take back from Vīs bloodstained garments. In my wretchedness I weep over my ailing heart; I rain blood from my eyes on my heart sore wounded; O lovers who cherish love, today I am the princess over all lovers! Out of the kindness of my heart I shall give you advice free: accept advice from me in friendly spirit: I am a warning to you, if you will take warning! See me and hear my plight, then strive no more in the practice of love! Forbear to plant the sapling of love in your hearts, for if you do you will surrender your lives to it. And if you do not know my plight, read it—it is writ in blood upon my cheek!

"Love lit a fire in my heart; the more I put it out the more it burned. I have filled the world with mud from the tears of my eyes; but the fire in my heart has not been damped by the water in my eyes. What kind of eye is this that is not visited by sleep? What kind of water is this that does not quench fire?

"I fancied to keep a sparrow hawk; I brought it up and petted it in a hundred ways; by day I kept it on my silvery wrist; at night I tied it nowhere but by my pillow; it learned to fly from my wrist and swoop upon the pigeons at its pleasure; I fancied it would catch game and always be my comfort. Suddenly it escaped from my wrist and was lost to my sight in the clouds. Now I am exhausted from dashing hither and thither seeking a sign of my escaped sparrow hawk. Alas for my past pains and the time that I have spent! Alas for my hopeful heart! Alas for all the great pains I have taken, for I have not eaten the fruit of my pains for so much as a single day! I shall wander the world like a caravan passenger, seeking to find some sign of my lost one. Both heart and lover have vanished from my breast; I shall not bide here bereft of lover and heart! I shall make stone my pillow on the mountains, because of the cruelty of that heart which is like a mountain of rock. My heart has deserted me; if I find a sign of it I shall give my wounded soul as a present for good news. Whilst my soul is thus full of smoke, how is my heart to be content with fortune? I am she of whom my lover has grown tired, I am she against whom fortune has become angry. You, Nurse, have killed me without a knife; for it was you who sowed the seed of love in my soul. You were my blind guide on this road: it is you that have flung me in the pit—now bring me out of it! Since it is from you that the pain has come upon me, it is right that from you also should come the cure.

"Prepare for the road; rise, do not tarry here; take my message, every word, to Rāmīn; say, 'Well done, ill-willed, disloyal youth! You have strung the bow of ignoble action; you have blinded the eye of truth; you have ruined the fortunes of chivalry. In nature you are like the scorpion—fatal to life; even when you come upon a stone you show your mettle. You are a snake, biting and only biting is your métier; you are a wolf, and your way is only to rend; from your nature shall emanate the selfsame deeds as you did before when you broke faith with those united to you by treaty. Wounded as I am by your actions, I still do not consider you worthy of this fault. Do evil to none, nor purpose evil; for when you do evil it will return upon your head. If love for me has altogether departed from your memory may you be ashamed before lovers! In the disgraceful mode of your departure from me you have forgotten your own fair words: your sweet words were like tulip petals; but under the tulip lay a black snake. If you have taken a new lover, let it be: may you have everything you desire in the world. Do not frighten me with desperation: not everyone who finds gold throws away silver: if you have dug a new channel in Gūrāb you should not shut off the water from the old; and if you have built a dwelling in Kūhistān do not destroy the old one in Marv. If you have planted a rose in the garden, may you have good fortune of it! but do not cut down the graceful box-tree[6] from its plot! Let new wife stay side by side with old lover; so that every seed may bear you fruit in the form of a different heart's desire.'"

Vīs with face like an idol spoke these words, a stream of tears flowing from her eyes on each cheek; you would have sworn that her eye were a Nourūz cloud ever raining upon a delightful upland meadow.

The Nurse, her heart burning for that beauty with idol face, said, "Spring of captivating beauties! Do not seat me on burning fire! Forbear to scatter rose water from your eyes on pomegranate flowers! For now I shall take the road to Gūrāb, I shall ever be without food and sleep on the road.[7] I shall try every artifice I know on Rām; perhaps I may deliver your soul from grief." Thus she spoke and took the road in the early morning, Marv became a bow and the Nurse the arrow shot from it—

78.

THE NURSE GOES TO RĀMĪN AT GŪRĀB. —an arrow which went its whizzing way from Marv the royal abode to the march of Gūrāb; when she came along the road to the march of Gūrāb the faithless prince came before her on the plain; hunting wild ass, stag, and boar like a furious lion; his retinue on the plain like a castle; its rampart every kind of game; some with necks broken, some with fore- and hindlegs snapped asunder, so many arrows stuck in their hides that you would have sworn the game was winged! The air was full of falcons, the plain of hounds, both speeding in flight and coursing. The one had emptied the air of birds, the other the ground of wild beasts. The mountains were dyed with the blood of the mountain goat; as the rocky crag was made into a narrow defile for the deer.

When the Nurse saw Rāmīn at the hunt her heart was filled with arrows by the cruelty of Rām; for when Rāmīn saw her on the road he neither asked about her journey nor inquired after that Moon; but said to her, "Filthy hag, spawn of demons! Teaching evil,

6. *G:* "violet."
7. *I. Mb:* "like the road."

pondering evil, of ill star! You have a hundred times deceived me with your spells, you have robbed me of as much sense and propriety as a drunken man! Now you have come along again suddenly like a ghoul, to cause me to lose my way. No wind of yours will see dust from me, no hand of yours take my halter any more. You might as well depart this spot, for your coming here is profitless and fruitless.

"Go and say to Vīs, 'What do you desire of me, why do you not become sated of disaster? From following the desire of your heart you have committed many sins; you have suffered sore affliction from ill fame. Now is the time to seek excuse; feel repentance and strive in goodness. We have both thrown our youth to the winds and gambled both worlds for a single desire. On the one hand, we have both become ill-famed; on the other, both become frustrated of our desires. If you do not purpose to turn back from this road, I shall not henceforth be your companion. Should we cultivate love for a hundred years more, see what will be left us at the end of it all!' I have received advice from sages of illumined heart and have sworn a firm oath before God by all that is good in the world; by the pure Spirit, the Moon and the shining Sun: I shall not seek any connection with her other than such as God may approve; I shall only then consort with her when I become the King of that earthly Moon. Who knows how many years shall pass till I consort with her? I have become the supreme example of the saying: 'Live, donkey, till the grass grows!' Much water shall flow in the streams before I attain that beauty of fairylike face. How long am I to sit hopefully waiting for one whom I see the spouse of another? The face of the sun would become black were it to live one single year in mere hope. My youth has been dissipated in this hope.

"I ever say, 'Alas for my life! Alas that my youth has made ready for the journey, and nothing is left to me of it but wind in the hand! In beauty it was like colored brocade, in stoutness like rocky Arvand.[1] It was the spring of my life; in beauty like blossoms in the garden. At the blast of the wind of love, my spring has become autumn; the bloom of my beauty has been plucked by the hand of grief. Whereas spring visits the garden yearly, my spring comes but once. That time—those days of youth—is past and gone when I cast my life to

1. See n. 1, p. 111.

the winds. If autumn might have the nature of Nourūz I might today recover the nature of that time!' Beware of speaking vainly to me, nor seek from old age the nature of youth. Return even now and say to Vīs, 'There is nothing better for women than a husband. God has given you a fine husband, the firmament of fortune and the sun of justice. If you are under a fortunate star, hold to him and reck but little of any man beside; for ill-starred as you are, you shall yet illumine the world by your good fortune. The King shall be your lord, I your brother; the world shall be your slave, Fortune your aid. On the one hand, you shall be of fair name in the world; on the other, you shall enjoy your will eternally.'"

Then he turned in anger from the Nurse; the plain became like a prison in her eyes. She saw no warmth in Rāmīn's words, nor excellence in his deeds. Once more she became blind and regretful, her agonized soul cut off from remedy.

If the Nurse's distress was such at the humiliation she experienced from heroic Rāmīn, see how that Moon was hurt, whose friend suddenly became her enemy! She had sown loyalty, and it brought up cruelty for her; her lover requited her with evil though she practiced good. The messenger came shedding tears from her eyes, dust rising from her lips, smoke from her heart. She had taken a letter sweeter than sugar; she brought back an answer more cutting than a dagger. A black cloud came and showered down rain—not rain, rather poisoned arrowpoints! A flash from far away struck the heart of Vīs; a veritable simoom set about the roses of her cheeks in her wretchedness. Her heart was wounded by the sword of cruelty, her soul tied with the chain of affliction. From the pain of her soul and heart she fell on her bed; her lofty cypress was felled. All her bed was filled with pain from her soul, her pillow full of yellow roses from her face.

Round her bed sat the beauties, wives of princes and champions: one of them would say, "The evil eye has wounded her"; another, "Some magician has her in his spell." Physicians learned in science were unable to diagnose her complaint: one would say, "Her complaint arises from black bile"; another, "All her pain arises from yellow bile."

Astrologers came from every city, the sages and soothsayers of Khurāsān; one would say, "This is the influence of the Moon in

Libra"; another, "This is the influence of Saturn[2] in Cancer." Sorcerers with familiars, charlatans too, all sat down brokenhearted on account of Vīs. One would say, "The evil eye has lit upon her"; another, "A Parī[3] has looked on her." None knew what had befallen her nor yet what suffering had made her ail so. The heart of the Moon was burning from the brand of Rāmīn; the heart of the King was writhing in pain through the Moon.

Jasmine-bosomed Vīs wept over her heart and shed tears like pearls with head hung low. When she was left alone away from the King of the world, she caused a river to flow with the blood from her eyes. She spoke words so touching that they drained patience from all hearts: "Why, lovers, will you not be warned? Why will you never listen to advice? Look on me, and beware of attaching your heart to anyone! For in the event you will accept any tribulation that overtakes your heart. Look on me, lovers, but from afar—for you will burn if you sit near me! A fire so fierce has settled on my heart because my lover's heart is of stone and steel. I may be excused if I call for help, for I am summoning help against that youth who knows no justice.

"I showed my wounded heart to him and said, 'I have been tried by affliction on your account.' Who knows how much evil he had done me? He performed one act of evil and multiplied it a hundred-fold in my soul. This lover that has now in the end become my enemy has rendered me desperate, frustrated of every desire. What good is there that man does to man that I did not do him in love? I threw hope and pains to the wind the moment I revealed the secret of my love to him; I sowed loyalty; why did I reap distress? I spoke words of praise; why did I hear curses? Seeing that my own fortune is in feud against me, need I cry out about an outsider, if it is thus? I have wrestled much with my inharmonious fortune, but there was no sorting stone with glass! Now I have become bereft of fortune and heart, and have inscribed my divorcement from both. I have laid my head on the pillow like the accursed because of the cruelty of that heart like a mountain of stone. Through my ill fortune nothing is fit for me but death; death is the only proper thing for one as

2. See n. 1, p. 63.
3. See n. 4, p. 60.

unfortunate as I! Since my lover chooses another before me it is better that my soul should taste death."

Then she summoned Mushkīn and revealed to him all the secrets of her heart, for Mushkīn was her secretary of old, always privy to the secrets of Vīs and Rāmīn. She said to him, "Mushkīn! Have you ever seen, or heard of, a more disloyal person than Rāmīn? Had hair grown out of my very nails I should never have suspected this of him. I little knew that water could arise from fire, or pure poison from pure nectar. You have seen how I have kept to the path of purity in sovereignty; now I am bereft of both; I am become despised in the eyes of both friend and enemy. I am neither a queen in queenship nor a saint in saintliness. Queenship is not for me to practice, nor the quest for greatness, nor the exercise of authority; year in, year out I have sacrificed heart and head and soul and property in the quest for Rāmīn. Now I cast about in the effort to gain union with him; now lament sorely from fear of separation from him. Even if I had a thousand dear lives I should not expend so much as one upon the question of Rāmīn. He wounded me sorely in his folly, but now he has quite broken my back. He knocked off many boughs from my tree, but now he has cut off my branch and pulled up my root.

"I was patient in the face of his hurtfulness; now the hurt of separation has robbed me of patience. This time he has done that to my soul in the face of which patience is not to be contemplated. The sword of his cruelty has cut off my head; the lance of separation from him has rent my heart. How may I be patient as my head is cut off? How silent as my heart is rent asunder? Can you imagine anything worse than that he should have gone, taken a wife, and then sent me a letter to tell me the 'good news'? 'I have planted and nursed a Rose, and cut myself off from myrtle, narcissus, and mallow flower.' Then he sent the Nurse away from the hunting ground, her heart all arrows; you would have sworn he had never seen her, or had perhaps suffered a hundred cruelties at her hand. Now I have fallen on my deathbed; the dagger of death is laid to my soul.

'Now, Mushkīn, dip your pen in musky ink and write a letter from me to Gūrāb. Look at my burning fever and cold sighs; record all my pain in the letter. You well know how to mold speech together and write all that is proper in a letter. Ponder your words well with wisdom: con them closely and from every angle: if you bring him back by means of your words, I shall be a mere servant before you as long as I live. You are learned and young men are easily deceived by learned words." When the wise Mushkīn heard this he made the whole world musky with his lore. He wrote a letter from Vīs of frustrated desire to Rāmīn of fair fortune and good name.

79.

VĪS WRITES A LETTER TO RĀMĪN AND BEGS A MEETING. The parchment of the letter was Chinese silk; the musk was of Tibet and the ambergris of Nasrīn;[1] the pen from Egypt and the rose water from Jūr;[2] the inkwell of ambergris-scented aloeswood from Samandūr.[3] The pen was as fine in point of slimness as was the figure of Vīs from having suffered hurt and wretchedness from Rāmīn. The scribe was more versed in sorcery than the city of Babylon; his words had sugar compounded in their very clay; his parchment fairylike as the face of Vīs; his ink sweetly scented as her lock: a scribe like her eyes in sorcery, words like pearls and sugar in his mouth. The heading of the letter was in the name of the One God, then the Contract and Bond were invoked:

"To her lover from the devoted sweetheart, who has evinced loyalty in her soul as nobly as might be; from a Moon hidden in love's wane to a Moon shining in the heaven of desire; from a garden ruined from end to end, to a garden blooming gorgeously from one side to another; from a branch all dried up to a branch whose fruit is moon and stars; from a mine worked and left devoid of ore to a mine scattering gems over the world; from a day that has come to the horizon of the west to a day raising its head from the east; from a ruby languishing in a dungeon to one set in a crown; from a rose plot that has suffered the simoom of separation to one that has blossomed in glory; from a sea become devoid of pearls and water to one teeming with water and radiant pearls; from a fortune as dark as muddied water to a fortune as renowned as the sun; from a sun diminishing every instant to a sun waxing greater till Judgment Day; from a love

---

1. Said to be an island producing ambergris. *Farhang i Ānand Rāj, s.v.*
2. Fīrūzābād in Fārs. Minorsky, *Ḥudūd ul-'Ālam*, p. 127.
3. In India. *Ibid.*, pp. 27, 87.

whose ardor has passed all bounds to a love which was once warm but is now cold; from a soul in torment, pain, and distress to a soul amid desire and good fortune; from a nature wary of desire to one awoken amid desire; from a countenance from which the glory of beauty has drained to one from which the glory of beauty radiates; from a face like brocade upon fire to one like brocade sumptuously figured; from an eye month in, year out sleepless and full of moisture to an eye month in, year out dry and full of sleep; from a true lover ardent in devotion and loyal to one flippant, shameless, and cruel; from a Moon become deserted and friendless to a King become ruler of the world I have written this letter in a plight so sore that soul has deserted body, body soul. I melt in the fire of separation; you sport in the banquet of joy; I have become the treasurer of the store of loyalty; you the vizier of the throne of cruelty. I hereby conjure you by love, friendship, and bond, inasmuch as we were inseparable companions and shared each other's words; by our acquaintance of years' standing, by our devotion and passion, to read this letter from start to finish and learn the details of my plight one and all; know, Rām, that this world is ever revolving: from it comes now weal and now woe, now suffering and now joy, now death and now life; well or ill the world shall come to an end for us, and then will come another world. Only a legend shall be left of us in this world, while in the next world God subsists eternal.

"All the world shall read our story and know all there is to know of us, good and bad. You know which of us is of ill repute, for they seek all their desires through ill fame; I was in purity as you saw me; you chose me out of all the world for my beauty. In purity I was like a dewdrop; in beauty like the petal of the tulip. No man but you had joy of me, fate had not cast dust upon me. I was like a wild ass in the prairies innocent of the snare and gin of the hunters. You were my hunter and gin-setter, you set gin and snare in my track. You threw me into the snare of disgrace; now you have cast me into the pit of loneliness. You deceived me and seduced me from the road, now you have broken faith with my soul. On the one hand I have found you a knave, on the other a traitor. You say, 'I swore a great oath that I would not have so much as the trace of a connection with Vīs'; but did you not also swear to me that you would not desert me till your dying day? Which of these two oaths am I to take as valid? which of these undertakings as binding? Your oath is like the flippant wind; your bond like running water. You are like brocade, taking on sheen of every color; or like a gold coin passing from hand to hand. Whom do you know like me in love? If you will not hold to me, to whom will you hold? See how much evil you did, to rob both yourself and me of reputation! First, you were guilty of seducing others' wives; you smeared the escutcheon of the house with disgrace. Second, you betrayed oaths and broke faith with those to whom you were pledged. Third, you deserted your faithful lover, without having suffered pain or hurt through her. Fourth, you spoke improper words to one for whom you are the only one in the world.

"I am that Vīs whose face is the sun, whose locks are pure musk, whose face is the blossom of spring, whose love is lasting; who is queen of the fair, moon of sorceresses, whose cheeks boast the moon, whose mouth nectar. I am that Vīs, I am she, who was as Bilqīs to Solomon.[4] There is for me in the world a king better than you: there is no Moon on earth for you like me. Every time you turn your heart from me you shall find me harsh when you come back! Do not so, Rām! for you will only suffer regret; you will find no cure for your pain but Vīs. Do not so! for you will become tired of Gul, and will not then gain Vīs by any amount of chivalry. Do not so! today you are drunk, in your drunkenness you have broken your compact with me. Do not so! for when you become sober you will be left without wife and mistress in the world. Many the day you shall moan before me, rub your cheeks in the dust under my feet; turn your heart away from hate to love, but seek me up hill and down dale without finding me. As you have tired of me and my cheeks, so you shall tire of Gul; I know it! As you cannot sort with me, with whom shall you sort? If you cannot play the game of desire with me, with whom shall you play it? I ever say, 'Any who is in the lists of love and is not suited by Vīs is suitable to die!' Let this be a sufficient sign of your ill fortune: it gave you a rose and took from you a rose garden; showed you a gleaming moon,[5] took from you a blazing sun. You preen yourself on possessing a Judas tree; little knowing that

4. See n. 2, p. 12.
5. *G:* "darkened moon."

242

you have lost a whole orchard. It seems you have forgotten all that bitterness in which you were bereft of patience and peace in desire.

"If you so much as saw me in a dream, you fancied you had attained kingship; if my perfume so much as passed by your senses, your body, were it dead, would be revived. Thus is man feckless and senseless: he forgets distress and joy. Again, you say you have lost your youth and are ever exclaiming, 'Alas, my lost life!' *My* youth has been lost in desire for you, as has *my* life in loyalty to you. I fancied you were a sugar-cane sapling and that I only had to plant you for you to yield sugar; I planted you, then tended you with care; but when you grew up you yielded me colocynth! When I recall the pains I took and the agony I endured from love of you, a fire flares up in my brain whereby a veritable Oxus flows from my eyes. How much distress and wretchedness have I endured, and in the end have had to drink this bitter draught! You dug a pit for me; the Nurse put out her hand, pushed me in, and herself sat at her ease! You provided the fuel, she lit the fire; and burned me in it to the delight of my enemies. I scarcely know whether to cry out because of you or the Nurse—for my pain originates from both. Although I have suffered disloyalty from you, and you have laid on my heart the brand of separation, caused my eyes to rain blood, made my lap a river in flood like the Oxus, I still cannot find it in my heart to commit you to God or rehearse your cruelty before him; may my eyes never witness pain for you, for pain felt by you afflicts my soul too. Now I shall recite letters on ten subjects, with phrases to make blood rain from the very pen: such that when a lover reads them, should he have a heart he will lose it!"

FIRST LETTER: *On Longing and the Pain of Separation.* "If the heavenly sphere were my scroll, all the stars my secretaries, the sky my inkwell, the night my ink, the letters of my epistle leaves, sand, and fish, and these secretaries wrote till the Resurrection my hope and desire for my love, I swear they would still not write one half of it, nor paint the dread I suffer in separation. Sleep does not visit me when separated from you; and if it does, the vision of you snatches it away. During this separation my plight has become so sorry that my enemy has mercy on me no less than my friend. Sometimes I

243

weep to comfort my heart; but you would swear I was damping fire with fire, and laying dust with dust, and curing every pain with pain. Here I am sitting with my misery, through separation; there you are sitting happily with an enemy. My eye weeps to see the halter of my friend in the hand of an enemy! You would swear this pain of exile is fire that burns nothing save patience! No one gets much sleep when it is hot: how then, say, shall someone rest in fire? I am the cypress that separation from you laid low and played into the hands of the enemy by felling; now the graceful figure you used to see is fallen prostrate on its sickbed. My friends, showing sympathy, sometimes come to visit me; but though they sit around my bed, I am so wasted that they cannot see me! Then, jokingly, one will say, 'Perhaps our patient has gone to the chase!' Longing has so reduced my frame as to make it invisible to the eye of the beholder. There was a time when they knew my plight from my cries; now I am so weak that I cannot even cry! Even should Death come and sit for a year I swear by your life he would not see my person!

"This is my only comfort in exile—that so long as I am in this plight I am secure from death! My care has become like a mountain range; the path of my patience up it has grown hard; may I never gain escape from my pain if I can muster patience in separation! How may patience survive in a heart which resembles nothing so much as burning Hell? When a heart has been drained even of its own blood, how is anything else to repose in it? They say, 'The soul is composed of blood'—all lies! I have no blood—how has my soul survived? My love, so long as you were in my embrace my body was like the branch, my breast the flower. Right enough that without you I should burn on fire—the barren branch always burns! Since you have gone, gone is all I desire; I fail to gain sight of you or peace; my desire is forlorn so long as I am forlorn in separation from you; it will not return till you return. My fortune is enraged against me: you would swear I were embattled against the sphere: without you, my world is in confusion like an army in disarray without its general. Time passes over me in separation like the cheetah stalking the deer on the plain. It is right that I should weep from this care: no fault to weep at such a plight! I am without friend, but care provides me companions in plenty! There is nothing I can do—but love sees to it that I am not idle! Without you I cannot fulfill life's desire: it is as though you were life itself to me; you planted the seed of desire for yourself in my heart; water it now from the spring of your constancy! Look on my face this once more and see whether you have ever seen such gold in the world!

"Though you be my sworn enemy, you will only have to see my face to have mercy on me. Though you are faithless and ill-willed, you will weep more than I myself from pity for me. They tell me, 'You are sick and ailing; seek out a physician to cure yourself!' If the patient's cure come from the physician—it is from the physician that my pain and hurt arise! My physician has played me false; I am left with this pain by his treachery; so long as I suffer this hidden pain I seek you, for it is you who know my cure. I long to see you, and cannot reconcile my heart otherwise. I will not relinquish the hope I cherish of fortune and of God that the blazing sun will return to me. If the sun of your face rises, the night of my care and tribulation will come to an end. Even old enemies have mercy on me: why should not you? Why should you not have mercy on me? Are you more hostile to me than my enemy? If you read this letter and do not come back, I shall testify to your mercilessness."

SECOND LETTER: *On Remembrance of the Lover and Seeing the Vision of Him in Dreams.* "My sweetheart, when you left me you took my heart from me as a hostage; why did you have to leave me and take a hostage from me as you left? I gave you my heart as a hostage so that you might know that without you I have no desire to live. My heart is with you wherever you are; it ever seeks health like the sick; how should a heart which is your fellow traveler and comrade transfer its love elsewhere? How may your memory fade from a heart whose very soul and sense you are? Though it has suffered so much bitterness through separation from you, you are dearer within it than the dear soul. What if you were disloyal and foolishly sought to be parted from me? I now hold your loyalty of all the more account and think no more of the cruelty you perpetrated. I am now merely the more loyal to you; I shall be so loyal and loving that you shall appreciate the extent of your cruelty and my love. Since disloyalty was your watchword, why did you always call me stonyhearted? I am indeed stonyhearted—but in devotion! Loyalty is forever inscribed on the stone! It is because this heart of mine has foundations of stone that loyalty abides in it. Were my wretched heart not of stone, love for you would not thus persist in it; in its loverhood my heart tasted wine of those lips and made me eternally drunk thereby; so inevitably, after the fashion of the drunk, if I see the moon I think I see the beloved, and if I see the sun as it rises it seems to me to be your face. I go and bow before the pine and say, 'How graceful is the stature of the sweetheart!' I kiss the tulip in April and say, 'How fair the face of the lover!' When the breeze brings the scent of the rose in the morning its perfume forewarns me of your locks; I tell my heart, 'The beloved comes! for that sweet perfume is the scent of his body!'[6] In dreams the vision of you visits me and shows me your face as I sleep; now I dally with your face, now live in dread of the arrows shot by your eyes; when I am sleepless you multiply my pain; when I sleep you lavish love on me. If you choose love for me in sleep, why are you in feud against me when awake? In dreams you are generous and loving; in waking hours miserly and murderous. In waking hours you will not come when I call—only so that my lamentation may be made the more! In sleeping hours you come uncalled, only to increase my sorrow! Seeing a vision of you in separation is only equaled by the day of union with you, lost to me forever; the day when I recall union with you only by the night that shows me your vision; once gone from me, what is it to me whether it be day or night? Today I find my eyelashes left in the same plight by both.

"I am left with only care from the sight of the vision of you; through care for you my heart is left sick; my heart so longs for you that it has become resigned to contenting itself with the vision of you; may there not be a kind of contentment even in such frustration, like a bird that is resigned to its snare? You would swear that my mother had offered up a prayer for me: 'May everything you seek be far from you!' For I am ever thus in love: happy even to see you in dreams. What drunkenness has overtaken this heart inured to care that it calls such care happiness? This is the extent of the joy it has

6. Cf. Avesta, Hādokht Nask II, 8, where the soul of the dead person smells the perfume of the *dāenā* (cf. n. 5, p. 95).

of its fortune, to see your face in dreams. If only my eyes could sleep and my soul see you in dreams!

"But I have not slept day and night since I saw you; from night to day I am frustrated of my desire, my darling! I have not slept ever since I was separated from you, so much blood do I rain from my eyes. See what a subtle difference Fate introduces between these two kinds of sleeplessness; one, sleeplessness from a surfeit of pleasure; the other, sleeplessness from a surfeit of pain! What if I remain awake for a hundred years, so long as my reputation in the world is for constancy! I have planted constancy so that my sleepless eye may water my field out of my eyelids! Constancy is like ore, love like the mine; it is no easy matter to work ore from a mine. If one day I pluck the hem of your garment you will suffer sore shame before me! My good faith will rejoice my heart, your bad faith break yours. If God is indeed the Judge at the Resurrection he will not leave the pains I have devoted to constancy unfruitful. He will speedily join me to my lover and erase care and distress from my heart. My pains will in a moment bear fruit for me in the shape of my lover, and wipe all care and distress from my heart."

THIRD LETTER: *On Seeking a Substitute for the Lover.* "Where are you, gleaming moon two weeks old? Why have you conceived lust for my blood? You prefer everyone to me; you are the only one for me in both worlds. They tell me, 'Why do you cry in vain and ponder so long upon a faithless lover? There is nothing like love for erasing love; why do you not take a lover fairer still than he?' He who speaks thus does not know that a thirsty man seeks water till he drops. Though rose water may be pure and sweetly scented, it is not like spring water to a thirsty man. It is an antidote that suits one whose entrails have been bitten by a gliding snake, not sugar! However sweet sugar makes the mouth, it is hardly as suitable for the wounded as an antidote! Now that they have succeeded in parting me from my sweetheart, my enemies have attained their dearest desire. No other person is any good for me, none other will do in his place. Once my hand has been severed by the dagger, what will it profit me to hew another even from precious ore? You are my sun in radiance; day will not dawn for me till you come; in the day of union, sun of the land, my breast was the shell and you the pearl. Once the shell is emptied of its pearl, it no more sees a pearl in its embrace; since it never again gains a pearl, right enough, then, that I should not take another lover! Everything in the world has its substitute; but I hardly think the pure soul has! For you there are a thousand entities like the soul; but to me you are the soul—and the soul has no substitute. If I seek a substitute for you I shall fail to find one; no moon is like my sun. In your absence I have refrained from washing my face and hair so that I may not wash your scent from my body. So long as your love lives so vividly in my memory, how is another to have joy of me? You would swear my stony heart was a caravanserai, a caravan of love for you within it; till they vacate the caravanserai there will no longer be room for another caravan! My body has turned to a hair from suffering distress; my heart to stone from practicing patience; I shall not afresh sow love in stone, for both my seed and my trouble will be fruitless. My love, though I am sick from separation, you are the eyes in my head, the light of my eyes. Do not foolishly seek to be parted from me, for only you are suited to me in the wide world. You are the partridge of cruelty, I am the mountain of care; the constant abode of the partridge is the mountain.

"I am March,[7] you glad Nourūz; these two must always be together. My breast is like a sea full of water, your mouth like a shell full of radiant pearls; I do not know how you have contrived to hold back from me, for the oyster shell never abstains from the ocean! You are the cypress of the stream, I the stream; deign to grace my bank! My love, you are a red rose, I a yellow; you blossom from joy, I from pain. Bring your red rose and lay it on my yellow, for in the garden these two roses are best together. My love, without you the soul has no worth: and if the soul be so, how shall the world be? My body is sleepless early and late; my heart like one asleep and lost to the world. They tell me, 'Go and take another lover! If he takes a star, you take a moon!' How shall I who have no luck in lovers seek a sweetheart from their midst? The love affair I have had is enough for me; I shall no more play at love with anyone; I am not so taken with this dye on my hand that I must dip my foot in it into the

7. Minorsky, *Iranica*, p. 192.

up? Now sleep deserts him on its account, now his hand is pricked by its thorn. Day and night he goes without food and sleep, now prunes it, now waters it. He endures all that care in the hope that one day he may see blooms upon it. Have you not seen one who keeps a nightingale so that it may delight his heart with its song? He gives it water and seed night and day, fashions its cage of aloeswood and ivory; he ever rejoices in it and is proud of it, in the hope that it will sing sweetly. Have you not seen how much dread and suffering one who takes to the sea suffers therefrom? He is ever without food and sleep, in the midst of waves and wind and water; he looks in vain for safety to every side; now fears for his cargo, now for his life. He traverses all that ocean in the hope that he may make a profit with his wares. Have you not seen how much labor one who works for jewels in a mine expends on it? He neither sleeps at night nor rests by day, nor do his pains ever see their last day; he is always humping stone and iron, endlessly engaged in hewing at the mountain; he braves all these discomforts in the hope that he may perhaps find a royal gem.' If life in the world consists of hope and concupiscence, everyone must needs have these two in him; so long as ever moon and sun rise, I shall have hope and concupiscence for your love. What does the tree of love resemble in my heart? A cypress of the orchard; its branches do not dry up in the hot season nor its leaves go yellow in the cold; it is always green and verdant and lustrous; you would swear that every day is spring for it. What does love resemble in your heart? An autumn rose plot, stripped naked and bare of foliage; its blooms and leaves departed, but its thorns left; I live in hope of a day when, through love, its spring blossom will return; constancy be its glorious leaves and blooms: its dry thorns be roses of a hundred petals; I descry in you three times as much hopelessness as I see hope in myself; I am like a thirsty branch in spring; you like the sky full of clouds and rain; I am a poor man haunted by distress and calamity; you a Korah ungenerous and mean. I cry ceaselessly in my pain—and the tragedy is that I know no calling but crying! 'How wretched the mourner who knows no calling but crying!' I am like a sick man whose soul, even in prostration and languor, will not give up hope of recovery. I am like a wanderer forlorn in the world, sick at the memory of his native land.

Sitting like a wanderer at the roadside I inquire for news of you in and out of season. They tell me, 'Give up hope of him, for hope will bear you fruit in the form of despair.' I shall go on replying forever, 'I live in hope, hope, hope!' I shall not give up hope of you, my fair one, till my dear soul abandons my body! Ever since love drove patience from my heart, my soul has been steadfast in this hope; my soul will not be quite burnt up in its torment, for hope of you dashes water on it now and again; if my hope fails, alas for my soul! for without hope I shall not survive for an hour."

FIFTH LETTER: *On Suffering Cruelty from the Lover.* "I saw you when you were not as proud as now; not so furious and obstinate; I have seen you such that if you so much as heaved a sigh the very moon in the heavens would have lost its way at it; in lowness you were as the dust of the road; at the mercy of enemy and foe. Your soul was in such torment that it was like Hell; your eye so full of water that it was like the sea. On any day when you wept even sparingly a second Tigris arose in the world. Now you have grown greater than Jamshīd; or even become the peer of the sun. Have you forgotten those days when I robbed you of patience and sense? Surely you have become aware of my inner heart, of how I adore you? Why are you as bitter as poison[9] to me whilst you are as sweet as nectar to all others? You are ever pleasant to all; why, then, do you increase in haughtiness toward me? You possess a hundred treasures of victory, state, and charm; right enough that you should pride yourself on such a wealth of treasure. What if you pride yourself on your own body? for my pride in you is more than my pride in myself. I pride myself in you, for you are worth no less; I shall sort with you even though you will not with me. But even though your face is spring blossom, roses ever in bloom on your cheeks, the spring of beauty does not last for anyone; the world gives one day and takes the next. Do not draw your bow so liberally on your lovers, for your bowstring will one day suddenly snap. And though you may have a quiver full of charms, do not shoot all your arrows at one lover. My heart is like a *kebāb*, you of fairylike face, thrust day and night into the fire of love. Leave the fire to blaze, but do not burn the *kebāb* you

9. *G:* "gall"; see n. 7, p. 138.

251

have roasted! Do not perform an action I never performed; do not dissipate my good name, for I never did so to you. I was once the object of affection that you are now; but I did not practice such haughtiness on you!

"There is no pleasure in love when it is attended by pride and haughtiness. Is not the pain of separation enough for my heart without your visiting on it the agony of your wariness also? You have raised yourself up to the heavens in pride; you have set fire to your own granary by your pride. You are human like me, not god-like; how long will you behave so pretentiously toward me? Even though you be lofty as the sun you will set again at night from on high. I crave of God a heart like yours, black, proud, false in love, and foolish; one with a heart like this will go unscathed; but the world will be scathed by it. I see you with a cheek like a gorgeously colored garden; I see you with a heart like a rocky mountain. I am grieved that your heart is thus; at the time of disloyalty it is as iron. Though you court separation, I shall not; though you speak coldly, I shall not do so; I shall plant constancy though you plant treachery; I shall bring water though you bring fire. My mother bore loyalty when she bore me; your mother cruelty when she bore you. Whatever cruelty was done me was done by my heart, for it went and sought loyalty in one disloyal. Inevitably you made it your target. Well done! Fire away with the arrow of your narcissus eyes! Fire away! so that they may say, 'Why has she done this? She bought calamity and has given her life as the price!' If they call Ārish an archer for shooting an arrow from Sārī to Marv,[10] you fire every moment a hundred flying arrows into my soul from Gūrāb! It is you, not Ārish, who deserves championhood; for you have passed Sārī by a hundred parasangs! You practice cruelty in so many ways—what a merciless and stony heart you must have! You have made my heart rich as Korah in pain of separation; you have made my cheek a River Oxus from the bloodshed of my eyes.

"Even more surprising is the fact that despite enduring so much cruelty I am not worn away; I must be made of iron! They tell me, 'Do not weep, for your body has become thin as a hair from weeping.' One who loses hope of the sun and its fiery nature and of seeing its

10. Minorsky, *Iranica*, p. 172; see n. 2, p. 176.

face weeps thus. Envious one, perhaps you do not know that in rain there is hope: spring is coming, when abundant rain falls; perhaps my love will return by means of my rain! Spring is coming, and I shall scatter flowers to greet it; when my love comes I shall scatter my heart to greet him. In separation from him I scatter pearls and coral; when united with him I shall scatter eyes and soul! If one day the Creator vouchsafes fair fortune, 'Happy the day that brings meeting!' If they sell me one soul for the price of a hundred, I shall scatter two hundred souls before my darling."

SIXTH LETTER: *On Calling Back the Departed Lover.* "My sweetheart, you have left me; what do you say, what is your command? You have not told me; you stole my heart and merely spurred your horse away, leaving me in a foreign city. You had no mercy on the poor wanderers left like sick men without a physician. Now I know that you do not remember me, that you are faithless in love and compact; you neither have mercy nor fear God; you never inquire after the health of the wounded. You do not say, 'How is that poor soul, who without me is lost in waves of blood?' Is this justice and love that I should die without you and you know nothing of it? Tell me, am I to direct my plaint to you, or complain of you, about the wretchedness of my plight without you?

"A pain has come upon me from separation which has no cure other than death. In the world there is no being a lover without grief; joy and loverhood do not go together. You take it hard that I complain of you: but I utter my plaint so that you may learn of my plight. Will you not tell me how you have the heart, my love, like an enemy, to practice cruelty upon a friend? Was it not enough to depart from me without going and taking another lover? I have had to live to hear this news, to suffer this injustice from you. Here I am suffering this treatment from you, while you sit without me by another lover's side! Have I become so low in your sight, have you become so wary of me? Are you not he that was spellbound by me, withered like the leaf in December? Am I not she who gave you back your life, attuned you to fair fortune? Are you not he that thought of nothing but me, and ever made the tincture of your eyes out of the dust under my foot? Am I not she who was the very mate of your soul, for this world held no joy for you without me? Why am I still the same today, but you changed? Anger proceeds from you, but love from me. Why have you become discordant in heart toward me; what wrong did I do that you abandoned me? Perhaps you trod the hard road with ease, for you bore but a light load of love for me! You were struggling in the sea of separation from me, you endured much suffering from the waves of grief; your heart clove to another lover since a drowning man will clutch at a straw! What if you have taken a new lover? This is no cause of astonishment to me; many the one who will eat vinegar at table though there is laid before him sweetmeat and sugar!

"Union with me was sweet as wine to you;[11] separation like drowsiness in its train. Now you are drowsy and turn from wine every time you catch my perfume. If wine has reduced you to this state, there is no antidote for you but wine! The first love of one's choice is as the very soul; beware of choosing anything in preference to a chosen soul! If you have opted for something new, hold to it; but do not vicariously hurt the old! Men's love is like jewels: the older they are the more precious; when a jewel is new it changes color; what is the difference between a badly colored jewel and a stone? Fresh love for a new lover is apt to change, like fresh color in a new jewel; a thousand stars are not like one sun; nor seven members like one head; nor a thousand siestas like the one of noon; nor a thousand lovers like a first love. I shall not find a lover to wound the heart like you, nor you one as constant as me. Neither can I cut my heart off from you nor you divorce yourself from me. In love you are the moon, I your sun; you shall be with me, I with you forever. Do not set store by your having gone far from me, or having become so radiant and full of light. You may much revolve but come back to me in the end; your light will fall on you as ever from me. Now, my lover with heart of stone, arise and come back! Do not multiply my distress and your own: for I shall henceforth be to you as wisdom to the soul and milk to wine. Separation from you is a fast lock upon the soul; only union with you may break it. Do not be agitated by the days that are past; begin loyalty and love from the beginning. What if you have purposed ill, and rooted up the sapling of love?

11. *I. Mb:* "union with you . . . to me."

Now that you have uprooted it, plant it anew; for this time it will yield you fairer fruit."

SEVENTH LETTER: *On Weeping in Separation and Bemoaning Loneliness.* "Cloud, you who weep at Nourūz, come and learn weeping from my eye! If your rain were like my tears, the world would be destroyed by one shower from you. I rain thus and still am ashamed; I would weep a hundred times as much; this grief is worth this much and more, but I am harassed by penury; I now weep bloodstained water and now blood; when neither are left, how shall I weep? On the day when I have none of either left I shall cry my eyes out in place of blood. I need my eyes to see you—without you if I have no sight it is no matter. I shall weep till I make the plain like a sea; I shall moan till adamantine rock becomes like collyrium. God forgive these two flooding eyes of mine, who are thus my companions every day! not rebellious against me like patience, not turned enemy and foe like my heart. In such a plight everyone seeks a friend; but my friends have deserted me. Patience there may be, but it fails to come to my aid; Fortune there may be, but it is Fortune itself that is responsible for my murder! My heart is trapped against its will in disaster; now patience has sent a message to my heart: 'I am patience, a heavenly scion; you took me and planted me in Hell. Heart, you are a Hell full of fire and smoke; thus it is that I have fled speedily from you.' Heart, since your life is a plague to you, it is pointless for me to bewail patience!

"Patience is a virtue in every pain there is; but in such a plight it is a vice in a lover. I do not wish to see the face of my patience; leave me to dwell without it. You have left me, my darling lover, patience and peace do not befit me. Should I become content in separation it would be a sign of disloyalty in me. I have staked heart and soul on my transaction with you; you are free to do with them as you will. In the sight of every lover who ventures love two hundred souls are not worth a crumb. Thus should the pursuit of love be, thus affection; if my pain arises from your cruelty, the more the one increases the more will the other. Sweet be the memory of the time when I had a lover like you in my embrace! Fate slept, good fortune

255

was awake; enemies few and hope abundant. The world is ever about this task of cropping happiness with the sword of Fate. It suddenly snatched you from my eyes, and they rained blood to see the robbery! I rain blood from my eyes because blood flows from a severed member. Without your face lamentation is my companion; the grief of separation has taken up its abode in my soul. In sympathy for me all my neighbors have fallen to lamenting to see my bitter lamentation; they say, 'Rest from lamenting so; you have burned our hearts; have mercy on us! We have seen many lovers in the world but none so wretched and prostrate as you!'

"But the idol-faced sweetheart has left me as shepherds in the plain leave their fire; left me alone here like the wayside shelter of a traveler. Was it not enough to set off on a journey away from me without going and taking another lover on the journey? So if I weep, I do so justly; such is my plight in face of the cruelty of my lover. Sitting on the throne of success I am like game wounded in the claws of a lion.[12] My heart says to me, 'You lament so sorely that in your moaning you are like an accompaniment to singers taking the treble line! If, lover, you are hurt that your sweetheart has taken another love on his journey, do you not know that your lover is the sun? Everyone lives in hopes of the sun! Now it is near, now far from you; light reaches you and others from it.' My love, I am in such sore distress that I do not know what I am saying to you. I am like a mother who has lost her child and has two hundred Mount Damāvands of grief upon her soul; rushing over mountain and plain like a madwoman, seeking her child in every nook and cranny of the world. I am unaware of pain and hurt even should a thorn suddenly prick my heart. I am astonished that you should countenance me being so prostrate and wretched! Even after all the pain and hurt I have suffered from you I cannot find it in my heart to complain of you before God; I dread the decree of Heaven; I do not dare harden my heart upon you. In my sorrow I shall only say this about the sore misery that separation has wrought upon me: may you have no happiness without me, may I have no life without you."

12. The text of G shows considerable variation from the Persian MSS in this portion of the letters.

EIGHTH LETTER: *On Asking for News of the Lover.* "I have a heart burning with my lover's brand; my weeping eyes are witness to my plight. I have a body meager as a hair, the world is as dark in my eyes as hair. Since day is to me as dark as night, imagine how dark night is to me. My eye will only then see day in the world when it sees that face that is the elixir of the soul. Ever since you have joined the caravan I prefer the sentry's calling to all others. I am ever a lookout on your road; you would swear I was a collector of tributes from caravans! Not one caravan passes me but I ask for a clue of you. I continually say, 'Who has seen that faithless one who knows nothing in the world but cruelty? Who has seen that soldier with face like the moon, whom God created to be a sweetheart? Who has seen that thief and robber of hearts that has spelled nothing but disaster for the world? Do you know how that spellbinder of hearts is? Is his love less today or more? Do you know what he has in his heart? Is he merciful to me or otherwise? Will he break faith with me again or not? Shall I meet him again or not? What does he purpose to do to me, whether good or evil? What does he say of me to friend and enemy? Is he pleased with me or offended? Does he purpose cruelty or constancy toward me? Does he remember me and say, "How is the one who remembers me month in and year out?" Does he ask anyone how I am without him? Does he treasure in his heart hope of union with me?' Though that sweetheart may not inquire about me, I constantly inquire about him day and night. He is the same as when I last saw him, the same stonyhearted false lover. The same rose-scented, rosy-faced beauty, the same bloodthirsty knight dedicated to bloodshed. Albeit he wishes me unhappy, desires every injustice for my soul, I wish him happy forever, secure from the injustice of Fate. What is the difference between one who brings me news of my sweetheart and the bearer of tidings of sovereignty? I hold that person as precious as my eyes, for his eye has seen the face of my lover. When he says, 'I saw him happy,' I am so happy I could lavish my very soul on him.

"I soothe the grief of separation by the very sight of his face; I hold him dear for my lover's sake. Every breeze that wafts from that land is sweeter to me than my dear soul; I know, when the wind is sweetly scented, that that lover of fairylike face is happy and well.

257

It brings me the scent of hyacinths from his locks and the perfume of wine and roses from those cheeks and lips. I heave a sad sigh from my wounded heart and confide my secret to the wind: 'Sweetly perfumed breeze of spring, you carry the scent of the locks of that beauty with face like an idol. Tell me, how did you find that graceful cypress, who ever keeps the soul of this poor slave in affliction?[13] You have delighted me with the scent of his lock, but have treated my heart cruelly: my wretched heart says, "Alas, that you have taken the scent of his locks elsewhere." Does he know how I am in separation, bereft of food and sleep and company? My body is lost in wind and rain through these cold sighs and weeping eyes! Is that beauty like me constant in love, or has he once and for all disabused his heart of love? When he hears my name, does he glow in happiness or grow angry from disloyalty? Breeze, carry my message to that Moon, which Fate suddenly snatched from me. Say, "You who have forgotten love for me, may you be shamed among lovers! Is this loyalty and love, that I should die without you and you survive? You are ever practicing chivalry in the world—do the chivalrous treat their bond thus? I have seen a thousand hearts wounded by cruelty; but never one like my own. In love cruelty is better than requiting my love with hate! You neither inquire so much as my name and style of any nor have mercy on this wounded soul of mine. You neither relieve me of the pain of separation nor acquaint me of your state by letters. I do not know how your heart is—mine is at the mercy of my enemies! My ear is so cocked for the door, my eye so trained on the road, that you would swear my house was a prison or dungeon! If a bird flies, darling of my heart, my wretched heart will fly from its place. Through that face as gorgeous as a peacock, my heart has become blue and fluttering as a pigeon." '"

NINTH LETTER: *In Which Writing a Letter to the Lover is Described.* "My sweetheart, cypress-tall, moonlike in face, of angel form, chain-like locks; how long will you mercilessly visit on me the grief of forlornness and the pain of separation? I conjure you to read this letter and know my condition all in all; I have mixed together ink

13. *I.*

☿ 258

and my heart's blood; and then written this indictment of cruelty. I call the letter 'indictment of cruelty,' since blood ever drips on it from the pen. As I recalled the disloyalty I have suffered from you in the day of separation, fire blazed from my seven members and burned the pens in my fingers; when I was left unable to contrive or find a remedy, I scattered rain on the pen from my eyes; by this resource I rescued the pen and wrote the tale of my doleful soul. But so much of my heart's blood did I weep from my eyes that I erased every word of it! See these faded letters: all the dots[14] on them blood from the eyes: the script of the letter is black as my fortune, its $n\bar{u}n$[15] bent as my back; the world has become a hoop round me like its $m\bar{\imath}m$,[16] my hope broken like its $j\bar{\imath}m$;[17] my frame is bowed like its $l\bar{a}m$,[18] but your stature straight like its $alifs$;[19] I would have us both drunk and happy, like $l\bar{a}m$ and $alif$[20] twined together. Oppression at your hands has become my occupation, my cruel one;[21] a blind alley like the $k\bar{a}f$[22] of the letter; I ever say, 'There is no way of escape before me' but you have no inkling of this blind alley! The heading of the letter is in the name of the Creator, the Lord who does his will with us. He has opened on me the door of love for you and he it is, too, that has set constancy in my soul; I have chosen him as judge in my case and called on him to intercede together with my letter. If you know my interceder and helper, have mercy on my heart, with none to accord it justice! I have no interceder but God; no pleader besides my letter. You previously craved quarter from me and sought pomegranate from the garden of my cheek. As I put my head in your snare and accepted every kind of message you sent, do you now forbear to string your bow mercilessly and remember the love of years' standing; as you read this letter, reflect that time was when my caprices were the wolf and you the sheep. Now you have escaped from the claws of my wolf, and it is you who crouch in wait for me like a wolf; as you read this letter, recall that time was when your fortune slept, love of me was like a snake; now you have woken from sweet sleep; it is I who sleep and you that have become

14. I.e., the dots of the Persian script.   15. Persian *n*.
16. Persian *m*.   17. Persian *j*.   18. Persian *l*.
19. Persian *a*.   20. Persian *l* and *a*, which form a ligature.
21. Readings of *I* and *Mb* combined here.   22. Persian *k*.

the snake. Read this letter thus carefully, and see whether you have ever witnessed such a manifold variety of hurt!

"I am that same lover, so precious to you, who shared so much pleasure with you; the same lover, so dear to you, who played so much at love with you; now I must write a letter and resign myself to helplessness; in the very city where I became queen and noble I have by my ill fortune become humble and a serf. Look on me, all who have sense, and no more plant love for any in your hearts! Look on me, all who are sagacious, and take warning from me! Do not accept a suit in love! My love, this suffices as rebuke for you that your name in the world is 'Ignoble.' What shall anyone who reads this letter say as he learns of my inmost heart therein? He shall say to me, 'God forgive you, loyal maid! for seeking so far the love of a disloyal lover!' But to you, 'God requite you, cruel youth! there was not in you so much as the scent of decency!' This love letter has come to an end; but I have infinite words to say to you; I have uttered a long plaint against my fortune, but this, so far as it goes, is only one thousandth part! My reproaches of you will never end; nor will my desire be gained by this discourse; sooner than speak vainly to you, I shall go and implore the Judge; send up my cry at the door of the One who has neither chamberlain nor janitor; beseech him, not you, for light, cultivate his friendship and not yours. He is the one to open the door he has shut on me; I need none other than him to open doors. I shall cut my heart off from all else but him; for he is better for me than everything in the world."

TENTH LETTER: *On Supplication and Craving Sight of the Lover.*
"Every night toward dawn I take before God a heart full of fire, a soul full of smoke, a body like a hair, and cheeks overlaid with gold; and rub my cheeks in the dust before him; my cry splits the vault of the hall; my wail makes a highway raid on Saturn; I cry as copiously as the cloud of March; I moan as plaintively as the mountain partridge. I boil as fiercely as the windswept sea; I tremble as violently as cypress and boxtree. I wash the blackness from the night with tears; and fill the earth down to the back of the Fish;[23] I heave so many sighs from the grief of my heart that the moon loses

23. See n. 2, p. 17.

that two-week-old Moon that eclipses the moon of my fortune; to that hollowed ruby that conceals thirty jewels within; to that pine branch that keeps the branch of my desire dry and fruitless; to that laughing rose petal that keeps me ever weeping; to that wild tulip that keeps my eye full of dewdrops; to those two strings of gems, those two bunches of ambergris; to that cheeky mountebank that keeps me ever unhappy in dreams; to that blossoming garden that lays waste the house of my patience; to that colored brocade, to that Moon and those Pleiades; to that cypress of rosy limbs that ever keeps my heart wounded; to those perfumer locks whereby the market of musk has been ruined; to that bewitching eye that keeps me sleepless and without food; to that moonlike cheek that keeps my soul full of fire with woe; to that two-week-old Moon that keeps me senseless and crazed; to that world-famed one that keeps me solitary, frustrated of my desire; to that rosy-faced, sweet-scented one who keeps me careering day and night; to those locks that practice rope tricks, that make me famous even in Shīrāz; to the caprice and rebuke of the youth whose glowing chin has robbed me of repute; to that pomp and glory that keeps my face like gold from distress; to that treasure of excellence that follows the craft of rancor against me; to that shining sun that surpasses the worldly sun in beauty; to that face like rose petals before which the rose casts its own in shame; to that cypress with jasmine face, like whom no jasmine breathes scent; to that victorious king, that unjust Moon; to that crown of cavaliers, to that youth the envy of spring itself; to him that is to me the soul of the world, to my young lover; to that moon of jasmine scent, to that cruel sweetheart; to the one I ever send greetings, without whom my eyes are like twin rivers. Greetings more than any number, more abundant than spring blossom, more than the sand of mountain and desert, the drops of the ocean and of rain; more than the plants of mountain and plain, more than the creatures on dry land and in the sea, more than the days of both ages, more than the stars in the wheeling sky; more than the manifold progeny of the world, more than the seed of Adam, male and female; more than the feathers of birds and the fur of animals; more than the words of state archives! more than we can think or ponder, more than our imagination or religion or craft; eternal greetings be from me upon you, from you constancy and love toward me. Greetings of friendship be from me to you, light from the Moon of your face on me! May it be so a thousand times over! This is my prayer; may good fortune say it Amen!"

80.

VĪS SENDS ĀZĪN TO RĀMĪN. Once the scribe had written the letter, bringing into play every device he knew; when Mushkīn had made the nib of his pen musky with ink, and in turn made the letter musky with the tip of his pen, Vīseh took the letter from Mushkīn and rubbed her twin musky locks upon it. The scent of the letter of Vīs carried for a whole parasang, and the perfume of her garments did likewise.

Then she summoned Āzīn and said to him, "You of as much worth to me as my own being, if you have till today been my servant, hereafter you shall be my noble brother; I shall hold you to be my peer in state, my confidant in love; I purpose to send you to Rāmīn, who is worth more to me than soul and eyes. You are my son, Rāmīn my lord; lord and son are dear to the heart. Do not tarry on the road, but hasten swiftly like the stone of the ballista and the flying arrow. For I shall henceforth have my eyes fixed on your road and shall be counting now the days, now the hours; so contrive that neither friend nor enemy see you; take my message and letter to Rāmīn.

"Give him my greetings more numerous than the stars and say, 'Ignoble oath breaker! So much suffering have I undergone at your hand, you evildoer, that I have a hundred times tasted the pain of death. Have you forgotten the oath and pledge which you swore and undertook two hundred times before me? What is the difference between that oath and the passing breeze? Between that pledge and the cloud of spring? You have treated my wretched heart as not even enemy would treat enemy. May all that you have done rebound upon your head in a place where no one shall come in answer to your cry! You may fancy that you have done this evil to me: I swear that you have done it to your own person! Your soul will not be able to face the arraignment, since it has chosen this action out of others! For they are reckoning these things jot by jot and after our time shall inscribe them in a register. Why have you divorced your heart from your friends, why chosen a sweetheart from the number of your enemies? You have wounded my soul like a dragon by choosing a sweetheart from a city of foreigners. Where will you find a lover like me, or a monarch like Shāh Moubad? A place as pleasant as Khurāsān, a strong refuge like Marv the royal abode? Have you forgotten the good you have had done you, and how you have been enabled to gain your every desire by me and the King? The only thing Moubad had of sovereignty was the name: you otherwise enjoyed every desire. As I had complete authority over his treasury, everything in it was at your disposal. You enjoyed your fill of his treasure, as well as of accouterments and stores without number. You did not mount other than choice steeds; you tied on no other but precious belts; you wore nothing but brocade of a hundred colors; brought from China, fairer than the Arzhang.[1] Of wine you drank nothing but flashing rubies; like Mars shining from the midst of the sun. Your servitors were picked from the number of the idol-faced fair; a sun like Vīs was in your embrace. Placed as you were in these circumstances, with all these riches and this high state, delightful, thrilling, enchanting, you gave me up for another; what have you gained after it all? what is your profit after all this loss? You have made no profit, but only dissipated your capital; you have made no gain, and are left without capital. Fate has robbed you of a hundred treasures, and now you scratch about for a farthing with a hundred pains. How ignorant you must be if you cannot grasp even this much—that you are in deficit after so much prosperity! In exchange for all you had, you now have but one thing only; like people who are left with lead in exchange for gold. In place of pure silver and natural gold, Fate has given you iron and brass. In place of pleasure and love, distress and wrath; in place of radiant pearls, mere glass. In place of reputation, stream water;[2] in place of pure musk, the dust of the lane. I am amazed that, if you are wise, you should thus countenance such an evil bargain for yourself! Why attach your heart thus to a Rose that will not last long for you? Is

1. See n. 3, p. 29.
2. Persian $\bar{a}b$ e $j\bar{u}$; $\bar{a}b$ e $r\bar{u}$ = "reputation" (lit. "splendor of face"). Persian $\bar{a}b$ means "water" but also "splendor."

one rose better or a blossoming garden? Is the rose of her cheek fairer than a two-week-old Moon?'"

When Āzīn heard the letter from beginning to end he straightway chose a swift-paced steed; like a mountain in height and girth; like a cyclone in running and galloping; rushing across the mountains like a flood; traversing the plains like a scouring ghoul; it mounted the heights like a leopard, rushed into rivers like a crocodile. Under its feet there was no difference between mountain and sky; to its eyes no difference between river and plain. On its back the rider took his ease on a journey, like a man sleeping on a bed. It rolled up the desert like the scroll of the letter and traversed the sky like a bird. He took neither food nor sleep on the journey, and came from Marv to Gūrāb in two weeks.

81.

VĪS LAMENTS HER SEPARATION FROM RĀMĪN. When charming Vīs dispatched Āzīn she lamented sorely at the pain and brand in her heart; whoever reads these pages will lose his heart, if he has any. "Where have my fortunate days of yore gone, when the Sun was in my embrace? How shall light come to me, separated as I am from the sun? I send two rivers flowing from my lightless eyes, for moon and sun have said farewell to me. If the sun has not departed from me, why has the world grown dark in my eyes? In the dark night I am sick and ailing; for the sick man's pain worsens at night. I did evil to none, lest I should suffer evil; why then am I now in this plight from ill fortune? You would swear a caravan of ill fortune reaches my heart every moment. My heart is like to split from the great pain that is in it; a pomegranate splits when its skin is full. The sun does not shine nor the wind blow in a heart tied around with so much injustice. It is ever cloudy in my heart; thus it is that a flood rains from my eyes. Clouds form and then part; why then do the clouds persist in my heart? This is why my face has gone the color of a coin; for the fields grow yellow from copious clouds. My tears have learned the scribe's art from this withered cheek, yellow as dye! They write in my blood the letters of grief variously in copybook hands. What kind of face is this whose color is like yellow dye? What kind of love is this whose scribes are tears? Love has lit a fire

265

in my heart and has burnt my heart with all its chattels. I am ever moved by pity for my heart at the trouble which afflicts it from love. If my wounded heart has committed some impropriety it has doubtless become thus through its own offense. What an evil ploy was this love! It has robbed me of heart and soul and youth. If it is I who have introduced it into the world, sufficient as my punishment is this brand of separation; a brand whose scar will remain on my soul eternally.

Where are you, my love with stature like an arrow? See me bent like a bow! In separation you are an arrow, I the bow; once flown, you will never return to me again. I writhe when I remember your cruelty; like those curling locks of yours, the color of box-tree. I tremble when I think on separation; like a sparrow soaked with rain. I have a heart united to your hand in treaty; but it has experienced from you nothing but breach of promise. How could you bear to aggravate its hurt, to steal its peace and cause it pain? Was it not ever to you loving as a mother? Did it not cherish love for you like a nurse? Did it not see the world with your eyes and ever dread that the evil eye might light on you? Was not the sight of you its desire and hope, was not your cheek its moon and sun? Was not your stature to it cypress and boxtree? Was not its very soul delighted by that boxtree? When did it prefer violets to your twin locks, or crunch sugar in preference to your lips? Why do you fight so against my soul, why recklessly shed my blood? Am I not she who was your heart's darling, my face your moon by night, your sun by day? Was not your love my constant companion, your per-fume ever the breeze that blew on me? Was not my face yellow from love for you, were not my tears bloodstained by your cruelty? Did I not release a river down my cheeks from separation, did I not lay a millstone on my heart from love for you? Are you not the only one for me in the world?[1] Are you not my sole desire in the world?[1] You saw me before I was a lover; if you were to see me now you would say, 'It is not she.' I am not the one you saw then, far from it—then I was an arrow, now I am like a bow. I have smitten my hands on my cheeks so much that that smiling pomegranate blossom has become a water lily. I water it with my sleepless eyes; for a lily will

1. *I. Mb:* "you are . . ."

not remain fresh without water. I lament till the nightingale laments in sorrow; I rain till the clouds rain on the roses. My eyes in redness resemble tulips; my tears like dewdrops on them; the tree of my pains has become fruitless; the body of my hope has been left headless. My heart is my enemy—alas for me! Why am I always seeking some remedy against enemies? How foolish I am to seek a remedy against my heart; for it is my heart that has quite dissipated my reputation. Had my heart not been my enemy, it would not have been so rebellious in my body. My heart threw itself on the fire when it became refractory; indeed, 'Fire is the desert of the proud!' Lament, my heart, for you deserve to see Hell on Earth! Fate has visited such ill fortune upon me that I weep year in, year out, and you burn. How may life be pleasant thus: I in water and you in fire? I shall make the world a sea by the tears of my eyes, and then launch a ship on it. I shall make my bloodstained garment my sail, and drive the ship along with the cold wind of my sighs. Since both wind and waves come from me, the waves will not be inhospitable to my ship. I shall be the compeer of the fish in the sea—for I am like a fish, always in water.

"I have sent a letter to my love, wrapped about with my bloodstained garments. He may or may not read the letter; may or may not learn of my distress; may forgive me for speaking of love, may seek reconciliation with me in reply. There can be no worse fate for lovers than to have to watch every day for a letter. The day of union, the time of joy, are past and gone, when I indulged in caprice and charm with my lover. Now my converse with him is a thing of letters, and sight of him a thing of dreams (if indeed I sleep!). I have had to live to see this day; and from that high degree have I fallen down to this! Why did I not drink fatal poison, why not die on the day of my good fortune? If Death had visited me then, perhaps my eye would not have witnessed such a day as this. Death for the soul on the day of success is better than this kind of life! World, this is your way; you ever reduce the desperate to wretchedness. The very wind which brings perfume from the garden does not bring me the scent of my lover's body. What evil did I do, that it has become thus to me? Perhaps even the wind that blows from your direction[2] is now

2. *I. Mb:* "your memory."

in feud against me! I see the spring blossoms of the earth in their pride, the soil covered in roses and brocade; spring has been denied me, since my pure soul is far from my body. The soil of the earth is better far than I; for it is visited by spring, but I am passed over."

82.

RĀMĪN REGRETS HIS MARRIAGE WITH GUL. When Rāmīn had consorted with Gul for a time he became sated of her company as well as intoxicated thereby; the spring blossom of joy withered, the wind of affection dropped, the bow of love was broken, the arrow of affection snapped. The embroidery of the garment of joy wore dull, the water of the spring of happiness became muddy. Rām's attachment to Gūrāb recalled the saying, "The cup pleases so long as the water is fresh."

Love of Gul was like wine, Rāmīn like a winedrinker: he drank blissfully of her whilst sober. The heart of the drinker longs for wine; he quaffs many a goblet and cup; in the end his heart becomes sated of drinking; in drunkenness, desire dies in his body. He does not care for wine even if it be nectar; since for him the nectar is laced with poison.

When Rāmīn had become somewhat sated, and it was a long time since he had seen Vīs, he went one day into the open country with the cavaliers; the world was like the lineaments of Chinese shrines from spring blossoms. He saw the tulip flaunting itself in the field, the nightingale singing on the bough. The earth was the color of thick brocade: violet, green, yellow, red, and blue. One of his companions, a maid[1] of fairy birth, had some violets and handed him a nosegay; Rāmīn's heart recalled the day he had made a compact with fascinating Vīs; Vīs sat on the King's throne, the sun shining from her face, the moon from her bosom. She gave Rāmīn a nosegay of violets[2] and said, "Keep this always in remembrance of me. Every time you see fresh violets remember this compact and oath." Then she uttered many curses on those who break oath and compact.

1. *G:* "a man."
2. Cf. *Tristan*, p. 282, *Tristan (B)*, p. 108, where Isolde gives Tristan a ring as a keepsake, and *Tristan*, p. 306, where he is reminded of the occasion when the ring turns up as he is prepared for marriage with Isolde of the White Hands.

Noble Rāmīn became so heartbroken that the world became dark in his eyes. The world was not dark, but his eyes; for smoke filled them from his burning heart; so much blood did he shed from his lightless eyes that rain did not drop from the skies that year. Tears drop the more from the eye of a person whose body care keeps wounded. Do you not see the dark cloud in springtime, which contains a flood of rain water more than others? When the memory of Vīs was renewed in Rāmīn's heart the fire of love increased therein. You would have sworn the sun of love had come out from behind the cloud of suspicion. When the sun comes out from behind a cloud its warmth is that moment the greater!

When love and loyalty showed their face in his heart, Rāmīn, faithless in love, strayed far from his companions; he dismounted from his horse brokenhearted, peace shattered in his heart, the color drained from his cheek. He kept saying, "My suffering heart, how long am I to see you like a man drunk without wine?" For a time he cursed the fate which ever kept his soul full of pain; now sick with distress in the city and in his abode; now far from house and home and friends; now having to possess his soul in patience in the company of a lover; now lament in exile from his love. Every moment he addressed his heart and blamed it for the burning in his soul.

He said to it, "Confused crazed creature, careless like Majnūn[3] of stranger and kin alike! You are ever like a drunken man, for you know neither good from bad nor right from wrong. What is the difference to you between ruin and garden, how does spring differ in your eyes from winter? No matter whether you rest on earth or brocade, in your folly you approve everything you see; you term cruelty as proper as loyalty; you consider desire as meet as reason. You are so malleable that you do not adhere long to any single compact; in your folly you take on all colors. You are ever the repository of the world's hurt; ever the ambush of the army of cares. Affliction has become your neighbor and taken up its abode in you; and has slammed the door of hope fast. You have come to Gūrāb, broken the treaty, and said to me, 'I have escaped'—but it is not so!

3. The lover of Leilā (see n. 5, p. 202); the type of the distracted lover in Persian literature.

It is not you who are drunk but I who am foolish and drunk; for I took passage on the sea with your fair wind!

"You said to me, 'Go, take another lover; divorce your heart from love of Vīs and loyalty to her; do not concern yourself on my account; for in the time of separation I shall exercise patience in the face of the pain of being denied the sight of her.' Filled with high hopes of you I cut myself off from my lover and chose another in her stead. Now you have left me drowning in the sea and have placed me on the fire of separation. Did you not tell me, 'Turn away from your lover'? When I did so, you brought up the dust of ruin from me. Did you not say, 'I shall be patient'? Now impatience has driven you crazy. I regret having obeyed your orders; having handed over my halter to your hand. Why did I conduct my affairs according to the promptings of a wiseacre like you? I have thrown both you and myself into humiliation. I fancied that you had escaped from woe; now I look again, you have become imprisoned! You have become as helpless as the silly bird that sees only the crumbs and does not descry the hidden snare. My heart, you broke faith with my soul, and then handed me over to the tender mercies of my enemies. Why did I listen to your advice, why hearken to your words? It is meet that I should be thus afflicted, for a foolish man deserves no other fate. It is only right that I should have become humiliated and a prey to care, for I put out the candle of my heart with my own hand; only right that I should have suffered care and distress, for I cut with my own hands the branch of happiness. I am like a deer with its foot in the trap; like a fish with the hook in its mouth. I dug a pit for myself with my own hand and cast the hope of my heart into the pit. What excuse am I now to offer before my sweetheart, how show her my heart burning with brands? How flippant, indecorous, and shameless would I be should I warm anew a frozen love! It was an evil day when I planted love and slew happiness with the sword of separation; ever since love has gained the upper hand over me I have not seen myself happy one single day. Now I am in exile like foreigners, now suffering separation like madmen. Fortune does not seek association with me; may no child be born with my fate!"

When Rāmīn had wandered a little from the company, the dust

of distress upon his cheeks, Rafīdā followed him secretly, eaves-dropping on his crazed son-in-law; the desperate Rāmīn was unaware of him; thus is the way of the desperate in love. Rafīdā heard all that Rāmīn said; then he went up to him and asked, "Light of the illustrious, why do you wear the garb of mourners? What desire is left that God has not granted you, why should a demon have brought distress into your thoughts? Are you not Rāmīneh, king of cavaliers? Is not your brother the sun of monarchs? Although you are the champion of the age and greater than sovereigns in renown, why do you yet ponder vain action and lament good fortune and happy days? You possess youth and a royal throne; what do you covet better than what you have? Do not be so discontented with your fortune, for discontent brings misery in its train. Once your head jibs at a silken pillow you deserve no pillow but the earth."

Sorehearted Rāmīn replied to him, "He who is well does not know the agony of the sick man. You are exempt, for you have no clue to my pain; when I lament you call me crazed. There is no delight like companionship, no pain so bitter as separation. A garment groans as you tear it asunder, the vine cries as you cut off its branches. My pain is not a whit less than theirs, when I experience separation from friends and kinsmen. For you, Gūrāb is your native city and abode, all in it are your children and relations; you are ever in the midst of friends, not like me wretched in a city of strangers; even if an exile be a king, he laments when he does not enjoy companionship. I need the world for kin's sake: 'all cures should serve for some wound.' Pleasant as delight and joy may be, a single friend is more precious than a hundred joys. Just as I covet all fame for myself, I likewise seek every desire for the sake of my friends. I envy you every time you come from plain or road; kith and kin are in company with you then, wife and children come to greet you. You are happy with them and they with you; you are all like a chain linked together. They all run round you, rejoicing one and all in good fortune like yourself. I have here no kith or kin, no lover or sweetheart or child. Once I was like you enjoying my every desire in the company of kith and kin and sweetheart; how sweet were those bygone days amongst all those fine friends; how sweet it was

271

that my affliction was from love, that I experienced different kinds of cruelty from my lover. Sometimes I was made brokenhearted by her two narcissi: sometimes made distressed by twin tulips: pain together with distress was sweet to me, for those narcissi were languorous and those twin tulips charming; how sweet was all that cruelty of the lover; how sweet to bite one's lip in agony. How sweet all her reproach in the time of union; how sweet when she veiled her face in flirtation; if she withdrew into the veil so much as one day in the week, she enslaved me like a prisoner.[4] How sweet to count kisses and swear an oath two hundred times on every excuse; how sweet when I called on God for rescue from her two hundred times a day; how sweet never to be one moment in the same state; now calling for help, now uttering blessings: then again I would repent of my words[5] and call down blessings a hundredfold upon her from my very soul; now to twine her locks, now to make a girdle of her arms.

"Those days were days of joy for me; yet I counted them as days of affliction. Sometimes I suffered distress from the roses of her cheeks; sometimes hurt from the narcissi of her eyes. Who should be hurt by a narcissus or driven to distress by a rose? For every injustice I suffered from her narcissus, I was awarded justice a thousandfold from garnet; when the hyacinth sprang an ambush on me, mallow flower steeped in nectar came to my rescue. I had no task in the wide world but love, no weight upon my soul save love's caprice. Why should a body engaged in such a task lament, why should a heart burdened with such a load writhe? My days were even as I have described; I had carried off the ball of success from every player; I had before me roses by the pannierload in the face of the beloved; and a whole store of musk in her hair. Now joy was to be savored, now the chase; now draughts of wine were counted, now kisses. Sometimes I had to say 'I am wretched in love!' sometimes 'I am laid low by passion!' My heart was happy at the very moment when I declared it sick and ailing. Now I am wretched, for that wretchedness is no more; now miserable, for that misery is past and gone."

4. Order here as in *I*.
5. *I. Mb:* "deeds."

🌿 272

83.

GUL LEARNS OF RĀMĪN'S REGRETFULNESS. When Rafīdā returned from the hunt, he divulged all the secret to Gul; how Rāmīn had sown wrath and reaped love, and had shown the very mettle he nursed in his heart. "Even if you try him forever," he said, "seek to win his heart and treat him kindly, at the time of biting he is the same old snake; at the time of rending, the same old wolf.' 'The bitter tree bears bitter fruit; although we may give it sugared water.' 'If you refine copper and brass a hundred times over they will not turn to natural gold by refinement.' 'If you put pitch in fire a hundred times over, it will never come up the color of milk.' Had Rāmīn been worth anyone's while, he would have evinced loyalty toward Princess Vīs. Since Rāmīn has proved unworthy of Vīs and of Moubad, it is not meet that you should be his spouse either. Rāmīn's heart is ever quick to become sated; he resembles a lion in his awkwardness and ill nature. Not having seen him at the side of others, you have chosen love for him in your ignorance. What is the difference between seeking love and uprightness from Rāmīn and planting fresh eglantine in salty ground? Why have you sought a compact from someone disloyal, why sought the savor of sugar from hemp? However, seeing that this was fated to come to pass, what is the use of wasting vain words on you?" When Rāmīn returned from the hunt, like the game he had an arrow lodged in his heart; a knot was tied in his brow; he had washed his cheeks with the tears of his eyes. In the joyous banquet you would have sworn he was a person without a soul!

The rosy-scented Gul sat by him, the market of the idol-faced fair ruined by her cheek. Straight in stature as a young cypress, but with tongues of flame shooting from the tree. As dainty in figure as a two-week-old moon, tulips and lilies blossoming on the moon. Fire rained upon every heart from her cheek, the arrow of Ārish[1] from the barb of her glance. Beside Rāmīn that jasmine-bosomed beauty was like a treasure of gems beside a corpse. His body was in its place, but his heart was not; he ever fetched up moans from his heart. In his heart he supposed that his plight was hidden from men; lamenting

1. See n. 2, p. 176.

in his heart in longing for his mate, he said to it, unknown to all: "What is sweeter than the banquet of the young with lovers sitting together in joy? This banquet and this festive hall are more distasteful to my heart than a house of mourning. My lover fondly imagines that I am even now in the midst of joy;[2] she little knows my plight, how wretched and brokenhearted I am. Maybe my darling now says, 'Rāmīn's love for me has grown cold.' She little knows my state in separation; cut off from the companionship of friends! My sweetheart now says, 'My faithless lover has left my side; has sat in happiness with another sweetheart and ruined the market of passion in his heart.' She little guesses that since I have left her side I writhe as copiously as her musky loop of hair! What, pray, has Destiny written on my forehead? What does my star purpose to do with me? What shall I experience at the hand of that cypress of jasmine scent, what from that eloquent Moon? There is no tyrant like her in the world, no victim of tyranny in the world like me. I have so much suffered humiliation that I am like the ground; I have undergone so much tribulation that I am like iron. I am quite worn away by manifold burdens and sufferings; have I not become an ass, fated to carry loads till my dying day?

"I shall go and cull a jewel from my mine and seek thereby the remedy of my soul. My pain arises from not seeing my love; now my cure is none other than seeing her. What wonder is this? Who has ever seen in the world a pain whose cure is effected upon seeing the cause of it? My happiness and pain alike arise from sight of her being sweeter to me than life itself. Why do I strive so much against my fortune? Why flee in the face of my plight? Why hide my pain from my physician? The more I struggle, the worse the calamity I provoke. I shall practice consideration toward my heart no further but shall noise its secret abroad in the world. The waters of separation have risen over my head; consideration is hardly apt for me in this plight! I shall go and say what I may to the beloved; perhaps I may wash the corrosion of cruelty from her heart. But so wasted by sickness am I that I may not live to see her face!

"I shall even now take the road for the city of my love, for if I die I shall die on my way to the beloved. At any rate they shall dig my

2. Cf. Tristan's soliloquy in the same circumstances, *Tristan*, p. 296.

grave by the roadside, and all the world shall know of my plight. Wanderers who see my grave shall sit for a time at its headstone. Once they learn my plight they will have mercy on me and mention my name generously: 'Here lies a wanderer slain by separation; may God have mercy on his soul!' Wanderers remember wanderers, for they remind them of themselves. Wanderers are wretched wherever they may be; this is why they cling to each other. I shall then be ashamed of death when I am killed by the hand of enemies; whereas if I die in grief for my love, I shall derive glorious fame from that death. Many the time I have wrestled with elephant and lion and worsted both in the fight. Many armies have I swept from their position, many enemies have I overthrown. The heavens kiss the ground before my reins, Destiny girds on the belt before my spearpoint; everything in the way of humiliation that I have inflicted on enemies, separation from my love has now visited upon me. I have escaped from the hand of wrath of my enemy but have become bound by the hand of love of my sweetheart. Death has never found its way to me; but now separation has proved to be its ambush. I do not know how I shall find my way from here all alone, taking with me no host or guide; I must go from hence alone, for it is not meet to take a host with me. Should I take a host with me on this journey, the King will become apprised of my enterprise. He will once more heap humiliation upon me, and I shall then gain no desire of Vīs.

"But should I fare forth alone, my road is fraught with terror; for the mountains are like a mine of silver from the snow, the plains are flooded with rain water, creatures wild and tame suffer a veritable Judgment Day from the cold. Now the country of Marv will be deep in snow, the air raining camphor on the cypress trees. In this hard season, this snow and cold, I do not know how I shall fare upon the road alone.

"And worse still than this snow and boggy road is the obdurateness toward me in the heart of that beauty fair as an idol. She bears me no mercy nor shows me her face; she will not come out on the roof nor open the door. She will not perform a single act of kindness toward me nor listen to any words of excuse. I shall be left brokenhearted like a ring upon the door, my soul will become desperate, all my troubles have been in vain. Alas for all my heroism and high fame, my bow, arrow, sword, and lasso! Alas for my throne, hall, and army, my realm, kingship, and state! Alas for my fleet steeds, my numberless comrades! A plight has fallen upon me from the world's hand in which I cannot seek aid from them! I do not shrink from javelin and dagger, I do not cross swords now with Faghfūr[3] and Caesar. It is that cheek like the sun that I dread; it is with a heart full of pain and burning heat that I do battle. I do not know how I shall acquit myself against my heart, how open the locked door by knightliness.

"Sometimes I say, 'My heart, how long will you struggle: shed tears from your eyes and dissipate your good name? With all others, the secret of the heart is happiness and joy; but all I see from you is burning and melting. Sometimes I am in the fire, sometimes in water; I neither enjoy happiness by day nor sleep at night; garden, palace, and hall hold no pleasure for me; neither pavilion nor seraglio nor the field. I neither gallop my horse on the plain with the champions nor play polo with friends on the field. I do not quest for fame in the battle of the cavaliers, nor do I follow my desire in the banquet of the squires; I do not sit happy with the nobles nor yet choose out one of the fair; in place of the modes of delightful melodies, blame comes to my ears night and day. In Kūhistān, Khūzistān, Kirmān, in Tabaristān, Gurgān, and Khurāsān, I am mentioned by every tongue, my name is on every mouth. Listen on every plain and by every river and they will be singing a song commemorating my plight; all the boys in the cities know it; the shepherds in the plain sing it. Women in the houses, men in the bazaar, sing my song[4] constantly. Whiteness has attacked the hair of my head, but still no glad tidings reach my heart. Is not that Hūrī of idol face far from me? Well then may patience and sleep and sense be far from me! So yellow am I that I am like a *dīnār*; so languid, that I am like a sick man. I cannot run so much as fifty yards nor draw my bow so much as a finger's breadth. Every day I gallop my horse you would swear my waist was like to break from weakness. My back, once of brass, is as good as wax; my fist, once of stone, mere wool. My steed, once

3. *Faghfūr* was a title applied in Persian to the Emperor of China.
4. See *Tristan*, p. 293, for the "Lay of Tristan."

276

swifter than the wild ass, has become like me feeble in its stall. I no more unleash the cheetah on the wild ass nor fly the hawk at the partridge. I do not try my strength with the wrestlers nor indulge in ever wilder carousing with the winedrinkers. My compeers ever rejoice in their good fortune, now marshaling the lists, now performing music. Some dally with gorgeous beauties in gardens, others enjoy the plain and mountain slope. Some adorn rose bower or hall, others tend garden and flower plot. Desire for the world has departed from my heart; you would swear my heart has gone to sleep like my fortune.

I am like a messenger, glued to the road day and night, I am like water lying month in, year out, in a well. I do not lay my body on the bed nor my head on the pillow; my felt saddle serves as both for me! Sometimes I wander with the demon in the waste, sometimes sleep with the lion in the reedbed. Neither have I known happiness in this world, nor shall I attain good name in the next. The sword of love has cut me off from the desire both of this world and of the world to come. Whilst others ponder charity and caress the souls of enemies with repentance, I am in the pit of love and the fetter of affection: you would suppose me a very child of affection! My heart, how long will you light a fire from love and burn me in the crucible of distress? My heart, you have carried imbecility beyond bounds; you have killed me of grief but have not[5] yourself died! My heart, you have become like poison, so unpleasant are you: you have become bereft of both worlds through love. May none in the world have a heart like you: so drunken, senseless, and foolish!'" When Rāmīn had striven with his heart awhile he fled melancholy from it; every time his heart heard admonition from him it fluttered like a bird with head cut off.

So melancholy did Rāmīn become at the banquet that he fled from it like a coward from a battle. He came down from his royal throne, they brought his fleet horse to him. He mounted his horse mighty as a mountain; you would have sworn wings sprouted from it. He sped out of the gate like the vanguard of an army and took the route and road to Khurāsān.

5. *I.*

84.

ĀZĪN COMES TO RĀMĪN FROM VĪS. Blessed is the wind that comes from the east! You would swear it rose from a garden; from Kharkhīz,[1] Samandūr,[2] and Fansūr[3] it brings the perfume of musk, aloes, and camphor. How sweet is the perfume of the breeze of the east! especially when it contains the scent of the sweetheart! A scent which comes from the fair sweetheart comes sweeter than the perfume of musk and ambergris. No scent of eglantine could have come from the garden as came the scent of Vīs to Rāmīn. He said, "This is no scent from the garden; it must be the perfume of charming Vīs. You would swear that the breeze that is privileged to pass by the sweetheart is armed with a perfumer's tray; what wind is this that gives the hope of better things to come?[4] and brings me news of my love?" As noble Rāmīn mused thus Āzīn of glorious fortune came to him: when Rāmīn saw Āzīn he recognized him from afar and galloped his bay horse up to him. The messenger dismounted from his horse; no horse, rather an elephant of Tukhār.[5] Āzīn advanced with beaming face and smiling, kissed the ground in front of Rāmīn. The scent of musk and the perfume of ambergris wafted from him— no, not the scent of musk and ambergris, rather the perfume of the sweetheart. How auspicious was Āzīn in Rāmīn's eyes! How delightful to him in turn the sight of Rāmīn! Each rejoiced at the sight of the face of the other, like cypress and boxtree in the spring. Then both tied up their horses and sat in a meadow on the verdant plain. The messenger made inquiries of him, about his fortunes in the past while; then he handed him the letter of Vīs and her shift and veil. When Rāmīn saw the letter of that silvery-bosomed beauty, you would have sworn the wild ass of the plain had sighted a male lion. His arms and legs grew weak with trembling, thought of the sweetheart carried him away; trembling seized his limbs so violently that the letter dropped from his hands. When he read the letter of his

1. See n. 1, p. 225.   2. See n. 3, p. 240.
3. In Sumatra. Minorsky, Ḥudūd ul-'Ālam, pp. 87, 228.
4. Cf. Avesta, Hādokht Nask II, 8.
5. I. Minorsky, Ḥudūd ul-'Ālam, p. 337. Professor H. W. Bailey suggests khel, "troop," for fīl, "elephant." I has "winged bird" for "elephant." See pp. 55, 163.

love he sent a flood of garnets dropping from his eyes. Now he pressed the letter of Vīs to his cheek, now pressed her garment on his heart. Now he would smell her bloodstained[6] garment, now kiss the letter scented with musk.[6] A cloud rose from his eyes whose rain was cornelian and gems. From the cloud lightning struck his heart; he found in his heart lightning fit to burn even fire. Sometimes he let fall from his eyes a stream of jewels, sometimes heaved a fiery sigh from his heart. Now he rushed hither and thither senseless as one possessed of a demon, shouted, and then again fell silent. Now he fell on his face beside himself, and weeping overcame him in his senselessness. When some little consciousness had returned to his soul, his mouth became the oyster shell of the pearls of his teeth; he said, "Alas, my sinister fortune! which has sown the seeds of distress and planted the branch of tribulation! which has cut me off from that young cypress, whose grove is palace and dwelling; cut me off from that shining Sun, whose heaven is seraglio and palace; robbed my eyes of that fair face, snatched from my ear those honeyed words; has given me in exchange for the sight of her a mere garment; in exchange for her words, a mere letter. My soul has found peace in this garment, the spring of my fortune has bloomed at this letter."

Then he wrote a fair reply, more glorious by far than brocade of fine weave.

85.

RĀMĪN SENDS A FAIR REPLY TO VĪS. The superscription of the letter bore the name of "Vīs of idol face; moon of lily breast and sun of jasmine perfume. Ivory idol, silvery moon; ornament of Kandahār, Chinese vignette; column of silver, crown jewel; graceful, lofty cypress, dome of ivory, tree full of blossom, garden of spring blooms, gorgeous spring, Moon fit to be ringed by a castle wall, sweet wine, antidote of the sense, Paradise of splendor, draught of nectar; sweet-scented rose, radiant pearl, royal silk, pure gem; Sun of the hall, Moon of the seraglio, star of the pavilion, branch of the garden; may I know no life without you; may you enjoy an eternal throne. I do not presume to see the moon of your cheek nor hear the nectar of your words. I am culpable, and fear that you may visit on me a

6. *I. Mb* has the epithets in reverse order.

fate that will rejoice my enemies. Although this sin is not in any way mine, it is still not meet to lay it upon you. You conjured up the dread demon of separation when you drove me from your side. You showed yourself quick to tire of love; you emboldened me to follow my own desire. This was not the idea I conceived of your love; I thought it[1] the heaven, and all the time it was the earth. You, if any, know that in love I laid the foundations of an eternal palace. You have ruined that splendid palace of mine, which ever increased my joy by its splendor. The sin is yours, but I proclaim you innocent; you are my queen, you may do whatsoever you will. I have resigned my heart to any way you may rule me; yours to command, mine to endure. My love, though I have become separated far from you, I have left my heart with you as hostage; my hostage is laid in your breast; how may I draw my head away from your yoke? I swear by your soul that since I am separated from you you would say I was in the jaws of a dragon. I have a heart full of pain from separation from you, and as witnesses to it my two yellow cheeks. If I am to produce witnesses before you, and bring friends with the witnesses, my two flooding eyes are sufficient as the friends; two friends are sufficient with two witnesses; you will see my two witnesses coated with gold; you will see the friends dabbled in blood. When I show you their faces you shall know the truth of their words. You will never witness other than truth from me; never see me falter in truth. You acted cruelly and experienced cruelty in return; practice loyalty and experience loyalty in return! Now that you have caused yourself to burn by your own hand and have sought excuse for the cruelty of the past, I shall begin loyalty in love from the beginning and devote my life to the task of loving you. You I shall acknowledge, and no other; you I shall desire,[2] and not this and that other. I shall scour the corrosion of your cruelty from my heart and purchase the dust under your foot at the price of my eyes. I shall not lessen in love for you, though you may diminish yours for me; I shall surrender my body and soul to you if you so desire. Why should I court separation from your face? why cut myself off from intimacy with the sun? why turn aside from the sun of your locks? What may I find sweeter than musk of Tibet? What if I undergo tribulation in your love?

1. *I. Mb:* "you."   2. *I. Mb:* "call."

'Treasure is not to be got in this world without pains!'[3] The heart craves Paradise and the Hūrīs from God; you, my love, are both the one and the other to me. Come, let us reck of this present world and never again recall the days that are gone. Consort with me like color with wine; for I shall consort with you like scent with the rose. You shall not be happy without me; I shall have no life without you. I have a dagger like a cloud raining poison; you have a glance like an arrow piercing the soul; when your arrow is joined to my dagger, how will any enemy escape with his life? So long as there remain sea and rivers in the world I wish you every kind of blessing. I have written your reply by the roadside and made the wording of the letter brief; for I come speeding after the letter; even if a hundred bonds should restrain me, I should snap them. I shall come hastening on the road as swiftly as arrow in the air or a stone dropping down a well." When Rāmīn's words drew to an end, Āzīn departed from him like the wind. Rāmīn, light of the world, followed in his tracks like a polo player galloping after the ball. Each took the road to Khurāsān; the labor of the journey seemed but light to them; like two flying arrows speeding toward the target, with a day between them.

86.

VĪS LEARNS OF THE COMING OF RĀMĪN. Although love is loss from beginning to end, tribulation for the body and pain for the soul, there are in it two joys at two several times; one happiness is at the time of letter and message; the other is the joy at the moment of seeing the sweetheart; the two happinesses are linked by infinite care. There is no sick man like the lover, especially when he is far from his love's embrace; sitting day and night like a sentry, his eyes glued to the road from which his love's letter and message may come.

Thus was the jasmine-bosomed Vīs; seated day and night marking the road by which Āzīn was to come; like a thirsty field in hope of rain or a sick man in hope of medicine. When she saw Āzīn hastening on the road she became as joyful as a garden at the April wind. So happy did she become at the sight of Āzīn that you would have sworn she had gained the empire of Egypt or China. Āzīn recounted all he

3. Still a common proverb in Iran.

had seen, how he had found the anguish of love greater than ever in Rāmīn. He told her of the woe that he suffered from desire, and the letter bore him witness in his words.

Here was a wonder: Vīs of the jasmine scent did even as Rāmīn has done with her letter; when she took it from Āzīn she planted a thousand kisses on it; laid it now on her eyes, now on her heart; made it sweet with honeyed kisses and musk-scented from her musky locks. She did not let that letter out of her hand for two whole days; she would now read it and now kiss it. Till Rāmīn came from the road, Āzīn was her courtier and comforter.

Then she decked her face like the moon and set flowers on the top of her musky plaits of hair; put on her head a crown of gold and gems, like some sun with the moon for diadem. She put on silk and brocade of divers hues, clothed the heaven in the radiance of the sun. You would have sworn her face was ornament within ornament, her body Chinese temple within temple.[1] Her two locks were the stock of a hundred cities of perfumers, her lips the cure for a hundred cities of sick men. In point of locks, she was fit to disturb the hearts of the young; in point of cheeks, the vexation of lovers' souls. Her locks twining down to her flanks were like Ethiopian troops wheeling over China. She was a statue beautifully hewn from musk, sugar, rose petals, and brocade; a paradise perfumed with roses and gorgeously hued; made of desire, ease, charm, and refinement. Her twin locks in scent and curl like ambergris and the letter jīm; her mouth like a bale of sugar and the letter mīm; the eglantine bloomed by the side of the jīm; the Pleiades were hidden in the midst of the mīm;[2] such a moon was the prisoner of love; her silvery body had gone gold on the surface; you would have sworn she was a dainty and charming figurine that the hand of love had placed on the fire!

Fever had fallen in the heart of her desire;[3] the ass of her joy was stuck in the mud. The knife of separation had penetrated to her very bone; the army of woe had fallen on her soul. She stayed on the roof of the pleasure dome of Moubad, mounting watch on every road. She was restless as a seed on a tray, fixing her eyes on her sweetheart's road. Night came, but no moonlight for her; in the night she knew

1. Or "spring within spring."   2. See notes, p. 259.
3. Persian *shetāb;* also "impatience" (lit. "haste").

no peace and sleep. You would have sworn her brocade bed was all through like rose stems full of thorns under her. At dawn her soul reposed a little; her heart became senseless and her eye slept. She leapt from sleep like one possessed by a devil and fetched up a sigh from her crazed heart. The Nurse took her and said to her, "What ailed you? What has some fearful ill-natured demon done to you?" The jasmine-bosomed Vīs trembled like a willow; or like the reflection of the sun shimmering on water. She said to the Nurse, "Have you ever seen a love like mine in the world, or yet heard of one? I have never experienced a night like tonight; my soul hovered on my lip a hundred times ready to depart; you would have said that bed of woven stuff under me was crammed with snakes and scorpions; my doleful fate is black like night; Rāmīn is like the moon in the night of my fate. Blackness will only then depart from my night when the moon of my fortune shows its face. Just now I saw the moon of his face in sleep; his hair filled the world with musk and ambergris; I dreamt that he took my hand and said with his sugary ruby: 'I have come to visit you in dreams, for I fear your enemy; I may not come when you are awake, for your enemy constantly guards you from me. They guard you straitly from me: but how can they keep our souls apart? Show me your face that I may look on it; for it is by the brand of your face that I am made thus. Do not be afraid; take me close in your embrace; for wine and milk are very sweet together. Your locks twine their ends like mail; remove the mail so that the moon may shine out from it! Make my breast ambergris-scented with your locks; make my lip sugared with your kisses. Seek loyalty and love toward me in your stony heart; speak endearments to me with your nectar lip. Do not be angry, for it would be a fault in you. "Sweet nature is better than a sweet face."' Having seen the face of my love in a dream and heard these words of his, why should I not be restless and helpless? Why should I not be ever melancholy? So long as my fortune keeps me from that Moon everyone will excuse this grief in me!"

87.

RĀMĪN COMES TO VĪS AT MARV. How splendid is Marv, the abode of Kings; land of the happy, splendid in summer and spring, autumn and winter. How can anyone who has been in charming Marv bear to live elsewhere? Especially when his lover is in Marv, how can he then live happily? This was the case of brokenhearted Rāmīn; cut off from Marv and from his sweetheart; not only far from friends and relatives but exiled from his old love. There is no place like the first, no love like the old.

When Rāmīn came to the land of Marv, every blade of grass was like a cypress in his eyes. Its ground was like Paradise to him, its branch like a Hūrī, its rose like perfume, its flower petals like camphor. In that land Rāmīn's soul was like the branch of the eglantine in the month of spring. You would have sworn that in the land of Marv the royal abode Rizvān had opened up for him the gates of Paradise.

As he came from the road to the castle of Marv, the watch caught sight of him from the roof of the pavilion. The watchman came down instantly, having joyfully espied Rāmīn on his horse. He gave the Nurse all tidings of him; her heart became free from care. She ran to Princess Vīs and said, "The antidote for your pain has come: the leopard of sovereignty has come stalking up! The lion of kingship has proudly approached: the breeze of Fortune has arrived, asking for a reward for good news; saying, 'The Spring of Monarchs has come!' The tree of happiness has borne fruit, tyrannical Fortune has turned just; the branch of love has brought forth new fruit; for the mine of union has yielded a jewel; morning has dawned from the bright east; the spring blossom of the country of desire has bloomed; hope of good luck has been vouchsafed by Fortune; the good news of joy has been vouchsafed by union; do you not see that the night has become like bright day, the world has become as gorgeous as the prime of the garden? Do you not see the branch of happiness blooming, do you not see the branch of care withered? Can you not see how the earth has become faced with brocade, the wind scented with ambergris? My Moon, raise your head from your pillow: open your eyes and see this world; the night was dark as your hair; now it has become bright as your face; it has become purged of the corrosion of care; the earth laughs from mountain to mountain. The world has begun to smile because of Rāmīn's face; the air become musky with his perfume. Rāmīn has come from the road

284

under a fortunate star; the Sun will join the Moon. Come and see the face of that fair youth; you would swear that you were looking at a son of the moon, standing in the audience hall begging audience; craving quarter from your wrath and anger. Your heart is wounded; he, too, is brokenhearted; doors are shut fast between you. Open your door to your sweetheart; increase the hope of him who prospers your soul!"

The jasmine-bosomed Vīs said, "The King is asleep; calamity lurks in his sleep; should he wake from his sweet sleep our affairs will be in a sorry plight; devise some stratagem whereby he may remain asleep and not know our hidden secret!" Nimbly the Nurse pronounced a spell over the King; you would have sworn he became dead upon his bed. Sweet sleep snatched him away like the drunken so that he had no clue to the world.

Then Vīs like a shining moon sat crouched at the aperture of the window; thence she espied Rāmīn's sunlike face; the flower of love blossomed in her soul but she practiced patience and kept her heart under control, did not show the turmoil that she had therein; she addressed all her words to his horse[1] and said to it, "Ransom of the Seven Climes, I tended you as my own child; why did you cut off from me love and bond? Did I not make your saddle brasses and girth of gold, your halter and bridle of silk? Did I not build your manger of marble and silver and keep it full of sesame all year? Why have you divorced your heart from my manger, why have you gone and chosen the manger of another? Now that I have seen all I have seen, kindness is not your desert. Alas for all the trouble I have experienced on your account! The stable you have found is your desert. You know well what tribulations you have suffered. 'He who does not deserve a manger merits thorns; he who does not deserve the pulpit merits the gibbet!'"

RĀMĪN REPLIES TO VĪS. When Rāmīn saw the Princess hurt, pouring poisoned words from her lips, from his soul full of anguish from pain and burning he addressed to her entreaties and thousand-fold excuses. He said to her, "Spring of lovers, in face the sun of the entrancing fair, paradise of sweethearts, throne of kings, ornament

1. Cf. Bowra, *Heroic Poetry*, pp. 157 ff.

of the fair, queen of moons, star of the dawn, brilliant moon, light of the land, sun of the lane, rose of a hundred buds, white lily, queen and desire of my heart! Why do you thus hasten to shed my blood, why turn your face away from me? I am Rāmīn, the equal of your very soul, you are Vīseh, my worthy sweetheart. I am Rāmīn, the king of the desperate; a very legend in the world for my love of you. You are Vīseh, moon of the fair; in eye and tress eternal queen. I am the same as you saw of old; the same fine loving sweetheart. I am the same as I was but you are not: why do you make your heart obdurate against me? Have you listened to your enemies' words, that your love like nectar has thereby become bitter to you? Have you allied yourself to my enemy? Have you kindled fire in my granary? Have you forsworn all those oaths and broken faith with my soul?

"Alas for that affection and hope which my soul expended on the culture of love! I sowed love in the garden of my youth, made my soul gardener; it worked my garden with happy heart and watered it with the tears of its eyes. It neither slept one single night nor rested one single day but wore itself away in constant gardening; when the spring of bright union arrived, tulips, mallow flowers, and lilies came up; there were masses of blooms in a hundred corners through its length and breadth; its perfume spread abroad like rubbed musk. Its planes and willows became shady; its myrtle and cypress spread their grateful boughs. Other varieties of trees blossomed, in beauty like the desire of the fortunate. Dove and nightingale began to sing in it; other birds, too, added their calls: loyalty spread a wall around; no, not a wall, rather a renowned mountain. At the foot of the mountain ran a sweet stream, at the side of the stream a golden meadow. The hill partridge rejoiced in it as a lion of the plain at sight of the mountain goat. Now the winter of separation has come: and with it the clouds and wind of disloyalty. The time of drought has come, in which every river has run dry. Month and year of blight have come on, and in them every bed has been ruined. Neither wall nor garden has survived, neither mountain nor river nor upland meadow. Vandals have uprooted its trees and knocked down its gate and wall. All its birds are now flown, partridge from the hill, nightingale from the plain. Alas for all those cypresses, roses, and willows!

Alas for the days of pain and hope! Our love was not of gold but of mud; once snapped it became fruitless and profitless. Heart was separated from heart, lover from lover; pain was piled on pain, trouble on trouble.[2] Now our ill-counselor has reached his heart's desire; may he be of ill fate and fortune like ourselves! Now our calumniator is free of the task of afflicting us; he may rest and sit at his pleasure. Now we have no messenger, confidant, calumniator, enemy, or eavesdropper. The Nurse does not suffer trouble nor you care; nor I pain in the heart nor Moubad hurt. No one is as culpable as I, for none is as black in fortune as I am. I lament this black sinister fortune of mine, for by it I am made weak in every member. My nature has become so full of excuses that a noble one is weak throughout. The demon of destruction would not have seduced me had he not wished black fortune on me.

"One in thrall to a demon will ever be in heart like me; blind and repentant; grasping in the place of fresh aloe and pure musk the bough of the willow and the desert sand. In place of pure gold and royal pearls I grasp potsherds and stones of the mountainside. In place of an Arab horse fleet as the wind I make do with a cheap Ṭarāzī[3] horse. My love, do not deal entirely in supposition; just for a moment practice love and reconciliation. Even though I may have committed an offense and done wrong, requite me with loyalty, affection, and love. The sin was in origin yours, my sweetheart; but in the upshot I have been visited with it. Today shall I seek excuse before you a thousandfold for the sin you one day committed. I shall offer up so many abject entreaties before you that I shall wipe away the corrosion of hurt from your soul. I shall always regard the fault as being my own, I shall practice excuse before you till my dying day. Now I shall say as I crave your pardon, 'I am guilty, guilty, guilty!' Now I shall say as I beg remedy from you, 'I am repentant, repentant, repentant!'

"You are my lady and queen over me; it is yours to visit me with punishment; but where then will be your generosity, your queenliness, magnanimity, and mercy? If you grudge me mercy and refuse to accept my prostration and excuse, I hereby grasp the bar of your

2. Lacuna in *I* here.
3. On Ṭarāz (in Transoxiana) see Minorsky, *Ḥudūd ul-ʿĀlam*, p. 119.

audience hall; I shall weep here in abjectness till I die. How am I to go elsewhere, for I know none to have mercy on me like you? Do not so, my Moon; spare my life; forbear to heap affliction further upon my soul!

"What if I once committed sin? Is there no sinner other than me in the world? Sins are committed even by elders experienced in the world; offenses are committed by learned scribes; even the fleet steed falls headlong; even the cutting sword blade goes blunt. Even though an offense emanated from me unexpectedly, do not lay upon me the brand of every refinement of cruelty! I am a slave, you a fair lady; do not in mere wariness fasten fetters upon me! I can bear every kind of cruelty from my love, other than that she should once and for all become wary of me. Even blindness is better for me than witnessing separation from you; deafness better than hearing words of abuse. May I never be far from you; may you never be patient away from me.

"My sweetheart, since you have made your heart obdurate toward me, life is but a light thing in my eyes. You are ever obdurate in your injustice; are not stone and steel obdurate? At the time of strife there is no love in your heart; are not steel and stone innocent of water? Fire has fallen on me from your heart; do not sparks fly from stone and steel? Everyone gathers round one who is burnt in fire; do you, too, come to my rescue, for I am burnt in fire. Even if you pour the sea itself on this fire that blazes in me it will not be diminished thereby. The world is full of smoke from the vapor of my sighs; my world has become as black as my fortune. The world is ever thus weeping for me; that is why tonight there is all this snow and rain. My heart is like a fire temple though my exterior is like a mountain of snow. Has God ever created an angel in the heavens all fire and snow like me? My snow does not melt even with fire; who has ever seen fire compatible with snow? Love has reduced my body to this state—half burnt and half frozen. It is ignoble to kill in the snow someone whose very soul is compounded of loyalty itself! I thought that you would rescue me from the fire; I did not know that you would cast me into the snow! I am your guest, Moon of two weeks; I have traveled a two months' journey in two weeks. People deem kind treatment meet for guests; they do not bury them thus in the snow! If putting me to death has become a light matter in your eyes, at least forbear to murder me thus in the snow!"

VĪS REPLIES TO RĀMĪN. Vīs of face as fair as the moon gave him a reply like a dagger dipped in poison: "Go, Rāmīn, abandon hope of Marv; consider both Marv and me nonexistent. Forbear to make this plea as you have done before! Remove this smoke, as you have removed the fire. Since you have broken faith, compact, and oath, where is the necessity for these spells, strings, and toils? You have deceived me once by your words; now you cannot do so again. Go and practice devices on Gul, if you like; practice toward her, if you will, constancy and love!

"You may be smart and adept at words: I am far from dull and inept! You have an ample repertoire of such spells: you repeat them in profusion over all and sundry. I have bitter experience of you and have heard not a few of your spells. I am sick and tired of hearing them and of being met with nothing but eternal spells! I have had my fill of your slights and spells and of your miscellaneous stock-in-trade! I shall not seek separation from Moubad nor practice disloyalty toward him; only he suits me in the world, for he loves me, faults and all. Not for so much as a day does he treat love as of no account or take a lover besides me. He is always a sincere constant lover—not like you, fickle and oath-breaking!

"Now he has the crystal cup in his hand; he is ever happy and drunk as is his heart's desire; for a king a happy state is meet; for you, any place, however it be, is meet. I am afraid that he may come into the seraglio and find that his rose has fled the rose garden. He will seek me and not find me sleeping in my place, and once more become suspicious of my activities. He will become aware of this notorious deed and of this congealed and sinister love. I am not willing for him to be hurt yet once more, for thenceforth I should have to fight with him for my very life.

"Enough for me the fear and tribulation I have suffered; have I not purged my soul of hope a hundred times over? What profit have I gained of all that tribulation? With what am I left after tasting all that bitterness? with what of all that oath-taking, save ill repute and despair? The King has been hurt by me, God the Creator himself

289

injured. I have squandered my youth for the sake of your love and have given up both worlds in exchange for ill fame. I ever wring my hands in regret, for I have nothing but empty air in my grasp. What I have to say will never come to an end; you shall never glean leaves and fruit from this branch.

"Return desperate through the door through which you have come; forbear to beat this cold iron in vain. The night is more than half gone; clouds have gathered, the storm worsens, a foot of snow has settled. Now spare your own life; go, lest you suffer a mortal disaster. May night be fair for you, day fortunate; may your lover always be Rose in name and Rose in face! May her bond with you so last in the world that you may have of it fifty children!"

When Vīs had abused him for a time and had reconciled her heart to not seeing him, she turned away from the window and hid her face; she did not grant him audience or speak more to him. Neither Nurse nor Princess remained at the window; the antidote to Rāmīn's pain was cut off.

Noble Rāmīn was left in the lane, at the mercy of his enemies, bereft of his sweetheart, and full of grief. Every creature had gained its resting place and peace, but brokenhearted Rāmīn was left without repose. He called on his God, sometimes crying out against his black fortune and sometimes against his lover. He said, "Pure and wise God, you are able to perform all that you will; you see me left helpless, exiled far from family and friends; there is a place on the mountain for sheep and goat; a refuge on the plain for wild ass and deer; here I have no resting place or abode; have mercy, I pray, on this wounded heart of mine. I swear I shall not turn hence desperate—and if I do I am no man. If I have no recourse but to die, it is better that I should die at the door of my love. Let everyone in the world know, then, that a lover gave his life for his love. Even were this snowstorm swords, the blustering wind tigers and lions, I would still not take one step back from here till my soul gained its desire. My heart, you are the selfsame heart that did not use to fear elephants or tigers, javelin and sword; why then are you now afraid of wind and rain? for both are surely your acquaintances. Do I not breathe out wind year in, year out when I heave my cold sighs? pile up clouds with the vapor of my aching soul?

"If that shining Moon were to return, what would be the difference to me between snow and showering rose petals? If my lip gained its desire of hers, if she made her bosom my refuge, I would have no distress on account of cloud and wind, the torture of this storm would vanish from my memory."

The brave Rāmīn thus spoke to himself, his mount up to the knees in mud. The horse had been drenched all night with rain, and the rider was in worse case than his horse from snow. All night Rāmīn's eyes shed tears, the sky dropping camphor upon his soul. All night Rāmīn's head was wrapped in weeping clouds; all night the wind swirled round his breast. On his body cloak, boots, and leggings were frozen stiff as iron from the cold.

All night Vīs wept in the seraglio, her rosy face all scored by her nails. She said, "What snow and cold is this whereby a Day of Judgment has befallen Vīs? Clouds weeping over the head of Rāmīn, are you not ashamed before that rosy-limbed youth? You have made his cheeks the color of saffron, his nails like indigo. You wail to me to have mercy on him, but you visit him with calamity by this wailing. Do not rain, clouds! Cease for a moment; do not heap on me care upon care. Wind, how long will you blow fiercely? Why should you not abate for a while? Are you not the wind which used to bring scent from him? and perfume the world with his sweet odor? Why do you not now have mercy on that body from which wild rose and lily borrow beauty? Deep, raging sea, you are but a slave before Rāmīn; however many royal jewels you may have, you do not count jewels like the hand of Rāmīn![4] However many sparkling gems you may have, you do not scatter jewels like Rāmīn's hand. You were jealous of that king of cavaliers and sent rain by the aid of the clouds; your weapons are but this rain water: his arms are all pure steel. If he escapes from here tonight, he will fill you with the dust of an army. How shameless am I, what a creature of spell and stratagem, that I sit at ease in the seraglio whilst a body nursed amid silk and brocade remains in the midst of snow and cold! The face of noble Rāmīn is a rose garden; cold is fatal to the petal of the rose." After speaking thus, she once again went to the window; the bright sun flashed a ray from the lattice. Again she said to his courser,

4. *I.*

291

"Noble steed! May you ever pace upon my eye! You are to me as a darling son: I cannot abide your suffering thus on such an ill day. Why did you choose a bad companion, ill-disposed to you? Have you not heard them say, 'First the companion, then the road'?[5] Had there been with you another than this youth of ill will, I would have found a corner in my eye for you; but now all your hope and pains have gone with the wind. There is neither audience for you in my presence nor resting place. Go back and crave audience and resting place of others! Ask the lost heart back from the stealers of hearts!"

"Go, Rām, do you too turn back from Marv; seek a physician and tell him of your complaint! Many the day I have sought audience of you and like a suppliant craved quarter from you: you did not grant me audience at your audience hall, nor did you give me quarter with my fellow suppliants. Many the night you have slept in comfort, not like me desperate and disturbed; you asleep amid silk and squirrel fur, I fallen on the road amid mud and mire! Now you have suffered the very evil you dealt to others; you have been smitten with affliction to match affliction! Delicate you may be, you stem of the lily flower; but you are hardly more delicate than I. Even should I have been seemly for you a single day, I never said to you, 'Suffer care on my account eternally.' Cut off the hope in your heart as I have done; through hopelessness I have attained repose. If hope brings on suffering, great relief comes from despair.

"I was that one who ever in hope launched my ship upon the sea; now I have escaped from the tempest of the ocean and have washed my soul clean of vain hope. By virtue of contentment I have chosen saintliness, for 'Contentment is the best Sovereignty.' Now that your luck is out with your old lover, go and hold to the lover you have newly taken! Old coins and rubies are of high repute; however, a new lover is precious! Now that you have cut off the head of love for me by your cruelty, a severed head will not grow again. If grass grows on my tomb, the very grass over me will nurse the hurt you have inflicted on my heart. Wise as I was in counsel, I yet did not know that love of the heart grows old. Do not seek love of me again, for youth does not return to the old.

5. Cf. *Tristan*, p. 312: "It is better to want for a companion than to have one from whom comes nothing but evil."

"I am she to whom you wrote the letter—that letter in which you covered my name with disgrace; I have suffered ill repute because of love for you and yet you were the only one with whom I indulged my desires. I did not seek any lover but you in the world, and as my ill fortune would have it you were one so miserable. You are like a mother whom a sinister ascendant decrees shall have one child, and that blind; failing to perceive her daughter's blindness, she is ever engaged in choosing a flawless bridegroom. If my heart is bent like a bow in love, my speech is straight in cruelty like an arrow. Your heart is like a target exposed to harm; move the target away from the path of the arrow. Go, lest you hear words to make your heart heavy; bitter as colocynth and wounding as keenly as arrows."

Rāmīn's heart writhed at her words; he pondered a reply to her in his heart. He said, "I do not know any mountebank like love, which snatches patience from the heart and drains color from the face. It snatches the heart away from a sober man as easily as a mountebank snatches purses from the drunken. Though my body has grown old, my love has not—'one can play a new tune on an old fiddle.'[6] In my body love for you is the pure soul; what fear has the soul of man of old age? Do not gibe at me for the abundance of my love; a sick man does not desire sickness. Do not abuse me, if you are healthy; for I did not crave debility of Fate. I made entreaty before you; you saw, but raised the flag of self-sufficiency. Why did I reveal the secret of my heart to you, why increase the distress of my soul? I am bold in revealing my heart's secret, you in stealing souls and hearts. Let none lay his heart bare, for in the event a day will befall him such as has befallen me. My sweetheart, if you have risen to become queen of idols, you, if any, know that a just queen is the best. Now that you have become rich in sovereignty spare a thought for the plight of the poor! If I have become sinful by virtue of love for you I am not thus deserving of blame; as long as lust lords it over the world, men's souls will not become sated of sin. Adam sinned in blessed Paradise; I am no more than one of his line.

"Sin is written on the head of the damned; sinfulness is compounded in his clay. Wisdom will not turn away the face of Destiny, nor bravery twist aside the hand of affliction. Be it someone bereft

6. Lit. "treble string."

of reason or yet someone sagacious, none wishes harm on himself. The sin of yesterday has left me together with yesterday; see how I shall cherish your love tomorrow! I shall plan for the morrow in very love, for no wise man tries to grasp at yesterday. If I have broken the compact in love, I know of no remedy but to seek excuse. Why should they know peace in a city where the apologies of the innocent are not accepted? If the excuse of one of low degree is proper, the more so is mercy from one of high estate. Have the mercy to forgive the sin I have committed, for I shall never haunt its neighborhood again. If those of low degree were not to demean themselves, the mighty would not have the chance to forgive. I have experienced much good at your hands, all save forgiveness and mercy. I committed my sin to try you, to see what mercy you had it in you to display. Have mercy on my sin and know that good actions are not lost in this world or the next. This shame is enough as my retribution, this ordeal enough of an affliction for me.

"Here I stand amid snow and rain; there are you with the eye of magnanimity fast shut. Here a heart full of tears because of mercilessness; there a tongue drawn like a sword. You say, 'I have never seen you; and even granted that I have, I have renounced you.' My sweetheart, do not seek separation from me; seek what you will, but not to be parted. I cannot stand the taste of this poison in my soul; I cannot bear this burden in my heart. Even were my heart of adamantine rock it would not be able to brook separation from you. It has no fear of disaster, yet dreads separation from you; it is you it craves of God, not me."

Vīs of the jasmine-scented bosom said, "Rām, bereft of wisdom, all you have of sagacity is the mere name. Once cruelty dashes its heavy brick on a heart the scar will remain forever. Your cruelty has remained in my heart, just as it has driven thence loyalty toward you. No one body contains both heathendom and religion; no single heart love and hate. Now that I remember your hundredfold cruelties, not so much as the scent of loyalty remains for you in my heart. You, if any, know how I served you; what distress I suffered in hopes of loyalty. Then how did you serve me in return? Killed me and consumed what you had killed. You went and chose another lover besides me; you did well, for you were no more than she deserved!

What other deed will issue from you than what you have already perpetrated? for like the vulture you have preyed on carrion. Well done! 'Give away a horse and take an ass!' How was one such as I worthy of you? Since salt marshes and sand were a fitting habitat for you, what need was there to decree for you palace and garden? I thought you a hunting lion and fancied that you would not trap other than the stag of the plain; I little knew you were an old fox and would with a hundred wiles catch a mere hare. Why having washed yourself thoroughly did you throw on your body dust and ashes? Why did you put down the goblet of wine and milk and set before yourself one of vinegar and garlic? Why did you rise from a fine-woven carpet and sit down on sackcloth and threadbare rug? Was it not enough that you forsook me, without taking up your abode in the city of enemies? Was it not enough to take another lover, without humiliating me before friend and enemy alike?

"Was it not enough that when you wrote your letter you compounded words of my very blood? And as if all this cruelty and wrath and hurt were not enough, you added to the load a further burden of ignominy: when the Nurse came to you, you drove her away and called her 'sorceress bitch' and 'spellbinder.' It is you who are the mountebank and spellbinder, not the Nurse; you are the sorcerer, you the one of many wiles. You took her for an ignorant mountaineer[7] and pronounced a sorcerer's abracadabra upon her; you cast a spell upon her and upon me; imprinted a thousand brands on our souls. You are a wizard with eyes like Zahhāk;[8] you practice both spells and necromancy. You perpetrated disloyalty; not so we; you broke the oath; we did not. You dwelt for some time happy in Gūrāb; now you have returned with lackluster countenance; you indulge ever in honeyed words, whose inner side is iron and their outer gold. I am that newly blossomed garden of a hundred colors against whom you uttered all those words of shame; I am that fine royal garden that was in your eyes but one huge fault; I am that spring from which you drank water and then disgracefully fouled the spring with earth; now that you have sorely suffered the tortures of thirst you come hastening to drink water of me! You should not

7. Minorsky, *Iranica*, p. 170.
8. See n. 2, p. 196.

295

have drunk from the spring and having once drunk fouled it with earth! for now you have debased the fountain, you will not again be able to drink its water."

RĀMĪN REPLIES TO VĪS. Once more Rāmīn replied to her and said, "Spring of Barbary and China! The world is like a turning millstone that the Creator has decreed should thus revolve. Its state never abides the same; sometimes it is March, sometimes winter. You and I are both children of the world; how can we remain in one state? Our body goes through revolutions like the world; now the infant, now the youth, at one time sick, at another healthy; even so now strong, now weak; sometimes endowed with possessions, sometimes without; now on a throne, now without a throne to its name. The body of man is weak and feeble,[9] being but a scrap of flesh and a handful of bone. In the heat it cannot abide the ordeal of being hot; in the cold it cannot stand the torture of feeling cold. When it is hot, it would be cold; when it is cold, hot. It seeks food, for it will grow in stature therefrom; then the selfsame body cries out from lack of food! Although concupiscence holds it fast in thrall, once you study it you will find it quickly tires of infatuation. Although it derives pleasure from its will, when it gains its will it is not up to it. In its frailty its desires are nothing but calamitous for it; thus ennui follows in the train of its desire. No sooner has its heart attained some ambition than the body becomes sated of it. Then again, should it fail to encompass its will, from the concupiscence in its heart it covets its heart's desire.

"Sometimes it is fierce and furious in desire; at other times when it has its will it becomes sated and dull. Once it has gained its desire no fury is left; once desire raises its head no dullness remains. No desire is sweeter than the love that is practiced with a cheek brighter than the sun; in every heart it grows so willful that that heart loses patience and peace. The heart is maddened by greed and becomes divorced from sleep and happiness. It can neither stand the capriciousness of the sweetheart in time of union nor bear the pain of separation at the time of being parted. Now it seeks to escape separation from her; now to separate itself from her anger and

9. With this passage compare Zaehner, *Zurvan*, pp. 171 ff., and *Tristan*, pp. 304 ff.

brutality. Since man is thus sorely weak, he is never patient in any single state.[10]

"My love, I am but one of the children of Man; how can I escape from the hand of desire? I orbit forever around you, for I have upon my head the bridle of desire. I sought you out when desire was predominant in me; it showed me all that was evil in the guise of good; afterwards, when you indulged in anger and capriciousness, you opened a new door by your faithlessness in love. I departed so as not to have to experience your wrath and caprices! and withdrew the partridge of love from your falcon. How could a heart that had gained its desire of you suffer from you in turn pain and humiliation? In the very city where it had been king and noble it would have had to be of low degree and humble. At the moment of departure I supposed that I would find it easy to live without you: I would choose another from amongst the fair of idol face and attach my heart to her in order to wash it clean of you.

"Nothing can burn the granary of love like love; as iron is broken with iron. When a new love visits the heart the stock of the old falls therein.[11] Whenever a new coin appears in the bazaar the worth of the old drops throughout the city. Since my friends one and all told me, 'It takes another love to break love; only love can cure love—there is no hewing an anvil other than upon an anvil!'—taking my friends' advice I went to Gūrāb, like a thirsty man searching for water over the wide world. Sometimes I sought some reminder of your face; sometimes I sought some comforter in separation from you. I saw on the road rosy-scented Gul; and fancied that I saw the shining moon. I had never seen an idol with that form or face, nor a rose with that scent and color. I attached my heart to love of that idol-faced beauty and told myself, 'Now I have escaped from love of Vīs.' But I was merely uttering spells over spells, merely washing blood from my heart with blood! I humored my wretched heart gently in every way I knew; I saw no profit of my humoring, for my heart merely grieved every moment. From love such a fire broke out in me that my body burned whilst my heart lamented. My heart knew no peace in my body, nor was there any end to its grief. If to

10. Cf. *Tristan*, p. 304.
11. Cf. *Tristan*, p. 303.

outward view I sat taking my ease, inwardly I wept at my separation. All that was left of my wretched body was a mere soul; I never for a moment slept or ate well. When without you I experienced a Judgment Day in my body I saw no remedy besides returning.

"You are to me good and evil, cure and pain, sweet and bitter, warm and cool. You are desire and affliction, pleasure and pain, grief and happiness, poverty and treasure. You are my eyes and heart, my soul and world, my sun and moon and sky. My love, do with me as you will, for you are sovereign and queen over me. I cry to you, for you are the Fire in my heart; to you I cry, for you are the judge over it. You are my enemy, you my friend; all you do is right, forbear to be cruel!"[12]

As the jasmine-bosomed Vīs wept on the edge of the roof, which became gorgeously colored from her face, her wretched heart did not reconcile itself to Rām; for there is no erasing an impression speedily from adamantine rock. Although her heart burned for Rāmīn, she wrought vengeance for her heart because of the envy of the past. When the fire of love blazed from her heart, Envy came and threw water on that fire.

She said to him, "Deceitful, eloquent youth who have thrown the ball of speech into the field! The wind is not to be trapped by entreaty, the brilliance of the sun is not to be hidden in mire. If you went to Gūrāb to escape my anger, seeking water throughout the wide world like a thirsty man, went to avoid facing my anger and capriciousness, took your partridge away from my falcon, sometimes sought a reminder of my face, sometimes a comforter in separation from me, having no recourse but another lover, whom you were to take to lessen your distress, I accept that all you have said is true; that you did not eat well nor lie down to sleep without care; but why did you write that wild letter, why abuse me therein? Why were you angry at the Nurse, why did you heap humiliation upon her as you did? What possessed you to drive her away from your presence like a dog in front of her enemies? I shall give you a word of advice, if you will hear it; hear and mark it, if you are of sagacious mind. Should you conceive a notion in your heart, leave the door open a little for peace; in war a wise man of sage counsel thus leaves the

12. *I. Mb:* "whatever you say is good coming from you."

door open a chink for peace; the demon has so cast wrath in your heart that he has gouged the niche of amity from your breast. Have you not heard that there are two demons of wrath always hidden in men's bodies; one says, 'Do this, and have no fear, for you will make great profit thereby'; once the deed is done, the other creature comes and says to him, 'Why have you done this?' That first demon rendered you silly, now the other demon has rendered you repentant.[13] You should not have picked a fight in the first instance only to find yourself now casting about for excuses in plenty! To commit no sin and be of clear conscience is far easier than to make excuses. To abstain from distasteful food is far better than drinking copious draughts of medicine. Had you only possessed this wisdom then, your tongue would have been that little shorter. Had I too possessed wisdom from the first, my companion in love would not have been such as you. As you have now become regretful, my soul has likewise become full of regret. I tell myself, 'Why did I look on your face, and having done so, why choose love for you? Now you are like water, I like fire; you properly broken in, I thoroughly wild and refractory. I shall not consort with you hereafter; water and fire sort but ill together!'"

Captivating Rāmīn said in reply, "The night of your anger has brought us on evil days.[14] This night I see two nights in the world: one from this murky tempest, the other from the anger of the beloved. How much pain has descended on me out of this night! My horse and I tremble on the brink of death.

"Why has my horse been arraigned along with me? He is not my accomplice. If you deny me bed and resting place, why do you grudge him a handful of barley and a wisp of straw? Entertain him with at least a handful of straw; rejoice my heart by saving his life. Let me be no friend or lover; merely suppose that tonight I am a guest. Good treatment is recognized as the desert of guests; they are not abandoned thus in the midst of the snow. I have thrown excuses out of court; I have now no excuse or pretext. All will call you unchivalrous should you say to me, 'Depart hence in desperation!' All noble and renowned men will attribute this to meanness, not to

13. Cf. *Tristan*, p. 306.
14. *I. Mb:* "made our day night."

rancor. Between us lies no blood, nor does there stand an ancient feud. This is mere scolding, not proper warfare; why do you wage such sore feud against my soul? You know well that the soul is not to be trifled with; why then do you mount attack upon your slave?

"I am not the man to flee from the cold; as long as there is breath in my body I shall fight it. I am not the man to turn back from your lane, even should I give up the ghost before your very face. What if I die in the snow? I shall win eternal fame among men. My name shall live forever for faithfulness should I in the last resort die before you. Without you I do not wish life; for thus I fail to attain to my desire. I have tried the world without you over and over again; I was alive in it in so far as a dead man may be said to be alive. Since then without you I am not of the number of the living, why should I desire to go on living without you? It is absurd for me to seek the world without you; for without you my very life is but a plague to me. Cruel winter wind! bring snow and take me quickly! Death amidst the snow is sweeter to me than the cruelty of fate and the anger of my love. Even a heart of stone and a soul of stoutest brass would not survive in the midst of so much snow."

The jasmine-bosomed Vīs said, "Faithless Rām, in the end you have been overtaken by affliction. This is the end of the sinner—one day he is caught in the trap. The wine that you have drunk will not come back to your cup; nor the bird that has flown return to your snare. Now you are homeless in Marv, a stranger to so many friends. You will not gain joy and desire of me; nor find so much as a place to lay your head in Marv. Better then to forbear to speak wild words; to seek rose and eglantine in salt ground. Since you have abandoned your former lover, sit rejoicing with your late love! Such a sweetheart as Gul sits waiting for you; why thus heartbroken? May Moubad's palace and hall be blest to his guests—guests that are distinguished, not like you, harbingers of eternal shame! I grudge you access anywhere at all: how shall I bring you into the King's house?[15] May there be no guest like you in his palace, that feels shame neither before him nor before God! May there be none other in his house like you, neither stranger nor relative nor brother. You are not now worthy of my lane, how should you be worthy of my face?

15. Order here as in *I*.

300

The more I drive you away from the door, the more you persist in saying, 'Here I am, your guest.' You are banished like a villager from a village when he hankers after being its headman.

"You have gone so far as to leave your home in winter; surely you knew that there would be snow and rain. Why did you account this journey mere play? why did you not make for yourself the needful preparations? Was not Marv your home, Vīseh your confidante? Why set off upon a journey in the winter without equipment? Your foolish heart has become your enemy; why has your blame lighted upon me? Well said the Dastūr[16] to Jamshīd: 'Let no man lament or rejoice over the foolish!' When you were not yet a commander or a general, you cherished my heart day and night. Now that you have become prince and lord, you have grown all at once heedless of me. You have put on your door the sign of indifference and have loaded me with scorn and jests. Do you now beg me to spare your life? I fear you want New Year in December![17] You fail to cultivate me in the hour of desire and delight; but only let wind and snow come, and up you come hastening to my side. Abandon hope of me, champion among heroes! Let me be free, for God's sake!"

Rāmīn sore at heart replied: "Do not so, my Moon, do not hurt me thus: is it not enough that you have driven me from you, is the arrow you have lodged in my heart not enough? Is it not sufficient that you have dissipated my good name and rehearsed my shame so thoroughly? Forbear to shoot the arrow of cruelty at me further; for you have wounded my soul and heart through and through. What worse tribulation than this could fall upon me, that you should say, 'I do not suffer you to be in my lane!'

"Why do you deny me passage? This is surely the palace of Moubad? Right enough that I should call you stonyhearted and foe, for you deny me the King's highway. It is unchivalrous to deny to your love right of way through city and road common to friend and enemy alike. Have you not just said that men of distinction leave the door open for peace in war? Why then have you no peace in your heart? Are you not compounded of clay as I? Now if you will

16. See n. 8, p. 38.
17. The Persian New Year begins in March.

not reconcile yourself to me, if loyalty has departed and what was to be has been, I must perforce depart hence and remain desperate, bereft of patience and parted from my lover. Give me a keepsake from your twin locks, give me a comforter from those two dusky nights of yours! Give me a loop from those two chains that steal the soul of youth and old man alike! Perhaps my soul may be saved by your scent even as my body has been wounded in your lane. Perhaps, once my soul has been ransomed, your heart in turn may become heavy in separation. You must have heard: 'The night is great with child; no one knows what it shall bear on the morrow.'"

Vīs of the moonlike form answered, "Sugar is not to be made from colocynth; fine silk does not come from stone, wine the color of Judas blossom from hemp. No iron ever becomes wax, no enemy a friend. Your words are to me mere gibberish; for I have for you neither leavened nor unleavened dough. Your wind will not blow me down, nor your might budge me from my place. I shall not become happy at your words, nor become carefree at the sight of you. It is no matter of a single hurt from you remaining in my heart that may be spirited away by a spell; you have spread the corrosion of hurt upon my soul; how may it be polished away with words? Your cruel barbs have lodged in my ear; there is now no way for further speech to join them. You have stuffed my ear by your own hand; how can I now hear your words? Many a time have I caught a smile from the face of union; many a time cried on the evil day of separation. Now I neither cry nor laugh; for my soul is not the slave of the love in my heart. My heart was a fox; now it has become a lion, for it has become sated of a lover like you. The lamp of love and hope that was brighter in my heart than the sun has gone out. That heart which was my enemy has departed; all things are changed in my body. My very eye that used to look at the color of your face, my ear that used to hear your words, one fancying it saw the sun, the other that it heard glad tidings, now that sun has become to the one like pitch, those glad tidings an arrow in the other. I have come to know that the lover is blind, for his fortunes are always sinister! Now I say, 'Triumphant fortune, will you not tell me where you have been till today? Now is the happy day for my body, now is there in my heart an eye that sees! Now can I savor the world, now know happiness in my spirit. I shall not fall into your trap nor sacrifice everyone for the sake of one ignoble soul!'"

Rāmīn resumed: "Jasmine-bosomed beauty, my heart was yours to give, it is yours to take: what if you have become sated of me and have sown in your heart the same old feud against me? I shall not become sated of you in my heart, nor can I find it in myself to become bold in seeking to visit cruelty upon you. From you may come fury—but from me sweet speech will be heard; from you may come abuse—but from me, love. I shall not turn my face away from you no matter how much you may hurt me; for I shall not find another like you. Even if you gouge one of my eyes out of my head, I shall lay the other eye before your hand. Your curses are like blessings to me, for your speech is like sugar in my ears. For all that you have abused me in disgraceful fashion I yet feel as though you have spoken in noble terms. Although you strive to wound me with words, and abuse me roundly in your fury, everything you say is sweet to my ears; you would swear it was the melodies of musicians I heard! When you fall silent, I say to myself, 'How wonderful it would be if she hurt me again! If once more she set her tongue to speech, if only to abuse me!' With the very words you employ to cure me you merely increase the old pain in my heart. Although I experience pain and hurt at your hand, I yet cherish hope of the day when I see your face.

"I ever say, 'Perhaps you will become reconciled to me and become the profit to set against love's loss.' Tonight, my love, I am like a man with a lion in front of him and an elephant behind; his heart is broken by the fear of both; affliction blocks his way on both sides. If I remain here, there you are, so disposed to me as to be like my enemies in feud against me; and again, if I depart from your presence I do not know whether I shall survive the snow and rain! I am stuck between two calamities: helpless in the face of two disasters. Although death is a disaster for the body, in such a plight it is my deliverance. If Death were now to take away my soul, my heart's pain would be over thereby. Though Death might wound my soul, at all events my body would escape from this travail. My body is drowned in the water of my tears, the world has become a hoop

303

around me like your locks. You hold my heart in that ambergris-scented lock; I do not know how I can depart hence in desperation."

Vīs of the moonlike form gave him a reply like sugar laced with poison: spoke to that exiled wanderer and transfixed the tears in his eyes with her glance. "Go, Rām, reconcile yourself to exile; pour on your heart the water of patience. The less you speak, the better; the less I see you, the better for me. You cause your soul vain vexation every time you try something already tried. Am I not disturbed in my senses and feeble-minded, thus far to try something already tried? The brand you have burnt into my heart is enough; the fountain you have opened from my eyes will suffice. If the Magian makes his fire blaze for a hundred years he himself will one day burn in it.[18] Try to bring up the ignoble or the wolf! There is no nature that improves through effort. Much have I tested you heretofore; you would swear that it was a scorpion or a snake that I assayed. Although to outward view you were broken in, you nevertheless showed your mettle in the fire.

"One half of my life has slipped away—and you say, 'Alas for my days of success!' Yes, one half of *my* life has gone by in pain and eternal shame; I would spend the remaining half in happiness; I have no wish to cast it, too, to the winds; what remains to me of all that former loyalty I sowed that should prompt me to take pains and sow further? I shall not practice love any further with those who know no love; for I have not turned enemy to my own body. My mother did not bear me for you, nor God create me for you. Are not the ten years of trouble I have suffered enough? and the vain distress I have undergone? How could there be more loyalty than I sought to practice—and what remains in my hand from seeking it? I practiced loyalty before and could not have done worse, for thus it is that I have a heart full of brand and pain. Everyone repents of cruelty; I am one that has fallen into this case out of loyalty! Loyalty has brought me such suffering that my nectar has become poison, my friend my enemy. How long shall a heart abide such harm and pain visiting it from love and hate? Even were it a mountain of

18. This verse is quoted, almost verbatim, in the *Gulistān* of Saʿadī (ed. Furūghī and Mashkūr [1344 H.S.], p. 32).

stone and iron it would not now have remained one instant in the body. Even supposing I had the will to practice love, you do not tell me how I am to do so with this heart! How should a heart that has escaped from fear and sprung from the snare once again set foot on your road?"

Rāmīn once more answered her, "Do not struggle so to extricate your head from the toils: you gain nothing in the end by these words; I fear you may have no soil in the spade of patience. Your tongue is not in step with your heart; your heart has no knowledge of these words. Your heart has no gift for patience; thus it has no clue to the words you speak. You are like a drum whose roll is fearsome; but within your skin all is empty air. Your tongue flaunts itself as tiring all too early—but your heart is not quite so bold. Your tongue is one thing, but your heart another, for one is colocynth, the other sugar. My God is not up in the heaven, my fair one, if your heart is not lovingly inclined toward me. But my fortune tonight is after my blood like an enemy. It has abandoned me in the snow like a lost soul, and left but a step between me and death. I shall not suffer myself to stay where I am any further, not court the anguish of snow and cold. You are foolish and may not have heard that 'a foolish friend is worse than an enemy.' Should even a fine child be foolish, it is proper to cut off love from it and sever relationship with it. Here am I in the midst of snow and cold, there you are in the midst of silk and brocade. You behold me in this plight and keep speaking honeyed words; what call is there for this protracted discourse? What time is this for all this haughtiness and capriciousness?

"My throat will be suddenly blocked by snow before in your haughtiness you have had the time to shorten your discourse. My place to die is upon the battlefield, with an army lying slain around me; why should I die a vain death in the cold? Why not take the way of safety? You do not desire me! Well, you are under no compulsion! As for me, I have no lack of sweethearts; let Moubad be in your embrace and may he have good fortune of it, but let me have another lover like you. Should I depart from your presence, know well which one of us will be damaged by this ill temper!

"Now I am going. Farewell! Go on playing this melody, so long as the lute does not break! I wish that you may be patient; 'what

305

better can the blind man wish than a seeing eye?' You Moubad's lover and he yours; may your fortunes be according to the desire of your well-wishers!"

The jasmine-bosomed Vīs said, "So be it; a thousand blessings on you! May your night be happy, your day happy as your night, your heart high, your fortune high as your heart. I am the fine lover you saw, whose like you had never seen or heard. My bright moon has not lost its light, nor has my musky hair become as camphor. The curl of my locks is no whit less twisted, nor have the pearls in my mouth lost their radiance. My cypress stature has not grown like a hoop, the silvery mound of my body has not become spare. If my cheeks were then a new moon, now I have become the Sun of the beauties of the world. The very Hūrīs of Paradise worship my cheeks; Rizvān himself is a ready customer for my lips. In face I am the Sun of the fair; in glance, past mistress of sorcerers. The rose itself is humble before my cheek, as the thorn is humble before the rose. The fir is bent before my stature, as gems beside my teeth are stones. In beauty of face I am Moon of Moons, as I am queen of queens in charm. No mountebank steals wallets from sleepers as I hearts from the wide-awake. No lion catches the wild ass, no cheetah the deer, as I capture even the sorcerer's soul with my glance. Charm itself borrows capital from my face; heathendom its stock from my hair. I have never been of small account in the sight of any; why have I become counterfeit in your sight?

"Although I may be wretched and feeble in your eyes, at any rate I am more than you say I am! Now you would have both Gul and me, so that your rose may be the bedmate of your lily; have you not, perhaps, heard the old sage's saw: 'A city governed by two Amirs will quickly come to ruin!' Where have you ever seen two swords sharing one scabbard, or night and day together in the same place? It is surprising that you call me foolish; it is you whose foot has been seized by folly. Had your heart not been senseless and foolish it would not have been writhing in this predicament! Let me be foolish—at all events I am rid of you. I belong not to you but to your overlord. Render God due gratitude and thanks that you are not, like Moubad, the husband of a foolish wife!"

88.

VĪS GROWS ANGRY, LEAVES HER VANTAGE POINT, AND SHUTS
THE DOORS ON RĀMĪN. When Vīs had given in full her reply to
Rām, her stony heart did not become broken in to love. She turned
away from the window and hid her face, saying to the watchmen
and sentinels, "Do not sleep tonight, but stay awake; be on your
guard one and all during your sentry-go; for tonight is a fearful
night—the world is in danger of being destroyed by the snowstorm.
From the high wind and the rushing of the rain you would swear
cavalry were charging! The world is raging like a furious sea; you
would swear the Flood was prepared! From the furious waves and
the rushing of the wind the ark is any moment like to crack! This
night is a Judgment Day for the world, bringing beasts and birds
within an inch of their lives." When Rāmīn heard his sweetheart
address the sentinels thus, "Tonight be ever on your guard, be one
and all wakeful and smart!" he abandoned hope of seeing his love,
for the wind was buffeting him all around; nor did he dare to stop
where he was, unable to move either hand or foot. Helplessly he
turned his horse's head, abandoning hope both of his life and of his
love. He went off into the snow like a mountain, greater than a
mountain the load of grief upon his heart. He said, "My heart, why
are you fearful, though you have been humiliated by your love?
It is often thus in love: the body of the lover is ever laid low. If you
survive this day, do not any more seek out the fair! You are free,
and the free man does not suffer his body to undergo humiliation
and injustice. Do not choose lover or friend after this, but sit burnt
as you are by the brand of the old lover. Lament the life you have
lost, and when you remember this lover, say, 'Alas, the pains and
times that are past! for nothing remains to me of them but regret!
Alas for all my pains and canterings! for I did not after all gain the
ball on the field! Alas for all my hope, which came to nothing like
the passing wind!' I told you, my heart, I ever said, 'My heart, turn
back from this road, for a pit will yawn before you thereon.' I said,
'Tongue, do not reveal your secret; do not divulge to your lover all
that is hidden in your heart; the lover will sorely humiliate us. All
too clearly did I foresee this day when once you had revealed the

secret to your sweetheart and divulged to her all that you hid, the lover would display all this capriciousness and haughtiness, for she has no pleasure any more in love. Silence would have been better for you than speech, but you spoke and now inevitably have suffered humiliation. What an excellent proverb did a lover once coin: "Silence[1] is the best policy even for birds!"'"

89.

VĪS REPENTS OF WHAT SHE HAS DONE. How astonishing, how deceitful is Fate, that thus holds us in thrall to her! Sometimes keeps us happy, sometimes sad; sometimes in love, sometimes angry; the wretch plays with us for all the world like a juggler with a bead! Perhaps we were not fated to have any but this portion, and had it not been so it would not have been right. Had our body not been tied to Desire, it would not have behaved haughtily to anyone, nor bowed its head to any in the world, nor assumed any of the world's burdens; it would have chosen deliverance from the fetter of its humanity and avoided all greatness save godliness. Had our nature been thus exempt from Desire, with whom would the world have been able to jest and sport?

Thus between Vīs and Rāmīn did the world contrive all that wrath following on love. When Rāmīn turned desperate away from Vīs, the Devil himself might well have given up hope of love between the two!

Vīs repented of what she had done; her sorrowing heart was wounded by its own hand. She rained tears like a spring cloud, sailed on the water like a ship. The roses of her cheeks became like clay in hue; from the pain in her heart she dashed stones upon her heart— no, not upon her heart, rather dashed stone on stone; in her cries she was like the high string sounding against the rest of the harp.

She ever said, "Alas for my sinister fortune! You would swear I was the tree that bears the branch of affliction. Why have I purchased care for my soul, cut my throat with my own hand? What ill is this that I have visited upon my own body? Why have I thus become my own enemy? Who now will put out the fire in my heart, whoever now knows the remedy for what is done?" She said to the

1. *G:* "patience."

Nurse, "Rise, and do not tarry! See my notorious plight and wounded soul! See whether this fate has ever overtaken anyone, any daughter been born of her mother with my fate! Faithful Fortune came to my door, and I drove it thence by force. The cup of nectar was in my hands, I was drunk from it; in my drunkenness I threw the cup away from my grasp. The black wind of cruelty blew dust on me: now the cloud of affliction rains pain upon me. Three times the moisture that rains from the sky is poured on my heart this night by grief. I have become impoverished of happiness; I have put out the lamp of my heart with my own hand. My Nurse, hasten like the wind; find my dear lover quickly! Take the reins of his horse, make him dismount, and say, 'You who departed hurt from me; there is no ambition without anguish; no love without reproach; in the soul hope and desire are found together; in love reproach and capriciousness go hand in hand. Your cruelty was true in fact; mine metaphorical, a thing of mere words. You will not find either love or love affair in which the lovers do not have words; why should one yearn for a lover toward whom one cannot be capricious? You were wounded by me in words; I by you in deed. If your deeds were right, why then were my words a fault in me? Assuming that it was right for you to do the deeds you did, was it not similarly proper for me to speak less or more as I deemed right?' Hold him, Nurse, till I come; for I shall make such excuse as is proper."

90.

VĪS SENDS THE NURSE AFTER RĀMĪN AND FOLLOWS. The Nurse went, swift as a flying bird; no harm came to her either from wind or from rain; a heart impatient with love fears neither cold nor heat. She thought the snow on the road rose petals;[1] she reached Rāmīn and stopped him.

Jasmine-bosomed Vīs was swaying like a cypress; her snowy body rushing through the snow. The splendor of the sun shone from her face, her perfume was redolent of spring blossoms. In the midst of dark night the world became like bright day; she made a garden in the midst of the snow by her face. The snow was ashamed before those silvery limbs; the wind before that musky tress; the snow was

1. Refers to Vīs in G.

hardly as fair as her limbs; the wind hardly as sweetly perfumed as her tresses. She shed pearls upon the ground from her eyes; from her hair, ambergris on the air. You would have sworn some Hūrī without leave of Rizvān had suddenly descended to Earth from Paradise, to save Rāmīn's life and lead him by fair fortune to his heart's desire.

When she came up to him she turned haughty and teasing and said, "Lamp of the noble! The composition of every clay is like yours; the nature of every heart like yours; everyone's heart writhes at hurt; everyone takes cruelty from the lover hard; everyone covets for himself fame and heart's desire: the more they have, the more they want. Just as now I visited you with cruelty, your cruelty was previously visited on me. If my cruelty rendered your heart sad, yours rendered mine likewise. See what you approve for yourself, and if you are wise, approve the same for everyone else. The world is now a friend, now an enemy; it smiles now on you and now on me. If your enemy is at your mercy today, one day you will be at the mercy of your enemies.

"Why should someone who is evil-doing like you take offense at a mere speech? In your ignobility you piled burden upon burden, in your lack of love you added deed to deed; see what you did to me: how often you took my good name in vain. What did I experience from you but evil-doing? See how much I had to hear that was odious! Was it not enough that you turned your back on the compact, and went and indulged in a love affair with another? If there was no remedy but doing away with love, where was the necessity for writing such a letter as you did? divorcing yourself from Vīs and the Nurse, multiplying humiliation and disgracefulness? What did you gain from the disgracefulness in which you indulged when you called me down so revoltingly? If you felt no compunction before your fine lover, did you not at least feel shame before God? Did you not swear oath to me a hundred times that you would never break the contract in love? If you can take an oath and then forswear it, why should I not proclaim the fact and stigmatize you as of base metal and faulty workmanship? Why have you perpetrated all these sinister deeds, the very rehearsal of which in words is shame? Have you not heard that the deeds of men are only disgraceful in consequence of men's words? Faults are disgraceful only in so far as they are enumerated: this is why the wise do not pick fault. Since you are unable to stand blame you should not have chosen other than the good. On every day look to the morrow; do not do evil lest you be tortured by its retribution! If you go to war you will suffer retaliation; if you throw a cup you will be hit by a pitcher. Once you sow destruction, you will surely reap it; if you speak to excess you will have to listen long![2] If you have sowed, now you have reaped the fruit; if you have spoken, now you have heard the answer.

"Do not be so sensitive, champion of braves! Do not twist your reins away from me; do not bear me a grudge and say 'This is not what I deserve.' At all events I am not responsible for your sin! It is proper that you should have been tried by the same pain as you yourself inflicted upon me. It is you who committed the offense and you who are angry: will you not tell me who has prompted you to be so bold? Act as judge and produce my offense! I do not know for what I am to seek excuse. Will you not say what fault there is in my body or what there is in my face and hair that is not fair? I still have a figure like a cypress covered in blossom; still a face like the moon, the hue of pomegranate blossom; I still have hyacinth steeped in ambergris; sugar set with gems; still bloom on my cheeks tulip and eglantine; still shine in my mouth Venus and the Pleiades. The splendor of the sun shines from my face; my perfume exudes a breeze laden with the scent of spring blossom.

"Will you not say what fault you know in me, other than sincerity of heart and beauty of face?[3] At the time of love, I am loving; at the moment of harmony, harmonious. Was I not born of the same mother as Beauty herself? Am I not of the same lineage as Nobility itself? Am I not the worthy daughter of Shahrū? Am I not the fair mistress of all beauties? The name of Beauty is my desert in the world; for the twist of my lock conceals the very snare of beauty, under every hair of my body a thousand hearts have fallen into the snare; the rose of my face is ever in full bloom; the tip of my lock is perennially scented with ambergris. If the spring blossoms so much

2. *I.*
3. Cf. the line of Ḥāfiẓ, partly quoting Sa'adī: "There is no fault to be found in your beauty save that a pretty face has no habit of love and loyalty" (*Dīvān*, ed. Pazhmān, p. 5).

as see my face they drop in very shame from the branches. You will never see any pomegranate blossom like my cheeks; ever fresh, perfumed, and in full bloom. You will never see any sugar like my lips; sweeter to hearts than life and possessions.

"If you have become weary of love and loyalty toward me and have wrapped up the carpet of affection, be chivalrous and hide it! Do not humiliate your sweetheart quite! Leaven your anger with a dash of conciliation: do not parade abroad your shortcomings in love. 'Not everyone who eats bread with meat ties the bones round his neck.' Sages term him a man indeed who can best hide the secret of his heart, whose very shirt knows not his secret; not even the hairs on his body are aware of it. So do you, too, confine this enmity within your heart, and forbear to display such anger and hurtfulness toward me. Do not block the road of happiness with rancor; do not quite snuff out the candle of love. Do not cut yourself off from love of an entrancing beauty like me; perhaps my love will one day stand you in good stead. The world never stays long in one state; after every day another day comes. If much wrath has overtaken you out of love, perhaps another day love will descend on you from wrath, just as after warmth comes cold, and again after cold, warmth."

Rāmīn, wounded to the heart, gave a reply as suited their plight: "My love, I have seen all your deeds and heard all your words; may the man perish who is ignorant in wretchedness: and who remains therein from his ignorance. I am not the man to mistake wretchedness and remain therein inactive. None other than a demon seduced me on to this road: I regret the direction given me by the demon. I traversed a road at its behest: for some time I suffered tribulation and wretchedness. I fancied that I would find a treasure by traveling on this road: I little knew that what I would find was fruitless pains! I dwelt happy and joyful in Kūhistān: my body free from pain, my heart from care. I divorced my heart from such great happiness: and embraced a road thus grievous. I deserve the wretchedness I have suffered: because I cut my heart off from all that joy.

"The silly heart prides itself on its sagacity; evil is the desert of one who cannot sort with good. 'Give the person you are testing a jewel; if he will not have a jewel, hand him an ember.' Fate gave me a jewel; when I threw it away it gave me in its stead an ember. I made a two months' journey and what did I see at its end? Ill fortune. I have deserved no end other than this; had it been otherwise it would not have been right. The moment I was ungrateful to Fate, Fate estranged itself from me. The moment I said, 'I feel no gratitude for anything,' Fate said, 'Then you are no friend of mine.' You did right to drive me from your side and call me nothing but mountebank and fool. Had my heart not been so foolish it would not have found itself writhing from attachment to an ignoble lover. Now turn back and do not cleave to me; abstain from love of me even as you have said.

"For my part, I go; till Judgment Day we shall not be joined together. I did not deny that you were like the moon in face; silver of forearm and musky of tress, queen and lady over the fair, watchful treasurer of the beautiful. Sorcery itself makes pretension to your eye; beauty itself gains profit from your face. You possess loops of musk trained over ivory; you own a crown for the moon, made of violets. In face you resemble a profusion of spring blossoms; in cheek you are like a Chinese figurine. But even though you be moon and sun, I do not wish you to shine on me at all. My love, you are the physician of the desperate, and you know their cure. After this, though my pain be sore, even should I die I shall not haunt your side. You have in your lip the water of life: you restore to the body life and youth. Even though I am faced with thirst, I shall die of thirst before I crave water. Even though love for you be a blazing fire, you shall not see it burn hereafter. Better for a fire that is all smoke to become embers, and that quickly.

"You have freely rehearsed faults in my body, two hundred times as many as even my enemy would find. Now you have forgotten those words, you have not stored them in heart or ear. You fail to see how you yourself have indulged in humiliation, and yet expect loyalty and love of me. It is you, jasmine-bosomed beauty, who resemble the woman who has a blind daughter in her arms, fails to see her daughter's blindness, and is ever choosing for her a faultless groom! You no less than I fail to see your own fault and are ever on the quest for a faultless lover! You always want to call the tune: you pick faults in everyone: what fault have you seen in me in your lifetime that you should evince such wrath and hurtfulness toward me? It is your heart that has become weary of love; why thus much call me lacking in love? You more than I wear the arms of false love: for your religion is mercilessness and meanness. If you had never seen my face, or ever heard tell of me in the world, it would still not have been right for you to be so merciless, to have inflicted all this humiliation in words.

"Leave aside that I am your lover of old, I have been in exile and on far journeys; the night has been dark but I have been without resting place or resource; caught in the grip of wind and snow and night, I have made many excuses for my sins; offered a thousand entreaties and cries for quarter; not so much as a word from you in the way of sweetness; not so much as one act of kindness. You did not grant me audience at your hall; nor in your cruelty did you grant me quarter. You left me in the snow and rain—and then drove me humiliatingly from your side. In your mercilessness you forbore to take my hand to rescue me in order that I might die in the snow! In your sore envy you failed to show me mercy; instead, you purposed my death like an enemy. Even had I exhibited envy toward you one single day, it would not have seemed to me to merit being a day of death! How shameless you are, how faithless in observance of oaths, that you hold the death of your friends as naught! Even if my death were pleasing to you, what profit would you gain therefrom? You have seen no profit of all your actions; you have come to suffer the same suspicion that you yourself have nursed. I have gained a handsome profit, for the perfidious has been distinguished from the faithful. There is at all events one consolation in affliction, that friend may be told from enemy thereby. Now that I have become aware of your nature, have become the enemy of your stony heart, your loyalty is like the Sīmurgh[4]—impossible to find; for you have a heart innocent of mercy, an eye that knows no tear. May none live to pursue love for you; for it is worth not a jot!

"Thanks to the just Creator for having delivered my soul from the fetter of love! I shall go and practice love no more with any; Gul of the rosy scent is enough for me in all this world! I shall go and be King beside her till my dying day, as she will till her death be Moon

4. A bird in Iranian mythology proverbial for unattainability.

314

at my side. Wherever there is a Moon like her, she deserves to have a King like me. Even if you traverse the world two hundred times, you will not find a Moon like her nor a King like me. Since Fortune has vouchsafed us the fair union we know, we shall live content with each other's love."

The jasmine-bosomed Vīs said, as she cried in turmoil, two springs of blood boiling from her eyes, her dress figured like the moon torn on her breast, the tulip-hued veil flung from her head, "You, dear to me as my own soul, desire of my heart and acme of my desire, you are the peer of beneficence for my fortunes, you are the compeer of joy for my soul; do not once and for all rend the veil of my fortune, do not render my soul a slave in love; forbear to break the branch of the tree of happiness; do not cast the moon of hope into the abyss! If I teased you a trifle, or behaved with envy toward you for an instant, do not make such recital of my envy, do not make to me excuses for separation. Since I have suffered pain for six months in separation, it was surely allowable for me to tease for a single instant! There is no separation without anguish; no love without reproach. In whosoever's heart fire burns through love, the lover's reproach is sweet. Reproach between lovers in union and in separation remains so long as their love survives. I gave a reply to you couched in metaphor; I fancied I but sported with you.

"Let my anguish now increase, then, with every day that passes, now that even those reproaches are in turn added to my cares! 'Should a stone fall from the heavens, it is like to fall on the heads of lovers'. Now I repent; why did I utter reproaches? for the anguish of my soul is thereby increased. I supposed that I was but teasing you; now that teasing has turned into an entreaty to you. If I went rather far in teasing, see how I shall seek to win you back! I vented feigned asperity upon you, and am left thus bewildered through it. If I gave offense by my teasing, now I have become like you trapped in the snow. As I was your confidante on the day of happiness, so have I become your companion on the day of affliction. You well know that I did not treat you ill; nonetheless separation has increased my care and pain. As I have suffered sore distress through separation from you, I shall not henceforth turn from you in play. Now I shall not drop my hand from your rein; I shall mourn in misery till I die. If you accept my excuse and forbear to stoke, by your fury, the fire that burns me, I shall be a mere servant before you till my dying day, and shall hold your behest equal to the command of God. And should I not thus practice love, you may desert me at any time. You may seek separation at any time, but may not seek intimacy. It is easy to cut a tree from the root; but it is not to be made to grow again once cut."

Rāmīn, light of the world, said, "After this, do not imagine that anyone will enjoy fruit of me; I shall forbear to practice love lest I suffer humiliation, lest I see the bright world dark through grief; why should one be mournful on the day of joy? or enslave one's free body? Many a day have I seen my body at the mercy of my enemy through sore humiliation! If humiliation is to overcome me, how right, then, that I should forbear to practice love with anyone. No place but Hell will befit me should I try something already once tried. I am free; and no free man chooses tyranny and injustice like a slave. No wise man plays the tyrant; no free man suffers tyranny. Even if the sun shines from your face, I have abandoned hope of your sun. Even were stone to become rare in the world, and one maund worth sixty maunds of jewels, I would buy a hundred maunds of it and lay it on my heart; perhaps I might thereby escape from this shame and disgrace! Even though a hundred treasures underlie union with you, it is still not worth the search at the price of all this suffering!

"I shall tear the heart from my body if again it indulges in love of either you or another sweetheart. Better for me even to be divorced from my heart, for it fancies everyone but me. Perhaps the best of my luck has lain in your love being tonight all hate.

"Many the task that is hard at the beginning, but Fortune yet leads it to success in the end.[5] Sometimes God rights events in a way that no one would presume to pray him to do. He it is who has so ordered my affairs this night as to dispose them in tune with the desires of my friends. I have escaped from those manifold words and excuses; from all that trial of pain, distress, and burning in fire. You would swear I had been a slave, and had become a king; that I was the earth, and had become the heaven and the moon. My soul has become so devoid of pain and grief that you would swear I am not

5. Line of *Mb* omitted, following *I*.

now of this world. So sober have I become after my drunkenness that I have awoken from the sleep of foolishness. My blind luck has now become seeing, my silly soul now become sage.

"Now that I have extricated my foot from the shackle of wretchedness, no grave will today receive my dust. Beware of cherishing the desire of seeing me any more pursue love: beware of supposing that you will again see me as you are wont to do, wretched and mournful; whoever has quite cut off his desire from the world will not thereafter be troubled by the slightest care on its account. I shall pass my life innocent of distress; I shall not henceforward seek gain merely to suffer loss. You too, if you are wise and sage, shall live like me and not know grief in your heart. You will practice wisdom and cultivate contentment; for 'contentment is the best sovereignty.'

"Even if you sow the seeds of love for a hundred years you will not have more than the wind in your hand of it all. No one has ever known peace in the practice of love; or ever trod a road other than that of difficulty. No one has ever followed this road to the end in the world; if you are reasonable my advice will be enough for you."

Jasmine-bosomed Vīs, hand in hand with Rām, was senseless as one drunk from the brand of loverhood. Her body trembling from the cold like a willow as she scattered rubies on grass from narcissus, she said, "You who are as precious to me as my eyes, moon of my night, sun of my day, the finest sweetheart love could require, the fairest king fame could demand, I have no wish for life without your face, I have no wish for success without attainment of your desire. I hurt you, and it was ill done; in grief at this deed I bite the back of my hand. Forbear to draw thus far the bow of anger and hurtfulness; do not knock thus hard the door of harm and distress. Come, let us make our hearts glad and recall each other for our good deeds. Let us no more speak of what is past, but cleanse our hearts with the water of love.

"Be not heavy at heart from the wretchedness that you have undergone and from the words that you have heard from me. Humiliation may come to you from your mistress, but not from one such as I, your darling and sweetheart! The renowned kings of the world kiss the very dust under the feet of a sweetheart. No war is involved in the reproaches of the fair, nor is any shame involved in the endurance of their caprices. Bear my capriciousness, for you have borne off my soul; exercise restraint, for you have stolen plunder. What will you do on the day of Judgment, for you will have the blood of one like me on your hands? What worse day may come for me than the day when I see neither heart in my breast nor the ravisher of my heart in my arms? What better for me than to have a heart as companion; and if no heart, at least a lover! You have stolen my heart and now purpose departure; you purpose to kill both heart and sweetheart! If you purpose to go, at least do not take this heart with you: for in this agony I shall rain fire upon it. How can you bear to court separation and cut off intimacy with my face? You were the one I termed faithful; now you have become altogether wary of me. Alas for all the compacts that you concluded, and once concluded, carelessly broke! I gave my silly heart much advice; I told it, 'Beware of attaching yourself to this faithless youth!' But, willful thing, it slid out of its bond; who can say what its plight became?

Why do you now keep me here so long? why render my languorous eyes bloodshot? If you are to turn away, do so quickly; for the cold is like to raise dust from the ruin of my soul. And if you are to turn away, my sweetheart, then take me with you; I am with you in foul times and fair, be it in Reyy or Khurāsān. Even should you rend a hundred veils upon me, and cut my hand from the hem of your garment, I shall yet grasp your hem and come with you; I shall not stay a moment with Moubad if you are gone. Even had I a heart like a mountain I should not dare so much as to contemplate separation from you. You purpose departure, shining sun, to leave me lost in the desert; how merciless you are, how lacking in love, how shameless, that your stony heart has failed to soften at these entreaties!"

The charming Vīs said these words and wept a river of tears on her breast from her eyes. Rāmīn's heart was not reconciled by her entreaties; so hard was it, you would have sworn it was of iron. The snow and the anger of Rāmīn both pledged themselves that neither one nor the other would diminish till day. When Vīs and the Nurse became resigned to despair, they turned from Rāmīn and departed.

318

91

VĪS TURNS FROM RĀMĪN IN ANGER; HE FOLLOWS HER. Vīs departed, and with her the Moon illumining the world; her heart full of smoke[1] and fire, her eyes of water; her body trembled like a willow from the cold, her heart turned away desperate from Rāmīn. She said, "Alas for me with my sinister fortune! You would swear it was in blood-feud against my soul! For my fate strives so mightily against me that one day it is likely suddenly to shed my blood. My nurse, do you know any who will be more ignoble than I should I further pursue love? If after this I nurture love, take your finger and gouge out my eye. My soul has become as helpless in my body as a lifeless corpse hidden under the earth. If my body should die of this sorrow, no grave in the world will receive it! Now that I am cut off from soul and sweetheart, what may I experience worse than I have done heretofore? Love has no disaster worse than this; 'there is no color beyond black.'" When charming Vīs was separated from Rāmīn, the air became like a raging dragon. Its snow was indistinguishable from fatal poison, for the heart froze instantly at its touch. A black cloud came, disposed its ranks, and blocked both breath and sight of the beholder; flung snow in eye and face, so that even an elephant would have been crazed by it.

It mercilessly blocked Rāmīn's road as the waves of the sea block the course of a ship. His body was in the snow, his heart in fire as he reproached himself for his anger and pride toward his sweetheart. He repented of his unpremeditated words and shed a flood of coral upon his breast.

Suddenly a shout escaped from him; you would have sworn his soul was riven from his body! Like the wind he twisted the reins of his horse, and found the jasmine-bosomed Vīs upon the road. He leapt from his steed senseless as one drunk and gave a cry like a soul forlorn; he said, "My idol, have mercy on me; do not heap distress upon my distress; my sin has become twofold through my folly, for evil appeared good in my eyes. I performed an act I knew to be ignoble; I have twice dissipated my good name before you. Now I entertain no expectation of the sight of you; my tongue is denied

1. *I.*

facility of speech with you; you would swear my heart was drunk from shame before you, that my tongue was knotted! Neither can I speak words of excuse nor again without you can I find the way in my plight! I am now left helpless and loverless; heart bereft of patience and body of peace. My tongue has fallen silent from shame before you; my soul senseless from love for you. The demon of wrath seduced my heart from the road; dullness overcame love. Now I have repented of my action; henceforward obedience on my part, command on yours! I shall become so solicitous and obedient that before you I shall be but the lowest of servants. If you meet my love with strife, I shall rend my breast with the dagger. I shall grasp the hem of your garment in the snow and hold it till both you and I are dead.

"There is no one for you in the world like me; once I am no more you should be no more; if it is right that I should die before you, why should I not grasp the hem of your garment in death? and seek at the moment of death a lover like you? At any rate we may rise together in the next world![2] With a lover like you I shall hold the reckoning of the bourn of resurrection as nought! You are my Paradise and Hūrī; who in the world seeks to be far from these twain? I am with you, you with me till eternity; I shall never divorce from you my hope and fear."

Wretched Rāmīn spoke these words and a bloodstained river poured from his eyes down his breast. Words they had a hundred times spoken they repeated from the beginning. They revived old cruelties and once more rehearsed them one and all. They recounted the cruelties they had experienced from one another, the harsh words they had heard from each other. Their talk lasted long; the world was amazed at what they did. The heart of Vīs was rocky as a mountain, her face as gorgeous as spring blossom. The rock did not soften at Rāmīn's words, nor did her spring blossom lose its color from the cold. When the standard of dawn came near the east, the talk of Vīs and Rāmīn was broken off. Rāmīn's heart was in fear of madness; the heart of Vīs burned in shame. For Rāmīn had gone mad from separation, Vīs been shamed by ill fortune.

When dawn came their talk was cut short; their lost hearts came

2. See n. 5, p. 95.

320

back to the road. Then they took each other's hands and from fear of enemies entered the pavilion. They washed their hearts of pain, their souls of grief, and closed the doors of palace and pavilion. Both bloomed for very happiness like roses; they lay down amidst ermine and brocade. You would have sworn the bed became a very heaven, and the two jasmine-bosomed lovers in it like the Gemini. In the bed but one body with two souls; like two shining gems in a single mine.

The pillow was all full of the Moon and the Pleiades, the bed of pomegranate blossom and eglantine. The beauty of their faces in the seraglio made it a picture gallery and a gorgeous garden. Face was laid on face like two pieces of brocade; hair upon hair like two musky chains. Here in the bed and there in those two fair faces were silk and brocade folded tenfold. Thus these two lovers, the desire of all, dwelt for a month; they rested from play neither by day nor by night, ever shooting the arrow straight on the target, ever intertwined like milk and wine. Sometimes they grasped the golden bowl brimming with wine, sometimes took a graceful cypress in their embrace. Sometimes they laid camphor and rose one upon another, sometimes laid silk and gold weave one on the other. Although their hearts were full of hurt, they sought manifold excuses for it through kisses.

The King sat on his golden throne, unaware of what Vīs and Rāmīn did. He did not know that Rāmīn sat day and night in his palace with his darling, ever drinking water from the same cup as she did, the head of reputation lopped by the sword of shame; his heart washed of the cares of the world and charged with love for the face of his sweetheart. Fallen into the snare through his own desire, he had gambled away both worlds for one sweetheart. One month's joy and fair fortune swept away from their memories six months of affliction.

May there be no love if it be not thus! wherein the lover drinks his fill of pristine fortune! How sweet is such love and happy state! Seldom does such luck befall the lover! This is the fortune that love deserves, so that love's hereafter may be all ease.

Many the day I have tried love; and never been as happy as this for a single one! Now time is changed from what it was; its best day is surely in the past!

321

92.

RĀMĪN MAKES HIS APPEARANCE BEFORE SHĀH MOUBAD.

When Vīs and Rāmīn had lived in happiness for a month like box-trees in the garden of love, the world grew pleasant and the snow and cold grew less, the vanguard of warmth advanced. Rāmīn, whose beauty illumined the world, said to Vīs, "It is meet that I should appear speedily before the King before he knows our secret, which may not remain hidden any longer." When the cunning youth had thought of this stratagem, he one night descended alone from the citadel and traveled one stage from Marv. When day broke he returned and appeared on the Marv road; he rode through the gate alone covered in the dust of the road; and, clad in the apparel of travel, he rode straight to the King.

They quickly bore tidings to the King that a great sun had shown its face; that Rāmīn, whose radiance blazed all over the world, had come from the road; in form like a cypress surmounted by the moon; having suffered not a little torment from the cold of the journey, and with his waist chafed by his belt.

When Rāmīn came before the King he bent the silvery cypress of his frame in adoration; the King rejoiced when he saw his face and inquired about his ways and days; Rāmīn, whose beauty illumined the world, said, "Your Majesty, illustrious King, high purposed in sovereignty! may triumphant fortune ever attend you; may your auspicious fortune render your enemies unlucky; may your will surpass the will of all; may your fame transcend all other fame. May your days be eternal in glory; may your good fortune be triumphant in kingship. It would require a heart greater than Mount Damāvand to be patient away from Your Majesty. You brought me up in my childhood, and now have raised my head above the Pleiades. You granted me riches and state, you are my father and my illustrious king; if I am careless whether I see you or not, know that I am of base metal. Lofty Saturn is proper to be sentinel to me if I be so much as a mere sentinel at your court. Why should I practice patience far from you? for I cannot abide the pain of separation. I delight in you, for you alone are my support; none other takes the place of you for me.

🦢 322

"Your Majesty, I went at your command to Gurgān and emptied its mountain and plain of wolves.[1] I so reduced Kūhistān with the sword that the lion there obeys the command of the deer. From Mosul to Syria and Armenia the King has no enemy left. By the King's aura of fortune my state has become so mighty that the world itself is the least of my slaves. God has granted me everything save sight of the illustrious King. When I am cut off from sight of him, you would swear I was in the mouth of a dragon. Although God in heaven is generous, he has not given everything to a single one of his creatures. Since I lived day and night in longing for the sight of Your Majesty that is food for the soul, I have galloped thus alone from Gūrāb, hastening like the floodwater from the mountains. I hunted on the way and devoured my prey like the black lion. Now that I have beheld the glory of this audience hall and have had the delight of seeing the King upon his throne, you would swear my heart has become a spring garden and that my single soul has become a thousand. I have realized all my hopes from Fortune, I have added a throne to the crown of Jamshīd.[2]

"At night I would feast with the King, and then set off once more upon the road. Then if the King be pleased to order me any other task, I shall find no way better than his behest. I hold his command so dear that I would lay down my life for it. In the eyes of the wise, I shall only then be alive when I have sacrificed my life at the King's command."

When the King heard from him these words skillfully put together, he said to him, "What you have done is good; you have shown forth righteousness and heroism. The sight of you is delightful to me; how shall I become sated of it in one day? Now it is winter and the season of cold; we should occupy ourselves day and night with nothing but calling for wine. When the days of fresh spring come there will be many companions for you on the road. I shall come with you to Gurgān to hunt, for in spring the house is wearisome. Now go and take from your body the apparel of travel, repair to the baths, and order other garments."

1. Persian gurgān: "wolves."
2. Possibly an oblique reference to the lineage of Vīs.

When Rāmīn departed happy from his presence, the King sent him many robes of honor. Noble Rāmīn remained there for three months; his eye saw nothing but the desire of his heart. Fortune granted him all he wished, he constantly saw charming Vīs in secret. He triumphantly indulged his heart's desire, but his desire remained hidden from the King. He constantly saw Vīs in secret, without the King having any inkling thereof.

93.

THE KING GOES TO THE CHASE FROM THE OLD CASTLE IN THE SEASON OF SPRING. When glorious spring pitched camp on plain and mountain and brookside, the world became in splendor like a garden, the earth like the sky in beauty. The old world became young again, and turned violet-haired and tulip-cheeked. The face of the land became like the treasure of the Khusrous[1] from abundance of brocade, gold, musk, and ambergris. The nightingale sang to the rose and trilled its song like a drunken lover. The violet bed twined its twin locks; the tulip border tied on its red robe. Game came down to the plain from the mountain passes; blossoms flowered at dawn from the branch. The rose came out like a bride from her litter and robbed the nightingales of peace. When the rose showed its face, the heavens constantly rained stars upon its crown. The world's water turned wine-hued from rain; the dust of the plain turned to sweet nougat from ambergris; the garden in beauty became like the fair; the branch in splendor became like the stars. The sky put on the garb of Nourūz and scattered a hundred kinds of gems on the roses. The narcissus celebrated with wine drinking, for it saw the world like a royal banquet. It took the gold cup in its silvery hand, like the crown of Khusrou in the hand of Shīrīn.[2] The breeze, when it passed by garden and jasmine bed, carried the perfume of lover to lover. The air scattered silver and jewels when the perfume of the rose wafted through it. It washed the back of the onager with the hand of the rain; it scoured the corrosion from the branches with the streams.

The environs of Marv became so lustrous that you would have sworn its suburbs were of Shushtar[3] silk; so much splendor grew

1. See n. 1, p. 29.   2. See n. 13, p. 101.   3. In Khūzistān.

apace through the rain that you would have sworn the very rain-drops were splendor in themselves.

At such a pleasant time, such a sweet moment, when the world was fresh and the days gentle, the King purposed to go hunting,[4] for at such a season city and house were wearisome. He quickly sent scouts and warned great and small in his army, "We purpose to go to Gurgān and for a space trap the boar and wolf; to bring down the leopard from the mountains, flush crocodiles from the swamps, unleash lynx and cheetah and feed both on deer."

When Vīs learned of the King's departure, the season of happiness became in her eyes a dungeon.

She said to the Nurse, "Do you know anything worse than that someone living should not wish life? I am that living creature who has become weary of life; I am wounded in a hundred places by the sword. King Moubad purposes to go to Gurgān: may his fate be sinister and his ascendant inauspicious! How shall I have patience in separation? How shall I escape from this calamity? If Rāmīn purposes to go with the King, my heart shall go with him. Should he take the road tomorrow, alas for me, for his horse will tread on my very eyes! With every step of his way, Rāmīn's horse will burn a brand into my dear soul. Once I am left far from that king among youths, you shall see me on the road like a lookout; I shall watch his road like a scout and make my eyes a flowing goblet. Sometimes I shall drench my collar with it, sometimes rain rubies and radiant pearls. Perhaps God will hearken to a prayer and turn aside this calamity from my soul.

"There is no calamity worse for me than the King, who is ill-willed and foulmouthed and rancorous. Perhaps I shall contrive to escape from him and not have to experience every moment the pain of separation. Now, Nurse, go to Rāmīn and tell him how thus and thus is my plight! Find out what he purposes to do with me, whether it be the desire of my friends or my enemies; if he purposes to go with the King tomorrow the story of my life will become short. Tell him, 'With all this pain of separation, who can survive till you return? See that you do not turn your face from me, for by the time you return you will not find me alive. Find from somewhere,

4. Cf. the episode in *Tristan*, p. 230.

anywhere, an excuse to remain at home; do not go with the King. Stay here in happiness: live without care, but fill his heart with grief! It is you who deserve fair fortune, he that deserves, month in, year out, blindness and tribulation.'"

The Nurse went before Rāmīn and rubbed these words into his wounds like salt. She told him all the message of Vīs, which you would have sworn was no message but rather an arrowpoint. Rāmīn's heart began to throb in distress; tears of agony started to drop from his eyelashes. He wept bitterly for a time at the separation, for did he not indeed spend his life in very wretchedness? Now pain, now distress, now fear; his heart had been cloven in twain by the hand of separation. Then he said to the Nurse, "Moubad has said neither yea nor nay to me; he has neither said anything himself nor sent me tidings; perhaps I have slipped his memory. Should he, however, order me to go, then it will be possible to find some excuse. When he departs, I shall stay in Marv, pleading an ailment in my legs.[5] My excuse shall be inability to walk. I shall say, 'Your Majesty is conversant with my ailment; hunting gives me vast pleasure, but a man cannot walk without legs. I fancy that Your Majesty knows that I am in pain and ailing. This is why you have not given me marching orders and I have, whether I like it or not, to stay in my place bereft of the King.' If this fancy be right, I shall remain in Paradise even on this earth."

When the Nurse gave Vīs this news it was as if she gave her tidings of succession to a throne! Her passionate soul lost its distress, the flower of happiness bloomed from her face.

94.

SHĀH MOUBAD GOES TO THE CHASE AND TAKES RĀMĪN WITH HIM. When the heavens gave the mountains saddlebrasses of gold and gave the earth a carpet studded with gems, brazen drums rattled out from the castle, gong, bugle, drum, and trumpet sounded forth. Heroes and cavalry swarmed out like blossoms from the branches of the trees. A great host surged from Marv like a fearsome wave from the deeps of the sea. Noble Rāmīn went before the King, without having prepared for the road in the customary and due manner.

5. Cf. *Tristan*, p. 230.

Before the brave champions the King said to him, "What new stratagem is this? Go, take what is necessary from the treasurer, for without you hunting is no pleasure for us."

Rāmīn departed crestfallen from the King's presence, like a fish with a hundred hooks in its mouth. As he prepared himself for the road to Gurgān you would have sworn a wolf[1] had rent his sheep! Unwillingly he took the road, his vitals wounded with the arrow, his heart with the javelin.

When Vīs learned of the departure of Rāmīn, peace altogether deserted her soul. She addressed to her burning heart, as she moaned, a sad lament at missing the face of her sweetheart: "Why should I not be distressed by loneliness, why not rain rubies upon gold? A heart accustomed to happiness and joy is now become like a partridge in the talons of a hawk. I shall not find a lover like the first, nor sow the seeds of love as in my first love. It would be a fault for me to be silent once bereft of my lover; right and proper for me to weep sorely in separation. If you do not credit my pain, my nurse, look at my red tears and yellow face. My tears are my words, my eyes my tongue: they tell the world my secret. How can I bear this pain and distress with one heart when the hearts of all are heavy thereat? I weep for my own soul, not for my sweetheart; for the sweetheart is gone. How may the soul remain here? How may a heart without patience find peace? when even with patience it would not bear this disaster."

When she spied Rāmīn from the corner of the roof, setting off upon the road all unwillingly with Moubad, his waist like a silken thread, girt round with his Kayānī[2] belt, the dust of the road on his locks, all color drained from his cheeks because of the brand of love for his sweetheart, having taken no farewell of his love, like one lost in salt desert or drowning in a river, the heart of Vīs boiled within her at the sight, and she said to it in her turmoil: "Farewell, my gay lover; farewell, cavalier of the army; farewell, dear companion; farewell, commander of the fair! You have gone without saying farewell to me, perchance you have withdrawn your heart from love of me. You have marched with the host: alas for my soul, for a host of cares has

1. Persian *gurg*.
2. Belonging to the mythological Kayānī dynasty.

327

attacked me! I tied my heart with a hundred steel chains; it broke them all and took the road with you. If my soul survives within me in separation I shall weep forlorn till you return.

"I shall send clouds of the vapor in my soul, the water of the tears of my eyes therein; I shall deck your camping-ground with water and greenery, I shall lay the dust of your road with rain; for your face is like spring blossom. Should not spring blossom have clouds and rain?"

As Rāmīn traversed one stage of the journey, he was not aware of the journey in his desperation. From the great care in his heart he knew nothing of it till he arrived at the stage. He lamented much on the road: lamentation is no surprise from the sick! In his lamentation he sang the words that men lonely for their lovers will sing:

"I lived to see a night like last night, when kisses were the arrows and the lip the target; now I see a day like today, when my soul has become the deer, separation from her the cheetah. Where has the joy and pleasure of last night gone, sugary cornelian and sweet pearls? The cruelty of so many years washed from the heart by silky breast and twin silver pomegranates; a garden on my face through the beauty of the face of the lover, the dark night like bright day thereby. Now that my eyes have seen such a night, how can I look on a day such as this? This is no day, but a fire temple for the soul, disaster for lovers' fortunes! May no lover have to experience such a day, whose affliction dissipates patience and burns the soul. If Time were a measurer it would surely reckon this day as a hundred years!"

When the King dismounted at the stage, the desperate Rāmīn went before him. There were a thousand witnesses in his face to the desertion of his body by patience and sense. He neither caroused with the King nor called for wine, but made the excuse of pain in his legs and departed. Thereafter day in, night out he was even thus: you would have sworn that his heart was in feud against his soul. His soul was full of pain, his cheek covered in dust; his whole body become a heart, and that heart all pain.

95

VĪS LAMENTS RĀMĪN'S DEPARTURE AND APPEALS TO THE
NURSE FOR REMEDY. When Rāmīn was separated far from charming Vīs, happiness and desire cut themselves off from her. She had
always been a moon: then she became a sun; like the sun yellow,
neither sleeping nor eating. She never rested from talking of Rāmīn
and recalling him; she tinctured her colored cheek with blood.

She said to the Nurse, "My nurse, devise some stratagem whereby
my departed faithless lover may return to me! From very love, my
nurse, have mercy on my soul, show me the way to union with the
beloved; for I cannot bear this affliction and have not the patience
to bear the pain of this separation. Hear my story, Nurse, for I shall
recite it to you like flowing water; I gave my heart away in folly;
now you would swear I am drunk from desperation without it. Do
not blame me for this desperation; for a very Judgment Day has
arisen from my soul. My heart has become as hostile as my enemy:
it ever sets fire to my granary: so helpless and mournful have I
become that I am at a loss in desperation about my heart. Now
impart some remedy to me, for I have no other like you to sympathize
with me. A fire broke out and fell upon me: it seized my heart and
now seizes the hem of your garment. Every fire is weak in face of
water: but mine has increased by the water from my eyes. I pour
spring floods upon it: who ever saw a fire waxing greater with rain?
Last night was such a trial for me that I would have sworn I slept
upon needles and thorns. Now it is day and time for breaking the
fast: but in my eyes it is as dark as pitch-black night. My day is from
the cheeks of the lover: my night from his tresses. I do not know what
is written upon my head, that Fate's handiwork with me should be
so sorely cruel! I shall go into the plain and wander with the shepherds, and shall forbear to haunt the society of my friends. A flood
shall arise in the city from my weeping; there will be an avalanche
from the mountains at my lamentation. I do not know what I am to
do, with whom to sit; whom in the world to see in my sweetheart's
stead.

"I shall not look at the world, but shall close my eyes; for I am
disconsolate at everything I see. What profit has my heart seen of all

I have undergone save that I am cut off from sleep and happiness?
I have tried my fortune countless times over: but have only been
wounded and saddened by it. I only increase the chaos of my fortunes when I try so far something already tried. You have heard all
my story: now see what may be the remedy of my plight."

The Nurse answered her and said, "One should never be at a loss
in a plight: what will come of all this weeping and lamenting save
that you will add grief to grief? Your compeers are happy and gay;
all proud in attainment of their hearts' desire. You are ever thus in
distress and pain; you have shattered my peace by your grieving.
The world should exist for the benefit of one's own soul: all medicine
be for some wound. Your pain and your cure are in your own hand;
why is your hand tied from the remedy? God has given you sovereignty, perfection, greatness, and authority. You have in your
house a mother like Shahrū; a helper and glorious brother like Vīrū;
you have a fine lover like Rāmīn, worthy of sovereignty and kingship; all your treasury is stocked with jewels; you are backed all
round by a formidable army. These are the very stuff of greatness;
seek greatness, and cut short this idle tale! You have visited much
evil upon Moubad and have tried him many a time. The demon in
his nature has not improved; nor has his fresh love grown old. He is
the same as of old, and you are the same; he will be the same toward
you to all eternity. Seek now, then, your remedy and cure—you
have the seed, the water, and the channel—before Moubad finds an
opportunity and hastens to take our lives because of the wrath in his
heart, for his heart is ever in feud against us three, like a lion in
ambush; you may be sure that one day, when he has found the way,
he will leap from the ambush. You will find no comrade better than
Rāmīn; place the golden crown upon his head, be queen and let
him be king; be with him like sun and moon together. There is no
king or commander of the age but will be your comrade in this
enterprise.

"Your first helper shall be your brother, then the other illustrious
kings. The kings are all in feud against Moubad, all ready to choose
Rāmīn and Vīrū. You have long treated your reason with consideration; you have suffered much affliction for the sake of your heart.
Now lay hold of a remedy in wisdom so that your cares may be

soothed. Do the deed now, if you may, for you will not find a better season than the present.

"There is no king or army in Marv; you have in your possession all the treasure of the King. What pains he has expended on this treasure! Now you have gained it all without lifting a finger. Buy with his treasure kingship and authority; for you have in abundance the price of kingship. Before he dines on you, breakfast on him that you may gain fame. If you wish to put this plan into effect, do not delay; send a letter to Rāmīn about your situation; tell him to desert Moubad and become the peer of the wind in speed. When he comes we shall devise a stratagem so that we may set about Moubad and bring him on evil days."

When Vīs of the jasmine scent heard these words, the tulip of happiness bloomed from her cheeks.

96.

VĪS WRITES A LETTER TO RĀMĪN. She called for parchment, musk, ambergris, and pen; and wrote a letter to Rāmīn eloquent of the pain of her heart; the words of the letter were so pathetic that blood dripped from their very letters. You lover who cherish love, send such a letter to your loving sweetheart; for if you read this letter to a stone, the twang of the harp will reach your ears from it. "From loving friend and wretched lover, to stonyhearted sweetheart wary of love: from slave desperate, without sleep and food, her heart entrusted to a king like moon and sun: from lamenting lover, sick and forlorn, at the mercy of her enemies and far from the desire of her heart: from a writhing servant burning on the fire, her world black, Fate recalcitrant: from a weeping servitor, unfortunate and wretched, with a bloodstained flood pouring from her eyes: from one of ruined heart and wounded spirit, with eyes of cornelian hue and cheeks of yellow; mournful, wretched, and in pain; every hair on her body become like a shackle; wasted, restless, wounded in heart, a river flowing from both eyes; do I write this letter in a plight so sore that there is none now so unfortunate as I.

"My body writhes and my eyes weep bitterly; my heart burns on the fire of affliction; my frame is like a burning candle raining teardrops; smoke rises from my heart like a black cloud. I am the intimate of calamity and the friend of grief, floundering in the ocean of separation. How wretched am I, weeping thus with one hand on my heart, the other on the pillow! The cornelian of my lips has become turquoise, the world's very heart burns for my soul. One eye, and a thousand clouds raining pearls! One soul, and a thousand kinds of tribulation! Separation has come and written all my hidden secrets in blood on my cheeks; now it has made my eye like a sea from abundance of water; sleep is now drowned in the moisture of my eyes. Since I find the abode of sleep full of water, how may I find sleep in water? I have rolled up the carpet of happiness with the hand with which I write this letter. My body has melted from suffering so much distress, my heart has fled from the surfeit of grief it has endured. How may I seek my desire of the world, for my soul has neither heart nor body left? Why have you taken away from me that face like the sun, which was as precious to me as soul and spirit? Since I have been exiled from your face I resemble only a hair of yours in thinness. By day the sun is the comforter of my grief, for it is bright and shining like your face; the stars comfort my grief by night, for when I look on them they are like your teeth—no, I am wrong—the grief that is mine is not one to be comforted by any. If a mountain experienced my woes, only blood would run down from it in place of water.

"My friends admonish me, my enemies blame me; from the multitude of their admonition and blame they have made me a by-word in the world—this is no love, but a cloud laden with grief; this is no separation, but a sword dipped in poison. Why should anyone attach his heart to love, why countenance this disaster for his soul? If every lover is to be like me, may there not be in the world so much as their trace—many the day I laughed at them: now I regret my laughter. I laughed at them like an enemy; now they weep for me. You saw me before I was in love; more radiant than the very sun in the sky. Now my cypresslike stature has become like a bow; the roses of my cheeks like saffron. Does not a laden branch bend? My body has bent under the load of affliction. I have become in form like a bent bow; the bloodstained tears of my eyes drawn upon my body like a bowstring. You have abandoned me here thus wretched; have departed and galloped the steed of separation. The dust which has risen from the hoof of your horse has settled in my eyes like arrow-heads. The vision of your face is in my eyes; through my eyes my soul sheds tears. They say to me, 'Why do you cry vainly? for you have become like a reed from crying! A departed friend is like the day that is gone; why nurture in your heart care for what is past and gone?'

"Now it is night and my sun has departed; the world is envel-oped in darkness. It is right that I should sit in hope that at dawn the radiant sun will return, departed spring return at Nourūz, my departed sweetheart also return one day. My fair love, of cypress stature and face fair as the moon, cavalier, hunter, questing after fame! In love I am she whom you knew, I hold my soul fit to be a sacrifice for love! One hair on your body is to me a hundred times more precious than my soul. I desire you and desire not my own soul. It is you I seek, not this and that. You have tried me much in love and you have been satisfied with me therein. Now I am as I ever was in loyalty to you; I bear witness to it with my bloodshot eyes. If you are uncertain of my loyalty, come and see these witnesses! Come and see my face, like a silver *dīnār*, royal pearls dropping thereon. Come and see my eye like the Oxus, the world full of blood from my two Oxus rivers. Come and see my figure bent, happiness fled from me and I from mankind. Come and see my plight, so sore that I am like nothing so much as one on a sickbed for ten years. Come and see my fortune, so catastrophic that you would swear my eye is blinded every moment. Come and see my love waxed ever greater, love like your beauty exceeding all bounds. If you haste to my side too late, when you approach you will find me no longer alive. If you would see my face again, do not rest, sleep, or tarry. As soon as you read this letter, return: traverse a three days' road in one; I shall lament till you come, ever seated on your road like a watchman. If my soul will not stand my distress and pain, I shall go mad from the pain of love. I crave from God night and day that I may again see your face, darling of my heart. Greetings from me, more than drops of rain, to that Moon, royal cavalier; greetings from me, more than the waters of the sea, to that youth of face like the sun and cypress stature! O God, keep my life long enough for me to see his face, then take it! If I give up the ghost from the pain of this brand, the world will meet its end in the smoke of my soul."

When desperate Vīs finished the letter, she dispatched a swift horse speeding toward him; a brave soldier of her retinue sped on a swift steed like a mountain, which passed over the mountains like a vulture, wrapped up the desert like the scroll of a letter; he neither slept by night nor rested by day on the road; but carried the blood-stained letter of that Moon to Rāmīn.

97.

RĀMĪN RECEIVES THE LETTER OF VĪS. When Rāmīn saw the letter of the graceful cypress, you would have sworn his face looked upon pristine fortune; he kissed it with his sugared rubies; put it to his languorous eyes and to his head. When he opened the seal of the letter and read it he scattered a flood of garnet from his eyes. The smoke of impatience rose from his soul, the water of grief rained on his cheeks.

He spoke words from his burning soul meet to be written in ink of gold: "My heart, how long will you deem this plight proper wherein you suffer months of grief, years of calamity? My heart, the man who seeks his desire and fame does not seek it with propriety and peace; the desperate man does not fear the cutting sword, the raging elephant nor the roaring lion, snow, storm, waves of the sea, rain, cold or heat. My heart, if you are a lover, why so fearful? Why ask of everyone remedy and cure? Who will hearken to your cry and lamentation? So long as you do not strive for yourself, who is going to strive for you? What is the point of love in such a weak state—you feeble in numbers and your enemies great? For every day's happiness you enjoy you will suffer a year's wretchedness and humiliation. Take on your head this heavy load; reveal this hidden secret from your heart. Now either the bonds must be broken or the head laid once and for all on the line in submission. I shall not find a brother better than my own hand; a better helper for my brother than the sword; I am no man if I exercise restraint any longer; let this secret become known! What can the world bring me worse than death? What can it rain on my soul but swords? How shall one who courts danger shrink from enemies, how shall a pearl diver abhor the sea? In the sea the pearl goes hand in hand with the crocodile; as in the world nectar is the co-mate of colocynth. The sword is the cup of the wine of desire, even as a lion lies in wait on the highroad to happiness. Battle past the lions and drink wine from the cup; for Nourūz follows December! Happiness is not to be found through ease; nor success through avoidance of travail.

"A trapper undergoes much trouble scouring over crag and mountain till he catches the game; there is no game[1] like sovereignty and authority; how shall a man take these easily? Since there lies before me fair game like sovereignty, since my sweetheart is one like charming Vīs of moonlike form, why do I struggle so sorely against my fortune, why do I not pour water on this fire? Why do I sit so long dazed, why do I not leap out from my ambush? I am trapped in a snare and my love likewise; we have resigned our hearts to pain and suffering against our will. Why not tear this snare asunder, cut in pieces the tree of shame? However, there is a due season for everything, a proper time and occasion for all exploits; the blossom that comes out in April is not to be found on the trees in December.

"Perhaps the day of tragedy has drawn to a close; that day may have gone, another dawned, the December of tribulation may have passed over us in our suffering and the spring of good fortune be here!"

When Rāmīn had spoken for a time in this strain, he writhed like a snake from the pain in his heart. His body was on the road but his heart in the arms of Vīs; the vision of Vīs hung before his eyes. Peace and patience were far from him till the night, dust from the smoke of his heart covered his lip. His eye was on the east, watchful of the moment when the host of Night should advance to open the way before him.

98.

RĀMĪN ENTERS THE CASTLE BY A STRATAGEM; THE DEATH OF ZARD. When only the smoke of night remained of the fire of day, and heaven wrapped up the crimson carpet of day, the sun departed on its red horse, the moon returned on its black charger, Rāmīn took the road from the camp, none to see him other than the moon

1. Cf. Introduction, p. xvii.

and the Pleiades. The envoy of Vīs preceded him with forty men, each one sufficient to take on a whole army. Now galloping, now cantering, like the Turkomans, he reached Marv from Gurgān in one week. When Rāmīn set out over the desert and only one day of the tribulation of the journey had passed, he dispatched the envoy of Vīs on the road and gave him many instructions for his mistress.

"Give her tidings of me in secret, for this time our plans are best kept concealed. Do not tell the secret other than to Vīs and the Nurse, for the Nurse is no less than our very profit and capital: tell her, 'Our enterprise at this time has become the tale of every tongue; I must never again see the face of Moubad; if I do I shall deserve every kind of torture. Tomorrow night keep watch in the castle; when one half of the night has passed, listen for me; devise some stratagem whereby I may come to you, show you the path to victory. Keep this matter concealed till my arrival; for I shall soon rend this veil.'" The messenger departed from Rāmīn, hastening on the road swifter than a falcon.

At that moment silvery-bosomed Vīs of rosy limbs was waiting quietly in the old castle of Marv. The entire treasury of the cunning King, too, was laid up in that castle; its warden was renowned Zard, who possessed more wealth than the King himself; chosen lieutenant of the King, his minister and brother; a second Korah in treasure and wealth. He was the guardian of charming Vīs, and at one and the same time ordered the world.

When the messenger came in from Gurgān he passed secretly through the gate into Marv. Then he put on a *chadur* like a woman and approached Vīs on muleback; for Vīs had the custom of giving every day a banquet for the women; the wives of the nobles used to go to her and spend a week in banqueting with her. The cunning man by this pretty trick contrived to find his way to Vīs behind Zard's back. He told her all Rāmīn's message, fair and sweet like pearls and sugar. Who can tell how great was the delight of Vīs, how relieved she was by the ploy of the ingenious man? You would have said a poor man had found the moving treasure[1] or that a dead man had found life again.

1. I.e., the treasure of Korah, supposed to be constantly moving farther down under the earth.

She straightway sent a servant to Zard to tell him, "My aura of fortune warned me in a dream last night that Vīrū was somewhat stricken by pain and languor; but now health has been restored to him. I shall go today to the fire temple, to light a fire to celebrate the happy turn of events. By my presents I shall increase the fuel of the Fire, in nobility, purity, and peace." The general said, "You do well to do so, do so always, perform good works and practice the works of the Religion."

Then Vīs set out with her friends, wives of nobles and the renowned, through the gates to the temple of the sun, one of the buildings of King Jamshīd.[2] How much blood did she spill of sheep, all of which she presented to the poor; how many garments and jewels did she scatter, what a flood of silver and gold did she pour from her palm! When Night spread its shadow over the sphere, the messenger went off and brought Rāmīn.

They emptied the hall of strangers; old Saturn became prostrate before Jupiter.[3] The secret remained hidden in the world; the wind did not lay a finger on the blossoming branch. Although a task may be formidable and hard, it will turn out successful if good luck attends it. Thus was it with Vīs and Rāmīn; happiness bloomed on the tree of affliction.

All the noblemen's wives departed, all strangers went out of the door. Vīs's men stayed with Rāmīn; then the warriors were straightway mounted on their steeds; forty of them, brave heroes to a man, with *chadurs* pulled over their faces like women. By this stratagem they passed through the gate, and from the fire temple took the road to the citadel. A party of torchbearers preceded them, a band of servitors and attendants; they drove the populace back from Rāmīn's way, and by this stratagem his fell deed remained hidden. By this device Rāmīn was brought into the castle; hidden in a *chadur* together with forty warriors.

Once he was in, they shut the door of the citadel; the sentries sat on the wall; they set up their challenges and calls, but failed to descry that the house of Vīs was full of enemies! When night grew dark as the soul of a false lover, you would have sworn it smeared

2. Minorsky, *Iranica*, p. 185.
3. See n. 1, p. 63.

smut and pitch on its face; the air grew murkier than the depths of the sea; the heavens as full of jewels as the deeps of the ocean; the army of the heaven came up from the east, like Alexander mounting from the darkness.[4]

The brave men leapt from their ambush and drew their daggers like a multitude of myrtle leaves. They set about the castle like a blazing fire, and all put the garrison to the sword.

Like a sleeping man up to whose bedside a leopard slinks, Rāmīn stole to his brother's pillow. Zard sprang from sleep and drew his sword, for he had the heart of a lion in prowess: he closed with Rāmīn like a furious elephant; death came up and came to grips with his soul; but then Rāmīn said to him, "Put up your sword; no harm will come upon your head from me; I am Rāmīn, your younger brother; forbear to put your soul on the fire because of hatred! Throw aside your sword and surrender your hands to bonds: for bondage is better for you than death and murder."

When the general heard Rāmīn's voice, he furrowed his brow in a frown and set his tongue to abusing Rāmīn, disgracefully miscalling his good name in his anger. He attacked Rāmīn like a ravening lion and struck a sudden sword-blow at the crown of his head. Rāmīn quickly put his shield to his head, the blade knocked off half of it. Then with his sword he smote Zard's head such a blow that his brains spilled out. He split his head in two at one blow and scattered the red rose of his blood on the mud.

When the ill-starred Zard was thus slain, the melee of the other fighters raged in the castle. The moon in the heavens did not peep from the clouds, for fear of blood being spattered upon it. A corpse was flung on every roof, there was a heap of dead on every slope. Many leapt from the wall of the citadel from fear of death—and did not escape it either! Many fought, from the rage in their hearts, for Vīs and did not live to tell the tale. The enemy wherever he might be found fell into a wretched plight; it was night for the enemy but day for Rāmīn.

When three parts of the night had gone, the world so ordered things that Zard's fortunes had fallen; a night as dark in color as

4. In Persian legend Alexander seeks the Water of Life, which is kept in subterranean darkness.

aniseed had given Rāmīn his desire forever. Although it vouchsafed him treasure and gems, it did not do so without robbing him of his brother.

If you look at the world, it is even thus. The poison of anger underlies the nectar of its love. Its rose is attended by thorns, its pleasure by grief; its desire by trouble, its profit by loss.

When Rāmīn saw Zard lying dead on the ground, he rent the garments on his breast and said, "My glorious brother, equal of my soul and eyes! Cut down with the dagger by my two hands, your belly torn by my javelin; killing you, my brother, is like breaking my back with my own hand. Even though I gain gold and jewels by the thousand, where shall I find a brother like you?" When Rāmīn had mourned long over the dead man and grieved sorely over him all in vain, there was no time to lament or suffer gloom, for it was the time of battle and questing for fame.

When Zard gave up the ghost through his ill fortune, his flock, without a shepherd, came under Rāmīn's mercy; the dagger was like a preacher delivering a proclamation; but its pulpit the helmets of heroes! It proclaimed Rāmīn King; the heavens breathed "Amen" to that proclamation. That night was one of the nights of glory, as precious to Rāmīn as the love of Vīs. The fortune of his enemies was as dark as the night; it vanished in the morning together with its companion in color. When day came, the fortune of Rāmīn rose and proclaimed his kingship the world over with panoply. In the dawn Rāmīn, light of the world, rejoiced and became glad in his fortune, sitting in public view with his sweetheart, his heart happy and his fortune following its own desire.

99.

RĀMĪN CARRIES OFF MOUBAD'S TREASURE AND FLEES TO DAILAMĀN. Then he quickly gathered from all over Marv all the camels and mules[1] that there were, took all the King's treasure, and left not so much as a thread of it in the treasury. He stayed two days in Marv, then took the road with his treasure and his sweetheart. He set Vīs in a golden litter, like the moon amidst the Great Bear and the Pleiades. Ahead were ten thousand camels and mules;

1. *G* adds "and elephants."

there was no reckoning the coin and jewels! On he came hastening along the road, taking the desert road by day and night. He made a two weeks' march in one, in two weeks the desert lay behind.

By the time word reached the King of Rāmīn's exploit, Rāmīn, glory of the world, was in Qazvīn. From Qazvīn he went to the land of Dailam, the flag of his fame reached the sky.

The land of Dailam[2] is a redoubtable place, wherein there is a host of Gīls and Dailamīs.[3] In the dark night their archers, shouting aloud, shoot men at long range. Some have bulky arrows and penetrate mail and armor by their shots. In battle they spin javelins as an archer shoots flying arrows. Their prowess in battle recalls demons: winged snakes shoot from their hands. In battle they hold broad shields, like a wall decorated with a hundred colors. As they are men of chivalry they fight manfully month in, year out amongst themselves. From the time of Adam till our day, innumerable kings, even rulers of the seven climes, have failed to conquer that land in triumph, nor have they imposed tribute upon that country. To this very day that tract has remained virgin, no king has wrought his will upon it.

When Rāmīn entered that kingdom in sovereignty, enjoying benevolence from fair fortune, once he had rested for two days from the fatigue of the journey, he took his ease reposing on the throne of fortune. There and then he spread a cowhide and laid on it purses of gold and silver like clenched fists. He threw a golden goblet on top of them, and with golden goblet scattered silver and gold. Since he had not only heart but coin to boot, he did not lack supporters and well-wishers. When he rained a shower of jewels the spring blossom of his fortune bloomed. His army was more numerous than leaves, sand, drops of water, and fish. The world with one mind rallied round him, not only round Rāmīn but round his countless coin. The nobles around him all obeyed his command, like Kishmēr, Āzīn, and Vīrū, like Bahrām, Ruhhām,[4] Sām, and Gīlū. Other kings from every quarter sent armies to Rāmīn; in one month his army

2. South of the Caspian. Minorsky, *Iranica*, p. 174. See also *ibid.*, pp. 12 ff.; *Encyclopaedia of Islam, s.v.* Dailam.

3. Cf. §3, p. 8.

4. Minorsky, *Iranica*, p. 165.

grew so vast that neither road nor waste could hold it. His chief general was Vīrū, his vizier and seneschal Gīlū.

100.

MOUBAD LEARNS THAT RĀMĪN HAS ABSCONDED WITH THE TREASURE AND VĪS. When they brought news to the camp the nobles did not pass the news to the King: for he was an ill-natured monarch, and there is no worse fault in kings than this! No one dared to tell him; all saw fit to hide it. For three days this secret remained hidden from him, all his affairs were set in disorder thereby.[1] When he learned of it the world fell about his ears; you would have sworn a Judgment Day had arrived for him. His favorable fortune fell out with him, reason hid its face altogether from him. He in no way knew what might be his remedy; you would have sworn his road was blocked behind and before. Now he would say, "I shall go to Khurāsān; may Rāmīn, Vīs, and Gurgān perish for all I care." Now he would say, "Yet if I retreat I shall become a byword for ignobility in the world. They will say of me, 'He has become frightened of Rāmīn, for otherwise he would not have come to Khurāsān.'" Sometimes he said, "If I do fight against him I do not know how my guardian angel will help me. My army is in feud against me, they will one and all choose Rāmīn as king. He is young, and enjoys pristine fortune too; the tree of his fortune reaches the sky. He has appropriated all my treasure; I am impoverished and he rich. I neither enjoyed the treasure nor gave it away; but laid it up— all for him! My mother cast me into this calamity by reconciling my heart to Rāmīn. Right enough that I should now be landed in misfortune, for having put into practice the admonitions of women!" He did not show his face to the army for a week, and traversed two hundred oceans of thought. In the end his decision was to fight with Rāmīn, like it or not. He felt ashamed to withdraw from battle and set off from Gurgān for Āmul. When he pitched camp on the plain of Āmul, the world became filled with flowers, so many were the accouterments of the army. From the tents the plain became like a mountain range, but a mountain range glorious as a garden!

1. *I. Mb:* "all Rāmīn's affairs blossomed."

101

MOUBAD MEETS HIS END WITHOUT BATTLE OR BLOODSHED.
However much we try the world, how are we to open the hidden
knot of its secret? Nothing is better hidden than its knot; nothing
is more current than its writ. The world is sleep and we are a dream
in it; why do we think to remain in it so long?

Its several states do not last for long; its nature is not always
accommodating. At the time of affection it does not know good from
bad; nor can it carry its affection for anyone through to the end.
There is no difference between one who listens to its talk of love and
one who expects a blind man to stand sentry. It displays a variety of
things: the inside true, the outside inverted. The whole thing is like a
conjurer's trick: the inside one thing and the outside another. What
does it most resemble? The building of a caravanserai, with a caravan
ever wending its way into it. Every kind of bird of passage enters it,
but does not rest in it for long. Whom does it most resemble? An
Archer with innumerable arrows before him; stringing his bow year
in, year out; but shooting the arrows into darkness. He does not
know how each arrow he lets fly from his hand has flown, or where.
You might think the world a handsome old woman, who throws into
a dungeon two hundred husbands a day. We seek its treasures with
a hundred pains, and after all neither we remain nor the treasure.
One moment you see an army and a king upon his throne; look
again, and neither army is visible nor king. You will see each day
that passes for us in the world accompanied by numerous men as
fellow travelers; once it has passed, another day comes, and another
horde of us comes with it. This is indeed a great wonder to me, and
I have turned melancholy from pondering it. I do not know what
this revolution of time is, nor these countless quirks it practices on
our souls.

A king ruling the world like Moubad, at whose hand the world has
experienced much good and bad, meets his last day in this wretched
humiliation, many a desire left frustrated in heart and eye. For,
when he moved camp to Āmul, he caroused with the nobles all night;
he sent robes of honor to the chieftains one and all and presented
accouterments of war, silver and gold to those of lesser degree. All

night he was drunk and happy on wine; see what was to be his rude awakening on the morrow!

As the King sat with the champions of the land, a cry suddenly arose from the army. It so befell that one side of the King's camp ran along a marsh. A boar[1] sprang out of a corner of it, in fury like a wild raging elephant. One crowd started shouting in front of it, another fell in after it in pursuit. The boar was maddened by the shouting and clamor and rushed into the King's camp; the King came out of his pavilion and mounted his polo horse, in his hand a black-feathered javelin which had sent many an enemy to his grave. He charged the boar like a male lion, then he hurled his spinning black-feathered javelin; it missed the boar, which threw itself like the wind on the legs of the King's horse. It roared in fury under the horse, and with a jab of its tusks tore its groin. Horse and King fell together, like sky and moon intertwined. No sooner had the world-conquering king fallen than the boar speared him with a fatal jab of its tusks; it tore him from navel to below the breast, the seat of love and hate was rent. The lamp of love went out in his heart, the fire of wrath went cold. The days of the King of Kings came to an end, the fortune of those who wished him well became black. See how such a king, with such power, was laid low at no cost.

World, I shall renounce you and no more listen to your deceit. Having tested your affection for others, I have wiped the corrosion of love for you from my heart. One would swear you were in feud against our souls. Say, what feud do you nurture against our souls, what is this disdain you have for our fortunes? Will you not tell us what we have done to you save eating a couple of crusts of bread here? See, is there any miser like you, who gives a mite and then takes back all? We never said, "Make us your guests here; and then make your heart hard against us!" You entertain us for two days, then demand our lives as the price! What is it you wish of us innocent people, that you shed our blood in a holocaust? If your nature is light, why do you evince blackness in your deeds? Why are you like a millstone ever turning, full of water and wind and dust? Since you have cast my fortune into the pit, what is it to me that you are so lofty? Even though I gaze at you eternally, you are the same old

1. Cf. Marjodoc's dream, *Tristan*, p. 219.

sphere, the selfsame water and earth; the same mountains, sea, and forests; evil as ever your deeds and nature. Any man who knows your nature calls you nothing but miser and ignoble. O God, I recognize you and not her! Better for me to call upon you in my every need! For Time is not worth what men suppose, nor yet the name they call her with the tongue.

102.

RĀMĪN SITS ON THE ROYAL THRONE. When tidings reached Rāmīn of Moubad, of how his ill star had laid him low, he thanked the creator of the world in secret for having disposed for Moubad such an end. No war was the pretext for his death, no blood had been spilled in the process. The days of such a king had come to an end and no offense lay upon Rāmīn. He prostrated himself a thousand times before God and said, "You who have favored my soul, you know how to open all kinds of doors. You know how to dispose such events; you banish from the world whom you will; you raise any you will to Saturn; I swear before you that as long as I live I shall seek to gain your favor. I shall seek justice amongst your servants; I shall always be upright and speak the truth; I shall order justice in my rule, I shall grant the desire of the poor by my well-doing; help me in my sovereignty; only you are fit to give me aid. You are my support, you my friend, in every enterprise; you my protector from evil eye and hand. You are my Lord, I a fettered slave; you, my Lord, vouchsafed kingship to me. You are my over-lord, I your servant; I am no more than your mere courier. Now that you have made me lord of the world, keep me under the protection of your canopy."

When he had for some time offered up entreaties to God and said much in this strain, he ordered the baggage to be tied up and the cavaliers of the host to mount; the roll of drums and the blare of trumpets arose; the army moved off like the Oxus River. Ripples of motion ran through the army like ripples through the clouds of April when the east wind blows. From the commotion the road became like the bourn of Judgment Day, from the mountains of Dailam to the city of Āmul.

Rāmīn, light of the world, with his sweetheart, came rejoicing and triumphant all the way. Amid rejoicing he entered the camp of Moubad on Saturday, the day of Rām. All the nobles went before him and cast gems on his throne. They all called him King of Kings and were dazzled by his glory and justice. His hand was like a spring cloud as it rained royal pearls; he took his pleasure in Āmul for a week; and every moment drained a fresh goblet in daylong carousing.

He gave Tabaristān to Ruhhām, chivalrous, fortunate, and illustrious. His lineage in Iran was Kayānī:[1] greatness was long-established in his line. Then he gave the city of Reyy to Bihrūz, his friend and true adviser; at the time when he fled with Vīs and avoided becoming embroiled in the snare of King Moubad, Bihrūz was his host in Reyy and kept him long hidden in his house. Good action was duly rewarded with good; for he was deserving of all good. "Do good and cast it on the waters; for one day you will recover it in the form of a pearl."

Then he gave Gurgān to Āzīn, his sincere and long-standing friend; at his court the general was Vīrū, and Shīrū was the seneschal of his palace: fierce elephants both and brave lions; in lineage brothers to Princess Vīs. When he had appointed a provost as ruler in each city and sent a protector to every march, with his army he took the road to Marv, for his face was a very antidote for Marv; the whole of Khurāsān put out festive stands, beauties with faces like fairies sat amongst them;[2] the whole of his road was like a garden, every hand cast jewels in his path. Every tongue called down blessings upon him, hearts were pledged to him in loyalty.

When King Rāmīn entered choice Marv he saw a Paradise with decorations massed in it; in beauty like the blossom of Nourūz on the trees; in fairness like the fortune of the lucky, the nightingale of a thousand strains playing the lute with its melodies; the blossoms the garments of the fair. Above hung a cloud of smoke from musk and ambergris, silver, gold, and gems raining from it. The decorations that had been put up remained for three months; people scattered down jewels from them day and night. Not only did choice Marv take part in these rejoicings; the whole of Khurāsān was even thus. For years people had suffered tribulation at the hand of

1. The Kayānīān were a mythological dynasty.
2. Lacuna in *I* here.

Moubad; after his death they gained ease. Once they had escaped from his injustice they rejoiced in the justice of King Rāmīn. You would have sworn they had escaped quite from Hell and now sat in the shade of the Tūbā tree.[3] Ill fortune is the end of the bad; their name remains eternally accursed. Neither perform nor meditate evil in the world; for if you do evil, evil shall be requited. How truly spoke Khosrou to the treasurers:[4] "God created the evil out of Hell. In the end he will return them to the selfsame matter from which he created them in the beginning."

When Rāmīn became a monarch pursuing and dispensing justice, the world was more peaceful than men asleep. Wherever his generals went they conquered the whole world by his aura of fortune. Whereas his enemies' pains were fruitless, the world from China to Barbary became his. A ruler was dispatched by him to every city, a margrave went to represent him in every march. All waste places were made fertile, a thousand cities and villages were founded. All men of evil mind were either on the gibbet or languishing in dungeon and gaol. He built a posthouse and shelter on every road, with a guard posted at the side of each. The world enjoyed peace from thieves and mountebanks, Kurds, Lurs,[5] highwaymen, and bandits. From the great bounty of silver and gold that he gave away, the very name of miserliness vanished from the world. From the abundance of gold, silver, and gems he bestowed, all the poor became rich. Injustice was forgotten in men's hearts; everyone who had been indigent became wealthy. No wolf sought advantage of a sheep, nor did sheep surrender in frailty to a wolf.

Every week he received his host in audience and gave them much noble advice; he sat the judges down in the judgment hall and extirpated the evil-natured root and branch.

In his audience hall kings and servants were as one, as were poor and rich. When a world-conquering king came before him, there was no difference at the time of seeking justice between him and an old woman. If a man of God came before him he was accorded honors like a king. In his presence a man of culture and learning

3. A tree in Paradise, according to Muslim belief.
4. Christensen, *L'Iran sous les Sassanides*, p. 124.
5. From Luristān, a mountainous region in southwest Iran.

was as precious as his eyes. In Iran everyone cultivated learning, so that secrets might blaze forth in his presence.

Rāmīn lived on earth for a hundred and ten years; and of those he was king for eighty-three. Amidst sovereignty, state, pomp, and wealth that illustrious king survived for eighty-three years; the earth grew prosperous through his justice, the age became happy through his glory. Under his aura of fortune, three things were lacking in the world: one, trouble; the second, pain; the third, grief. Sometimes he nourished his soul with knowledge, sometimes rejuvenated his body with pleasure; he now took his ease in Khurāsān, now hunted in Kūhistān.

Now he would be in prosperous Tabaristān, now go to Khuzistān and Baghdad. He opened a thousand springs and canals, and founded by their side many cities and villages. One of those cities which has survived is Ahvāz, which he then named "the city of Rām";[6] though it is now called Ahvāz, it is known under the name of "Rām" in registers. He was a king of good life and fair name; for in the language of those days the word for fair was "Rām." Never has there been a king so lofty as he: nor has there been one to play the lute so melodiously;[7] see how finely he designed the harp—who has ever made a discovery better than his design? The clue to that blessed one having designed the harp is the fact that he named it "the Rāmīn harp."

When Rāmīn's sovereignty was established, everywhere from Moon to Fish was filled with his justice. He handed the world over to the silvery-framed Vīs and made her his sovereign. He had two sons of that beauty of moonlike form; fair as their mother, brave as their father; two royal children, their names Khurshīd and Jamshīd; the world pinned its hopes upon their glory. He gave the land of the east to Khurshīd, the land of the west to Jamshīd. He gave to one Sughd, Khvārazm, and Chughān;[8] to the other, Syria, Egypt, and Qairuvān.[9] The world was in the hands of charming Vīs; but her special fief was Āzerbaijān. Likewise all the lands of Arrān and

---

6. *G:* "Ramin-ahvarukmia." Minorsky, *Iranica,* p. 175.
7. See Introduction, p. xvii.
8. Places in Transoxiana. Minorsky, *Ḥudūd ul-ʿĀlam,* p. 114.
9. See n. 1, p. 143.

Armenia were in the hands of that jasmine-bodied beauty. They remained together for years in sovereignty and fully indulged the desires of their hearts one and all. They tugged the halter of their lives for so many years that they even lived to see their children's children.

103.

THE DEATH OF VĪS. When Vīs had lived with Rāmīn for eighty-one years, only dregs remained of wine, husks of musk: the head of the graceful cypress became bowed, its back crooked like a bow. Even though someone has no enemy in the world, once you look keenly his enemy is none other than the world itself! How well said Nūshirvān the Just[1] when old age shot an arrow into his heart: "The world has done to me in my old age what no enemy has ever succeeded in doing. I wonder that I should have relied upon the world, it has first broken my back and then slain me!"[2] Although Vīs received loyalty from the world, she also experienced cruelty from its revolution. So weak did she become by its revolution that her seven members became beyond control. Then Death suddenly came out of its ambush and snatched away that wasted Moon.

Rāmīn's heart became a mine of grief from his distress for her, his eyes doleful at the blow. He said, "My choice, illustrious spouse! soul of my body, precious to my soul! You have left me branded with loneliness, you have spurred on the horse of separation. I have not in all the world seen any as loyal as you; why have you all at once become indifferent to me? Did you not often make compacts with me that you would never desert me for so much as a day? Why have you gone back on a treaty made by your own hand? and mixed loyalty with cruelty? Loyalty has been observed by a lover loyal as you; but cruelty has been perpetrated by this cruel age! Hardly surprising that it has been cruel to you; who has ever experienced loyalty from Fate in this world? You have expunged loyalty from the world; you have gone and taken loyalty with you. The pain of old age was enough for my heart; now you have laid the fetter of captivity upon my body as well. Why have you laid another pain

1. Khusrou Anūshīrvān, the Sassanian ruler of the sixth century A.D.
2. Cf. the line of Saʿadī, *Gulistān*, ed. Furughī and Mashkūr, p. 16, l. 5.

348

upon me and given affliction a passageway into my soul? My eyes swept the dust from your feet; now you lie helpless, sleeping under the dust.

"Your sweet voice used to say, 'Rām, may my body be the dust under your feet!' Now I have had to live to see the day when your silvery body has indeed become the dust under them! With you this sovereignty of mine was sweet; even with all this treasure my heart rejoiced in you: now this world is nothing but a calamity for me; it is preposterous for me to seek the world without you. Am I to rend the garments on my breast in distress for you? pour dust on my head to lament your death? For I am old and you know that it is not proper that such humiliation should be courted by the old; my heart bears a heavy load of grief for you; my eyes rain jewels at separation from you. I shall keep both the one and the other in pain and tears; but I shall not visit suffering upon my hand and tongue. It is right that my heart should suffer distress and my eye have its lashes ever dabbled in blood. But it is not meet for me to rend my garments with my hand; or to utter a string of lamentations with my tongue. Patience is a virtue in the old; especially in separation from spouse or lover. Although my tongue is long-suffering, my heart ever increases in restlessness. Whilst I have my heart boiling within me from distress, I yet keep my tongue silent and innocent of speech." Then he ordered the construction of a royal *dakhmeh*[3] such as was worthy of his fine wife, raised from the fire temple of Burzīn:[4] the top of its tower built up to the Pleiades. In shape it was redoubtable as a mountain, in ornamentation fashioned like a gorgeous Paradise. Fire temple and *dakhmeh* were both likely to inspire the envy of Rizvān. When he had completed both fire temple and *dakhmeh*, see how he made his preparations for the next world.

104.

RĀMĪN SETS HIS SON ON THE THRONE AND HAUNTS THE FIRE TEMPLE TO HIS DYING DAY. At the beginning of the year, on the

3. "Tower of silence" for the exposure of the dead.
4. H. Massé, *Wîs et Râmîn* (Paris, 1959), translates: "et l'on y entretint le feu sacré, venant du temple de Berzīn." See Minorsky, *Iranica*, p. 164 and note, p. 185. On Burzīn see n. 3, p. 76.

fortunate day of Nourūz, the world became turquoise-colored by victorious fortune. Rāmīn summoned his son, Sun of Princes, and the nobles; set him on the throne before him and called him monarch and king of the world. He set the crown on his head in triumph and said to him, "Illustrious king of the land, may this Kayānī crown be fortunate for you, likewise this throne and royal seat; God has given me dominion over the world; I have given this gift to you: be worthy of it as you may. I have tested you in prowess and have always been happy at the result; I have given you the crown of sovereignty, for you have the proper will to rule. My son, my years have exceeded a hundred; the world has passed over me: what was to be has been. Now it is eighty-three years that I have been the joy of my friends, the plague of my enemies. Now it is meet that you should exercise sovereignty; for you are of pristine fortune and young. You have long seen me engaged upon this kingship; discharge it even as I have done. Everything which God asks me on the Day of Judgment I shall demand of you before the Judge. Good name is better than fine desire; so act that your end may be good."

When he had given Khurshīd the golden throne, he cut off hope from throne and crown and kingship. He descended from the royal throne and went to the *dakhmeh*, the throne of the next world. He took up his abode at the fire temple and dwelt there; he attached his pure heart to God. God that day granted him kingship when he chose contentment and saintliness. Although before this he had been a prince, he was ever the slave of desire. The world carried out his orders and he in turn from the craving of his heart was the obedient servant of desire. When he disabused his heart of this world's desire, he freed his body from desire and his heart from care; be sure that a heart which has escaped from the hurly-burly and desire of this world has escaped eternal punishment. As the king rested for three years from his cares, he showed his face to none in the world.[1] Sometimes he sat on the *dakhmeh* of his sweetheart and wept day and night from the pain in his heart. Sometimes he offered up entreaties to God and suffered care on account of the sins he had committed. Old and decrepit as he was, he did not rest for three years from weeping and lamenting. He ever proffered excuse to the Judge and

1. *G* ends here.

regretted the deeds he had done. When he craved mercy from God you would have sworn that the smoke of grief rose from him; in three years that fragile body assumed the color of a strand of saffron. One night he was craving pardon of God; all night long he had washed his cheek in blood; when no strength remained in his body, at dawn God called him to his side. He gave God a soul washed clean, which had escaped from the hand of many enemies.[2] His son, Sun[3] of monarchs, came, and with him the nobles and well-wishers; they carried his body to Vīs and laid the two illustrious remains side by side. Their souls were joined together, they saw each other's spirits in heaven.[4] In heaven those two constant souls were once more joined as bride and groom.

The world lays an ambush for us night and day; you would imagine we were deer and it a cheetah; we wander and scamper in the grazing ground, fondly fancying that it is unaware of us; we say, "We are wise and ingenious." Can any wise man be thus confused and helpless? We do not know whence we have come nor where we must hie from hence. We have to bide in two worlds: one transient, the other eternal. We pin our hopes on this transient abode and do not reck of that abode which is eternal.

Though we mark well that we only pass this way, we still do not believe our eyes; how foolish, how confused in mind are we, not to cleave to the permanent to the exclusion of the transient! We seek the accouterments of eternity in a dwelling where we spend a mere moment. Who are we, with our inverted nature, to call the world infamous? The world is the fetter, and we are happy in our chains; we do not seek intimacy with our Lord, the Lord who created for us two worlds, one perishable, one eternal; the Lord to whom the entire two worlds are as a speck of dust is to us. Happy is the man who takes him as a friend and reckons all things on the basis of carrying out his behest! Happy he whose end is good, happy he who leaves behind a good name! Even as we glean tidings of those who have passed away, tomorrow perforce they shall glean tidings of us. We who have sought reports shall ourselves become a mere report;

2. Or, "and escaped from . . ."
3. *Khurshīd.*
4. Cf. n. 5, p. 95.

we who have spoken idle words shall become mere idle words. They shall tell of us in the world as we have told the tale of Vīs and Rāmīn. I have told a tale as fresh as spring blossom: each verse in it as gorgeous as a bloom. My fine fair friend, perfect in beauty and of pure-based nature; read out this pretty story, for your friends' happiness will be increased thereby, a story far pleasanter to scholars than a gorgeous garden! I desire you to recite my poetry so as to know its worth. When you read this poem, man of letters, crave forgiveness of God Almighty for my sins! Say, "O Lord, have mercy on the youth who composed this beautiful tale; it is you who accept excuse from your servants; forbear to visit his words on his soul!" The blessings of our Lord and his mercy be upon the Prophet, his companions, and his house!

105.

CONCLUSION. The sun of happiness has risen, the sky of high fame has cleared. The breeze of victory has begun to blow, the spring of joy has come in its train. The cloud of fortune has overlain all borders, felicity rains on all subjects. It is a propitious festival and a happy time, the age rejoices and all are happy. The earth is clad in a mantle of colored silk, the sky in a canopy of golden clouds. I see the world filled with light, far removed from the disasters of the sphere.[1] The spring blossom of sovereignty and command has bloomed triumphantly in the months of Mihr[2] and Ābān.[3] The day of felicity has begun to lengthen at the very time when the night starts to grow longer. The flower of fortune has begun to smile when the sweet basil has withered in the world; the world is renewed and fortunes changed; perhaps God has re-created the world! The drop of bounty rains from its clouds, the seed of joy sprouts from its soil. The heaven knows no influence save justice; surely Mars and Saturn have fallen from it! When did the heaven have such influence? When did the world know such pristine fortune? Surely the shadow of night stems from the glory of the Humā,[4] as the light of

1. The text is disarrayed in *I* from here on.
2. September–October.
3. October–November.
4. A fabulous bird whose shadow is auspicious.

day from the glory of God! The tongue of everyone you see is uttering thanks; the soul of everyone you see is seeking love; surely the dread of death has departed from people, and everyone has found his heart's desire! Justice and truth so illumine the world that you would swear men's night was day. Men lovingly inclined are happy and rejoicing, men versed in literature held dear and treated generously. It is as if this time were the garden of the age, and the realm a stately cypress therein—a cypress whose radiant color remains both in autumn and in spring. Now the good are like flowers in spring, the evil-minded like rose stems full of thorns. A monarch whose throne is lordship itself is a very ornament of kingship for Isfahān: Isfahān is like eternal Paradise, the palm of the hand of our lord and ruler its Rizvān: a lord aided by justice and religion, Abū'l Fath Muẓaffar ibn Muḥammad, pride of Khurāsān for good name, judge over Isfahān by the order of justice. The age has made his regime a cynosure, felicity has bowed before his face. The chronicle of his fame has passed the Oxus, the banner of his will reached the heavenly sphere. One so noble has emerged from this low world as ruby from rock, pearl from oyster shell. At the time of light, moon and stars are to him as idols to men; precious to every heart as wealth, pure as the soul, and renowned as reason. Never, Majesty, does the moon shine like your counsel, or reason itself rival your mind. You surpass even the prophet in one respect, that unbelievers do not reject description of you. Your generosity ever titillates the heart; the simoom of your wrath melts the soul. You are a sea; and when the sea is rough, who dares try conclusions with it? When you say, "Arrest such and such a one," the seven members of the heavens tremble. Though you dread fire on the Judgment Day, you venture fearlessly into fire. At the time of questing after glory you rain a shower of arrows as copious as a shower of rose petals in spring. Shifting sands are like purslane to you; the raging sea a rivulet in your eyes. You have a person grand and worthy; why do you count it as naught on the day of battle?

You have no fear of disaster, but shrink from shame; you cultivate learning and see to the poor.[5] I see your nature fraught with nobility, your hearing attuned to culture. With so much nobility and good

5. *I.*

353

works you are like to hold off the decrees of Fate from the world! Happy the one whose worthy son you are! Happy the one whose fair lord! What action springs from your excellence! What progeny from your line! All are worthy and renowned, refined like gold and polished like ruby. Your noble stock resembles the east, for nothing comes from it but moon and stars. Culture derives pride from a seeker after art like you; eloquence derives pride from an orator like you. Nobles are mountains, he the high sphere of heaven; see the distance between one and the other! The ways of nobles are pain to the soul; the ways of our lord antidote and cure. No delay is to be detected in him at the time of generosity, nor defect in him at the time of virtue. The glory of God orbits round him like the line of the compass round the center. His policy is a rampart round the realm, his compact the spring blossom of the garden of pride. Since his propitious fortune is wakeful, all the world is like someone between sleep and waking. His mind and heart are moon and sun; his command and awesomeness lightning and thundercloud. The world's pleas are like demons, the liberality of his hand like the Qur'ān. He has slain men's desire and pleas: the gold of his liberality is the blood-price of the one and the other. The hand of the age has a sword with which it takes his enemies, called Envy; the envious man suffers more blame than benevolence, for he is ever the enemy of government—more than all a government paramount such as this which has six hundred servants like Narīmān.[6] I shall not say, "May he have no enemy"; let him have one, but that one powerless! May this generous blessed monarch live long! so that beneficence, learning, justice, and faith may live long! May justice and faith last as long as he, may fortune call him whom he calls!

Growing in the garden of the realm like a pine are three jewels like three blazing stars, nobility written on their faces, goodness compounded in their ways. It is no matter for surprise if they are like you, for the fruit of the palm is no other than the date. The eldest of them is an ocean of learning, a world of chivalry, and a mountain of clemency. Reason acknowledges that he is a prince, Abū'l Qāsim 'Alī ibn Muẓaffar; apple of his father's eye in scholarship, pride, and

6. The father of Sām and great-grandfather of Rustam.

adornment of his house in perfection; the smell of milk still lingers on his mouth, but I know no knowledge that is a closed book to him. His words are the spring blossom of the tree of learning, his excellence the ornamentation of the house of generosity. His face is graced with modesty because God created him of very saintliness; embodied in him the very proof of perfection; showered on him the rain of his favor. The world has fixed its hopes on his excellence, more than on the light of the sun. As light radiates from the sun, so does the ordering of kingship radiate from him; when his perfection translates itself from potentiality into action, the splendid are aghast at his splendor. Crowned kings come to do homage before him and rub their cheeks in the dust of his hall. May this son live so long as the world lasts and delight his father's heart by his success. Younger than he is the glorious lord Abū Naṣr, glory of the time and ornament of the age. Having beheld the vision of his forebear, Heaven professes itself the slave of this descendant. That glorious star is indeed like a star; great when its nature is known, though small to outward view. In aspect he is like Zū'l-Fiqār;[7] for he is both small and renowned. Child as he is, he has all the wisdom of the old; small as he is, he has all the nature of Amirs. By the sugar sweetness his speech contains he shows many signs of fortunateness. Many the proud deeds he shall perform! Many the praises he shall hear! Heaven daily decorates a crown for him, for moon and sun are a fitting diadem for him! The age inscribes rescript and realm in his name and ever ties his standard in victoriousness. Fortune and success are in harmony with him, the panoply of good luck seeks him out. May it be even as I have said, blessings light on him and on his father!

Younger than he again is another champion, Abū Ṭāhir Muḥammad ibn Muẓaffar; speaking in the cradle like Jesus, a prodigy in infancy like Moses, spellbinder of unbelievers and enemy of the base. Like Jesus, talking even from the cradle, like John the Baptist, practicing judgment in infancy. Though he be tiny to outward view, he is mighty in intelligence when the inner truth is known. At first glance he is like fire: but his strength and awesomeness are great. He is in the springtime of his life; this is why he is like a blossoming

7. The sword of 'Alī, cousin and son-in-law of the Prophet Muḥammad and fourth Caliph.

bud; when the heavens learn of this bud, sun and moon will become his slaves. As sure as the hawk's chick is a hawk, son will be as exalted as father.

May both the eyes of evil be closed on all three, may the tree of their life grow forever, son rejoicing in father's sway, father delighting in son's culture!

You who have carried the scroll of your fame above the moon and brought down from the sphere the star of your desire, who sit triumphantly on the throne, the seats of enemies shattered in dread of you, I have brought you a Mihragān present,[8] fluent as the water of the spring of life. At this festival no subject has brought a present better than your servant's; by your order I have composed a romance beautiful as a blossoming garden; it is graced by proverbs of wisdom like fruit, sweet ghazals[9] like spring basil; you are prince of the nobles of the age, so I have prefixed your name to this story; I began the work with your name and have set the seal of your name on its end. See how fortunate this story is; the spring splendor of your name is its crown and throne! You would swear this volume was a world, for it has your name at both ends. Its beginning and end east and west, your name orbiting it like the sun. You well know that poetry composed like this will last so long as there is verse and poesy. Through the glory of your name your servant's words shall be on every tongue till the Resurrection. Their youth shall last forever, for they have drunk the water of life from your liberality. Whenever you seek verse, there should be a poet like me before you. If you obtain from all others strung pearls, you shall obtain from me moon and stars set on thread;[10] when I gallop the steed of verse into the field, the Milky Way is the pitch of my polo stick. My style is brilliant as Sirius; in conceits like the crown of Kisrā[11] in gems; especially when the field is such as this—dedicated to you and in memory of Vīs and Rāmīn. Though I have expended much labor, it is no one day's favor that I have had to acknowledge. My lord, the night of my labor is at its end; now the morning of your

8. Mihragān is the festival of the autumnal equinox.

9. Lyric poems: the reference is presumably to the songs of Rāmīn. See Introduction, p. xii.

10. *I.*   11. Khusrou Anūshīrvān; see n. 1, p. 348.

satisfaction has dawned; I have trod the long road of ill fortune, but now I have reached the stage of victory.

Generous prince, since I first saw you I have become so that I know no task but joy; I am ever joyful and drunk through your liberality; you would swear some elixir has come to my hand! Why should I not delight in your felicitous countenance? for I am independent of all thereby. You are the sun, and when I sit before you it is only proper that I should not look at lamp and candle. You are the sea, and I a pearl fisher; it is from you I seek pearls, not from spring and stream! My mouth eats sugar from speaking my thanks to you, my tongue rains jewels from praising you. As I rejoice in you year in, year out, may your life be blessed with every fortunate state! May your fortunes be glorious, may your lot ever be to follow your will! You have become Khusrou, your heart's desire Shīrīn;[12] your enemy the target of arrow and javelin. So long as there is destiny in the world, may the span of your life be eternal; so long as there is felicity in the heavens, may your felicity increase. May your will and command ever be current, your fortune and luck ever young; may your night be day, your day Nourūz; your head invested with the color of triumph and your fortune victorious, the cords of your life tied to the day of Resurrection; prosperity seated with you as your courtier; your heart, hand, door, and face open; your throne and dais and table spread; in your hand now the pen, now the dagger; now the tresses of the fair, now the flask of wine; may such custom and institution as I have described prevail; this is your servant's prayer: may Fortune say Amen to it!

12. See n. 13, p. 101.